Spectre of War

Based on Historical Events

David Lee Corley

DEDICATION

Dedicated to all the men and women that fought and
sacrificed for their country.

Table of Contents

"War does not determine who is right—only who is left."

— Bertrand Russell

The Enemy of My Enemy

US Embassy - Saigon, South Vietnam

The rain came down in sheets, flooding the streets of Saigon. Granier sat in the back of a jeep, water dripping from his boonie hat. The jeep's driver turned onto Tu Do Street, passing American GIs headed to the bars and brothels that lined the neon-lit alleyways. Granier grunted, thinking how soft the Americans had become.

Granier's jeep pulled up to the imposing gates of the US Embassy and was waved through. He stepped out and hurried inside, water running off his poncho. He refused to use an umbrella like the other civilians. Even though he was a CIA officer, he was still a soldier at heart. He wanted his hands free for fighting.

After being cleared by the Marine guards at the embassy's main entrance, Granier took the stairs up to the ambassador's office. He walked down the plush carpeted hallway, lit by crystal chandeliers that seemed out of place in this war-torn country.

Inside, four men waited around the sleek teak table:

3

US Ambassador Ellsworth Bunker, General Abrams, head of MACV, Theodore Shackley, CIA Chief of Station, and Robert "Blowtorch Bob" Komer, head of the Phoenix Program. Komer, Granier's direct boss, motioned for him to sit at the end of the table. Bunker took control of the meeting and said, "We have been tasked to make a final recommendation to Washington as to the fate of the Phoenix Program. With the final drawdown of US troops approaching, there are many in Washington that want it shutdown permanently. They say that while it has been useful, it is too dangerous to be turned over to South Vietnamese intelligence. There are fears it could become a tool for settling personal vendettas, extortion, and human rights abuses if mismanaged. The US could be blamed for its future misuses since we were the ones that started it. As one of the program's original developers and the current head of operative training, we thought your input might be useful, Officer Granier."

Granier grunted that he understood. "You understand that we are not questioning the program's success in dismantling the Viet Cong's infrastructure. We've crippled their recruiting abilities and support leadership," said Shackley.

Granier grunted again.

"Do you have anything to say beside a grunt, Officer Granier?"

"Sure," said Granier. "You want my opinion... I say shut it down –"

"I would have thought you would have been more protective of the program," said Komer.

"I wasn't finish."

"Well, then by all means... go on."

"Shut it down... and Saigon will fall within one year

of our final departure."

"That's a pretty bold prediction," said Abrams. "The ARVN aren't just gonna roll over when we leave. They have one of the biggest and best equipped militaries in the world."

"Without Phoenix the Viet Cong will regain control of the south within a few months. They will recruit by the hundreds of thousands. And when they're ready, they will attack mercilessly with North Vietnam's help. They ARVN won't be able to stop them. Before Phoenix, we were losing the war to the Viet Cong. Phoenix stopped them."

"So, you would have us turn the program over to the South Vietnamese?" said Bunker.

"Not exactly. You're right that Phoenix can easily be corrupted if placed in the wrong hands. But not all South Vietnamese would use it for personal vendettas, extortion, or human rights abuses. We have thousands of South Vietnamese operatives in the program right now. They're doing great things to protect and save their country. There is no reason that should stop after our troops leave."

"So, how could Washington be reassured that it won't become an albatross hung around America's neck?" said Bunker.

"It's gonna be tricky, no doubt. But if we can show the South Vietnamese leaders that the program will only work if used correctly, they'll want to keep it running at an optimum level."

"That's a pretty tall order," said Komer. "Once our military leaves for good, they'll be no reason for them to do as we say. Oversight won't work if there's no big stick."

"I don't disagree. It's highly likely that the South

Vietnamese will revert back to their old ways of doing business once we're gone."

"So?"

"I've thought a lot about it. The only way to keep Phoenix uncorrupted is to convince the South Vietnamese leaders they're dead without it."

"And you think we could do that?" said Abrams.

"I know it's wishful thinking, but yes. We can do it as long as it's a priority."

"How would you suggest we do that?" said Shackley.

"First, we take all current American Phoenix operatives, and we integrate them into the South Vietnamese Phoenix program. They become advisors, not operatives."

"Wouldn't that create a huge intelligence gap until the South Vietnamese are trained?"

"Yes. I didn't say this would be without risk. But I think we can manage it somewhat. The American advisors would be carrying out the same missions but would be using the South Vietnamese as the operatives."

"I'm not sure that would be wise as we pull the last of our troops out of the country. They would be exposed," said Abrams.

"I agree. So, we'll have to do it in stages. As the US military ramps down, Phoenix ramps up."

"That might work," said Bunker.

"Second, we need to provide oversight as long as we can. We need to recruit the best South Vietnamese operatives possible. Like we are doing now, but at ten times that recruitment rate."

"Is that even possible?"

"We have a lot more resources now, than when we

started. We take some of the best South Vietnamese operatives currently in the program and use them as our recruiters."

"That's gonna draw away even more intelligence resources," said Abrams.

"It will. We need to be careful. But the South Vietnamese recruiters will be our best hope for recruiting quality intelligence operatives within Phoenix. If there is one thing I've learned in my current post, it's that they know their people far better than we do. We need to take advantage of that."

"What else?" said Shackley.

"We need to make damned sure we put the right South Vietnamese intelligence officer in charge of the program. I'm talking exhaustive interviews and background checks. We need to understand how the man thinks before we put him in charge. And we need to do it all covertly without him knowing."

"And?"

"Finally, we need to provide our own covert oversight. The South Vietnamese are not going to like that if we're found out. But I think it's essential if we expect them to defeat the Viet Cong."

"But even if we do find something is wrong with the way they're executing the program there isn't much we can do. No big stick, remember?"

"That's true. But there are two sides to persuasion – the stick… and the carrot. And America still has a lot of carrots to give South Vietnam as long as our leaders are willing to withhold them if necessary."

"How long do you think it would take to get the South Vietnamese Phoenix Program running on its own?" said Bunker.

"If we're aggressive, two years."

"That's too long. We'll be out of country by then."

"Alright. You tell me. How long do we have?"

"Six months," said Shackley.

"That's pretty tight. But I suppose we can have a basic program up and running in six months, then fill out the number of operatives required over the next year or two."

"And you think we can do this?" said Komer.

"I don't think we have a choice. South Vietnam falls without Phoenix."

"You've given us a lot to think about. Can you stay in Saigon a few days in case we want to meet again?" said Bunker.

"I'll make it so, Mr. Ambassador."

Two days later, Granier was summoned back to the embassy. He took the familiar route to Komer's office, wondering why Blowtorch Bob had requested an urgent meeting.

Inside, only Komer awaited him. They sat across from each other at Komer's desk. "I'll get right to it," Komer said. "After careful deliberation and consultation with Washington, we've decided to move forward with transitioning Phoenix to Vietnamese control."

Granier nodded, keeping his face neutral.

"It won't be easy, as you pointed out. The White House has concerns about corruption and human rights abuses once we pull out." Komer templed his fingers. "But we agree that dismantling Phoenix altogether would be disastrous."

He eyed Granier sharply. "You made a convincing case that, handled correctly, the program is South Vietnam's best chance at countering the Viet Cong once we depart."

Granier remained silent, sensing what was coming next.

"I'll be blunt. We want you to head up the transition." Komer held up a hand to stall Granier's protest. "I know it's a hell of an ask. You'll have little support on the ground as our presence draws down. And you'll face resistance from certain ARVN factions."

His gaze bored into Granier. "But if anyone can pull this off, it's you. Your experiences with the OSS, CIA, and Phoenix make you uniquely qualified."

Granier grimaced, mind racing over the overwhelming obstacles. Then he thought of the Alternative - Saigon overrun by Viet Cong, South Vietnam in Communist hands. The choice became clear.

Looking at Komer, he rasped, "I'll do it." Then he added wryly, "But you owe me a drink when this shitshow is over. Top shelf only."

Komer barked a laugh. "Glad to hear it. I'll hold you to that drink. Top shelf only." His expression turned serious again. "Now let's talk details..."

They hammered out a strategy for the transition. It would not be smooth, Granier knew. He would face resistance and setbacks. But with grit and cunning, he might just pull off the impossible - handing Phoenix to the Vietnamese without it becoming a weapon for tyranny.

Granier left the embassy in the rain. The future of South Vietnam rested on the quietly determined warrior's shoulders.

Saigon, South Vietnam

Granier sat in his Saigon office, poring over personnel files of American Phoenix operatives. He needed to select just the right men to train the South Vietnamese counterparts who would soon fill their roles. Standards would be high.

A knock on the door frame made Granier look up. Staff Sergeant Mike Voss stood at attention. "Reporting as ordered, sir."

Granier waved him in. Voss had an impressive record: Marine scout-sniper in Korea, recruited for covert operations in Laos before joining Phoenix. The wiry man with rugged features sat down as Granier skipped pleasantries.

"Sergeant Voss. Your file indicates extensive experience in long-range reconnaissance. Your sniper totals are high, as are your target interdiction counts in Phoenix."

Voss nodded. "I go where needed and do what must be done."

"This assignment requires more. Your duty will be training, not operations. The South Vietnamese must internalize Phoenix as their own, not as some American creation. For that, they need teachers, not crusaders."

Voss looked skeptical. "With respect, sir, the V.C. body count comes before cultural sensitivity."

Granier's eyes bored into him. "Not in this case, Sergeant. Our mission is to train the South Vietnamese Phoenix operatives. That's going to require patience and understanding."

Sitting back, he retrieved Voss's file. "Your platoon commander called you the most stubborn trooper he'd ever met. I cannot afford that. This assignment requires flexibility and restraint."

Voss bristled but maintained composure. "I'll admit adapting doesn't come naturally to me. But I aim to carry out any mission to the utmost."

Granier closed the file. "How do you feel about the South Vietnamese taking over a program you helped build?"

Voss considered his response. "If you think it's best, I'll make it work. My job is getting the enemy, not politics."

Granier appreciated the honesty. Granier was not looking for weak-minded soldiers that would obey his ever whim. He wanted warriors and warriors were not always easy to control. It was the nature of the beast. He saw potential beneath Voss's blunt exterior. With careful guidance, that tireless dedication could make him an excellent instructor.

"How's your Vietnamese?"

"Passable, sir. But I'm working on it."

Granier grunted, then said, "Very well, Sergeant. You're assigned to the training cadre. Dismissed."

As Voss left, Granier felt the weight of his decisions. Choosing the right mentors could determine Phoenix's future - and with it, South Vietnam's.

Aircraft Hangar – Saigon, South Vietnam

The cavernous aircraft hangar was filled with the murmur of hushed conversations. One hundred American Phoenix instructors sat at tables reviewing stacks of personnel files - the records of thousands of potential South Vietnamese trainees.

Granier paced between the rows, answering questions in his trademark grunts and terse phrases. He was pleased to see the instructors taking their task seriously, debating qualifications and suitability of each candidate.

Sergeant Voss waved Granier over to his table. "This recruiter notes the candidate is too timid. But excellent marks at intelligence school. Thoughts?"

Granier scanned the file. "Some roles need reserved types. Analytics, not operations."

At another table, Captain Morris raised a file. "This man was passed over for promotion twice. Disciplinary issues?"

"Troublemaker when young. But creative thinker. Bends rules, gets results. We ain't looking for choirboys," Granier nodded approval.

The afternoon wore on. Some candidates were quickly set aside - rumors of drug use, petty crime, family VC connections. But most files revealed promising, if flawed, recruits.

Granier noted each objection and endorsement. He began to recognize the instructors' strengths - who focused on intelligence versus field skills, unconventional thinking versus discipline.

By end of day, neat stacks of files sat on Granier's desk. The selections were critical; these men would soon become the local eyes, ears and hands of the South Vietnamese commander running Phoenix. Their competence and his could determine the country's fate.

As the hangar emptied out, Granier sat alone pondering the silent files. Somewhere in those pages might be a future Nguyen Van Thieu, or a corrupt double agent. Finding the gems would test every skill he had honed over decades of war.

After the last instructor left, Granier closed the giant

hangar doors, then retreated to his spartan office in the corner of the hangar. He settled behind his metal desk. He unlocked and opened the bottom drawer.

Inside lay a small stack of personnel files – his shortlist for the Vietnamese officer who would command Phoenix once the Americans departed. This decision weighed heaviest of all.

Granier riffled through the first few files, immediately discarding two candidates. One had past involvement with a notorious death squad. Another came from a powerful family notorious for corruption.

He paused on the file of Major Pham Van Nguyen. Covert background checks found no red flags no rumors of impropriety, clean finances, praised by colleagues. A promising profile.

Digging deeper gave Granier pause. Nguyen's thinking was rigid, tactical rather than strategic. And officers under his command complained of hyper-criticism.

Granier set the file aside. Micromanagers did not inspire men or instill loyalty. And Phoenix would require flexibility to walk the grey lines of counterinsurgency.

The next file was Colonel Tran van Huong, current head of South Vietnam's counterintelligence force. Granier knew him as intelligent and professional, though some viewed him as too calculating in pursuit of promotion.

Unlike the other candidates, Huong fully grasped the power of Phoenix, both for good and ill. He seemed to recognize the need for oversight and discipline.

Granier weighed the risks. Huong was ambitious but had not abused his current powers. Perhaps it was idealism, but Granier's instinct told him Huong could handle the temptation.

He placed Huong's file atop the short stack. The decision was critical - and final. Granier could only trust his judgment and watch events unfold.

He locked the files away and headed to his quarters in darkness. The coming months would reveal whether his choice preserved South Vietnam or doomed it.

US Embassy – Saigon, South Vietnam

Granier sat at a table in a secure room at the American embassy, joined by Komer and Shackley. Before them sat Colonel Tran van Huong, Granier's pick to lead the South Vietnamese Phoenix Program. As the panel watched Huong, Huong watched the panel. There was little trust in the room filled with spies. But everyone understood the importance of the Phoenix Program to South Vietnam's survival.

Komer reviewed his file. "Colonel, your leadership skills are well-regarded. But commanding Phoenix requires utmost discretion."

"I am aware of the sensitivities," Huong said tersely. "And I am no stranger to covert operations."

"Even so, misuse of Phoenix could have disastrous consequences," Komer pressed. "Assassinations, intimidation—such tactics can backfire."

Huong's eyes narrowed. "With respect, you Americans do not grasp the enemy we face. Ruthlessness is required when confronting VC barbarism."

Shackley cleared his throat. "Care must be taken. Winning hearts and minds is still critical."

"Hearts and minds!" Huong retorted. "You speak as

if the Viet Cong can be gently persuaded. They understand only force... or better, death."

Komer bristled at the outburst. "That attitude will lose this war, Colonel. Phoenix cannot become a license for brutality."

Huong slammed a fist on the table. "Do not lecture me about how to defeat my enemy, Mr. Komer! You will withdraw to safety across the ocean while we remain to fight. We will do what is necessary to protect our people."

A tense silence followed. Komer regained composure. "You're right - it is not my place to dictate how you secure your country."

Huong gave a curt nod and the questions resumed. He was not an easy man. He described his vision for Phoenix - precise, ruthless and under absolute control. No method would be spared in destroying the Viet Cong, but operations would not spiral into uncontrolled vengeance.

After two intense hours, Huong departed. He had stood his ground and told the blatant truth when asked. Granier gave an approving grunt. "Strong spirit - exactly what Phoenix needs with Americans leaving."

Komer and Shackley sighed but agreed. For better or worse, Huong would lead Phoenix harshly. Whether South Vietnam survived or not could depend on that iron will.

Granier hoped they had chosen wisely. The fledgling Phoenix's wings were spread - where it soared or plunged rested in Huong's hands now.

Jungle, South Vietnam

The stifling Vietnamese jungle echoed with the sounds

of training. Under Granier's watchful eye, American advisors put squads of South Vietnamese recruits through grueling exercises in stealth, tracking, interrogation, and tactical combat.

Sergeant Voss stood before a group practicing covert movement. "Charlie's got eyes and ears everywhere. Step lightly, stick to shadows and foliage." He demonstrated weaving silently between dense ferns.

The trainees tried to mimic his ghostly grace with mixed success. Voss made them repeat the drill until even the clumsiest recruit could slip through unseen.

Nearby, Captain Morris supervised interrogation training. "The key is reading body language - a darting gaze, nervous ticks. Spot the lie amid truths."

The recruits took turns interrogating each other about a staged VC cell. Morris corrected them when they missed a deceptive tell or pushed too aggressively, violating protocol.

At the firing range, marksmanship improved daily. And in makeshift classrooms, advisors lectured on analyzing enemy networks, surveillance, recruiting informants.

By the end of each eighteen-hour day, exhausted recruits stumbled back to their barracks. Though training was grueling, motivation remained high - every man had lost loved ones to the VC and hungered for payback.

Gradually, Granier noticed progress. Squads executed ambushes flawlessly. Interrogations extracted hidden intel. Surveillance teams tracked targets undetected for days. The raw recruits were becoming a hardened Phoenix cadre.

But challenges loomed. ARVN commanders still

excluded American advisors from some missions. And rumors said some South Vietnamese ignored rules against extortion and looting.

When he could, Granier made example of offenders with latrine duty and public reprimand. He could only hope such discipline instilled morality along with skill. Much remained uncertain as Phoenix prepared to leave the nest.

The day arrived when Granier and his advisors stepped back and ceded full control of operations to their South Vietnamese counterparts. No longer American-guided, Phoenix was reborn as the autonomous Phung Hoang program under Colonel Huong.

The first weeks were marked by successes. Acting on solid intelligence, Phung Hoang teams eliminated numerous high-level VC cadres and sympathizers who had long eluded capture.

But it soon became apparent that old habits die hard for some ARVN commanders. Phung Hoang agents in certain provinces began indiscriminately detaining or executing any civilians suspected of VC ties, with flimsy evidence.

When reports reached Huong, he immediately dispatched internal inspectors to identify and harshly punish those responsible. "We must excise this cancer before it spreads," he told Granier grimly.

Meanwhile, VC propagandists were hard at work portraying Phung Hoang as ARVN's terror weapon against innocent peasants. Sympathetic civilians began withholding intelligence that could target VC infiltrators.

"Hearts and minds are key," Granier warned Huong. "Brutality only drives people into VC arms."

Huong nodded, but his eyes remained hard. "Then we shall educate them on who the true enemy is."

Granier could only counsel strategic restraint and hope Huong took heed. The fledgling Phung Hoang remained balanced on a knife's edge - apt to fall either into unchecked violence or impotence against a growing VC threat.

Saigon, South Vietnam

Granier entered Huong's office at National Police Headquarters, expecting a routine briefing. But the colonel's grim expression told Granier something bad had happened. "What happened, Colonel?"

"One of our interrogators has uncovered a Viet Cong assassination plot," Huong said without preamble.

"Who is the target?"

"Your countryman, Lucien Conein."

Granier went silent, jaw clenched. Granier hated Conein with every fiber of his being. Conein had attempted to kill Granier on several occasions. He had some mixed-up notion that Granier was a double agent working for the enemy. There had been rumors floating around that Conein, since retiring from the CIA, was buying up American weapons on the black market and selling them to the highest bidder. Part of Granier felt Conein deserved his fate and hoped the VC succeeded.

But another part of him knew that he had little choice but to save his adversary. Saving Conein was the strategically wise choice. Letting a high-profile American get assassinated would damage South Vietnam's reputation and endanger the Phung Hoang program's success.

Still, the thought of Conein being gone once and for all was intriguing…

Huong continued, "Our source says the VC mean to eliminate Conein so they can resume buying the American weapons on the black market themselves."

"When will it happen? And how?"

"We are not sure yet. The interrogation is continuing, but the informant's information seems to be limited."

"Do you know where the plot originated?"

"The interrogator traced it back to a VC cell operating near Cam Ranh Bay," Huong replied. "We are still connecting the dots to identify the operatives in the plot. How do you wish to proceed?"

Granier's internal debate raged. His duty said protect Conein. His instincts said good riddance. Finally, duty won out. Granier met Huong's gaze, face grim. "We put Conein under surveillance while we dig for more information."

Huong nodded agreement. "I thought you would say as much. We cannot let the VC win. I will use every resource at my disposal to uncover this plot. I assure you we will flush out the operatives before they can strike."

Granier knew the odds were good that Huong using the Phung Hoang program could skillfully intercept the assassins. But darker possibilities troubled him. Perhaps certain figures in South Vietnam or the CIA wanted the hit to succeed and Conein silenced...

After leaving Huong's office, Granier considered whether to tell Conein about the plot. Part of him thought it better Conein remain ignorant. Forewarning could cause Conein to alter his patterns, scaring the VC hit team into hiding.

However, the smarter play was likely informing Conein. As much as Granier hated Conein, he knew that Conein was an excellent counterintelligence operative. He could be an asset in identifying the assassins if he knew to be vigilant. And if Granier withheld the truth, he risked Conein's death being blamed on South Vietnam.

Granier found Conein holding court with Corsican mobsters at one of their Saigon restaurants. It was one of Conein's known hangouts and as usual Conein was already well lubricated on the legendary Corsican aperitif– Vin Mariani, each bottle of fortified wine mixed with six ounces of cocaine. Arriving alone and unarmed, Granier felt he was entering a den of wolves.

Conein noticed him and whispered to a brutish bodyguard, who frisked Granier roughly before letting him pass. Patrons eyed Granier as he approached Conein's table. "What do you want, Granier?" Conein sneered.

"There's a Viet Cong plot to assassinate you. I came to warn you," Granier said tersely.

Conein's laughter echoed through the restaurant. "Half of Asia wants me dead! You'll need more than rumors to interrupt my drink."

"I don't give a shit if you listen to me or not. I'm doing my duty, you pissant."

"Watch your mouth, Granier. You're in my territory. I could have you killed, and nobody would say a word."

"Maybe, but I'd lay odds I could take you down with me before I go. It might even be worth it."

"So, why warn me? Why not let the Viet Cong do your dirty work?"

"Believe me, I thought about it. If the VC succeed in icing your ass, it will embolden them and embarrass the South Vietnamese government. I can't allow that, even to see you in the grave."

"A true patriot. Why should I believe this ain't some bullshit trap you devised?"

"To what end? If I wanted you dead, you'd already be dead. I don't need a trap. I have a sniper rifle."

"And everyone would know you did it."

"Look... you assume that I think about you enough to devise some plan to kill you. But the fact is I don't think about you at all. I've moved beyond your bullshit, Conein. Karma's gonna take care of you. It's just a matter of time."

"Karma can kiss my grits. You've delivered your warning. Now, get your ass out this restaurant before I have you hung on a meat hook and filleted for a late dinner."

Granier laughed, turned, and shook his head as he walked out.

Stepping into the night air, Granier felt damp sweat under his shirt. Whatever came next, they would remain enemies in this life and the next. Some rifts run too deep to mend.

Huong's men watched Conein from discreet distances as he went about his shadowy business in Saigon. He moved like a prowling tomcat through the bustling streets, seeming oblivious to the eyes on him. They watched as he met shady contacts at cafes, exchanged briefcases stuffed with money at hurried back-alley exchanges, and visited storefronts that served as fronts for his illicit operations.

Some nights he gambled with ARVN generals, Asian crime bosses, and Americans of dubious employ until the early hours. Other times he disappeared into opium dens or brothels forbidden to outsiders.

The agents tracked Conein's meetings with gun runners, drug smugglers, artifact dealers and spies of all allegiance. He moved easily between Saigon's various underworlds, conducting machinations that served only himself.

After years evading adversaries, little escaped Conein's notice. He began picking up the tail, spotting the same faces nearby too often to be coincidental.

One afternoon, Conein ducked into a narrow alley. When the Vietnamese operative pursuing him entered, Conein pinned him against the wall, knife edge brushing his throat. "Why are you tracking me?" Conein hissed, pressing the blade tighter when the frightened man hesitated.

"Colonel Huong's orders," the agent finally admitted. "To protect you from VC assassins."

Conein held the operative's gaze, reading his face for deception. Seemingly satisfied, Conein released him, then flicked the knife in a sudden slash across his cheek. "Tell Huong I can take care of myself," Conein said as the operative stumbled back, hand clutched to his dripping face. "If we meet again, I'll take your eyes as a remembrance."

The operative fled. Conein cleaned his blade, then disappeared like a specter into Saigon's shadows. The cunning old smuggler was an enemy, ally, or wild card - depending on need and circumstance.

Huong was livid when the operative reported how

Conein had knifed him. "Damn him! Conein cannot be allowed to assault my men with impunity!"

The operative hung his head, ashamed to have been bested. "He moves like a viper, Colonel. I did not see the blade until it was too late."

"You are lucky to be alive!" Huong seethed. He turned to his deputy. "Issue an arrest warrant for Lucien Conein immediately on charges of assaulting a police officer."

Granier entered the room. Seeing Huong's fury, he asked, "What happened?"

Huong stood grabbed the operative's head and turned it to show Granier the long wound, "Conein," said Huong.

"I should have warned you. He can be a mean bastard."

"No matter. He will pay for what he has done."

"Yes, and he should… but not right now. With respect, Colonel, arresting Conein now could doom the operation and lose the assassins' trail."

Huong's cheek twitched, but he held his tongue.

"Conein is a snake, no doubt," Granier continued. "But what we are working on is bigger than Conein. We have a chance to take down a key component of the Viet Cong network. Conein must remain free until the threat is neutralized."

"So, he does this and gets a pass?"

"No, he should pay for what he done, but when the time is right."

He met Huong's fiery gaze. "Bringing him to justice won't matter if a VC bullet finds him first. Focus on the larger mission for now."

Huong weighed this, then sighed and nodded reluctantly. "We shall continue our surveillance for the time being."

He turned to his beaten operative. "But Conein will answer for this insult when the vipers striking at him are in their graves. His day will come."

The operative bowed, comforted by his commander's promise of future vengeance against the American who had dishonored him.

Nguyen, a Viet Cong operative, lay prone on a rooftop, peering through binoculars as Conein exited a small restaurant below. He and his VC cell had been tasked with tracking Conein's movements for the past week.

They observed him discreetly, blending into the crowds as they ghosted him through Saigon's congested streets. When Conein met contacts, Nguyen's partner Minh got close enough to eavesdrop and snap photos with a concealed camera.

At night, they broke into Conein's apartment and installed microphones. From a safe house a few doors down, they recorded his phone calls, learning the web of Conein's criminal associations. His schedule, vulnerabilities, and connections were meticulously documented.

After two days of surveillance, Nguyen noticed something new - they weren't the only ones watching Conein now. He spotted the same operatives near Conein too frequently to be chance.

"Government agents," Minh speculated. "But why the sudden interest in Conein?"

Nguyen wondered the same. Someone must have tipped off ARVN intelligence about the assassination plot. Careless chatter by the loose-lipped recruiter perhaps.

When Nguyen reported the surveillance, his

commander was unconcerned. "We proceed as planned. The government rats will scatter once their American master is dead."

The tracking continued, now with greater care to avoid the ARVN agents' notice. Nguyen was confident their hand-picked assassin could evade the police and eliminate Conein. Soon, very soon, the crucial arms pipeline would be theirs.

Minh sat in the safe house listening intently through headphones. The equipment before him was wired to the microphones concealed in Conein's apartment. Minh monitored all of Conein's conversations for intelligence.

Most were mundane - boasting to his fellow criminals, flirting with mistresses, arguing over debts. But this call caught Minh's attention.

"Mr. Chou, so pleased you accepted my invitation to Saigon," Conein said smoothly. "I believe Taiwan can greatly benefit from what I have to offer."

Minh recognized the name - Chen Chou, a deputy defense minister in Taiwan. He grabbed a pen to take notes.

"I believe we can come to a mutually beneficial arrangement regarding the equipment you require," Conein continued. "Discreetly of course. Shall we say 9pm tomorrow at the Cercle Sportif?"

Minh jotted down the meeting time and location. Supplying Taiwan would cut into the VC's own arms acquisitions from Conein's pipeline.

After finalizing details, Conein rang off. Minh smiled coldly. His commander would be pleased - they could eliminate Conein and sabotage this alliance in one blow.

Tomorrow night, the Finnish Valmet rifle Conein himself had unknowingly provided for the assassination would be used to end his meddling and loose lips once and for all.

Minh left immediately to report to his commander. The kill team would be readied and sent to the Cercle Sportif to intercept both Conein and the Taiwanese official. Soon the pipeline would flow to the revolution.

Granier entered the interrogation room where a handcuffed VC agent sat bruised and bloodied. Colonel Huong stood facing the man.

"Tell Officer Granier what you just revealed," Huong ordered.

The agent kept his eyes lowered. "Conein is meeting a Taiwanese defense official tonight to broker an arms deal. The plan is to kill both men during the meeting before they can seal the arrangement."

Granier felt his pulse quicken. This was the break they needed. "Where and when is this meeting?" he demanded.

The agent shook his head. "I don't have that information. Truly, all I know is the assassination is planned during their meeting tonight. They have a sniper team."

Granier cursed under his breath as he turned to Huong. "We'll need to cover every venue Conein uses for his deals. And keep him under tight surveillance."

Huong nodded. "We will deploy additional men. My interrogators are also working every angle to uncover the meeting point."

"There isn't much time."

"My men can work quick when needed."

"Alright."

Huong gripped the agent's shoulder firmly. "And this one's usefulness is not yet exhausted. We will learn what we need to stop this plot."

The agent paled at the implied threat. Granier's mind raced with the new intelligence. He had to prevent Conein's death tonight along with an innocent official. "I'll coordinate surveillance teams," Granier said. "We cannot lose Conein's trail before the VC assassins reveal themselves."

The showdown neared, but the assassins still held the advantage. Granier could only hope they did not slip the tightening net. Granier and Huong worked urgently to determine the location.

Granier's past knowledge of Conein gave them some leads. "His favorite spots are the Corsican mob boss's restaurant in the old quarter, the Cercle Sportif club, and the rooftop lounge of the Continental Hotel. He does all his deals at one of those locations."

Huong dispatched agents to all three venues to scout security and identify vantage points. He also put word out on the street for informants to report any hints of the meeting.

The interrogators worked in shifts trying to break the VC agent, while other analysts combed Conein's phone records for clues.

Around noon, an informant called Huong's office. He had heard from a chef at the Cercle Sportif that Conein booked their private dining room for 9pm that evening.

"That's it!" Granier exclaimed when Huong relayed the news. "You can control access and surveillance at the Sportif. We need to prep an operation immediately."

Huong agreed and rapidly issued orders. All exit points would be covered by plainclothes agents. The perimeter would be monitored for approaching assassins. And Conein would be escorted to ensure he reached the meeting safely.

An hour before the meeting, Granier entered Huong's office and opened a locked cabinet, removing his customized Model 70 Winchester sniper rifle. Though other sharpshooters were in place, Granier wanted oversight personally.

He headed to an apartment building with an unobstructed sightline to the Cercle Sportif's entrance. The residents had been quietly evacuated earlier that day.

Granier ascended alone to the top floor. Entering an empty unit, he approached the window facing the club. He cut a small viewing slit in the rice paper screen, then set up his rifle on a bipod.

Lying prone, Granier peered through the scope at the French colonial style building below. Huong's men were discreetly positioned around the perimeter and at the entrance.

Granier chambered a round, then focused on the front doors. The meeting was set for the second-floor dining room near the front of the building. Houng had arranged for the private dining room Conein had originally booked to be flooded with water from a leaking coupling on a pipe. The private dining room near the front of the building was the only alternative. Granier mentally mapped fields of fire to cover the exterior balcony and stairwells.

Slowing his breathing, Granier waited patiently, letting the familiar rituals of preparation calm his mind.

He became one with the weapon, an apex predator stilling all motion before the killing strike.

By 9pm, the trap was set. Now they had only to spring it on the VC cell to stop the murders. But with so many lives at stake, Granier knew the margin for error was razor thin.

When Conein's car arrived, Granier tracked him with his scope as he entered the building. Moments later, an unmarked vehicle dropped off the Taiwanese official at a side entrance. The pieces were in motion. Now to wait for the assassins to reveal themselves.

Granier's eyes methodically scanned nearby rooftops and windows. His crosshairs lingered on any hint of movement. Tuning out all distractions, he would be ready when the bullets began flying.

Surveying all the surrounding buildings, Granier saw no signs of the assassins. Huong's men seemed to have the perimeter securely locked down.

Granier stayed vigilant but couldn't shake a feeling something was off. The shadows held too much stillness, devoid of any subtle threats.

Granier watched through his scope as Conein and Mr. Chou were escorted to the private dining room on the second floor. Conein was laughing and boasting, while the Taiwanese official seemed reserved.

As they entered, Granier again scanned the windows, balconies and nearby rooftops again. Still no sign of watchers or a sniper nest. Something felt off, but he couldn't place it.

He radioed Huong. "No visual on shooters yet. But stay alert. My gut says we're missing something."

Inside, a waiter appeared with a cart of covered silver platters. Granier's instincts blared a warning, but it looked identical to the other serving carts going in and out. The waiter left the room.

Moments later, Conein emerged looking irritated, heading for the bar. Granier watched him gesturing angrily to the bartender about his drink order, then throwing the drink in the bartender's face before marching back toward the dining room.

Suddenly, the second floor of the club exploded in a massive fireball, blowing out the windows. Granier shielded his face from the shockwave. Screams echoed from within.

Rushing to look through his rifle scope again, Granier saw only flames and smoke pouring from the dining room. The bomb must have been hidden in the cart, set to detonate after the waiter escaped.

Huong's voice shouted over the radio, demanding status from his units. But the VC cell had slipped through their perimeter unnoticed, costing innocent lives.

Sickened, Granier watched Conein rush from the building unscathed yet again. But any relief was replaced by crushing failure. The assassins had outplayed them all, anticipating their trap and striking ruthlessly at the weak seam.

Chaos erupted on the street as dazed patrons fled the bombed club. Coughing from the smoke, Conein staggered toward his car.

Gunfire erupted as two VC agents appeared, cutting off his escape. Innocent civilians were mowed down in a hail of bullets. Conein dove behind a flower bed for cover, pulling his pistol.

The assassins advanced, firing VALMET submachine guns. Conein returned fire, forcing them to take cover behind the concrete planters.

Granier immediately centered his crosshairs on the

first agent, who rose to spray another burst at Conein. Granier gently squeezed the trigger until the rifle cracked. The VC gunman dropped with a crimson burst.

Swinging his barrel, Granier tracked the second assassin as he pulled a grenade from his jacket. The man pulled the safety pin and arched back to hurl the grenade. His head exploded from Granier's second shot. The live grenade dropped to the sidewalk and exploded hurling the assassin's corpse into the air. It landed with a thud.

With both killers down, Granier quickly scanned for additional threats. No more emerged - only panicked patrons fleeing from the devastated club.

Conein broke cover, pistol ready until he verified the assassins were neutralized. For once, the unflappable smuggler seemed shaken as he viewed the bloody aftermath.

Granier kept vigilant overwatch as Huong's men swarmed to secure Conein. The VC cell may have slipped the initial trap, but their desperate last gambit had failed.

As Conein was escorted to safety, Granier finally exhaled, adrenaline ebbing. The shadowy plot had been thwarted, but only due to fortune as much as skill.

Conein was brought to a nearby safe house under heavy guard. Granier soon arrived, sniper rifle slung over his shoulder.

"Ah, fuck. I knew it was you up there," Conein remarked bitterly. "I suppose you expect a thank you."

"I expect nothing from you except misery and lies, Conein. It's your nature. Can't change nature," Granier replied coldly.

Conein poured himself a drink with a shaking hand. "We've tried to kill each other so many times. Perhaps it's fate we're both still breathing."

"If so, fate has a poor sense of justice."

"Justice?" Conein laughed harshly. "As if men like us can judge. We're all damned in the end."

Granier turned to leave. "Some more than others. This changes nothing between us."

Conein raised his glass in mocking salute. "Wouldn't dream of it. See you in Hell, brother."

Stepping into the night, Granier forced thoughts of Conein from his mind. The man was a plague - endlessly troublesome, impossible to be rid of. Granier could only keep fighting the damage left in his wake.

Their twisted destiny would continue, enemies locked in orbit until the inevitable final violence. But for tonight, Granier took cold comfort that Conein's shadow had not yet fallen over Vietnam irreparably.

Operation Lam Son 719

Pentagon – Arlington, Virginia

The mood was tense inside the Pentagon briefing room as General Abrams stood before the Joint Chiefs, Secretary Laird, and National Security Advisor Kissinger. Behind him, a wall map of Laos. "Gentlemen, the monsoon rains have cleared, giving us a window to strike at the heart of the Ho Chi Minh Trail before the mud returns. I propose an operation where ARVN forces will spearhead a ground assault into Laos to capture Tchepone and sever the enemy's logistics network."

Abrams circled Tchepone on the map. "Tchepone is the nexus connecting the NVA's supply lines, troops, and warehouses. Disrupting it would cripple communist operations in South Vietnam. This operation is also an opportunity to prove that

Vietnamization is working by putting the ARVN's training to the test in a major assault."

"Laos is a lost cause. Why send in troops now?" said Kissinger.

"A successful offensive will boost ARVN morale while striking a blow against the NVA's operations in the South. I plan to deploy 17,000 ARVN troops with armor, artillery, and airborne units. U.S. forces will provide airlift, logistical, and combat support."

Secretary Laird asked, "Exactly what kind of support will we provide?"

"The AC-130 gunships will be key to protecting the ARVN troops as they engage with the NVA," Abrams replied. "The three miniguns in each gunship will disperse and destroy any human wave assaults by the NVA. The gunships' advanced night observation and targeting capabilities along with the two Bofors 40 mm guns aboard each aircraft will enable them to dismantle anti-aircraft sites and bunkers along the trail that might threaten the ARVN advance."

"How many gunships will be available?" asked Laird.

"We'll have three AC-130 Spectres airborne each night for close air support, plus three flare ships to illuminate the battlefield if needed."

Kissinger spoke up. "And if three prove inadequate?"

Abrams outlined contingency plans for additional airpower, but concluded, "I believe three gunships and their sensors can provide the necessary fire coverage given the terrain and enemy deployment. We'll also have 175mm M107 self-propelled guns set up in South Vietnam along the border to provide extended fire support. They have a twenty-four-mile firing radius that will protect the ARVN as they first enter Laos and can reach all the way to Tchepone our main objective."

After further discussion of logistics and contingency options, the Chiefs approved Abrams's bold plan, now codenamed Operation Lam Son 719. D-day was set for February 8th when the first ARVN armored convoys would cross into Laos to begin their advance on Tchepone.

US Embassy - Saigon, South Vietnam

Tom Coyle stepped into the dark-paneled office, taking in the familiar smell of polished wood and cigar smoke. Behind the desk, Theodore Shackley, Saigon's CIA Station Chief, glanced up from a report, his sharp gaze betraying the analytical mind of a veteran CIA operator. "Coyle, good to see you. How's that new navigator working out?"

"Green as hell, but he'll learn. Had to stop him trying to calculate our position with a sextant though," Coyle chuckled.

Shackley gestured to a chair and Coyle sat down.

"Can I get you a drink?" Shackley offered motioning to a crystal decanter with an amber liquid.

"No. I'm good."

"I'll get right to it then. Operation Lam Son 719 is a go. The brass is finally taking my advice to cut the Ho Chi Minh Trail at Tchepone. ARVN's going in hard along with U.S. air and arti support."

Coyle leaned forward. "Risky putting the ARVN in charge but could be a big win if they pull it off."

"It's a gamble, but Vietnamization needs a field test. If it works, we can start bringing more of our boys home." Shackley pulled out a map, circling an area with his finger. "High command wants it straightforward - a hammer blow along the trail to Tchepone. But I aim to add a dagger in the back of the NVA. That's where you come in."

Shackley slid the map across the desk, circling an area west of Tchepone with his finger. "This will be your personal zone of operations once the main attack goes in. You'll have free rein to pursue any targets that present themselves in this area."

Coyle studied the map, rubbing his chin thoughtfully. "No restrictions or oversight? You're giving me a long leash."

"You got a problem with that, Coyle?"

"No. Just the opposite."

Shackley leaned back. "A long leash for our top dog. This is an off-the-books operation. We need chaos and confusion, not bureaucracy. Hit their reserves, supplies, anything that supports the defense of Tchepone. Maximum damage."

Coyle traced his finger along the western hills depicted on the map and said, "I can do that. What about SAMs and anti-aircraft?"

"Air Force is assigning two Wild Weasels to take out the SAM sites ahead of each strike. In addition, we are sending an escort of two A1 Skyraiders armed with napalm to take out any anti-aircraft gun emplacements.

"That should do the trick."

"I should think so. We are going to give you and your crew the highest priority when it comes to assets and resources. We have high expectations."

"My Spectre can do a hell of a lot of damage with free rein."

"That's what we were hoping. No restrictions, no oversight. Just wreak havoc on their reserves, supplies, anything to fragment their response. This is your show, Coyle. Light 'em up."

Coyle offered a slight grin. "I'll take that drink now."

February 8, 1971 – Border Area, Laos, and South Vietnam

The dawn sky lit up as US artillery shells screamed overhead, crashing into the jungle on the Laotian side of the border. Lieutenant Colonel Ly stood frozen, momentarily deafened by the barrage. Around him, hundreds of ARVN tanks and armored personnel carriers stood silent in their staging areas, waiting for his order to advance into Laos.

Ly tensed as more artillery rounds screamed overhead, a high-pitched wail that pierced the pre-dawn darkness. Seconds later, thunderous booms echoed across the landscape as the M107s 175mm and the Long Tom 155mm shells found their targets across the border.

Though the guns were behind him, each explosion flickered like a strobe light along the horizon. Ly tracked the intermittent flashes, picturing the deadly shells arcing high over the dark jungle canopy before plunging back to earth.

Salvo after salvo fired, filling the sky with shells. Orange bursts rippled across the blackness, momentarily illuminating the Laotian valley the ARVN forces would soon advance into.

The M107s and Long Toms pounded continuously, raging steel hailstorms walking back and forth across planned routes of the ARVN infantry's advance and suspected enemy concentrations. Blooms of fire overlapped until the horizon was a pulsating wall of light.

As the initial bombardment concluded, sporadic follow-on barrages targeted bunkers and gun positions, denying respite or repair to whatever NVA forces remained. The artillery had spoken, heralding the ARVN assault to come.

As the last shells from the artillery faded, a new rumble filled the air. Ly peered into the predawn gloom; his eyes drawn east toward the rising sun. There, just over the horizon, he could make out tiny pinpricks of orange light periodically blossoming against the dark jungle canopy.

The blooms of fire grew steadily, accompanied by a distant, ominous thunder. Ly knew that each eruption of light marked another deadly load of bombs from a B-52 Stratofortress striking NVA positions arrayed along the Laotian border.

The strategic bombers were softening up the enemy defenses in preparation for the ARVN ground assault, pounding troop concentrations, bunkers, and anti-aircraft batteries. From this distance, Ly could only see the afterglow of the explosions. But he could well imagine the devastating impact of the saturating carpet bomb strikes.

As false dawn gave way to morning light, the tempo of the aerial bombardment increased. It became a constant rumble interspersed with rising columns of gray smoke from the pulverized jungle. Ly steeled himself, knowing the time was approaching to drive into the maelstrom and engage whatever enemies remained. Ly felt the apprehension in his gut give way to resolute purpose. He radioed to his company commanders. "Get them ready to move out."

The commanders barked orders and men ran to vehicles, scrambling aboard. Ly pulled himself into the cupola of his M113 armored personnel carrier, surveying the mixed force of tanks, armored cavalry, and mechanized infantry. Over 17,000 ARVN soldiers would participate in the raid across the Laotian border, the largest ARVN operation of the war.

With a final check that all units were reporting ready, Ly gave the order to advance. With a roar of diesel engines, the armored column lurched forward, crushing bushes as they moved from paved roads to the mud track leading into Laos.

Two hours later, Ly squinted through sweat-filled eyes at the trail ahead. The B-52 strikes had obliterated whole swathes of jungle, leaving only mangled tree stumps and craters surrounding the path. Intelligence reported NVA units concentrated near the border, but aerial bombardment had surely depleted their numbers and softened their defenses.

The rumbling roar of diesel engines drowned out the buzzing jungle as the armored bulldozers crawled forward. Looming up ahead, the cratered dirt road was blocked by mounds of earth churned up by carpet bombing.

Sergeant Tran stood sweating in the morning sun, one hand on his holstered pistol as he watched the bulldozers approach the obstacle. Days of monsoon rain had turned the road into a muddy quagmire, but now B-52 Arc Light strikes had made it completely impassable.

The lead bulldozer pushed into the cratered zone, its thick front shield and armored cab protecting the driver from any undetonated ordnance. The giant blade began steadily pushing tons of mud and debris, carving a path through the wasteland of bomb craters.

Following 100 meters behind, the second "D9" bulldozer worked in tandem, smoothing the ground so vehicles could once again pass. The engines roared as thick columns of exhaust spewed from the vertical stacks.

From his vantage, Tran could see they were making steady progress. Within an hour, there would be a lane wide enough for trucks and armor.

The rumble of the bulldozers was a sound he had come to welcome. It meant a path was being cleared to advance, to resupply, or to medevac the wounded. Wherever bombs fell, the armored dozers arrived after to carve a roadway through the aftermath of destruction.

They were ungainly beasts, but their presence gave Tran reassurance. The bombers blasted the way open. These machines made that opening passable again.

Riding in a field modified M113, Captain Nhu, the lead company commander, scanned the treeline ahead through binoculars as his column approached the clearing.

The South Vietnamese called their armored personnel carriers "Green Dragons" and used them like light tanks in addition to troop carriers. To improve the survivability of the M113s against enemy fire, ARVN crews implemented field modifications using salvaged armor. Much of this extra armor plating came from decommissioned WWII-era ships that had been sunk or scrapped.

The additional armor plates, often over an inch thick, were welded or bolted onto the front, sides, and top of the M113s. This helped protect against rifle and machine gun fire, shrapnel, and low-velocity anti-tank rounds.

Particular attention was paid to increasing armor around the top-mounted .50 caliber machine gun position. Thick armor shields salvaged from ship hulls were installed to better protect the exposed gunners. This allowed them to continue providing suppressive fire even under enemy attacks.

While not able to withstand larger anti-tank weapons, the extra armor gave M113 crews and passengers greater protection and confidence. It also lengthened the lifespan of these armored workhorse vehicles in the face of constant ground fire and ambushes during mobile operations.

From his vantage point on top of the M113, Nhu spotted fresh footprints in the mud that indicated the NVA had recovered here after the bombardment. "Ambush possible ahead," he radioed to his platoon leaders. "First platoon probe forward."

Moments later, machine gun fire erupted from the trees. Green tracers laced the air as RPG rockets screeched past, detonating against the trail behind them.

"Ambush left!" Nhu ducked down, calling for suppressive fire. His men returned fire as he radioed the tanks forward. Nhu ducked down into the hatch as machine gun fire ricocheted off the armor. He keyed his radio handset.

"All units suppress those treeline positions!" Nhu ordered. His men complied, raining fire back at the NVA ambushers.

Nhu switched channels on the radio. "White Tiger, this is Dragon Six, we are under heavy fire and require armor support forward on the left flank, over."

The tank commander's response crackled through static. "Solid copy, Dragon Six. White Tiger moving up now."

Nhu rose back up through the hatch, steadying himself on the .50 cal. The tanks would add some heavy firepower and help them punch through this kill zone. He just needed to hold on a little longer.

The lead tank, an M41 Bulldog, churned into the clearing, turret swinging toward the treeline. Its main gun boomed, high explosive rounds ripping into NVA positions. Enemy machine gun fire sparked harmlessly off the tank's frontal armor.

Nhu kept up a steady stream of fire from the .50 cal as the tank ground forward along the left flank. In the treeline, muzzle flashes still winked as the entrenched NVA fired an array of small arms and machine guns. RPG rockets continued to snap overhead, but the ambushers were having to adjust their aim to account for the advancing armor. The fight was wild and furious.

The lead tank reached the treeline and rotated its turret sideways. The long barrel of its 76mm cannon trained on the bushes for a brief moment before belching flame. The high explosive shell tore through the foliage and detonated, silencing one of the machine gun nests.

Another roar resounded as the tank fired a canister round, spraying thousands of metal flechettes into the treeline that scythed down exposed enemy fighters. Its machine guns chattered, stitching the woodline.

Under the tank's barrage, Nhu saw his opening. "All units, charge forward through the clearing!" He ordered. The armored column revved and surged ahead, firing all weapons. Dirty grey smoke obscured the scene as HE and phosphorous rounds turned the treeline into a churning meat grinder.

Within minutes, they broke through to the far side, leaving a litter of enemy dead behind. Nhu exhaled, tasting gunpowder in the air. A hard fight, but they had survived first contact. Now to push deeper into Laos and seek out the enemy's heart.

Ubon RTAFB - Ubon, Thailand

The sun sank low on the horizon, casting long shadows across the tarmac of Ubon Royal Thai Air Force Base. In the fading orange light, the AC-130 Spectre gunship sat fueled and loaded on the flightline, its distinctive flared tail and underwing 40mm cannons making it instantly recognizable.

Inside the aircraft, the preflight checklist was nearing completion as Coyle and his crew made final preparations. Coyle sat in the left-hand pilot's seat, adjusting his night vision goggles and studying the coordinates for the mission - targets across the border in Laos that would soon feel the might of the Spectre's heavy firepower.

At the navigator station, Captain Mills carefully plotted the route and reviewed no-fire zones and potential abort locations. Across the narrow aisle, the fire control officer, Lieutenant Walker, flicked switches to arm and test the guns, while the loadmaster Chief Rollins ensured pallets of extra ammunition were secure and ready to feed the hungry cannons.

Like a brooding beast stirring to life, the AC-130's hydraulics hummed and vibrated as the crew brought the ship's systems online. Coyle checked the time - ten minutes to takeoff. He keyed the intercom.

"Listen up. We've got some high value targets across the border that command wants removed from the map. Ambush positions, supply dumps, anything feeding the NVA war effort over there. Our mission is to leave as big a mark as possible on Charlie with our special package."

Mills looked up from his charts. "Wild Weasels and Skyraiders should be airborne shortly."

Coyle nodded, catching Rollins's eye. "I want those guns singing all night. We don't return home until we expend the last round or Jolly Green arrives to pull our asses out."

A round of grim chuckles answered him over the intercom. These men knew the risks and welcomed them. All were volunteers for this CIA covert war.

Outside, the throaty roar of turboprop engines split the humid air as a pair of A-1 Skyraiders taxied past, laden with napalm canisters. Two F-100 Wild Weasel jets rolled onto the runway, primed to hunt any enemy SAM sites that dared threaten the gunship.

"Pilot's starting engines," Coyle called over the whine of the port turbine spinning to life. One by one, the four Allison turboprops rumbled to power, their propwash rippling across the tarmac.

Coyle eased the throttles forward, and the AC-130 began to roll, laden with its lethal payload. Lift-off was seconds away. Under the cloak of darkness, they would range deep into enemy territory to serve up vengeance from the sky. Coyle lived for these missions - just him, his crew, and the guns. Time to fly.

The landing lights flicked off as Coyle gently lifted the AC-130's nose, feeling the heavy gunship become airborne. He banked away from the airfield, dim instrument panel lighting illuminating his weathered features.

They climbed to orbiting altitude, the blacked-out Spectre vanishing into the night sky. Far below, the lights of Ubon receded into the distance.

Mountains – Eastern Laos

Coyle tracked the navigation systems as they crossed into Laos, entering the patchwork of enemy anti-aircraft positions, supply lines, and troop concentrations that comprised the Ho Chi Minh Trail network.

Up ahead, the F-100 Wild Weasels were making their first supersonic pass over the target area, probing for surface-to-air missile radars. Coyle listened over the radio for any call-outs. Hearing none, he nodded to Mills. "Plot our first target run - the supply depot at coordinates two-niner-alpha."

Mills relayed the heading change to Walker in Fire Control as Rollins unlocked ammunition belts to feed the hungry 40mm cannons.

Coyle banked the AC-130 onto the attack heading, watching through night vision goggles as the supply depot came into view. The infrared radar had detected the structures and heat signatures, but Coyle would aim the guns manually.

Centering the crosshairs over the clustered buildings, he called out "Guns, stand by!" Moments later, Coyle squeezed the fire control trigger, feeling the aircraft shudder as streams of red tracers arched downward.

The 40mm shells exploded through the depot, walking from one structure to the next. Fuel drums burst into fireballs, ammunition popped and snapped. Coyle kept his aim steady, engulfing the area in flame.

Satisfied the target was destroyed, he released the trigger. "Shackle, get the guns reloaded," he ordered as he banked the AC-130 around for another pass.

Through the green glow of the night vision goggles, Coyle watched for any remaining signs of life. There were none. The night vision combined with the Spectre's firepower made for a lethally accurate and stealthy attack. Charlie never saw them coming.

Eastern Laos

The UH-1 helicopters swooped low over the jungle canopy, flanked by Cobra gunships as they approached the landing zone deep in enemy territory. Lieutenant Danh checked his gear one last time and shouted final instructions to his platoon before they touched down. "Lock and load! The LZ will be hot!"

The ARVN paratroopers chambered rounds into their M16 and M60 machine guns as the choppers flared for landing. Danh could see smoke already rising from the clearing as pre-assault bombs and rockets impacted around the perimeter.

As the skids sank into the tall grass, Danh leapt out, his platoon following. Gunfire cracked from the treeline to the west. Danh snapped shots back as he bounded toward the cover of a large crater, his men fanning out amidst the din of Hueys departing and Cobra gun runs supporting his position.

When the last trooper was down, Danh radioed Battalion. "Blue Falcon is on the ground. Advancing to phase line Bravo."

"Roger, Blue Falcon," came the reply. "Good

hunting."

Danh motioned his platoon forward toward the tree line where the ambushers were hidden. The paratroopers advanced by rushes, using bomb craters as cover. Rifle and machine gun fire lanced out toward the treeline, answered by muzzle flashes from NVA trenches and foxholes.

Danh targeted one flashpoint and dropped a grenade into the nest, silencing it with a thump. As they closed within fifty meters, he signaled his point squads.

"Assault through the trees on 3...2...1...Go!"

The ARVN troops breached the treeline as Cobra gunships made danger-close strafing runs. Danh exchanged fire with an NVA soldier in a spider-hole, cutting him down before a burst of AK fire ricocheted off his helmet.

His men were through and clearing trenches with grenades and bayonets. After ten brutal minutes, the enemy fire slackened as the surviving NVA pulled back deeper into the jungle and took up positions along a treeline.

As Danh's platoon advanced on the treeline, the thumping of rotor blades grew louder. Two Cobra attack helicopters crested the trees, banking hard over the ARVN troopers.

The lead Cobra dove toward the enemy positions, its chin-mounted 20mm cannon spewing shells that tore into the treeline like a chainsaw. Its rocket pods rippled in succession, unleashing a volley of 2.75" high explosive warheads that exploded in fiery bursts within the NVA trenches.

The wingman gunship rolled in right behind, miniguns chattering as it saturated the area with thousands of rounds per minute. Tracers ricocheted and sparked through the foliage like hellish fireflies.

The Cobras made pass after pass, pounding the enemy positions to soften them up for the ARVN ground assault. Tracer rounds from the NVA's 12.7mm heavy machine guns streaked by the banking helicopters, but their armor deflected the desperate return fire.

As Danh's platoon hit the tree line, the gunships shifted to make danger close runs, strafing within mere meters of the friendly troops. The fury of the rocket and cannon fire tore holes in the NVA's defenses, allowing the ARVN paratroopers to punch through. Within minutes, the surviving communists were pulling back deeper into the jungle. The ARVN were driving the communists back as they had been trained to do. Vietnamization was working as planned.

Foothills, Eastern Laos

Sergeant Nguyen waved his squad forward up the trail. Despite some sporadic contact earlier, he felt cautiously optimistic. The NVA had been caught off guard by the operation's speed and ferocity.

His men seemed content as well, with the occasional joke or banter breaking out. After months of reactive engagements, it felt good to take the fight forward into enemy territory.

As the column entered a narrow gorge, Nguyen grew watchful, scanning the silent slopes.

A rumble like distant thunder gave him pause. Seconds later, mortar shells screamed in, tree bursts ripping through the canopy above. Cries erupted from his squad as white phosphorous rained down.

"Take cover!" Nguyen yelled, diving for a crater as

more salvos impacted up and down the column. Men screamed as WP coated their bodies, metal fragments slashed through the trees.

Nguyen huddled in the pit, trying to raise Battalion on the radio. Another barrage of mortars cratered the trail, bracketing the lead tanks as they advanced. Through the smoke, Nguyen saw tails of recoilless rifle fire lance out from the hillside, penetrating the thin armor of a personnel carrier as it made its way forward.

His radio squawked to life. "Red Dragon, pull back! You're in a kill zone!" Nguyen watched helplessly as the APC took another direct hit, erupting in a fireball.

Grabbing a dazed private, Nguyen retreated down the trail, urging his decimated squad to follow. Wounded men limped past as gunfire raked the column from all directions. It was chaos, a rout. All pretense of advance had been shattered in minutes.

Reaching a damaged M41 tank, Nguyen took cover behind its steel treads, breathing hard. Through the ringing in his ears, he heard the whine of turbines - Skyraiders arriving on station to expend their ordnance.

Napalm blossomed along the ridge line, searing flesh and foliage. The pooling forest fire bought them respite to drag the wounded back. Defeat was bitter, but Nguyen felt only duty remained.

Politburo - Hanoi, North Vietnam

The mood was tense inside the dimly lit chamber as General Giap unfurled his maps before the Politburo members. Operation Lam Son 719 had begun, with columns of ARVN forces supported by American artillery and airpower now advancing into Laos.

"The South Vietnamese and their American advisors have made a grave miscalculation," Giap declared. "They rely heavily on long-range artillery stationed within South Vietnam, unable to move batteries into Laos without escalation."

He traced a line along the border. "Our scouts confirm the American long-range guns have a maximum range of twenty-four miles from their current positions. Here, northwest of Tchepone, we are safely beyond their reach."

Le Duan, General Secretary of Communist Party of Vietnam, leaned forward, intrigued. "What do you propose, General?"

"A change in strategy. We will pull the bulk of our forces back beyond the range of the American artillery and establish reinforced bunkers and ambush sites along the expected enemy approach."

Giap pointed to the rugged terrain surrounding Tchepone. "Our anti-aircraft units will similarly reposition out of artillery range, but remain close enough to protect our main formations. We will turn this area into a kill zone of interlocking fields of fire. When the South Vietnamese armor pushes beyond the twenty-four-mile artillery umbrella, we will spring the trap, hitting them from camouflaged positions in terrain we control. Their artillery bombardments cannot touch us there. But we will bleed them dry."

"And the American fighters and bombers?" said Le Duan.

"Our anti-aircraft forces will exact a deadly toll on American aircraft once they are forced to operate beyond the range of their artillery," Giap continued. "Without artillery suppression, enemy pilots will face barrages from massed machine guns, missiles, and automatic cannons concealed in the rugged terrain. Every mile deeper into Laos will increase the risks and attrition for American airpower."

Le Duan nodded approvingly. "The South Vietnamese rely heavily on helicopters and close air support. If these become prohibitively costly to employ, it will further isolate advancing ARVN units."

"Correct," replied Giap. "We will make the skies as lethal as the ground, bleed white both their armor and aircraft. This ring of steel and fire will squeeze the life from their futile invasion."

Le Duan considered this, then replied. "Make it so, General. Now is the time to draw the ARVN deep into our web, cut them off, and inflict the kind of psychological defeat from which they cannot recover. Force Washington to reconsider this escalation."

Giap rolled up his maps. "I will reposition our forces immediately. Have patience, and we will repay this aggression with interest in due course. The steel ring around Tchepone will tighten like a noose, strangling the South Vietnamese. We will make Lam Son 719 their graveyard."

The generals departed, committed to executing Giap's adaptive strategy. By ceding ground, they aimed to lure the ARVN into an inescapable kill zone where massed firepower could not reach. Patience and preparation were about to blunt an enemy's bold gambit and turn confidence into despair. The winds of war were shifting.

Khe Sanh, South Vietnam

Private Tran stood in swirling red dust as the throaty roar of helicopter turbines washed over the staging area. All around him, hundreds of Huey UH-1 troop transports were spooling up, rotor blades cutting the air over the assembled ARVN paratroopers.

Tran adjusted the magazine pouches crossing his chest, counting each loaded M16 mag out of habit. His hands trembled slightly from anticipation. A hand clasped his shoulder. "Stay sharp in there, brother," said Corporal Kham, his squad leader. "Today we make history."

Tran nodded, grateful for the steadying reassurance. He was young, fresh from jump school. Today would be his trial by fire. The biggest air mobile operation of the war, with nearly 300 ships carrying over 8,000 paratroopers into the heart of enemy territory - the plan was audacious, putting the ARVN's best airborne troops atop the NVA headquarters at Tchepone in one stroke.

"Mount up!" came the order. Tran filed aboard the Huey, finding a seat and gripping his rifle tightly. He could see Cobra gunships hovering nearby, bristling with rockets and miniguns.

At the radio signal, the armada of transports lifted off in a swirling cloud, wingtip to rotor tip. They turned west, racing low over jungle canopies toward Laos.

Inside, the paratroopers sat silent, each alone with his thoughts. Tran recited a silent prayer, hoping it would not be his last. Their lives were in the hands of the pilots now.

Without warning, the helicopters banked hard right, breaking formation as plumes of smoke marked the impact of anti-aircraft fire. They were taking fire, the enemy alerted to their approach. Red tracers arced up from the jungle.

The Cobra escorts peeled off, diving to suppress the

gun positions with salvos of 2.75" rockets and streams of minigun fire that churned the terrain below into shredded plant matter.

More rockets streaked in from the NVA, proximity fuses detonating shards in all directions.

Their Huey jinked and veered wildly, the pilot dodging the deadly flak. Tran gripped his seat as inertia threatened to slam his body hard against the cabin wall. He caught glimpses of other helicopters trailing smoke, whether from battle damage or countermeasure decoys he couldn't tell.

Then suddenly they were over the clearing, green LZ smoke billowing below. "Get ready!" shouted the crew chief. The Huey flared hard and hit the ground. "Go go go!"

Tran leapt out, rifle sweeping for targets as he dashed for the treeline. Other helicopters were touching down, disgorging their cargo of camouflage-clad troops under heavy fire. Withering automatic weapons fire laced out from concrete bunkers across the open ground.

Cobras Dueled with 37mm anti-aircraft guns, trading salvos back and forth that lit the sky with criss-crossing vapor trails. Paratroopers spilled from shot-up transports riddled with holes. The enemy had been ready, turning the Landing Zone into a free fire kill box.

Under the press of returning rotor wash, Tran joined the other ARVN fighters rushing forward, determined to carry the LZ or die in the attempt. Bayonets flashed as they closed with bunkers in vicious hand-to-hand combat.

This was the hell General Abrams had unleashed them into. Tran banished all thoughts but the primal drive to survive. Kill or be killed, one way or another, the battle for Tchepone would be won this day.

His lungs burning from exertion, Tran helped overwhelm another bunker in fierce close quarter combat. The air was filled with screams and acrid gun smoke. Under the Cobra gunship's strafing runs, the paratroopers finally cleared the LZ.

Joining his squad, Tran rushed forward into the adjoining village - a maze of small houses and shops. Movement flickered in windows as NVA defenders popped out to fire before disappearing.

A paratrooper ahead took a sniper round cleanly through the neck, collapsing backward without a sound. Tran's squad returned fire onto the rooftop, driving the sniper back into cover. The ARVN paratrooper was dead. No time for sentiment, the battle raged on.

"Grenades, then clear those buildings!" Kham yelled, hurling frags through doorways before his men flowed inside, firing on full auto under the pressure of the assault. Each structure became its own savage brawl.

By the time they emerged back into the streets, Tran was dazed, ears ringing and rifle barrel scorched from continuous fire. The fighting devolved into small knots of ARVN and NVA exchanging frantic volleys on street corners and alleyways.

Cobras roared overhead, the downdraft from their rotors ripping at torn prayer flags hanging from damaged pagodas. The NVA were falling back deeper into the communist logistics hub under the fury of the multi-pronged air assault.

Kham radioed in their position to the battalion commander. "Be advised, LZ Bravo is secure. We are advancing northward along phase line blue."

The acknowledging squawk was barely audible over raging gunfire. It didn't matter. Tran knew their orders - keep attacking until the enemy's grip on Tchepone was broken or you are dead. Nothing else existed in this tempest of violence.

He loaded a fresh mag and scanned the road ahead. The battle was far from won, but they were driving forward under iron resolve. Today, the Republic's airborne elite had come to conquer.

South of Tchepone, Laos

"Red Crown, this is Rambler flight, two Phantoms requesting clear hot for attack run, over."

The airborne battlefield controller responded in a cool Texas drawl, "Rambler flight, Red Crown. Cleared hot on assigned target echo-bravo, friendlies danger close from IP to target. Roll in heading 0-2-0, cleared to expend all ordinance on target."

"Copy clear hot, rolling in heading 0-2-0 for target echo-bravo."

The lead F-4 Phantom banked hard right over the jungle, lowering its landing gear to reduce speed as the pilot aligned on the bombing run heading. The Number Two jet on his wing matched the maneuver perfectly, maintaining tight spacing.

In the rear cockpit of the lead Phantom, Captain Tran continuously scanned the instruments, keeping them flying straight and level as his pilot visually acquired the target coordinates.

"Tally target, I have visual on the trucks and supplies," came the callout over intercom. Tran pressed a button, arming the 500-pound bombs slung under each wing. "Bombs armed and ready," he reported.

At five miles out the pilot called "Pickle!" and Tran hit the bomb release, feeling the aircraft jump up as four thousand pounds of high explosives dropped free. He kept the Phantom steady as the bombs tumbled toward earth.

Seconds later, brilliant flashes strobed across the jungle canopy.

As the last explosions faded, Tran heard his pilot mutter "Good hits." The bombs had landed right in the middle of the target area - a North Vietnamese Army supply depot and staging area for units operating near Tchepone.

"Two's bombs away, good effect on target," reported the wingman over the radio. More detonations flashed across the valley as the Number Two Phantom's payload found its mark.

"Red Crown, this is Rambler Lead declaring guns guns guns," the pilot radioed, arming his 20mm cannon. The Phantoms swooped back around, dropping lower for a strafing pass along a line of camouflaged trucks.

Tran tracked the target through the optical sight, calling out small corrections until red tracers converged on a fuel truck, touching off a fiery secondary explosion. Fireballs mushroomed up from the NVA motor pool as 20mm rounds ignited fuel and ammunition.

"Rambler is Winchester and RTB, thanks for the help Red Crown," the flight leader radioed as they climbed away from the devastated depot, safe from any retaliatory fire.

Tran exhaled, feeling the post-combat rush

subsiding. Another successful strike mission under their belts. The tangle of jungle and cloud flew past the canopy as they turned south for home.

Tchepone, Laos

Machine gun fire rattled off the sides of the M113 as Nguyen's squad approached the outer defensive lines of Tchepone. Through the periscope, he could see the sandbagged bunkers and trenches guarding the approach to the small city that served as a vital NVA logistics hub along the Ho Chi Minh Trail.

This heavily fortified objective was their target - an enemy strongpoint they had to seize. Nguyen dropped down into the personnel carrier as an RPG round detonated against the armor plating. Outside, the rumbling of tank treads told him the assault had commenced.

"Listen up!" He shouted to his men over the din of battle. "We punch through the bunker line, then dismount and clear those trenches on foot. Watch for antitank teams trying to flank the armor. Expect fatal funnels and crossfire."

The men nodded silently, faces taut with tension. Nguyen strained to hear the radio as orders were given. Their company would be right behind the tanks, ready to exploit any breach.

With a lurch, the APC surged forward. Through the ports, Nguyen watched tracer fire crisscrossing the gray dawn sky. The lead tanks were engaging the bunkers at close range, turrets traversing rapidly to distribute high explosive rounds along the line.

One bunker erupted in a direct hit. The heavy .50 caliber machine gun flung backwards out of its firing slit. Another took a round straight down the gun port, silencing it permanently.

Green tracers continued to pour from other bunkers, forcing the tanks to button up. Hatches sealed, the armored wedge steadily ground forward, tracks churning the earth into wide furrows.

"Dismount!" Nguyen yelled, as his APC reached the smoking breach point. He led the squad out into a withering storm of incoming fire. The trenches were still manned, rifles and machine guns spitting lead from their reinforced log and earthworks.

Weaving through the bullets, Nguyen dove into the nearest trench, firing on the move. An enemy soldier rose in front of him, only to be cut down point blank. Nguyen felt the man's dying breath hot on his face as he plunged his bayonet into the next defender.

The paratroopers cleared the trenches in savage close combat. By the time Nguyen emerged back topside, his uniform was stained dark with blood that wasn't his own.

The outer defenses were taken. After consolidating the position, they moved deeper into the city along rubble choked streets. Bullets whizzed out from buildings and alleyways as NVA snipers exacted their toll before pulling back into the warren of fortifications.

A heavy machine gun hammered from a first story window, pinning down an ARVN squad caught in the open. Reacting quickly, Sergeant Thu rolled a grenade across the pavement into the building's open front door. The explosion silenced the nest.

They leapfrogged forward by bounds, one unit suppressing ahead as another bypassed to take out pockets of resistance. Each city block became its own bloody battle.

From above, helicopter gunships pounded buildings housing NVA strongpoints, filling the air with smoke and concrete dust. The fight became a hellish urban slog, room by room, block by block.

By late afternoon, Nguyen's company had seized the central market district. They took cover inside a pagoda as sporadic harassing fire continued from hidden defenders. The fighting had devolved into a deadly cat-and-mouse game.

Nguyen took stock of the men, passing out captured rice and dried fish. Most were once fresh-faced academy graduates. Now, hollow eyes stared back through mud-streaked faces. The brutal realities of their choice bore down upon them.

As dusk approached, orders came down to continue the advance under cover of darkness. Tchepone would be taken, no matter the cost.

Nguyen steeled himself for the night's work ahead. The infantryman's war allowed no rest. Eyes peered from the shadows, waiting for the cloak of night. But so too did the enemy.

AVRN Headquarters - Saigon, South Vietnam

The ceiling fan clicked slowly overhead, circulating the humid air inside the ornate office. General Abrams wiped his brow with a handkerchief and turned to his South Vietnamese counterpart, General Minh.

"Our spotter aircraft confirm that ARVN armored forces have advanced beyond the twenty-four-mile range of our M107 batteries inside South Vietnam," Abrams said, tracing his finger along the Laotian border on the situation map spread atop the desk.

Minh nodded grimly. "This will make providing fire support more difficult. Our own artillery lags far behind and has trouble maneuvering in the muddy terrain."

Abrams leaned back, considering his response. The South Vietnamese had relied heavily on the big American 155mm and 175mm guns to soften resistance ahead of their advance. Now his forces would be isolated, beyond that protective umbrella.

"It's a concern, but we can compensate with increased airpower," Abrams said. "I'm diverting additional sorties from the 7th Air Force to provide close air support. Tac air will have to fill the gap."

Minh looked unconvinced. "Our route forward remains heavily defended by anti-aircraft weapons. You have seen the toll taken already on helicopters and low-flying aircraft. Can your pilots accept those risks?"

"My boys know the stakes. We'll attack SAM sites and flak guns aggressively to keep a corridor open for airstrikes. And the B-52s can still reach targets with stand-off bombing."

"But your plan depends on securing and establishing a forward firebase. If the advance stalls before then, your aircraft may not be sufficient without artillery." Minh replied.

Abrams waved a hand. "My advisers report morale remains high among the ARVN troops. Once we take Tchepone, securing your supply lines, victory will be imminent. Airpower has not failed us yet in Vietnam. I have faith it won't start now."

Minh still looked troubled but nodded. "I pray you are right, General. We are committed fully now - there can be no turning back. Quyet thang!"

Abrams smiled at the "determined to win" motto.

He clasped Minh's shoulder reassuringly. "Quyet thang! We won't abandon you halfway. I guarantee airpower will prevent this offensive from faltering."

Privately, he harbored a flicker of doubt about that reassurance. But it was too late for reservations. The battle was joined. Now they had to trust bombs and bullets over blood and sacrifice to carry the day.

North of Tchepone, Laos

Thunder rumbled in the distance, masked intermittent pops of rifle fire. Captain Nhu peered through the cupola as sheets of rain obscured the surrounding jungle. Somewhere out there, NVA troops lay in wait within their hidden bunkers and trenches.

Earlier that morning, the lead ARVN units had crossed the twenty-four-mile range limit of the American long-range artillery batteries hunkered within South Vietnam. Now the only artillery support would come from the shorter-range ARVN guns struggling to advance along muddy roads into Laos.

Nhu knew they were driving deeper into the teeth of the enemy's prepared defenses. He ducked into the personnel carrier as the radio crackled.

"All Dragon units, be advised you are entering Zone Red," came the voice of Battalion Commander Ly. "Expect heavy resistance. Proceed with caution and maintain tight intervals."

Nhu nodded to his driver. "You heard the Colonel. Keep us buttoned up and don't let gaps form."

The convoy of tanks and APCs churned ahead, tracks throwing up rooster tails of rust-colored water. The road had degraded into a sloppy trail, canopy tangled tightly overhead. Ideal ambush terrain.

A burst of green tracers zipped from the undergrowth, striking the vehicle ahead. Nhu grabbed the .50 caliber machine gun and returned fire at the treeline as RPGs screamed overhead, slamming into the mud-bogged rear tank.

"Stand by for air support!" Nhu radioed to Ly as he continued to rake the trees with suppressive fire. In response came only static. "Dragon Six, do you copy? We need air support on our six, over."

Ly's response came through broken and distorted. "Air units encountering heavy fire...multiple gunships hit...air cover unlikely..."

Nhu felt his gut tighten. No air cavalry or medevac. They were deep in the belly of the beast now. "Advance to contact!" he ordered his driver. "Keep moving."

The column slowly ground forward as Nhu continued to spray the treeline, pushing through the ambush zone. They had lost five vehicles, with three more damaged but moving. Far steeper costs lay ahead.

By late afternoon, lead elements were approaching another clearing when withering machine gun fire erupted from concealed bunkers across the tree line. Heavy ZPU anti-aircraft guns added to the deluge of fire, their quad-barrels spewing armor piercing rounds that tore through the lead tank's light armor.

Nhu watched helplessly as the stricken M41 Walker Bulldog twisted and went up in a fireball, mortally wounded. He ordered his vehicles to pull back and find cover, trying desperately to call for artillery suppression. But they were well beyond the protecting umbrella of the American M107s and the ARVN howitzers were still bogged down and out of range.

Hunkered at the edge of the clearing, Nhu weighed

their options as darkness approached.

The NVA had executed Giap's strategy masterfully, allowing the South Vietnamese forces to overextend then attacking at carefully prepared points along the methodical advance.

Nhu realized Ly had only one choice - withdraw the battered column before it was cut off completely. They had ventured recklessly beyond safe limits, and were now paying the price.

Nhu radioed Ly, recommending immediate withdrawal before they were encircled. Ly's response came back resigned. "All units pull back, we are breaking contact and retreating from this valley."

As the ARVN column began withdrawing, NVA artillery suddenly opened up, cutting off the muddy trail behind them with a curtain of shrapnel and churned earth. They were pinned down, denied their escape route under intense barrages.

From the jungle, telltale smoke trails marked the firing of recoilless rifles. Their 57mm rounds pierced the thin armor of the M113s with ease, turning the armored personnel carriers into flaming coffins.

Nhu ducked reflexively as a round blew through the front slope of his vehicle, ripping apart the driver before exploding out the rear in a spray of molten shrapnel.

"Dismount!" he coughed through the smoke, as surviving crew bailed out of the stricken APC. Together with the other survivors, they took what cover they could in craters and under vehicles. It was a rout, the kill zone tightened completely around the shredded column.

Through it all, Ly's voice remained steady on the radio, directing aircraft to mark their position with smoke and calling for danger close fire missions. Help too long in coming.

Greed

Central Laos

Coyle banked the AC-130 gently onto its attack heading, double-checking the coordinates for the enemy command complex nestled deep in the Laotian valley. Tonight's target was a high value one, and the route in would be filled with danger. Coyle radioed the lead F-100 fighter jet and asked if they had any contact.

"That's an affirm. We're spiking radar emissions bearing one-six-five for ten. Looks like an SA-2 Guideline site."

"Roger that," Coyle replied. "Clear us a path in."

The Wild Weasels surged ahead, arming their AGM-45 Shrike anti-radiation missiles. Three miles from the target, they detected the radar source - an SA-2 command truck hidden under jungle canopy. Missiles streaked from the Weasels and a fireball etched the night as the truck, radar, and missiles were annihilated in fiery explosions.

"Magnum, target destroyed," reported the Weasels as they broke away. Now it was the Skyraiders' turn.

The propeller-driven attack aircraft swooped in low and slow, hunting for anti-aircraft guns guarding against the gunship's approach. Tracers arced up toward them from a tree line, promptly met with a deluge of high explosive rockets, napalm, and cannon fire. More explosions flashed across the valley as the Skyraiders neutralized bunkers and gun pits with deadly precision.

"Path is clear, all threats suppressed," the flight leader radioed. "She's all yours. Bring the rain."

Coyle rotated the AC-130's aft radar, locking onto the command complex below. Changing the gun selection switch, he activated the 40mm Bofors cannon and lined up for the attack run.

"Guns hot!" Coyle called, then squeezed the trigger. The Spectre shook as high explosive rounds tore from the guns, lancing into the structures clustered 2000 feet below. Thunder reverberated through the valley as the 40mm shells detonated in rapid succession, engulfing the enemy position in smoke and flames. Return fire winked impotently into the night sky as the installation was pummeled into fiery ruin.

Coyle banked the AC-130 away from the burning remains of the enemy command complex. His ammunition stocks were still decent after the first strike.

"I'm going to hit the supply depot at coordinates four-five-seven before we head home," he told the crew.

Coyle radioed his escorts to inform them of the new target. The pilots came back with negative responses. They were short on fuel.

"Just make sure the route is clear. We'll make the assault and return to base without escort," radioed

Coyle.

Pushing ahead of the gunship, the Wild Weasels and Skyraiders confirmed the route was clear then peeled away to refuel, leaving the gunship to conduct one more attack alone.

Coyle put the AC-130 into a pylon turn above the supply depot tucked into a valley. He unleashed a punishing barrage from the 40mm cannons, walking explosions through the storage bunkers, fuel, and ammo caches. Fireballs bloomed as secondary detonations added to the destruction.

Pulling away from the smoking target, the AC-130 shuddered violently as shells tore through the right wing. The number four engine erupted in flames, hit by concealed anti-aircraft fire. The number three engine was smoking badly when the prop locked up coming to an abrupt stop. Two more shells pierced the cockpit punching through the radio in a shower of sparks. "Dammit!" Coyle cursed, knowing that he had gotten greedy by assaulting an extra target without his escorts.

Over the din, flight engineer Wilson shouted, "Number four engine is on fire! Fuel line must be ruptured!"

Glancing at the temperature gauges, Coyle saw the number four engine severely overheating. "Cutoff fuel to number four!" Coyle yelled back.

Wilson flipped the fuel shutoff switch for the damaged engine. "Fuel off now!"

The fire died down as the fuel spurting onto it was cut off. But some flames still licked the wing surface.

Alarms blared as Coyle struggled to keep the damaged AC-130 airborne. "Find me somewhere to put her down!" Coyle shouted to Mills, the navigator.

Mills frantically scanned his maps, searching for a viable place for an emergency landing deep in hostile territory. "There! An abandoned Lima site five miles west of our position."

Coyle banked the crippled plane toward the coordinates as Mills provided heading and altitude instructions. Surrounded by dense jungle and steep mountains, the old airfield was their only hope for survival.

Black smoke trailed from the shredded wing as Coyle guided the aircraft lower, preparing for an emergency landing. Without radio, no one would know their location or situation. But if they could get on the ground in one piece, they'd have a chance.

Coyle fought to keep the stricken AC-130 in the air less than fifty feet above the jungle canopy. The rest of the crew strained to look out the windows, searching for any sign of the small landing strip hidden in the jungle below.

The plane strained to stay aloft, with only two working engines. Coyle wrestled the yoke, the shredded right wing making the gunship want to roll and dive.

"I see it, ten o'clock low!" the loadmaster yelled. Squinting through the smoke, Coyle could barely make out the dim outline of the neglected runway tucked between vine-choked trees. His heart sank as he realized how short the runway was - no more than a few hundred yards carved out of the jungle.

With no other options, he coaxed the crippled AC-130 into an unsteady descent toward the neglected airstrip, knowing their margin for error was razor thin. If they overshot or landed long, the unforgiving jungle waited to consume them.

The lumbering aircraft hit the cracked tarmac hard, skewing to the right. The aircrew bounced into the air and tumbled across the deck like bowling pins. Ignoring the jarring impact, Coyle desperately applied full left rudder and brakes, using every bit of strength to keep the gunship tracking straight.

Hydraulic fluid leaked out across the runway from the aircraft's shattered systems. The trees loomed closer as the wounded plane bled off speed at an agonizing pace. "Come on, come on!" Coyle growled through clenched teeth, muscles burning from the tension.

At the last possible second, the AC-130 screeched to a halt, its nose just two feet from an unforgiving tree trunk. As the adrenaline rush receded, Coyle sat back, breathing hard. That had been too close. But by razor-thin margins, they'd made it down intact. Wilson grabbed the fire extinguisher and yelled, "Make a hole."

He opened the cargo door, jumped out, then crouched under the plane's fuselage to get to the right wing. With the wind pressure gone, flames rose as the engine fire gained power once again. Putting the nozzle next to number four's engine panels he unleashed the extinguisher. Ten-seconds later, the fire was out. Only smoke rose to the sky.

With the aircraft now powerless and motionless on the abandoned runway, the crew let out relieved breaths, glad to have survived the harrowing landing. They all knew how much fate had smiled on them.

A lone pair of eyes watched the smoking aircraft from the concealment of the jungle.

Saigon, South Vietnam

The mood in the ornate Saigon office was tense as General Abrams confronted his South Vietnamese counterpart, General Minh. "I don't understand your insistence on declaring victory and withdrawing from Laos," Abrams said. "We have the enemy on their heels now. This is the time to press the advantage!"

Minh shook his head wearily. "Press with what advantage? My troops have been devastated taking Tchepone. I lost some of my best airborne troops. Each day in Laos brings new casualties we cannot sustain."

Abrams leaned over the map table. "If you pull back now, the North will just filter more men and supplies down the Ho Chi Minh Trail again. We have to exploit this opportunity to interdict their logistics network at its source! It's the only way you can win this war."

Pacing to the window, Minh replied, "Your president has made it clear Vietnamization is the policy going forward. No major US ground forces will deploy to Laos. Without your manpower, how long can a prolonged campaign succeed?"

"You underestimate your army's capabilities," Abrams countered. "With ample American air support, ARVN can disrupt the enemy's supply lines indefinitely. I'll personally vouch for any resources you need."

Minh shook his head. "Words and promises only carry so far. Every day in Laos costs me soldiers while the communists reinforce. And the rains will soon turn the terrain into a swamp. My forces will be trapped and at the mercy of the NVA."

Abrams clenched his fist on the table before speaking again in a measured tone. "I ask that you leave at least a battlegroup in Tchepone to interdict the trail junction. Don't surrender all the blood spent taking it without purpose."

Minh considered this reluctantly. "I can perhaps keep a battalion. But the rest must withdraw back to Vietnam before we lose our window. You know my requests for reserves were denied in Saigon. Without reserves, we are over committed."

Abrams bit back his frustration. He had pushed for greater commitment, only to be overruled by cautious politicians. "A battalion will have to suffice, then. With airpower, they can do real damage to NVA logistics."

Minh nodded solemnly. "I will make it so. But pray this token force does not become a liability should the communists concentrate their strength. We have won a battle, but not yet the war."

The two generals shook hands, tension lingering between them. Abrams knew the invasion force would soon be a shell of its former might. He could only trust airpower and a single understrength battalion to now stem the flow down the Ho Chi Minh Trail. It would have to be enough.

Abandoned Lima Site, Laos

Inside the damaged AC-130, flight engineer Wilson examined the shredded radio, shaking his head. "No chance of fixing this. It's been gutted. You know... the Lima site might still have a functioning radio."

Coyle nodded. "I doubt it, but it's worth a shot. Mills, take Walker and search the Lima site on top of the hill. Look for anything we can use."

As they headed up a steep hill toward the Lima site, Wilson and Coyle stayed with the aircraft, inspecting the damaged engines. They surveyed the four Allison turboprop engines, two on each wing of the AC-130.

Wilson inspected the damaged number four engine caked with fire extinguisher powder. "So, what do you think?" said Coyle.

"Severe fire and shrapnel damage to number four engine. All the wiring is charred. It's a goner. But the number three engine seems in fairly good shape except for some severed control cables and fuel line damage. If I can salvage components from the number four engine, I may be able to get three running again."

"A three-engine takeoff on a short runway?" said Coyle.

"Take it or leave it."

"I'll take it, but we're gonna need to lighten the load."

"Oh, and we're gonna need some more hydraulic fluid. We lost about half when the lines were severed."

"Okay. I'll get working on finding some."

"There should be some drums of hydraulic fluid in the maintenance huts."

"How long is it gonna take to fix number three engine?"

"I don't know. Maybe two or three days."

"Make it two. We're in enemy territory and I'm sure the NVA are hunting for us after what we did to their command complex."

"Good point. Two it is. I'll get to work."

The rest of the crew took stock of their limited armament and dire situation, deep in enemy territory. They had survived the landing, but rescue was uncertain. Danger lurked in the surrounding jungle. They knew the NVA and Pathet Lao would be searching for them and the abandoned Lima site with its airfield was an obvious place to look.

Rollins tallied their armament - just two M16s, five pistols, four grenades, and a flare gun. In small arms their options were limited. They did have the heavy weapons in the gunship and plenty of ammunition.

Coyle ordered Rollins to remove one of the 7.62mm miniguns from the AC-130 to use for perimeter defense in case of attack. He sent the two door gunners, Pierce and Owens, to patrol the surrounding jungle and watch for any enemy movement. So far they seemed alone, but that could change quickly.

Walker and Mills headed uphill through dense jungle to the abandoned base. Reaching the dilapidated buildings, every piece of equipment had been destroyed or removed. The radio was gone. But they grabbed some tools and spare parts that might be useful.

The mid-day sun beat down on Coyle as he approached the sagging maintenance building at the edge of the abandoned airfield. With the AC-130's hydraulics badly damaged, he needed to find any reservoirs of fluid they could salvage before trying to take off.

Stepping through the open doorway into the gloomy interior, he spotted a pair of fifty-gallon drums marked "Hydraulic Fluid" and "Engine Oil" stored against the far wall. But as he drew closer, Coyle saw with sinking disappointment that both containers had been tipped over long ago, their precious contents long since leaked out into the cracked concrete floor.

Crouching down, he could see the dark stains where the puddles of fluid had spread before eventually being absorbed into the thirsty ground. Even the spigots on the upturned drums hung empty, not even a drop remaining. This maintenance shed was a grave for the lifeblood his damaged plane so desperately needed now.

With a sigh, Coyle stood up, wiping the dust from his knees. As he turned back toward the door, a flicker of movement caught his eye. A shadow had shifted on the wall near the entrance.

"Rollins? That you checking on me?" Coyle called out, thinking one of his crew had followed him to the shed. But no reply came back. Uneasy, Coyle slid his hand to the grip of the .38 revolver on his shoulder holster.

The jungle beyond was still, no sign of who or what had moved. As he stepped forward, a shape filled the doorway, sunlight dazzling his eyes.

"Your gun." The words were slightly accented but clear enough. Blinking, Coyle made out a young Laotian woman, steel in her eyes and an old revolver leveled at his chest. Her finger was on the trigger and her aim looked steady.

"Do you know how to use that?" Coyle asked calmly, assessing her stance. In response, the woman expertly cocked back the hammer on her rust-pitted pistol.

"I'll take that as a yes." Slowly, Coyle drew his .38 out by two fingers and handed it over grip-first. The woman slipped it into her belt and produced a coil of rough rope. "No do what I say, I shoot you in head," she said bluntly.

With the gun still trained on him, the woman motioned for Coyle to turn around. He felt the rope bind his wrists tightly behind his back. Testing the knots, he found them secure but not circulation cutting. "Why are you doing this?" Coyle asked.

In response, she pressed the muzzle against his back. "No speak. Quiet." Coyle clamped his mouth shut, realizing conversation was not part of her plan.

"Walk," she ordered, gesturing with her revolver toward the dense jungle beyond the shed. With the gun at his back, he complied, picking his way through the foliage at the treeline before being directed deeper into the shadows under the canopy. His captor followed silently, vigilant for any tricks.

Coyle's mind raced, calculating the odds of overpowering the woman to escape. But she kept a healthy distance, never growing complacent. They were isolated miles behind enemy lines. His crew had no idea he was even in danger. For now, Coyle could only bide his time and gather intel on where he was being taken and why. "I'm Coyle. What is your name?" said Coyle quietly.

"Quiet," said the woman.

"I just want to know what to call you."

The woman moved swiftly behind him and pistol whipped the back of his head. Stunned by the strength of the blow, Coyle went down to his knees.

"You no quiet," she said.

"I be quiet."

"You walk."

Coyle struggled back to his feet and resumed his journey, walking in front of the woman. She keeping her distance so she could not be attacked without warning. After a few minutes...

"Keo," she said. "Name Keo."

Not wanting another whack on the back of the head with her pistol, Coyle nodded that he understood. They moved through the jungle, Keo occasionally pointing them in a new direction. Coyle finally stopped, turned, and said, "Where are you taking me?"

"Go. Walk."

"No walk until you say where we go?"

Keo again cocked the trigger on her pistol, threatening. "Go ahead and shoot. I'm not moving until I know where we are going."

Keo took a moment to consider, then said, "Trade you with Pathet Lao."

"For money? I have money I can give you. More than Pathet Lao."

"No. For daughter."

"Pathet Lao have your daughter."

"Yes. They take her after kill husband. He American like you."

"A soldier?"

"No. Aid worker. Good man."

"Why did they take your daughter?"

"She tall like husband. She good worker in mines."

"What mines?"

"Copper. In jungle. They take all children that can work. The others they kill."

"Your husband tried to stop them?"

"Yes. I think. I not know."

"How many children did they take?"

"Maybe forty. I not know. Many die. Mine dangerous. Jungle dangerous. Pathet Lao dangerous."

"Yeah. I get it."

"You walk now?"

"Yes. I walk."

Coyle started walking again. Keo uncocked her pistol and followed. "How you know they trade?" said Coyle as he continued to walk.

"They hate Americans," said Keo. "They hate my husband. They trade daughter so they kill you."

"Yeah. I don't think they do what you want."

"They kill you for sure, for sure."

"Oh, yeah… they kill me for sure, for sure. But they gonna kill you and your daughter too."

"You not know."

"I'm pretty sure, for sure. You think about it."

Coyle stopped talking and gave Keo time to think as they walked through the jungle. "They kill me because my husband American?" she said.

"Yeah. And they kill your daughter because she half American."

"They not know."

"They not stupid. They will figure it out."

"Maybe."

"Can you take that risk?"

Another long silence as they walked. Keo's mind racing. Trying to figure out if Coyle was lying. "Why you look at cans?" she said.

"You mean drums in shed?"

"Yes, drums."

"We need hydraulic fluid for plane."

"Drums empty?"

"Yes."

"Pathet Lao empty."

"Probably. Do you know where there are more drums like that?"

"No. But I know where plane crash in jungle."

"A plane like our plane?"

"No. Small plane."

"Did it burn when crash?"

"No. Just crash. Man driving die in jungle."

"Was it a Skyraider?"

"I not know. You want? Fix plane?"

"Yeah. For sure, for sure."

"Good. You get my daughter; I show you plane."

"Okay. But you show me plane first. When we get your daughter, Pathet Lao chase us. If our plane work, we escape. You understand?"

"Yes. I understand. How I know you tell truth? Maybe you fix plane and leave. Not give me daughter."

"You don't know me. But I always keep my word."

"You good man?"

"I try to be. You're holding the gun. It's your call."

"Yes. I have gun. I think about it."

"Okay."

As they continued through the jungle, Coyle saw movement up ahead. He stopped and motioned for Keo to be quiet. He pointed up ahead. Keo strained to look but saw nothing. Then, a rifle barrel pressed against the back of her head. She froze. "Drop your pistol," said a man's voice.

Keo dropped her old pistol on the ground at the same time reaching for Coyle's pistol hidden under her shirt. Coyle reached out and stopped her. "Not this time," he said taking his pistol back. Owen stood behind them with his M16 pointed at Keo and said, "What the hell happened, Coyle?"

"What can I say... she got the drop on me."

Pierce, also holding an M16 walked out of the jungle in front of them and said, "You ain't ever gonna live this one down. Captured by a woman?"

"I don't know. She's a pretty tough woman... and brave."

"What do we do with her? Take her back to the airfield?" said Owen.

"Not yet," said Coyle kneeling to pick up her pistol. "We need to do a little recon."

Coyle handed Keo her pistol and said, "I keep my

word. For sure, for sure."

Keo thought for a moment, then nodded and said, "I think you good man."

"Why don't you show us where the Pathet Lao are keeping your daughter?"

Keo nodded.

As dusk settled over the jungle, Coyle checked his revolver one last time before nodding to Keo, Pierce, and Owen. Under the cover of fading light, they began stealthily approaching the Pathet Lao camp located deeper in the dense undergrowth.

Moving slowly from tree to tree, the group paused just outside the perimeter, concealed in thick foliage. Coyle peered through a screen of leaves, surveying the busy enemy camp. Armed Pathet Lao guards patrolled the camp while an officer shouted orders.

At the center of the camp stood a row of large bamboo cages, roughly constructed from lashed-together poles. Dirty, haunted faces stared out between the bars – Montagnard children, some perhaps no older than nine or ten.

Coyle felt his jaw tighten. He watched as more teenage prisoners were led out of a jungle trail into the camp, their hands bound with rope. Exhaustion and hopelessness were etched on their gaunt faces. Prodded by rifles, the prisoners shuffled over to the row of cages, heads down in defeat.

The camp commander shouted another order and guards began cramming the captive children into the crowded confines of the bamboo prisons. Desperate siblings called out to each other as they were separated between cages. In minutes, the barred rooms were packed wall to wall with emaciated prisoners.

Keo scanned the dirty, haunted faces visible between the bars. Suddenly she gasped, seeing a girl of around twelve - her daughter Suen.

Overcome with anguish, Keo started to rush forward from cover, but Coyle grabbed her, clamping a hand over her mouth to silence her cry. Keo bit down on his hand, but Coyle held firm, pulling her back into the jungle. Owen and Pierce folded back, ensuring that they weren't being followed. Once again undercover, Coyle kept Keo pinned until her primal rage subsided.

When her body went limp, Coyle slowly released his grip. Regaining composure, Keo allowed him to pull her deeper in the jungle. Owen and Pierce followed. "We'll come back for her. I promise," whispered Coyle in Keo's ear.

Just after dawn, Coyle, Pierce, and Owen, led by Keo, made their way down a nearly invisible trail through the oppressive jungle. Dense vines and creepers clutched at their clothes, trees looming over them like silent sentinels.

Breaking through a wall of foliage, they emerged into a small clearing. A decaying moss-covered shape rested there, slowly being absorbed back into the living jungle. Creeping vines curled around fractured wings and tail while muddy water pooled in the buckled fuselage.

Coyle let out a low whistle as he inspected the corroding remains of the Douglas Skyraider. Judging by the condition and model, it had been downed here for years, long before their own arrival. The pilot must not have survived, unable to radio his position before perishing alone in the wilderness, miles from rescue behind enemy lines.

Approaching the nose, Coyle could see the familiar silhouette of a 750-pound iron bomb still suspended under the collapsed starboard wing, its fins and tail corroded but casing intact.

Other signs showed scavengers had already stripped many useful parts over the years. The radio was gone. But there were other components that might yet prove serviceable. It was a slim chance, but one worth investigating.

Coyle turned to Owen. "You and Pierce get back to the airfield. Tell the others what we've found. Bring the fifty-gallon drum in the maintenance shed and see if you can find a funnel or pan so we can drain the hydraulic fluid. Bring Wilson and his tools."

The two men nodded and headed off. Drawing his knife, Coyle began hacking away vines to uncover more of the fuselage and access interior components shielded from the elements. If providence allowed, this downed relic might just provide their damaged bird with a new lease on life.

Time passed swiftly as Coyle became absorbed in his task. Keo stood watch with pistol ready, eyes and ears tuned to the surrounding jungle. The danger never fully receded here even for those who called this land home. Her mind was troubled. She had upheld her end of the deal, guiding them here. But would these foreigners truly keep their word to help liberate her daughter in return?

Her people had been abandoned before by American promises. As the day waned, Keo could not quiet her worries. Finally, she spoke, "When fix your plane, will you help free the children as you promised? Or will you fly away and leave them to darkness?" There was ache in her voice.

Coyle turned to her with compassion. "On my honor, I will keep my pledge. Your people's trust was betrayed before, but not by me." He met her eyes. "Those children will be freed, no matter the cost. And your daughter will be returned to you. I swear it on my life."

Keo searched his face, then nodded slowly. Perhaps this man's word could be believed. But only action would banish lingering doubt. For now, she could only hope and help however possible. The children's fate hinged on promises in a world where promises often died.

Footsteps eventually signaled the aircrew's arrival. Wilson wasted no time assessing the wreck. His expert eye quickly detected wiring, sheet metal, mechanical linkages, and electronic components worth retrieving. Coyle, Owen, and Pierce went to work bleeding the hydraulic fluid from the aircraft into the fifty-gallon drum. At one point, Owen and Pierce took turns blowing into the tubing pushing the remaining fluid out the opposite end. It was slow work. The smaller aircraft had less hydraulic fluid than the gunship. They needed every bit they could salvage.

By dusk, Wilson had an inventory of scavenged parts and a plan of action. "It'll be tricky, but I think we can modify some of these to get number three operational again."

Coyle clapped his shoulder. "You've done tougher repairs before. Let's pack this up and give it our best shot."

The jungle had reclaimed this fallen aircraft long ago. Now, piece by piece, it would surrender its bones to resurrect another bird so it could once again reclaim the sky. What fate took, desperate innovation now restored.

Wilson laid down his wrench, having finished the patchwork repairs on the AC-130 to the best of his abilities. The gunship was still battered, but flightworthy again - barely. Wiping the grease from his hands, Wilson looked over to where Coyle, Keo, and the rest of the crew were gathered, voices low as they finalized the plan to rescue the caged children from the nearby Pathet Lao camp.

"I don't like going in at night," Rollins said. "Too hard to maintain situational awareness. Those prisoners are just kids and they're gonna be scared. Once they're free there is no telling what they'll do. They could try and hide in the jungle and we'd never find them."

Owens nodded. "Yeah, but night makes it easier to infiltrate the camp without being seen. I say we strike under cover of full darkness."

Keo drew a crude map in the dirt. "Two guards here. The rest sleep at night."

Coyle considered the rough diagram, pondering their options. A night raid would maximize secrecy, but day would allow tighter coordination and allow them to keep an eye on the children. Both had advantages and risks. "The thing that worries me is not the infiltration of the camp or freeing the children. We can take out the two guards quietly. As long as we don't wake the other soldiers we should be good. Keo, you need to keep those kids quiet."

Keo nodded.

"What really worries me is what happens when the Pathet Lao figure out that the children have been freed. They're gonna be on us like white on rice. Even if we make it back to the airfield, we still gotta take off and that's not gonna be easy with a bunch of communists shooting at us."

"And we don't even know if number three engine will start," said Wilson.

"I know, but we can't risk testing it. It's too damned loud. We're just gonna have to have faith that you worked one of your miracles and got it right the first time. How sure are you, Wilson?"

"I don't know... maybe eighty percent."

"So, we're gonna need a plan to slow down the communists if Wilson needs some time to get number three running."

"That's a lot of ifs, Coyle," said Rollins.

"Well, we just gonna have to get lucky. That's all," said Mills.

"Did you bring your lucky rabbit's foot?" said Pierce.

"Nah. Lost it in high school. I gave to Nancy Geller after we had sex for the first time," said Mills.

"Bad move."

"Not at the time."

"Okay, let's focus," said Coyle. "Anyone got any bright ideas on how we can slow down the Pathet Lao?"

"Well, I got one. But it's gonna require a bit of heavy lifting to make it work," said Rollins with a slight smile.

Under the moonless jungle canopy, the Pathet Lao camp was still except for two guards lazily making their rounds. Inside the bamboo cages, the captive Montagnard children slept fitfully, exhausted from the day's work in the mine.

Making hand signals, Coyle directed Pierce and Owen to circle around behind the patrolling sentries. Silent as shadows, their knives flashed in the firelight. The guards collapsed without a sound.

With the sentries down, Coyle and Keo emerged from hiding. The camp remained quiet, only gentle snores rising from the surrounding lean-tos as the soldiers slept unaware. Time was now critical.

Keo rushed directly for the children's bamboo prison. She scanned the small forms desperately until she spotted Suen's beloved face. "Suen!" said Keo a little too loudly as she grasped Suen's hands through the cage. Tears of joy flowed freely down both their cheeks.

Coyle watched wanting to get Keo moving. But he knew it was hopeless. The mother and daughter needed a moment. He pulled out his K-Bar and cut the first cage open. He motioned for the children to keep quiet as they left the cage. Walker was waiting in the jungle ready to guide them.

The brief reunion grounded Keo's swirling emotions. She had to free the others quickly, before the camp awoke. With renewed purpose, she cut open the cages while Coyle returned to keeping watch.

The children emerged into open air, confused and wary. "This way, hurry! Your families await!" whispered Keo urged them towards freedom.

One by one, the children disappeared into the jungle like spirits until only two remained. As Keo freed the last boy, his leg caught on a trailing vine and he tripped with a cry.

Hearing the cry, a soldier emerged from a hut, fumbling with his rifle. Coyle was faster, knocking him out cold with a blow from the pistol grip. The silence had been shattered. Now speed was everything. Pierce and Owen ran to help Keo with the children.

"Go!" Coyle hissed. With her hand wrapped firmly around her daughter's hand, Keo fled with the last child as angry voices carried through the camp. Owen gestured urgently and they melted into the bush just as the first wild shots chased their heels. More screams and commotion erupted, but the jungle shrouded their escape.

Keo urged the children onward through the dark jungle, their bare feet flying over roots and stones. Behind them angry shouts grew closer as the pursuing Pathet Lao slashed through clinging vines. She clutched Suen's hand tightly as they slipped through the concealing jungle. The dream of liberation had begun. Her family was still fractured, but Suen gave renewed strength and hope on this perilous path.

Coyle stopped momentarily at the tree line, letting Keo and the kids gain some distance. He raised the flare gun skyward and fired.

The brilliant magenta flare arced over the shadowy canopy. Forward, its glow would alert his aircrew to be ready. Now their survival depended on evasion and defensive preparations.

Coyle took off running as the flare drifted down through jungle leaves. The vivid phosphorous temporarily lit the night, banishing darkness.

Angry voices sounded behind Coyle as flashlights stabbed through the underbrush. The hunt was on. But his crew had been warned.

The kids gasped for breath, some crying in fear and exhaustion, but Keo would not let them falter. "Keep moving!" she insisted. "Do not stop!"

Keo urged the children forward as Coyle protected

the group's rear, pistol raised. Behind them, the angry pursuers drew steadily closer, rifles cracking.

At the caravan's tail, Owen peeled off and vanished into the brush. Minutes later rifle shots flashed from the jungle, followed by confused yelling. The tactic worked - Owen had drawn some soldiers astray.

But more pursuers remained doggedly on the trail of the children. Again, Pierce broke from the group, firing blindly into the dark before moving to set up another ambush. Another cluster of Pathet Lao took the bait, breaking away toward his shots.

Coyle pressed the flagging children onward. The jungle assaults had bought precious time, sowing confusion among their hunters. But threats remained. They had to reach the airfield before the soldiers reorganized.

Keo led them in evasive weaving, using the darkness as cover. But still their hunters clung to the trail. The air filled with gunfire and screams as two worlds collided in this hunt - one chasing shadows, the other salvation.

Coyle fired several rounds blindly over his shoulder. His pistol clicked empty. The enraged Pathet Lao were just yards behind, close enough he could hear their snarled threats.

Ahead, Keo led the exhausted children into a moonlit clearing. No choice now but to cross the open ground and hope the far treeline offered sanctuary.

"Go, go!" Coyle yelled, stopping to scoop up two stragglers by their waists. Bullets whipped by them as he ran full tilt, the kids' legs flailing. Lungs burning, Coyle focused everything on reaching the far side ahead of the bullet storm.

Twenty more yards. A burst of gunfire tore up dirt

beside them. The Pathet Lao were within range and there was no cover to protect them. Suddenly a voice rang out - "Hit the deck!"

Coyle dove forward, shielding the small children beneath him. He scanned for the voice's origin as gunfire erupted back in the direction they had come.

Just inside the treeline! A dark figure knelt behind the flashing muzzle of a minigun pirated from the gunship. The deafening roar filled the night as the weapon unleashed a torrent of fire into the exposed Pathet Lao. It was Rollins behind the gun with Mills beside him ready to feed him more ammunition.

Coyle pressed himself and the children flat, making themselves small as the steel storm raged above them. Screams mixed with the Gatling gun's fire.

Finally, the gun spun down. Popping his head up, Coyle saw carnage across the clearing – dozens of Pathet Lao lay in the field, motionless.

Coyle rose with the two children and pushed them toward Keo. "We've got to keep moving. There not going to stop. More will come."

Pierce and Owen emerged from the underbrush to wave Coyle forward. Keo waited with the children further back in the sanctuary of the dense brush.

Rollins set the minigun on the ground next to the remaining ammo cases. He set a grenade next to the firing mechanism and pulled the safety pin. As the grenade's handle flipped away, Rollins called out, "Fire in the hole" and ran to catch up with the others. The grenade exploded destroying the Gatling gun and setting off secondary explosions as the ammunition cooked off.

Coyle took a child's hand in each of his own and headed for the airfield ahead.

Pure exhaustion weighed down every step as Coyle led the group out of the jungle onto the airfield tarmac. Behind them, two nightmare hours of evasion through the predawn darkness. Ahead, salvation awaited - if their battered aircraft could get airborne one last time.

Keo shepherded the children toward the waiting AC-130. Coyle did a quick headcount as they climbed aboard – thirty-two tired but grateful young lives saved. Now to make sure those lives didn't end here.

He conferred quickly with Rollins, Owens, and Pierce. "Dump all the weapons and ammo outside. We need to shed every ounce possible for takeoff. Leave nothing for the enemy." The men got to work as the others took their seats inside the aircraft.

In the cockpit, Wilson was already going through pre-flight checks. The turboprops coughed and belched smoke as he fired them to life one by one. Engine three sputtered and flamed out. "Dammit," said Wilson.

Coyle leaned into the engineer's shoulder. "I'll take her. Keep trying on number three." Wilson nodded and they switched places. Outside, grenade blasts signaled the destruction of any weight deemed non-essential.

Hands dancing across the controls, Coyle coaxed the damaged aircraft to life. The engines were rough, wounded bird barely hanging on, but running. But not even Coyle, with all his experience, could take off with only two engines. Not with a load of children as cargo. Physics wouldn't allow it. "How are you doing there, Wilson?"

In response, number three engine belched fire and smoke as it groaned to life.

Wilson gave Coyle a thumbs up. They were as flight-ready as possible under the circumstances.

Coyle opened the side window and called out, "Get your asses on board!"

Coyle released the brakes and taxied the listing gunship toward the runway as the eastern sky brightened. Morning brought a new chance for the desperate and daring. Pierce and Owens were the first to reach the door and hop into the aircraft as it rolled.

Without warning, gunfire cracked from the treeline. Pathet Lao soldiers had tracked them! Rounds ricocheted off the aircraft as the gunners tried to prevent their quarry's escape.

"Go go, get us airborne!" yelled Rollins as he ran toward the cargo door. As Rollins reached the door, a bursts of automatic rifle fire stitched across his back. Owens grabbed his hand as he crumpled. Owens tried to pull Rollins inside, but he was too heavy. "He's dead," said Pierce.

"We don't know that," said Owens refusing to release Rollin's body as his boots dragged along the tarmac.

"Let 'em go, Owens," said Pierce. "It's what he would want."

Owens held on for another moment, then released Rollin's arm. The lifeless body fell to the tarmac and tumbled several times before stopping, motionless. Pierce had been right. Rollins was dead.

Grinding his teeth, Coyle pushed the trembling throttles to max. The wounded plane lumbered down the runway, gradually gathering speed. The jungle treeline approaching fast. The enemy gunners adjusted their aim, bullets piercing the thin metal skin.

Keo used her body to shield her daughter. The

children cried in fear as tiny shafts of sunlight appeared one after another through the aircraft's metal skin.

Coyle and Mills watched the jungle near as the gunship reached the end of the runway. "Now," said Mills.

"Not yet," said Coyle keep the plane on the ground for as long as possible as they gained speed.

Moments later, the battered wings bit air. The AC-130 heaved itself skyward, drips of oil and hydraulic fluid trailing like blood. Coyle banked away from the bullets nipping at their heels. Against all odds, they had escaped.

Keo embraced her daughter, both weeping with joy and grief. No elation at bucking the odds could erase all they'd endured. But deliverance was the first step in healing.

Coyle leveled the aircraft, mind reeling from flashbulb memories of their savagery and salvation below.

Ubon Airfield, Thailand

The AC-130 touched down hard on the tarmac in Ubon, Thailand. It was far from a graceful landing, but any safe arrival was miracle enough given the damage the aircraft had endured.

As the cabin door opened and the stairs lowered, the thirty-two liberated Montagnard children peered out anxiously. But instead of armed pursuers, they saw smiling aid workers waiting to receive them on the safe haven of friendly soil.

Keo guided the kids down onto the miraculously solid ground. Some laughed and cried with joy. Others remained solemn, old beyond their years. All had lived lifetimes in the days since capture. Their road ahead would be long.

As the last child exited, Coyle and his crew descended from the aircraft. Though battered, their heads were held high. Quiet handshakes and embraces were exchanged, wordless reflections on their intertwined fate.

In halting English, Keo took Coyle's hands. "You keep your promise. " Deep emotion choked her words. "You give me hope."

"It was the right thing to do," said Coyle.

"I sorry about Rollins."

"Me too. But he knew the risks and I think he would do it again if he had to. It was a good cause and he was a good man."

Keo smiled through tears. They embraced fiercely, two kindred spirits joined briefly on the winds of war. Then Keo turned to rejoin the children, helping ease their transition back to light.

Laotian and South Vietnamese Border

Captain Nhu pressed his men forward along the muddy trail, shrugging off the sting of shrapnel in his arm. Once high, morale was now sinking along with their prospects. After brutal ambushes and bloody assaults, the armor and air cavalry of Nhu's company were reduced to a weary handful. The NVA bunkers and machine guns waited around every bend.

Not far ahead, Lieutenant Colonel Ly grimly assessed his ravaged battalion. Barely a quarter remained of the confident force that invaded weeks prior. They had reached the limit of human endurance.

At the rear, Sergeant Nguyen kept the wounded

moving as best he could. With medical supplies exhausted, only those who could walk or be carried had hope of seeing home again. Their pride in taking the fight to the enemy was gone. Now the war was a gnawing pit in their stomachs that grew with each fruitless sacrifice.

By March 25th, the remnants had withdrawn into South Vietnam, the land they sacrificed so dearly to occupy abandoned without victory. Doubts arose about ARVN readiness and the wisdom of America's shrinking commitment. For Ly, Nguyen and Nhu, the battle left scars both visible and hidden. But war allowed no time to lick wounds. The secret conflict would grind on in jungles and villages, claiming more souls who dared believe in a future of freedom. The winds of war spared none.

Operation Lam Son 719 ultimately ended in strategic failure for South Vietnam and the United States. Despite early success in penetrating into Laos and capturing the logistical hub at Tchepone, ARVN forces suffered heavy losses from NVA ambushes and could not advance further against determined resistance. After a two-month struggle, the South Vietnamese were forced to withdraw back across the border, unable to sustain the offensive. They left behind a battalion-sized element at Tchepone, but it too was defeated in the following months.

The operation resulted in estimated casualties of 3-5,000 for ARVN forces, a severe loss for South Vietnam's military capabilities. The US suffered 214 soldiers killed along with the loss of 168 aircraft, including 101 helicopters and twenty fixed-wing planes.

Though exact figures are uncertain, North Vietnamese casualties likely ranged from 10-15,000 killed in action. NVA anti-aircraft units also scored a major victory, claiming eighty-one US aircraft shot down according to their records.

The losses revealed how exposed South Vietnamese forces were beyond the range of American artillery and air support. And the increasing cost of US air missions highlighted the growing capability of communist anti-air defenses.

Militarily, the casualty exchange ratio heavily favored the North Vietnamese. But strategically, Hanoi gained only a temporary reprieve as Washington refused to alter its withdrawal timetable despite the setback. Still, the losses shook confidence in Vietnamization, laying bare lingering ARVN deficiencies.

The operation cast further doubt on claims of Vietnamization progress. ARVN forces proved unable to maintain themselves so far from home support without major US ground involvement, which President Nixon refused to authorize. Casualties were extremely heavy for the South Vietnamese, while US air support took punishing losses from NVA anti-aircraft defenses. Morale in South Vietnam suffered a blow, foreshadowing struggles ahead. Though depicted initially as a success, the Lam Son 719 invasion highlighted the limits of Vietnamization and weaknesses still remaining in ARVN's capabilities. The war's conclusion remained distant.

White House – Washington DC, USA

The thick stage lights caused Nixon to perspire slightly under the TV makeup as technicians made final adjustments. In a few moments, he would be speaking to the American people about the war in Vietnam.

An aide handed Nixon a glass of water and he sipped it carefully to avoid smudging the precisely applied powder and lipstick. Appearances mattered greatly for how his speech would be received.

At the signal from the director, Nixon shuffled his notes one last time and looked directly into the bright glare of the camera. Millions were tuned in to hear his nationwide address. "My fellow Americans, tonight I come before you to discuss our progress in ending United States military involvement in the conflict in Vietnam."

Nixon adopted a confident tone, communicating command and conviction. "As we implement the process called Vietnamization, responsibility for fighting is steadily being transferred to South Vietnam's armed forces. Their recent offensive into Laos demonstrated that our training efforts are working."

He gestured for emphasis, holding his head high. "South Vietnam's army is now capable of defending its country with our advice and material support. Accordingly, I am announcing an additional withdrawal of 100,000 US ground troops, to be completed within the next six months."

Pausing, Nixon shuffled to the next page of his typed speech. "I promised you an honorable end to our combat operations in Vietnam. We are following the timetable I outlined. As South Vietnamese forces grow stronger, more of our brave fighting men can come home."

Nixon looked back into the camera. "Much hard work remains. But the progress we have achieved is proof that America's sacrifices in Vietnam are not open-ended. Our ally's success confirms they have the training and resources to defend themselves."

"We will keep our ironclad commitment to South Vietnam's independence. But as their strength increases, our combat role can decrease. I urge all citizens to welcome home our returning soldiers who have served with honor. They have earned our eternal gratitude."

Nixon set his notes down. "The light at the end of the tunnel may still be dim, but this new withdrawal shines as a beacon of hope that Vietnamization is succeeding. The road ahead remains difficult, but working together, we will reach journey's end. Goodnight, and may God bless America."

The camera light switched off and technicians began removing Nixon's microphone. He sat back, hoping his address had convinced the public that Vietnamization was working as promised. Buying time was critical - time to hand over the war's burden before dissent at home became unmanageable. Perception was as important as reality in politics. Now, he had to ensure this latest withdrawal was executed smoothly, backing up his claims of progress. The end was still far off, but he had taken another step toward.

Mary Ann

March 28, 1971 - Quang Tri Province, South Vietnam

The monsoon rains had turned everything to mud. As Sergeant Mike Collins slogged through the muck toward Fire Support Base Mary Ann, he couldn't help but think that this place was Hell on earth.

Collins had seen a lot of combat in his two tours in Vietnam. A gruff NCO from Iowa, he'd volunteered for special operations forces after his first tour as an infantryman. The constant danger and stress had hardened him into a pragmatic soldier who got the job done no matter what.

Though he could seem cold on the exterior, Collins cared deeply about the welfare of his men. He'd learned the hard way that in war, compassion was a liability that got people killed. Feelings had no place on the battlefield, only discipline, vigilance, and violence of action.

Some labeled him an old-school hard ass. Others saw him as a lifer who cared about his troops, if only by driving them hard in training to keep them alive in combat. Collins didn't care what the rear echelon pencil pushers thought of him.

He'd seen Mary Ann built from the ground up, from a vacant hilltop to a sprawling firebase. He'd survived dozens of enemy assaults in the previous months. He'd be damned if he let the NVA take Mary Ann on his watch.

Situated in Quang Tri Province near the demilitarized zone between North and South Vietnam, FSB Mary Ann was a vital strategic position for the Americans. It allowed artillery support for patrols along the Ho Chi Minh trail and provided a forward operating base to launch attacks into enemy territory. Its proximity to the North Vietnamese Army and the Viet Cong made it a constant target.

The hilltop firebase was alive with controlled chaos. Soldiers scrambled to reinforce battered bunkers and replace sandbags chewed up by shrapnel. The sickly sweet smell of cordite hung in the air, mixing with the mineral tang of mud and unwashed bodies. All around the perimeter, AN/PRC-25 field radios crackled with reports and requests for fire support. Artillerymen sweated over their 105mm and 155mm howitzers, getting targeting coordinates from forward observers. Helicopter crews trotted to their Hueys and Cobras, rotors already spinning up to launch counterattacks.

In the tactical operations center, Captain Miller and his staff marked maps and plotted troop movements. The TOC was dug deep, reinforced with timbers and sandbags. But it still shook with each mortar or rocket impact, maps dancing on the plywood walls as dust sifted from the ceiling. The men inside barely noticed, caught up in the intricacies of defending the firebase. Artillery calculations and logistics took focus, leaving no room for fear or doubt. Necessity and training fused them into a cohesive fighting force.

Collins ducked into the bunker, shaking the rain off his poncho. The shelter was cool and dark after the sweltering humidity outside. A few candles flickered, casting shadows on the tired faces of the men inside. They were an engineer company tasked with keeping the base operational and improving its defenses. It was a never-ending job.

"How's it looking out there, Sarge?" asked a baby-faced private. Collins recognized him as one of the new arrivals, still shiny and optimistic. That wouldn't last long in this place.

"It's a goddamned swamp," Collins grumbled. "The shovelheads shelled the perimeter again last night. Took out a section of the wire."

He saw the nervous looks exchanged between the young soldiers. Mary Ann was all that stood between the NVA's artillery and the cities below. If the base fell, the Communists could rain shells on Danang and Hue.

Collins turned to the company commander, Captain Miller. "We need to fortify the eastern bunkers and get that wire replaced. I've got sniper teams sweeping the tree line, but Charlie's apt to probe our defenses anytime."

Miller nodded, arms crossed. They were stretched thin, with too many vital positions to shore up and not enough men. "Do what you can, Sergeant. I'll get you some men from HQ platoon to help with the digging and wire."

Collins scowled. More half-trained bootcamp kids would only slow them down. But beggars couldn't be choosers.

He spent the next hour organizing teams to rotate

in and out of the downpour, repairing damaged bunkers and replacing sandbags. Mortar fire rumbled in the distance, indistinct through the hiss of rain. The clouds pressed down oppressively, reducing visibility to less than fifty yards. Cold mud sucked at their boots, the earth literally trying to swallow them up.

When the call came over the radio that the wire crew needed support, Collins had a gut feeling trouble was coming. He grabbed his gear and slogged out past the perimeter into the maze of shell craters beyond. Staying low, he led a squad through the mire, senses straining for any sign of enemy movement.

The trees erupted without warning, green tracers slicing through the rain. Collins dove for cover as enemy mortar rounds slammed in, geysers of mud fountaining up where they hit. The NVA had them zeroed in.

"Return fire!" Collins yelled. The chatter of M-16s answered the Communist AK-47s. Leaping up, Collins unloaded on full auto into the tree line until his magazine ran dry. A dark shape lurched out of the shadows toward him, dressed in black pajamas with an AK leveled from the hip. Pulling his pistol like a gunslinger, Collins dropped him with a burst from his .45 before he could fire. Training until his fingers bled, repetitive motion, muscle memory, - these were the things that made a difference in a firefight. Collins didn't need to think, he just reacted.

Collins dove behind a shell crater, dropping another AK-carrying soldier with a burst from his rifle. The staccato answering fire from his squad told him they were still in the fight. Scrambling through the mud, Collins moved laterally, trying to flank the enemy position. He spotted a dark hole torn in the perimeter wire, evidence of how the NVA infiltration team had slipped through.

Popping up, he threw a frag grenade at the hole then hit the dirt. The explosion flashed and boomed, shrapnel shredding the surrounding brush. Collins signaled his squad to concentrate fire on that sector. With any luck, the grenade had bought them a brief lull.

They leapfrogged forward, one fire team laying down suppressive fire while the other maneuvered. It was tough going through the thigh-deep muck. The ominous silence told Collins the NVA were still there, waiting.

As he crouched behind a large rubber tree, a cry split the air behind him, followed by thrashing in the mud. Whirling around, Collins saw a wide-eyed private trapped hip-deep in mud, clutching at his blood-soaked neck. An enemy sniper had nearly decapitated him with a single round through the gap in his helmet and flak jacket.

Collins crawled to the dying man, but it was no use - the major arteries were severed. "Dammit, hold on! Medic!" Collins shouted, knowing it was futile.

The private's eyes glazed over as a final wheeze escaped his lips. Collins slammed a fist into the mud. The ambush had been planned perfectly, luring them into a prepared kill zone.

Signaling to his RTO to direct a squad to hit the trees from the flank, Collins used his last grenade to lay down covering fire. Under the crackle of the grenade, he thought he heard a scream from his right flank. Gunfire erupted from that direction - it sounded like Corporal Willis's fire team.

Charging forward, Collins bowled over a young

NVA soldier who popped up in his path. They tumbled into the bloody mud and Collins dispatched him with his K-bar. Surging to his feet, Collins saw Willis and two of his men locked in close-quarters battle against half a dozen NVA regulars. One of Willis's men was down, the other firing wildly with his pistol.

Collins keyed his radio mic to call for help but took an AK round in the shoulder, spinning him around. He returned fire with his .45 one-handed while drawing his K-bar again with his left. Another enemy fighter charged him bayonet-first. Collins side-stepped and slashed upward, opening the man's throat in a crimson spray.

He staggered toward Willis's squad just as a grenade blast hurled Willis and his surviving soldier backward. Collins watched helplessly as the NVA surrounded the two wounded Americans to finish them off.

Pure fury boiled up inside him. He was not losing any more men today. With a primal scream of rage, Collins charged right at the enemy soldiers, firing his .45 and knife clenched in a death grip. His world narrowed to the three NVA fighters standing over his men, who turned in surprise at the mud-covered madman barreling down on them.

Collins tackled the first man, driving his K-bar to the hilt into his chest. The others were hampered by the close quarters as Collins spun, using the impaled enemy as a human shield as the second soldier emptied his AK at Collin and the dead soldier. He fired point blank into the second man's face as he was trying to reload his AK, then charged the third before he could bring his AK to bear.

They went down in the mud and Collins dispatched him with a slash to the throat. Gasping for air, covered in a mix of mud and blood, he quickly checked on the wounded Americans. Willis and his soldier were still alive, though both seriously injured.

Collins radioed in for an emergency medivac as he tried to patch them up. He would keep them alive by sheer force of will until the choppers arrived. Hearing movement behind him, Collins whirled with his .45 raised. Two of his squad members emerged from the jungle, equally muddy and blood-spattered.

"Damned good to see you guys," Collins said with relief.

"We eliminated the sniper and reinforced the wire," one replied. "Is anyone else still out there?"

Collins listened intently to the sounds of gunfire back at the base camp. "I don't think so, but we need to get these wounded out."

With the perimeter reinforced for now, Collins focused everything on keeping Willis and the others alive. He silently vowed that FSB Mary Ann would stand, no matter what it took. That would be his revenge for his fallen men... survival of the firebase.

The medevac choppers arrived in a swirl of beating rotors that whipped the jungle foliage into a frenzy. Collins helped load the wounded into the Hueys, then climbed aboard himself. He took one last look at the blood-soaked mud where they had battled the NVA infiltration team. Satisfaction washed over him knowing they had eliminated the threat, for now.

As the helicopters lifted off, Collins peered out the door to survey the firebase below. Plumes of smoke rose from multiple impact points across the base. He could see soldiers still reinforcing bunkers and stringing new rolls of concertina wire. The fight was far from over.

Collins checked on the two wounded from his squad. The medic had started IV fluids and dressed their wounds, but both men were pale and shivering from blood loss. Collins put a hand on each of their shoulders.

"Hang in there. You're going to make it," he said. He hoped it wasn't an empty promise.

At the field hospital, Collins helped unload the casualties, then allowed a medic to patch up his shoulder wound. He went in search of Captain Miller. He found the company commander looking utterly exhausted, still covered in mud, and his hand bandaged from a deep cut.

"What's the situation, sir?" Collins asked.

Miller ran a filthy hand over his face. "Everything is still contested. D Company just repelled another push at the eastern bunkers. But we're critically low on 105 ammo and claymores."

Collins spat on the ground. "I need to get back there. My guys are still in the fight, but they're outnumbered."

"Everyone's outnumbered," said Miller looking at Collins's bandaged shoulder. "You're wounded, Sergeant."

"It's a through-and-through, sir. I'm okay. Give me a supply of grenades and bullets and I'll make sure those bastards regret the day they messed with Mary Ann."

Miller managed a tired smile. "I believe it. Get cleaned up and rearmed. We're airlifting reinforcements in at dawn."

As the sun crested the jungle canopy, Collins was on the first Huey back to the firebase. It was time to take the fight to the enemy.

The Hueys swept in low over the firebase, rotors beating down the smoke drifting across the shell-pocked landscape. Staring out the doorway, Collins could see soldiers in foxholes hugging the earth as the choppers landed quickly, disgorging fresh troops and ammo.

As Collins jogged toward the eastern bunkers, the incoming mortar barrage started. Round after round rocked the base, sending geysers of mud and shrapnel high into the air. Men dove for cover, cowering low until the barrage ceased.

Picking themselves back up, the troops hurried onward to their positions. The enemy was signaling their intent to test Mary Ann again today. Collins intended to give them an even bloodier reception than yesterday.

Captain Miller waved Collins over as he passed the tactical operations center. "Sergeant, we've got reports of a large enemy force amassing in those tree lines to the east. They'll be coming at us in brigade strength soon."

Collins spat on the ground. "Let 'em come. We'll stack them up like cordwood."

"That's what I want to hear," Miller said. "Now get to your sector and make sure your men are dug in deep and ready."

Collins arrived at the eastern perimeter as his platoon sergeant finished positioning the reinforcements in their foxholes and bunkers. He moved amongst them, dispensing last minute advice and reassurance. Most were FNGs - fucking new guys - never having faced combat before. Collins knew the next few hours would age them a lifetime.

He ducked into a bunker, peering through the firing slit at the tree line 300 meters away. Through the lingering mortar smoke, he could see dark shapes moving, zig-zagging between the rubber trees. The NVA were coming, and this time they would force a decisive engagement.

Collins turned to the wide-eyed private next to him on the machine gun. "Get ready, son. You see anything move out there, don't hesitate - just squeeze that trigger. And may God have mercy on their souls."

The kid nodded, swallowing hard as he flicked off the gun's safety. Collins leaned close and spoke low and calm: "Listen to me. You can do this. I know you're scared - any man with sense would be. Use the fear to sharpen your focus. We hold this line, whatever it takes. You got it?"

The private nodded, reassured. That was Collin's job – keep his warriors confident and alive. He would do his best, but he knew it wouldn't be enough. More of his men would die. It was a shitty situation, but there was no getting around it. Charlie wanted the firebase and his men stood in their way. It was that simple. In war everyone wanted something, and the only real question was how much they were willing to pay for it.

The coming battle would test them all like never before. As the first communist mortar rounds began falling amidst the perimeter wire, Collins said a silent prayer. Lord, bring us strength.

The first enemy waves emerged from the jungle 300 meters away, sprinting hard under covering mortar fire. "Fool's courage," said Collins to himself as he signaled for his machine guns to open fire. Tracers sliced through the morning mist like scimitars. The Claymores they had sown across the beaten zone erupted in thundering steel storms, cutting down dozens of NVA at a time.

Still they kept coming. Like locusts, another wave emerged from the trees to replace the fallen. RPG rockets streaked in to blast craters in the perimeter berm, opening paths for the attackers.

Collins ran up and down the line, directing fire. "Conserve your ammo! Aim for the leaders and machine gunners first!"

He unloaded barrage after barrage from his rifle until he could feel the hot barrel on his face. Beside him, the cherry private fired the M60 relentlessly, teeth gritted as 7.62mm casings piled up around his boots. When the gun abruptly fell silent, Collins looked over to see the kid struggling with a jammed round.

Collins placed a hand on his shoulder. "Slow down, breathe! Don't force it."

With Collins walking him through, the private cleared the jam in seconds and resumed firing. The gun chattered on as Collins slapped a new magazine into his rifle and got back into the fight.

Captain Miller's voice crackled over the radio net, directing 53mm recoilless rifle fire from one of the towers onto enemy formations. Skyraiders screamed in overhead, dropping napalm and cluster bombs that erupted in fiery shrapnel. The earth shook under the nonstop bombardment.

As fast as the Americans cut them down, more NVA emerged from the jungle. They scuttled like spiders under the defensive wire, slithering into shell craters, and then dashing for the bunkers before being mowed down. It was like they have already accepted their deaths and the only question was how many Americans they could take with them before their final breath.

Grenades cascaded in, blasting sandbags to shreds and collapsing timbers. The air was choked with dust and cordite. Everywhere Collins looked, the enemy was breaching. He shot two more NVA bolting through a tear in the wire, then bayoneted another who jumped into his hole.

"Ammo! I need a mag!" Collins's radio man, Pfc. Hernandez, tossed him one. Slap, lock, rack, and Collins was back in action, picking off an NVA machine gun crew that had set up behind a berm. He glanced back at the firebase's interior line - at this rate, the outer perimeter would be overrun within thirty minutes.

Captain Miller's voice sounded over the radio, strained with desperation. "Viper lead, this is Python 6 - danger close fire mission, danger close! Level that treeline, now!"

The ground heaved as a full artillery battery unleashed on the jungle. Tree bursts devastated the woods, eviscerating dozens more NVA troops. But still they kept coming.

A massive secondary explosion erupted as the artillery strikes detonated an NVA ammo depot hidden in the jungle. The blast wave rippled out, knocking soldiers off their feet even hundreds of meters away. Collins watched a mushroom cloud rise and dissipate - the firebase had just received a brief reprieve.

"Hernandez, get over to 2nd Platoon and see what they need," Collins ordered his RTO. "We're getting flanked from the east!"

Suddenly a cry arose from the inner perimeter - "Sappers in the wire!" Enemy commandos had penetrated the final line of defense. Collins could hear

Captain Miller directing the quick reaction force to counterattack and seal the breach.

But more NVA were still rushing the outer bunkers. Collins leapt up with his .45 and ran from position to position, rallying the defenders. Men bled from shrapnel wounds, covered in a slurry of mud and blood, but they kept fighting with pure adrenaline.

An RPG round screamed in and exploded atop a bunker, collapsing it in a cloud of dust and timbers. Collins felt hot steel slash across his back. He stumbled but kept moving, pushing the pain from his mind.

Coming upon a wounded private propped against a sandbag, Collins helped brace him up. "Where's your squad?"

"Dead... RPG got 'em," the kid gasped through bloody lips. He couldn't have been more than nineteen.

Collins grabbed more ammo and stuffed it into the private's flak jacket. "Use it well. Aim for the breach. Help's coming."

Leaving the private to cover a breach in the wire, Collins sprinted for the CP. He arrived to find Captain Miller bleeding from multiple shrapnel wounds but still directing the defense. His face was hollow, eyes sunken.

"We're out of time and ammo, Sergeant," Miller said. "If we can't hold them off for the next fifteen mikes, Mary Ann falls."

Collins racked his brain. Artillery was almost exhausted, air power stretched thin. Suddenly, he had an idea - it was desperate, but their only chance.

"Sir, that creek bed to the west...we could pull back and draw them into an L-shaped ambush. When they funnel in, drop Willie Pete all along the bend - fry the whole regiment!"

Miller considered it. Then determination flashed across his face.

"Do it, Collins. We'll give you whatever covering fire we can."

Collins quickly outlined his plan to the platoon leaders, directing squads to peel off section by section and fall back to prepared positions along the creek bed. They would draw the advancing NVA into a kill zone and unleash white phosphorus grenades from the high ground, incinerating the enemy.

As word spread, the defenders began their tactical retreat, alternating bounding overwatch maneuvers to cover one another. Collins led from the front, never taking his eyes off the tree line for signs of pursuit.

Within fifteen minutes, the outer perimeter was abandoned, sandbags still smoldering from the intense bombardment. Spider holes, torn wire, and mangled bodies were all that remained. The NVA cautiously advanced behind a final barrage of mortar fire, retaking the ground so many had died for that morning.

Collins waited, concealed along the creek bend with 2nd Platoon. Across from them, Captain Miller and a squad of volunteers had stayed behind on the slope above the tree line, drawing the enemy forward. Collins watched as the NVA took the bait, emerging cautiously from the jungle into the open. They filtered into the creek bed by the hundreds, guided by Miller's decoys.

When the bulk of the force had entered the ambush zone, Miller's voice crackled over the radio: "Python 6 to all stations - Light 'em up!"

Collins gave the signal as Willie Pete grenades rained down on the enemy, turning the creek into an inferno. Screams rang out, accompanied by the sizzle of flesh. From three sides, the Americans poured unrelenting fire into the kill zone.

The NVA attack disintegrated into pandemonium, men scrambling over each other to escape the scalding white flames. They lost all cohesion, fracturing into disorganized individuals. The ambush was brutally effective - within minutes, the threat to Mary Ann had been eliminated entirely.

In the sudden silence that followed, Collins found it hard to comprehend they had survived. This small firebase on a remote hill had endured onslaught after onslaught, solely through the resolve of the men manning its defenses.

Mary Ann would stand, bloodied but unbroken. And Sergeant Mike Collins would forever remember the heroes who made it possible.

As the Americans retreated from Vietnam, the firebases along the border were turned over the South Vietnamese or abandoned. More and more, the South Vietnamese moved their troops to protect the cities rather than the countryside. Even Khe Sanh Combat Base was eventually abandoned as priorities shifted. With the border more porous, weapons, ammunition, and reinforcements poured into South Vietnam. The writing was on the wall for whoever bothered to read it.

The Study

1967 – Prince George's County, Maryland, USA

Andrews Air Force Base bustled with activity that crisp autumn morning. Ground crews in fatigues hustled to prepare the fleet of aircraft standing on the tarmac. The low rumble of idling engines mixed with barked orders and banter.

The Secretary of Defense's plane waited on the tarmac as a limousine pulled up and Robert McNamara stepped out, buttoning his suit jacket against the autumn chill. He looked across the tarmac and saw a silent procession of coffins draped in flags were being unloaded from a transport just arrived from Vietnam. It was a sight McNamara witnessed often lately on trips to Andrews. The seemingly endless line of young lives lost stirred an unease that McNamara could not dispel. Another fact-finding mission, another tally of body counts and bombing reports. How many more until this war was won? Or was it unwinnable from the start? Doubt gnawed at the edge of McNamara's mind.

"Morning, sir," his aide said, hustling up the stairs behind him as he entered the aircraft. "We should land in Saigon at 0700 local."

McNamara gave a curt nod as he settled into his leather seat. He loosened his tie and sighed, anguish concealed behind horn-rimmed glasses. The war he helped escalate was spiraling out of control. But he was trapped - duty bound to see it through, yet increasingly certain that each bombing run and troop surge only dug the hole deeper.

1967 - Santa Monica, California, USA

The RAND Corporation's boxy modernist building sat just off the sun-dappled edge of Santa Monica's Palisades Park. The crisp lines and geometric shapes embodied RAND's ethos of rationality and order. Inside, the airy spaces hummed with focused activity. Analysts and researchers strode purposefully between offices, debating equations, hypotheses, and methodologies in urgent tones. The building was an intellectual hive dedicated to systematizing policy through objective facts and data.

As a former Marine officer, Daniel Ellsberg found RAND an ideal environment to apply his analytical mind to America's defense. He would arrive early and stay late, immersed in the rarefied thought bubble, clacking away on his typewriter. Ellsberg's conviction remained firm. The war must be won, and he would help systematically analyze how to achieve victory.

Though seemingly worlds apart that autumn day in 1967, McNamara and Ellsberg shared key traits that would drive them toward a fateful collision. Both men were intelligent, analytical, and driven - prestigious Harvard graduates who believed in the power of facts and rigor. They had faith in rational decision-making processes to shape policy and strategy. McNamara had helped run Ford Motor Company using statistical analysis before joining Kennedy's cabinet. Similarly, Ellsberg applied his Harvard PhD in economics to defense policy matters at RAND. Both wanted to "get the numbers right," believing that cold hard data was essential to guide America's military apparatus. This shared faith in quantitative rationality was about to be profoundly challenged, bonding the two men together over a course neither could foresee.

McNamara's years of immersion in the harsh realities of the Vietnam War had planted seeds of doubt in the data-driven Secretary. Ellsberg, in contrast, remained insulated in his theoretical think tank post, belief system still intact. But it was only a matter of time and exposure before Ellsberg's analytical mind reached the same troubling conclusions as McNamara.

June 17, 1967 – Pentagon, Arlington County, Virginia, USA

Robert McNamara sat at his large mahogany desk, the late afternoon sun slanting through the window behind him. The secure phone rang, startling him from his reverie. "Yes...thank you, I'll be right down."

McNamara straightened his tie and headed briskly down the E-ring corridor. The building bustled around him - uniformed officers clutching stacks of reports, clerks ferrying classified files - yet McNamara felt utterly alone.

He entered the secure conference room, taking his seat at the head of the long table. His generals and advisors regarded him expectantly. McNamara cleared his throat. "Gentlemen, the current situation in Vietnam demands clear eyes. To that end, I am commissioning a comprehensive study of our involvement going back to the 1940s. Every decision, every rationale. No judgments, just facts."

The men glanced around uneasily. McNamara continued. "I don't need to tell you this war has become murkier the deeper we wade in. To find our way out, we need to understand how and why we arrived at this moment."

He looked around the somber room. "No more half-truths gentlemen. Let this be a record we leave to history - unvarnished, objective truth, as best we know it."

His reasons weighed heavier than the men knew. McNamara sought clarity on the tangled path that led to where they were. But deeper down he sought redemption. He had silenced his own doubts too long while sending young men to die. This report was a last grasp at reconciling his conscience before fate closed the door.

The generals knew secrets that could ruin them. They feared the truth.

But McNamara was undeterred. He knew truths that already ravaged his soul. This act would not erase the damage done. But perhaps the light of understanding could guide them out of the darkness ahead.

McNamara hoped to illuminate that path for others. The study would be a beacon for future leaders -

Example over pride, compassion over ego. Proof that admission of error shows strength, not weakness. To make sense of the senseless, with clinical hindsight. And perhaps, to better understand himself - how the best of intentions can lead astray.

He had decided to purposely not tell President Johnson and Secretary of State Dean Rusk what he was planning on doing. If asked, he would tell others that he was only collecting documents, not undertaking a comprehensive study. He would deceive to reveal the truth.

The generals held dark secrets. But McNamara grasped the study's true purpose - a light through fog of war for those who would follow. The first step towards peace is truth.

Santa Monica, California

Daniel Ellsberg sat in his RAND office, engrossed in a report on Vietcong troop estimates. The phone rang.

"Ellsberg speaking."

"Dan, it's Mel Gurtov over at the Pentagon." An old colleague. "Got a study commission here I think you'd be perfect for. McNamara just set it up—full review of Vietnam decision-making back to the 1940s."

Ellsberg's interest was piqued. "A major lessons learned exercise?"

"More than that I think," Gurtov said. "McNamara's looking for an unvarnished account, warts and all. First time this kind of in-depth review's been undertaken mid-war."

"And you want me on the team?" Ellsberg asked.

"Your analysis chops are just what we need. I know

you've been clamoring for more data-driven review. Here's your chance."

Ellsberg leaned back in his chair. A ground-up study of the entire Vietnam engagement—the analyst in him hungered for such an opportunity.

"You know I've always believed we can't remedy mistakes if we don't face them openly," Ellsberg finally said. "Count me in, Mel."

After hanging up, Ellsberg felt a twinge of doubt. What if the unvarnished truth contradicted the prevailing narrative? But he pushed the thought away. Getting the facts right was what mattered. Wherever those facts led, the conclusions would speak for themselves.

Little did he know where those conclusions would take him. For now, the chance to systematically analyze Vietnam policy was irresistible. The die was cast.

January 1968 - Pentagon

For months, Ellsberg and the other thirty-five analysts, half of them active-duty military officers, the rest academics and civilian federal employees, had immersed themselves in the trove of classified documents, compiling a comprehensive chronology of Vietnam decision-making stretching back over two decades. Interviews were conducted, timelines assembled, cables analyzed. The vault-like basement room in the Pentagon was strewn with papers - classified cables, old memos, interviews with former officials. The analysts worked around the long table, piecing together the unvarnished history McNamara had requested.

"Let's discuss 1945," Ellsberg said, pacing at the

head of the table. "These cables clearly show we knew Ho Chi Minh had popular support among the Vietnamese people."

"That's right, we recognized him as a nationalist first, communist second," another analyst replied, shuffling through documents.

A third analyst looked up from interview notes. "Now hold on, while Ho may not have formally allied with communist powers yet, he was committed to communism well before 1945. His ideology was clear."

"Fair point," Ellsberg conceded. "But the cables also suggest our leaders believed Ho's communism was not of the strictly Stalinist variety. They saw it tempered by Vietnamese nationalism."

"So, are you suggesting we could have pulled him away from communist orbit if we'd backed him in '45?" the second analyst asked.

Ellsberg paused, considering the magnitude of the question. "I don't know. But it appears there was a window where supporting Ho's independence aims could have avoided pushing him deeper into communism's embrace. A window we chose to close and seal Vietnam's fate."

"It's easy to say that now," the third analyst cut in. "But in 1945, the administration was laser focused on keeping France aligned with NATO against the Soviets. And France desperately wanted its colonial possessions back."

The first analyst nodded. "The cables show U.S. leaders viewed European security as the priority. So, they held their nose and supported re-imposing French colonial rule in Vietnam, despite America's own anti-colonial beginnings."

Ellsberg sighed. "A short-term gain for a long-term

pain. If we had only backed our ideals instead of Cold War realpolitik in '45..."

Heavy silence filled the vault. The analysts grappled with the truth - earlier moral courage could have spared the US from war in Vietnam.

The work continued. As the disparate pieces came together, a sobering picture began to emerge at odds with the official narratives. The domino theory, the Gulf of Tonkin incident, the early escalations - the classified records revealed realities more complex than the public was told.

Draft papers filled the Pentagon conference room. Ellsberg scribbled notes as the analysts debated which cables and documents to include. The classified histories were open before them, revealing troubling truths at odds with the official storylines.

"How can we possibly include this Cable 243 business from 1945?" one analyst said. "It clearly contradicts the domino theory justification."

"But Secretary McNamara said this has to be an unvarnished account," another replied. "We have to include what the documents show, even if it's inconvenient."

Ellsberg spoke up. "I have to agree. Our duty is to the facts and evidence, regardless of perceptions."

"Easy for you to say, you're just a contractor," came a retort. "Some of us plan to keep working here after this study."

"So you suggest we omit relevant facts to avoid rocking the boat?" Ellsberg asked pointedly.

The analyst held Ellsberg's gaze before looking away. "No...no, you're right. The truth matters more than our jobs. It's just...this isn't what I expected to find."

"None of us expected it," Ellsberg said. "But here we are. All we can do is follow where the data leads. Even if it contradicts where we began. Right?"

Murmured assents rose around the room. The classified histories made one truth abundantly clear - the path that led them to this war was far different than any of them had believed.

January 1969 – Pentagon, Arlington, Virginia, USA

McNamara sat at his desk, reviewing his resignation letter one last time before signing. Though he'd known for weeks President Johnson intended to replace him, seeing the words formalized his departure as Secretary of Defense. After signing and neatly folding the letter, he sealed the envelope just as an aide knocked.

"Mr. Gelb is here to see you, sir."

"Send him in."

Leslie Gelb entered holding a single binder. "Here is the full Vietnam study, Mr. Secretary."

McNamara took the slim binder, surprised. "This looks rather short, doesn't it?"

"Oh, that's just the table of contents. The bulk of the work is right here, sir." Gelb gestured and assistants wheeled in hand-trucks bearing stacks of boxes. They began removing the contents – typewritten pages, photocopied cables and memos – neatly stacking them into multiple towering piles on McNamara's desk.

"That's it, sir. The full Vietnam study you commissioned, all forty-seven volumes."

McNamara regarded the mountains of paper somberly. "What's the final page count?"

"Just over seven thousand, sir. It's quite

exhaustive... as you requested." Gelb hesitated. "I know you're headed out soon, but I hope you'll get a chance to review some of the findings. I think you'll find it illuminating."

McNamara ran his hand over the piles. The smell of fresh photocopies wafted up. "I'll do my best to look it over before the transition. But as you know, my plate is overflowing at the moment."

"Of course, sir."

McNamara stood, walking over to gaze out the window at the Potomac. "You know, when I commissioned this study, I hoped it might bring clarity. Now I wonder if anything can make sense of it all."

Gelb didn't know how to respond. "We aimed for an unvarnished record, sir. I believe that's what we've produced."

McNamara turned, managing a small smile. "I'm sure you have, Les. And I appreciate that. Hopefully others can learn from our experience, even if..." His voice trailed off, eyes fixed on the mountains of history weighing down his desk.

The two men stood awkwardly for a moment, years of history hanging between them. Then McNamara showed Gelb out. Alone again, he eyed the mountains of paper that embodied his hopes - and now his fading grip on a war that defined an era.

Wrapped up in preparing for his new position as the head of the World Bank, McNamara would never read the study he had commissioned.

February 1969 - Santa Monica, California, USA

Dumbfounded, Ellsberg sat in his office at RAND. "He barely looked at it, Dan," Gelb said over the phone. "Seven thousand pages summing up years of work, and I don't think McNamara even read a single page."

Ellsberg leaned back in his chair. "But he commissioned the study. Why wouldn't he want to review the findings?"

Gelb sighed. "My sense is the war has moved far beyond what the study covers at this point. He's got enough current crises without sifting through old history."

"So what happens to it now?"

"It gets filed away I suppose," Gelb said. "Another government report that gathers dust."

Ellsberg stared out his office window at the California sunlight, considering the implications. All those classified documents, the exhaustive research, for what? A report bound and forgotten?

"We worked to get the unvarnished truth out there," Ellsberg said. "But if no one reads it..."

Gelb interrupted, "I better go, Dan. We'll talk soon. I'm sorry how this thing turned out. A shame really."

After hanging up, Ellsberg sat silently for a long time. They had sought to shed light on the opaque history of Vietnam decision-making. But it seemed fated to remain obscured.

Somehow, Ellsberg knew he couldn't let that happen. The truth mattered - not just for McNamara or Gelb, but for the nation. He began mentally sorting through his options. The study couldn't remain buried if there was any way he could expose it to the public.

Princeton University - April 1968

Ellsberg took his seat in the lecture hall among scores

of students and academics gathered for the "Revolution in a Changing World" conference. The Vietnam War raged on, fueling anti-war sentiment across the country. Princeton had organized this symposium to debate morality, justice, and strategies for change during tumultuous times.

As the first speaker took the podium, Ellsberg scanned the room. Intellectual luminaries and student radicals rubbed shoulders, drawn together by opposition to the war. Ellsberg noticed John Roche, special advisor on Vietnam under Johnson, seated toward the front.

The lecture soon opened to a vigorous Q&A session. A student stood to challenge Roche on the morality of the war. Ellsberg saw Roche bristle as the young man questioned America's role in the conflict. An uncomfortable energy rippled through the hall.

During a break, Ellsberg approached Roche. "That got a bit heated back there," he said. "The students mean well, but they can be zealous."

Roche nodded, smoothing his tie. "I know they think they're advocating for peace. But naiveté leads to disaster, as we've learned."

Ellsberg held back a retort, thinking of the War Room arguments he'd observed in the Pentagon. Who was more naive - the students or the policymakers?

"Well, I appreciate you coming to engage with them," Ellsberg said politely. He rejoined the lecture with much on his mind. The students desired sweeping change, while men like Roche sought to uphold the status quo. Ellsberg found himself questioning which side he fell on. The lines no longer seemed so clear.

After the last lecture, Ellsberg sat despondently in the

crowded cafe when a woman approached his table. "May I join you? I'm Janaki."

"Daniel," he said shaking her hand. "You're taking classes here?"

"Yes. Full load. Are you here for the lectures?"

"What gave me away?"

"Grey hair. Just a little."

"Gives me away every time. So, what classes are you taking?" Ellsberg asked, stirring his coffee.

"The regular courses like geometry, English lit, history, plus several on Gandhian philosophy and nonviolent protest," Janaki replied enthusiastically. "Learning about Gandhi's life has been fascinating. You'd think I would know all that stuff from India, right? But they don't teach it that much in the schools. At least not in depth as they do here."

"What draws you to his teachings?"

Janaki's eyes lit up. "Oh, his steadfast commitment to nonviolence, of course! And his ability to defeat injustice through compassion, moral courage and the power of truth paired with love."

"That's inspiring," Ellsberg said, nodding along. "We could use more of that approach today."

She spoke passionately about the power of truth paired with love. Ellsberg found himself nodding along.

Over time, they began discussing the anti-war movement and Ellsberg's disillusionment. He slowly opened up about the secret study and his frustration at failing to spark action by leaking parts of it.

"Truth alone often isn't enough," Janaki said thoughtfully. "One must convey it with compassion."

Her words resonated deeply, kindling courage

within him. After several hours, Ellsberg felt seen and understood by this wise friend who spoke of nonviolent resistance. Janaki helped crystallize the path forward - he would find a way to share the full truth compassionately.

"I believe you've shown me a different way, my friend," Ellsberg said in parting. "Thank you."

Washington D.C. - October 1969

Ellsberg joined the swelling crowd massing near the Washington Monument, many clutching signs decrying the war in Vietnam. He had convinced himself he was on a fact-finding mission, but there was something else driving him to the protest. A need to hear the other side of the argument. He felt conspicuous in his button-down shirt and slacks among the sea of tie-dye, jeans, and anti-war slogans. But he pushed down his discomfort, letting the energy of the protesters wash over him.

As the march began, Ellsberg fell in step. He observed the diverse mix - students, clergy, veterans - all united in their call for peace. Protest chants and songs echoed against the marble facades lining the route. It was his first mass demonstration, and Ellsberg found himself inspired.

"First protest?" the young man asked, noticing Ellsberg's buttoned-up attire.

"Is it that obvious?" Ellsberg smiled sheepishly.

The student grinned. "You'll get your sea legs. What brings you out today?"

Ellsberg considered his words. "I'm here to learn. Hoping to better understand multiple perspectives."

The young man nodded thoughtfully. "Opening

your mind is the first step. Once you start really seeing the truth of this war, I think you'll know where you stand."

They walked on, Ellsberg pondering the comment. He admired the protesters' conviction but couldn't shake his analytic instincts to see all sides. Still, the student was right about one thing - seeking truth with an open mind was essential. Wherever that led, Ellsberg knew he would follow, even if it meant leaving old loyalties behind.

When angry shouts arose ahead, he craned his neck to see counter-protesters waving American flags and jeering. The two groups stared each other down, potent with simmering confrontation. But police stepped in to defuse the tension and the march continued on.

Ellsberg mulled the encounter as he walked. He understood counter-protesters' patriotic loyalty but couldn't abide their refusal to question. Didn't true loyalty require facing hard truths?

Near the Pentagon, the march halted and speeches began. Ellsberg listened intently. When the rally dispersed, he had found his tribe - those who sought truth undeterred by fear. And with his inside knowledge, perhaps he could now help amplify their dissenting voices.

September 1969 – Santa Monica, California, USA

Ellsberg paced his office, rehearsing what he would say. He and Russo had been colleagues at RAND for years, working closely on projects related to the war. Russo was one of the few people Ellsberg trusted completely. But what he was considering could put

Russo at grave risk.

A knock at the door - Russo ducking his head in. "Dan, what's up?"

Ellsberg waved him in, closing the door. He rubbed his palms on his pants, mouth suddenly dry. "Tony, what I'm about to say stays between us."

Russo cocked his head. "Of course, Dan. What's going on?"

Ellsberg took a breath. "I want to get the full Pentagon Papers study out to the public. Everything. I...I think I need your help."

He held Russo's gaze - months of building pressure led to this moment.

Russo blinked, processing. "You're talking about releasing thousands of pages of classified documents? That would be a massive leak."

"I know it's asking a lot. You can say no; I'd understand completely. I just ask you keep our conversation a secret."

Russo sighed, running a hand through his hair. "I took the same oaths you did. But I also swore to defend this country from enemies both foreign and domestic. If you feel this is necessary..." He met Ellsberg's eyes. "Alright my friend, I'm with you."

Relief washed over Ellsberg. He was no longer alone. He had feared condemnation or rejection. But Russo understood - sometimes loyalty required dissent.

They clasped hands firmly. A silent pact sealed by moral necessity, promising peril ahead. Like a breached dam, the decision unleashed forces that could no longer be contained.

As the last RAND worker bee said goodnight and left, Ellsberg glanced down the dim hallway before waving

Russo over. They entered the document storage room, flipping on a single light. Cabinet drawers slid open soundlessly as they swiftly gathered classified records - cables, memos, reports - on the Vietnam War going back decades.

With arms piled high, they stole down the deserted corridor toward the copy room. Ellsberg loaded pages into the machine one-by-one, listening for footsteps over photocopier's rhythmic whirring. The process was painfully slow. Russo watched the door, neck prickling.

The photocopier fussed and whined, slowly reproducing several copies of each illicit page. Military secrets once reserved for high-level eyes now churned out in replica, bound for the public.

As hours passed, Ellsberg's eyes strained in the harsh light. But his hands kept steadily feeding documents. Russo whispered that dawn was breaking; they had to wrap up.

Back at the office, Ellsberg tucked the night's yield into a locked drawer. Hurriedly re-shelving the originals in their file cabinets, the two conspirators emerged into early sunlight muffling yawns. No one had glimpsed their clandestine mission.

Every night, they returned to repeat the ritual - scanning, copying, concealing. Two covert scribes, transcribing truth's scripture to share with the people. The danger grew with each cache of copied pages. But once begun, they could not turn back.

Night after night they worked, until the entire study had been duplicated. Arms weary, they added the last sheaf to the towering stack in Ellsberg's office. Russo wiped his brow and sat down heavily.

"Well, that's seven thousand pages of classified documents. I'd say we just photocopied ourselves decades in prison." He laughed, a tinge of nerves in it. "So, what now?"

Ellsberg regarded the mountain of paper - his monument to truth or folly, he wasn't sure.

"To be honest, I'm not exactly certain yet," he admitted. "This project has consumed me so completely; I haven't thought much past completing the copying."

Russo raised an eyebrow. "You don't have a plan for distribution?"

Ellsberg sighed, leaning against the cabinet. "I've got some general ideas - leak it to the press piecemeal to get public attention. Maybe find an anti-war congressman to read it into the record. But nothing concrete yet."

He clasped Russo's shoulder. "I know it's asking a lot to trust me without all the answers. But thank you, my friend. I couldn't have done this without you."

Russo held his gaze. "We're in it together now. We'll figure the next steps out."

Ellsberg nodded, looking back at the mountain of truth waiting to see sunlight. The path forward remained unclear, but he had to believe their faith would be rewarded.

Among other things, the documents showed that the Johnson Administration had systematically lied, not only to the public but also to Congress. Ellsberg kept the documents secret only showing them to a few people he thought necessary to reveal them to the public.

Throughout 1970, Ellsberg tried to persuade several

U.S. Senators, including William Fulbright and George McGovern, to read the study on the Senate floor, because a senator could not be prosecuted for anything he said on the record before the Senate. While both senators were impressed by Ellsberg's dedication and the report, neither accepted the challenge. While noble, what Ellsberg had done was considered treason.

Running low on options, Ellsberg decided to release a couple of copies privately to Marcus Raskin and Ralph Stavins at the Institute for Policy Studies in Washington DC. As more time expired, Ellsberg knew that the chance of his mission being discovered grew with each passing day. It wasn't the Ellsberg feared going to jail for what he had done. It was that he feared the study would hidden away or possibly even destroyed to keep it from the public. The thought kept him up at night.

Desperate, Ellsberg contacted the New York Times correspondent Neil Sheehan, who he had earlier in Vietnam. When they met in Boston, Ellsberg insisted that Sheehan only take notes on what he read while in his apartment. For several days Sheehan complied with Ellsberg's request, until the exhausted Ellsberg went on vacation to the West Indies leaving Sheehan with the documents so he could continue his reading.

With Ellsberg away, Sheehan struggled with himself - uphold a promise or reveal vital secrets?

As a reporter, his duty was to publish the truth. But as a man, his word meant something. He had looked Ellsberg in the eye and agreed to his terms.

Sheehan agonized over betraying the man who risked so much to share these revelations. But keeping truth buried - wasn't that the greater betrayal?

In the end, conscience overruled obedience. Having

read only a fraction of the documents, Sheehan knew the importance of the study. The people deserved to know what their leaders hid about war's terrible costs.

On March 2, 1971, with hands almost shaking, Sheehan packed up the documents in several suitcases and left.

At the copy shop, waiting for the pages to reproduce, his stomach churned. Each whirring pass of the machine sealed his Judas kiss to Ellsberg.

But the resolve solidified - the reporter eclipsed the friend. The story was everything now, more vital than any pact. Sheehan would not hide truth in shadows, no matter the promise broken. His rational was that Ellsberg really wanted the report revealed even though he wouldn't admit it. He had risked all. Publishing the report was natural outcome of his endeavors.

Sheehan returned Ellsberg's copies to his apartment, then placed his copy of the documents in several suitcases before going to the airport.

At the airport clutching stolen truth, Sheehan said a silent prayer for Ellsberg's forgiveness. Then he boarded the plane, leaving remorse behind on the tarmac. The story that could end a war flew with him.

He flew his copies to his home in Washington DC, where he stored one set, then flew to New York to face his editor with the biggest story of his career.

June 13, 1971 – New York, New York, USA

The soaring *New York Times* building on 43rd Street bustled with reporters pursuing stories and dodging editors. But on the executive floor, a tense meeting unfolded in a quiet conference room.

Floor-to-ceiling windows looked out on the

glittering Manhattan skyline. The polished oak table was strewn with copies of the classified Vietnam study and scribbled legal notes. About a dozen men sat around the table in suit jackets and rolled up sleeves, their voices echoing off the wood-paneled walls.

At the head sat *The Times'* grizzled executive editor, his lined face creased in a frown as he listened. To his right was the paper's seasoned legal counsel, bald head gleaming under the glass chandelier as he pointed out legal risks.

The iconic *Times* logo bearing the newspaper's motto "All The News That's Fit to Print" was etched onto the glass wall behind them. As the lawyers outlined prosecution dangers and editors argued democratic duty, each side appealed to that motto's legacy, wrestling over where to draw the line this time.

"Publishing top-secret documents could put us all in legal jeopardy," the head lawyer said. "The government will come down hard."

"But this material could expose years of lies about the war," the editor countered. "Don't we have a duty to inform the public?"

"We do, but we could also endanger lives and national security by revealing secrets."

"Our reporters have been through the study exhaustively and found no threats to life. Only revelations about how five presidents misled America into an unwinnable war."

"That context won't matter if we're prosecuted under the Espionage Act," the lawyer rebutted.

"So we're supposed to prioritize avoiding prosecution over serving the truth?" the editor asked in exasperation.

Back and forth the debate raged. The lawyers

outlined dire legal risks, while the editors argued historical importance.

"At some point, we have to decide if getting this information out is worth the consequences we'll face," the editor said. "I believe the people's right to know here outweighs the fallout."

The lawyer slowly nodded. "Publish a few excerpts first to test the waters. But once this genie is out, there's no putting it back in."

The editor took a deep breath. "Then let the light in. We'll print a first installment next week."

The revelation Ellsberg set in motion would soon be picked up by history's tides.

After weeks of heated discussions with their attorneys, the editors of *The New York Times* published the first of nine excerpts from the 7,000-page collection of cables, reports, and analysis that would soon be called the Pentagon Papers.

After reading the front-page story, Ellsberg was shocked when he realized what Sheehan had done. He knew it was just a matter of hours or even minutes before he would be arrested. He wasn't sure if there was still a role for him to play in the release of the documents. He gathered his set of the documents and fled. He avoided the FBI agents hunting him for thirteen days while he decided what to do.

Finally, Ellsberg gave the documents to his former colleague at RAND, Ben Bagdikian the national editor of *The Washington Post*.

Ellsberg admitted publicly his role in copying and releasing the Pentagon Papers. He said to the press, "I felt that as an American citizen, as a responsible citizen, I could no longer cooperate in concealing this information from the American public. I did this clearly at my own jeopardy and I am prepared to answer to all the consequences of this decision."

A few minutes later, he surrendered to federal authorities at the U.S. Attorney's office in Boston. Not long after, Russo was arrested in California.

Together, Ellsberg and Russo were charged under the Espionage Act of 1971 and other charges that carried a total maximum sentence of 115 years in prison for Ellsberg and thirty-five years for Russo.

On June 26, 1971, US Senator Mike Gravel was given 4,100 pages of the Pentagon Papers which he received from Bagdikian. Three days later, Gravel stood on the Senate floor and entered the papers into the Senate record.

President Nixon requested and received a court order to prevent *The New York Times* from publishing its articles on the top-secret documents. It wasn't until June 30th that the U.S. Supreme Court allowed *The New York Times* to resume publishing its articles on the documents.

The release of the Pentagon Papers embarrassed the Kennedy, Johnson, and Nixon administrations. Donald Rumsfeld explained the fallout, "To the ordinary guy, all this is a bunch of gobbledygook. But out of the gobbledygook comes a very clear thing.... You can't trust the government; you can't believe what they say; and you can't rely on their judgment; and the—the implicit infallibility of presidents, which has been an accepted thing in America, is badly hurt by this, because It shows that people do things the president wants to do even though it's wrong, and the president can be wrong."

January 3, 1973 – Los Angeles, California, USA

Daniel Ellsberg and Anthony Russo sat side-by-side at the defense table as Judge Byrne entered and proceedings began. The cavernous courtroom was packed with reporters and observers. The long-awaited trial over the Pentagon Papers leak promised high drama involving secrets at the highest levels.

"Mr. Ellsberg, Mr. Russo, you stand accused of espionage, conspiracy, and theft of government property," Judge Byrne addressed the defendants. "How do you plead?"

"Not guilty, your honor," Ellsberg replied steadily. Russo echoed him in solidarity.

As the trial commenced, the prosecution characterized the leak as a reckless betrayal that damaged national security. The defense portrayed it as a selfless act of conscience to inform public discourse.

Judge Byrne presided studiously, allowing each side ample time to state their case. His even demeanor and sharp questioning kept proceedings orderly. But the defense soon exposed improprieties in how the case was handled:

Ellsberg was denied the chance to explain his motivations for leaking. The judge ruled Ellsberg's intentions were irrelevant to whether he broke the law.

It was revealed that White House "plumbers" broke into the office of Ellsberg's psychiatrist, Dr. Lewis Fielding, seeking damaging information.

Finally, the prosecution had withheld evidence that Ellsberg's phone conversations were illegally wiretapped by the FBI without a court order.

Judge Byrne listened gravely as each revelation emerged. Ellsberg and Russo watched nervously, hoping the judge would act on these violations of justice and civil rights.

During the trial, Judge Byrne met with John Ehrlichman, White House counsel. Ehrlichman offered Byrne the directorship of the FBI. Byrne refused until the trial had concluded. Byrne was criticized by many for even agreeing to meet with Ehrlichman during the case.

During a recess, Ellsberg turned to Russo. "However this ends, I'm grateful you stood by me, Tony. I got us into this, but you didn't hesitate."

Russo clasped his shoulder. "We wanted to do some good. Now let's hope the judge believes in true justice."

After emotional testimony, the trial concluded. Far more than two men's fate hung in the balance, but the fate of truth itself.

On May 11, 1971, Judge Byrne looked out solemnly over the packed courtroom. After months of testimony and shocking revelations, the trial now rested in his hands. "I have endeavored to listen to each side fairly," Byrne began. "Yet this case has brought improprieties to light which I cannot ignore."

He cited the White House break-in of Dr. Fielding's office, the wiretapping of the defendants without a warrant, and the prosecution withholding of evidence.

"These gross misconducts and illegal actions have incurably infected the proceedings," Judge Byrne declared. "In light of the totality of the circumstances, I cannot allow this flawed case to stand."

A murmur swept the courtroom. Ellsberg and Russo braced hopefully.

"Therefore, given the governmental abuses and the defendants' able representation, I order all charges dismissed against Mr. Ellsberg and Mr. Russo." Byrne banged his gavel decisively. "This deeply troubled case is dismissed in the interests of justice."

Euphoric relief broke over the defendants. Justice had prevailed over corruption, aided by their willingness to follow conscience whatever the risk. Byrne's verdict validated their faith - the truth, once brought to light, could not be buried again.

Operation Chenla II

The roots of the Cambodian Civil War stretched back decades, to the French colonial era when nationalist movements began emerging across Indochina. In Cambodia, anti-colonial sentiments swelled under French rule, eventually exploding into open conflict with the First Indochina War in the 1950s.

Cambodia gained independence in 1953, but the country remained deeply divided. Right-wing factions with ties to the old French puppet regime held power in Phnom Penh, while leftist insurgents allied with North Vietnam and China operated from jungle strongholds. By the late 1960s, the communist Khmer Rouge had gained strength under the leadership of Pol Pot. They aimed to topple Cambodia's US-backed government through guerrilla warfare.

In 1970, Prince Norodom Sihanouk was deposed in a coup led by General Lon Nol. Sihanouk had tried to maintain Cambodia's neutrality amid the Vietnam War, but Lon Nol threw his support behind the US and South Vietnam. In response, Sihanouk allied with the Khmer Rouge against the new government, ushering in full blown civil war.

For years, the Khmer Rouge chipped away at Lon Nol's army. They steadily expanded their control over the Cambodian countryside while also battling US forces along the Vietnam border.

1971 – Cambodia

Colonel Seng Ros stood on the parapet of the ancient temple, looking out over the jungle canopy stretching to the horizon. The stone ruins were a welcome respite from the suffocating humidity of the Cambodian lowlands. A light breeze rustled through the nearby trees, carrying the trills of tropical birds.

For a moment, Seng Ros allowed his mind to wander to simpler times. As a boy, he had once come here with his father, when Cambodia was still a peaceful kingdom unravaged by war. Now at thirty-five, Ros commanded an army battalion charged with rooting out communist insurgents in this remote northern province.

Footsteps sounded behind him, and Ros turned to see his second-in-command, Captain Prum, approaching. "Any word from Regimental headquarters?" Ros asked.

Prum shook his head. "The radio is still down. This damned jungle and the humidity, play havoc with communications."

Ros grimaced. Operating blind out here made him uneasy. He knew the Khmer Rouge were on the move, trying to cut his battalion off from Phnom Penh. Without new orders, it was impossible to know where to deploy his men.

"Sir, the villagers say Khmer Rouge troops were seen across the river two nights ago," Prum added. "If they cross in force..."

He trailed off. There was no need to finish the

thought. If the communists attacked in numbers, Ros's battalion could be swallowed up by the jungle. Overrun, just like dozens of others before them.

Ros turned back to the vista before them, brow furrowed. His battalion was spread dangerously thin across three villages, trying to provide protection. But the Khmer Rouge controlled the countryside - they could strike anywhere, anytime.

"We need air support," Ros said finally. "With helicopter gunships, we could punish any force that dares attack us."

Prum hesitated before responding. "Colonel, you know we've been denied gunships. Phnom Penh is hoarding all air power to defend the capital."

Anger flashed across Ros' face. "So, they leave us to the wolves out here? This is exactly how the communists will nibble away at us, biting off one isolated battalion after another."

He paced the ancient stones, frustration boiling inside him. His superiors were blind, refusing to see the coming disaster if the Khmer Rouge were not checked.

"Sir, what about the Americans?" Prum began delicately. "Perhaps if we requested aid directly?"

Ros considered it. The US had so far avoided major involvement in Cambodia's civil war, but they were eager to strike communist sanctuaries near the border. Securing American air support was risky, but could be his battalion's only chance for survival.

After a long moment gazing out over the endless jungle, Ros turned to his second-in-command. "Very well. Send a message requesting helicopter gunship assistance from the nearest US base. Stress that it's urgently needed to interdict Khmer Rouge troop movements."

Prum nodded. "Yes, sir, right away."

As his captain hurried off, Ros hoped he was not making a grave mistake entangling his men with the Americans. But with enemies closing in, they were fast running out of options.

The Khmer Rouge battalion marched swiftly along the jungle trail, motivated by the prospect of victory. Their commander, Colonel Phan, had assured them the riverside village ahead was lightly defended. By day's end, it would be theirs.

Phan urged his men onward. Intelligence said no Cambodian troops were within ten kilometers. They did not expect an attack this far from the capital.

The rhythmic thudding of helicopter blades grew in the distance. Phan felt his stomach tighten. Surely those sounds were from across the border in Vietnam, not here in their controlled territory.

The choppers thrum swelled through the jungle. They were close. Too close. "Helicopters, from the river!" Phan yelled. "Disperse, take cover!"

The battalion scrambled off the trail, diving into the brush as two US Bell AH-1 Cobras crested the treeline. But it was too late - the Khmer Rouge column was exposed in the open.

In the lead attack helicopter, the American crew chief spotted movement below. "Raven 1 to Raven 2, we've got a target, you see 'em down there in the clearing?"

"Copy Raven 1, tally multiple foot-mobiles, they're Charlies for sure. Weapons free, let's light 'em up."

The gunships banked into attack runs along the length of the column. Their turret-mounted miniguns spun up and unleashed streams of fire into the jungle below. Dozens of 2.75-inch Hydra rockets fired from their M261 launch tubes, their foldable fins flipping open as they screamed toward the troops below.

The Khmer Rouge never had a chance. The sheer volume of lead from the aircraft's miniguns and shrapnel from the exploding rockets overwhelmed any attempt to take shelter or defend themselves. The aircrew's aim was dead on. Communist flesh was shredded in the merciless barrage as hundreds fell.

From the ground, Phan could only watch helplessly as his battalion was decimated. The Americans had caught them utterly unprepared. In mere minutes, the choppers passed back over the treetops having reduced the Khmer Rouge to a bloodied ruin.

Phan knew then the village could not be taken today. US airpower had appeared from nowhere to wreak havoc. It was a harsh lesson in the new realities of Cambodia's civil war.

Ros stood on the old temple parapet once more. The sunlight glinted off the winding river in the distance, now host to a new sight - American gunships patrolling up and down its length.

Their arrival had been like divine deliverance for Ros and his beleaguered battalion. Each day the helicopters flew out on sorties, hunting Khmer Rouge guerrillas in the surrounding jungle. Just knowing that heavy aerial firepower was on call 24/7 had done wonders for morale.

Footsteps behind signaled Prum's approach again. "Colonel, our scouts report the Khmer Rouge have halted their advance. It seems they are hesitating to amass forces within range of the gunships."

Ros nodded, lips curling in a smile. "Just as I hoped.

Those communist rats have already gotten a taste of what the gunships can do."

"Have the Americans said how long they will remain?" Ros asked.

"No word yet. I suspect they are focused on Vietnam and this is a temporary deployment."

Ros's smile faded. He feared Prum was right - the Americans would move on as suddenly as they'd arrived. The gunships were a stopgap, not a permanent advantage.

"Then we must make the most of them while we can," Ros said. "Order constant reconnaissance along the river. If we can catch major Khmer Rouge elements in the open again, I want them hammered without mercy."

With the US helicopters above, Ros finally felt like he was taking the fight to the communists rather than awaiting their next blow. He was determined to make them pay dearly for every inch of Cambodia they hoped to control.

Phnom Penh, Cambodia

Brigadier General Lon Non stood before his assembled field commanders, preparing to outline Operation Chenla II. The task was daunting - retake Route 6, Cambodia's critical overland link to the port of Sihanoukville. Without Route 6 it was only a matter of time until Sihanoukville fell to the Khmer Rouge and Cambodia's key supply route with it.

"Gentlemen, as you know our last offensive failed to dislodge the Khmer Rouge from Route 6," Lon Non began. "But in the intervening months, our army has been transformed."

He continued, "Over 100,000 new FANK troops have been trained by advisors from the American and South Vietnamese militaries. They will reinforce our ranks for Chenla II along with heavy artillery and air support from our allies."

The previous operation six months ago had quickly bogged down. FANK's armored spearheads lacked infantry support and were decimated by guerrillas with RPGs.

"For Operation Chenla II, we will take a different approach," Lon Non continued. "A massive artillery barrage will soften enemy defenses before the ground assault begins. Our infantry will advance under the cover of heavy air support. This time we will take the fight to the Khmer Rouge with strength in manpower, artillery, and airpower," Lon Non emphasized.

Lon Non gestured to the map marking FANK units along Route 6. "General Mok's division will attack here, towards Treng. General Binh, your forces will push south to link up with Mok. Together you will drive the Khmer Rouge from the highway."

Lon Non looked around the room. "With our expanded forces and allies, we will liberate Route 6 once and for all. The port of Sihanoukville is the gateway to Cambodia's future. We must seize it. Questions?"

General Binh spoke up. "Sir, the Khmer Rouge owns the jungles. They will not retreat easily, even under bombardment."

Lon Non nodded grimly. "You are right, general. This will be a bloody slog all the way down Route 6. But we must succeed - Sihanoukville and the southwest will be isolated if the port road stays in their hands."

The brigadier general made eye contact with each

man. "It comes down to this - we are staking everything on victory here. I expect your very best. Dismissed."

The field commanders rose and departed, their morale boosted by the American training and support. Retaking Route 6 remained a daunting task, but now the odds were in their favor.

August 20, 1971 – Route 6, Cambodia

Dawn broke over the Cambodian countryside, the morning stillness shattered by thunderous artillery barrages. All along Route 6, FANK guns opened fire on Khmer Rouge positions dotting the highway.

At a forward firebase near Treng, Brigadier General Lon Non watched the salvos through binoculars. The earth trembled under the intense bombardment meant to soften up the communists.

Lon Non checked his watch. H-hour for the ground assault was nearing. He nodded to his radio operator. "This is Brigade, commence attack."

With that order, FANK forces began their advance down Route 6 led by tanks and mechanized infantry. Their goal was to link up and clear areas already pounded by artillery.

FANK Sergeant Kahn banked the T-54 tank off the highway onto a muddy dirt track leading into the jungle. Enemy fire had pinned down the infantry advance ahead from concealed positions in the treeline.

Kahn's orders were to blast through and take out the communist bunkers with the tank's heavy cannon. The 100mm gun should be more than enough to finish the job.

"Driver, half speed," Kahn ordered as they bounced through the dense underbrush. "No point rolling up unannounced. We'll let them know we're here soon enough."

The T-54 crunched forward until Kahn could make out slit trenches dug beneath the trees. Communist troops manned recoilless rifles and machine guns, raking the highway periodically.

"Target, front! Range 200 meters!" Kahn called out. "HE round, load!"

The gunner chambered a high explosive round and took aim. The cannon roared, shell blasting into the trenches and detonating. Dirt sprayed high as the position was ripped apart.

But return fire quickly rang out, antitank rounds glancing off the T-54's sloped armor. The Khmer Rouge were skilled at concealment, concealing multiple fighting holes.

"Target right, load canister!" Kahn spotted muzzle flash from a recoilless rifle concealed behind a termite mound. The close-range shell tore the nest apart in a hail of shrapnel, neutralizing the threat.

One by one, Kahn methodically knocked out bunkers while his loader kept the cannon fed. After fifteen relentless minutes, fire from the treeline petered out. Kahn and his crew had busted the communist ambush site.

Satisfied, Kahn ordered the tank to reverse out. The accompanying FANK infantry could now advance behind the tank's opening barrage. T-54s were proving their worth supporting the Chenla II drive down Route 6.

Lon Non listened as progress reports crackled through.

So far, his divisions were gaining ground rapidly under the cover of fire support. Having learned lessons from their defeat months earlier, FANK troops moved cautiously from village to village rather than surging ahead.

FANK Captain Ratan edged through the jungle underbrush, his eyes darting for any sign of the elusive Khmer Rouge. The fighting this morning had been intense as his unit cleared villages along Route 6. Now an uneasy quiet hung over the area.

A rifle shot cracked from up ahead, followed by voices shouting in the Cambodian dialect. Ratan froze, signaling to his men to take cover.

Creeping forward, they spotted a Khmer Rouge squad crossing a clearing 100 meters away. Ratan's unit opened up with a fusillade, cutting down several of the exposed communists.

The survivors scattered but quickly regrouped, returning disciplined fire. They knew these jungles far better than the FANK troops. What began as a lopsided ambush soon turned into a blistering close-quarters firefight.

Bullets whizzed overhead as Ratan's men dashed between trees and termite mounds, struggling to outflank the elusive Khmer Rouge. Both sides exchanged volleys at near point-blank range, neither able to finish the other off.

After a bloody half hour stalemate, the communists disengaged and melted back into the jungle having bought time for their comrades to retreat further down Route 6. Despite FANK's advance, the Khmer Rouge were making them pay for every foot.

Ratan could only catch his breath as the firing

tapered off. Chenla II would be won through dozens of small skirmishes like this. He knew his men had the toughness to endure. Strengthening his resolve, gunships soon roared overhead pursuing the fleeing communists - a reminder that aerial firepower would help tilt the scales in this grinding war.

Lon Non heard aircraft approaching - the air cavalry had arrived. Waves of helicopter gunships swept over the battlefield hunting Khmer Rouge attempts to counterattack. When the enemy was spotted, the choppers swooped in raking the jungle foliage with minigun fire.

By late afternoon, messages arrived that the two FANK divisions had successfully met up halfway down Route 6. Lon Non allowed himself a grim smile. The offensive's first phase had succeeded, thanks to thorough preparation and heavy firepower.

Yet harder fighting loomed ahead. The Khmer Rouge were too entrenched along the highway to dislodge easily. Chenla II would be a major battle stretching over weeks or months.

FANK battalion commander Sophan radioed to the circling US fighter jets overhead. "Ripper flight, we have Khmer Rouge bunkers one klick west. They're pounding our advance from the treeline."

"Copy Ripper lead, tally target area. Rolling in hot." came the reply.

The F-4 Phantoms swooped low over the jungle, releasing bombs directly onto the communist positions. Flames erupted from the tree line as the heavy ordnance exploded.

From their hidden bunkers, the Khmer Rouge

commander roared to his anti-aircraft battery. "Don't let up, fire! The imperialists cannot hunt freely in our skies."

His men needed no urging, firing furiously at the American jets with 12.7mm heavy machine guns and 37mm flak cannons. Tracers lit up the sky as the F-4s jinked and banked to evade the barrage.

"Damn, these guys are really bringing the heat today," said Ripper 3 through the radio. "Ripper lead, recommend we loiter at max range for strafing run."

"Copy, let's switch to sidewinders and take these bunkers out from distance."

The Phantoms roared back out of range before swooping around to re-attack. Missiles lanced from their wings, corkscrewing towards the jungle canopy.

Blasts rippled through the treeline as the bunkers were smashed by direct missile hits. But still the Khmer Rouge gunners refused to retreat, quickly dragging out spare machine guns and readying them despite the pounding.

"Their fortifications are too hardened, we need to burn them out," Ripper lead called. "Napalm run on my mark."

The jets thundered over disgorging flaming jelly over the jungle. With a whoosh the tree line became an inferno. The Khmer Rouge guns fell silent, flames consuming the bunkers and choking the air with oily black smoke.

From the ground, Sophan's battalion cheered as America airpower turned the tide once more. The communists would keep resisting, but their hold on Route 6 was being pried loose mile by bloody mile.

But that night, Lon Non let his headquarters staff

celebrate the initial gains. Morale and momentum were critical, thanks to his American advisors Lon Non knew. For now, Operation Chenla II was off to a solid start.

Phnom Penh, Cambodia

Over the next week, the FANK offensive down Route 6 continued grinding ahead. The combined arms approach of armor, infantry and air support kept the communists off balance.

By employing lessons learned in their earlier defeat, the revamped Cambodian army was making steady progress reclaiming the vital highway. Villages and sections of road were taken mile by mile against stiff Khmer Rouge resistance.

In the capital of Phnom Penh, Lon Non followed events closely from headquarters. While heartened by the gains, he knew the hardest fighting still lay ahead. The communists would fight ferociously to maintain control of their sanctuaries along the Vietnamese border near Sihanoukville.

Lon Non pondered his next moves. The highway south passed through the Cardamom Mountains, ideal terrain for ambushes. He would need to use SCOUT reconnaissance teams to probe ahead and identify communist positions to bombard.

The brigadier general remained confident in the expanded FANK army. Bolstered by American training and firepower, they were becoming an effective fighting force. If that continued, Cambodia had a chance to survive the civil war, despite the Khmer Rouge's early gains.

The liberation of Route 6 and the south would take

every ounce of FANK's strength. But for the first time, Lon Non believed victory was possible. Cambodia's future now hinged on completing the bold stroke of Operation Chenla II. All their sacrifices would mean nothing if the highway lifeline remained in communist hands.

The toughest test was still to come. After years of setbacks, a glimmer of hope had emerged.

Kampot, Cambodia

By the third week of Operation Chenla II, the FANK divisions reached the outskirts of Kampot, a provincial capital halfway down Route 6. Taking the town would be key to securing the southern half of the highway.

Brigadier General Lon Non flew down to General Binh's forward headquarters to review the offensive's progress. Looking at the maps, it was clear Kampot would not be taken easily. The communists had fortified the town which was surrounded by hilly terrain perfect for ambushes against any assault.

"Our aerial reconnaissance shows they have interconnecting trench networks and bunkers throughout Kampot," General Binh briefed. "And the hills are surely packed with mortar and recoilless rifle positions covering all avenues of approach."

Lon Non frowned as he studied the defenses. A direct frontal attack would be bloody. But leaving the town in Khmer Rouge hands was unacceptable given its strategic location.

After some thought, Lon Non traced a line along the hills to the east of Kampot. "If we move forces through here under cover of night, we can flank the town from the high ground at dawn."

He looked up. "At first light, we hit them with an artillery barrage and airstrikes from the east while simultaneously assaulting from the highway. That should allow us to break through while they are off balance."

General Binh considered the plan and then nodded. "Yes, I believe we can penetrate their defenses using simultaneous attacks from two directions."

Lon Non knew it was a risk splitting their forces. But the payoff of catching the Khmer Rouge by surprise could tip the scales when tackling Kampot's formidable fortifications.

The stakes were high, but the opportunity was there to gain the upper hand against a dug-in enemy. Lon Non had faith his troops were up to the challenge after their recent successes.

"Issue orders to shift forces into the hills tonight under cover of darkness," Lon Non instructed. "At dawn, we attack Kampot from east and west with all we've got."

The battle for Kampot, and control of Route 6's midsection, was about to commence in full fury.

Predawn darkness shrouded the hills east of Kampot. FANK infantry picked their way silently through the jungle, guided by scout units towards attack positions. Everyone's nerves were taut knowing a ferocious battle loomed at first light.

As the sky lightened, Brigadier General Lon Non gave the signal over the radio. Artillery batteries surrounding Kampot opened up, raining shells onto the communist bunkers and trenches. Minutes later, aircraft swooped in dropping bombs and napalm over defensive strongpoints.

Under the fiery barrage, FANK infantry and armor assaulted Kampot from the main highway to the west. Simultaneously, the forces in the hills emerged from the jungle and attacked from the east, hitting the reeling Khmer Rouge defenders from both sides.

FANK Captain Ratan moved stealthily through the Kampot side streets, leading his platoon towards the sound of gunfire downtown. Earlier they had assaulted from the hills east of the city, completely surprising the communists.

Over the radio, Ratan heard his commander Colonel Seng Ros coordinating the attack. "The 2nd Battalion has central market secured. Prisoner reports Khmer Rouge headquarters nearby, in municipal building."

Ratan glanced at the street signs and waved his men forward towards the government complex. Rounding a corner, they encountered a Khmer Rouge machine gun nest set up at an intersecting alley.

Hitting the dirt, Ratan's radioman called for support. "Bronco 1-1, need air on target fifty meters southeast!"

Within minutes, an AH-1 Cobra gunship made a strafing run, obliterating the nest with minigun fire. Ratan took advantage of the chaos to lead his platoon in a charge, rushing through the intersection towards the main square.

Once inside the municipal building they swept room to room finding only abandoned weapons and maps. The Khmer Rouge commanders had slipped away. But the headquarters' capture meant the enemy chain of command was disrupted.

Ratan smiled in satisfaction. The audacious assault into the city from the rear had been a textbook maneuver. He felt pride in how far the FANK army had come with American training. This hard-fought victory at Kampot would be remembered as a key triumph on the long road to liberating all of Cambodia.

Fierce urban combat erupted as Cambodian government troops fought from street to street, building to building. The communists recovered from the initial bombardment and mounted stiff resistance. Rocket and small arms fire raked the advancing FANK soldiers.

FANK tanks rumbled through Kampot, blasting structures harboring Khmer Rouge holdouts. Slowly the defenders were compressed into a tighter perimeter in the town center. By late morning, Lon Non's pincer attack was succeeding in overrunning communist positions district by district.

In the afternoon Lon Non received a radio message - FANK troops from east and west Kampot had linked up, bisecting the Khmer Rouge zone of control. Although mopping up operations would continue for days, the tide had decisively turned.

Lon Non allowed himself a moment of satisfaction. The daring plan to envelop Kampot had broken the stalemate when a frontal assault would have cost hundreds more lives. It was a showcase for how far the Cambodian army had come with new tactics and training.

After this hard-won triumph, Lon Non knew spirits would be high among his men. The rest of Route 6 now lay open and victory in Operation Chenla II was coming into sight at last.

Two months later, Colonel Seng Ros peered through his binoculars at the tree line along Route 6. His battalion had advanced only a few kilometers south of Kampot when communist resistance had intensified.

Ros turned as Captain Prum approached, his expression grim. "Still no contact with 2nd Battalion on our flank. It's possible the Khmer Rouge has cut them off."

Ros grimaced. After Kampot the offensive had bogged down again in brutal jungle fighting. Intelligence indicated the communists had rushed reinforcements south to protect their sanctuaries near Vietnam.

A burst of AK-47 fire sounded from the treeline, followed by sniper shots. Ros and Prum ducked reflexively.

"Sir, we walked into a hornet's nest here," Prum said. "The enemy knows this jungle and our lines are exposed."

Ros slammed a fist on the sandbag wall in frustration. Two months grinding down Route 6 and now they had lost momentum. Perhaps treasonous officers in Phnom Penh had leaked FANK plans and positions.

"Get Brigade on the radio," Ros said. "We need air support to sweep the jungle ahead of us before the Khmer Rouge cut this highway for good."

An hour later, Ros listened grimly as Prum returned. "No aircraft available - the capital is their priority. We're on our own out here."

Ros felt icy anger grip him. After coming so far, the high command was leaving his battalion stranded without support. The initiative was slipping away by the hour as communist reinforcements flowed unchecked into the area.

Unless the tide turned quickly, Chenla II could end

in disaster along this contested stretch of Route 6.

Captain Rattan led his weary company up the jungle trail in the Cardamom Mountains. Over the radio, he heard his battalion was pinned down trying to force the mountain passes.

Reaching a ridge crest, Rattan spotted a concentration of Khmer Rouge fighters firing from bunkers concealed on the valley walls and slopes. He grabbed his radio.

"Steel Rain, this is Tiger 1-1, request fire mission on enemy bunkers at grid 829560!"

Static answered. The mountains wreaked havoc on communications. Rattan hurriedly set up the portable satellite radio to reestablish contact.

Minutes dragged by, but the American advisor responded, "Tiger 1-1, negative fire mission - all assets diverted east to support capital defense."

Rattan's face fell. No artillery or air support would save them. Looking to his men, he said simply: "Fix bayonets." Their ammunition was low, but their courage remained high.

With bayonets affixed, the company of 100 men charged down the slope towards the communist positions. Taken by surprise, the Khmer Rouge hastily organized to meet the thrust.

The Khmer Rouge commander called to his machine gunners, "Cut them down before they get through!"

A murderous crossfire erupted from concealed bunkers on the valley walls. Dozens of Rattan's men were shredded in the first volley, the rest throwing themselves prone in the high grass.

Rattan crawled forward, rallying his surviving

soldiers. "On me, we can still break through!"

As they rose to advance again, the Khmer Rouge had zeroed in their heavy weapons. Another scything hail of lead tore through the exposed company. Even Rattan's bravery could not overcome the devastating fire.

Within minutes, Rattan and nearly all his men lay dead or dying on the blood-soaked ground. Their bold bayonet charge had been swallowed up, breaking against entrenched communist troops dominating the high valley.

The Khmer Rouge commander nodded in satisfaction. The mountain passes were secure. These chokepoints had halted the imperialists' advance and turned the tide of battle back in revolutionary favor.

With air power grounded and artillery silent, the communists had seized the advantage. The unfinished highway through the Cardamom Mountains became a killing ground, ending Chenla II's bold momentum.

Rattan could only utter a final prayer as his life ebbed away - that Cambodia's future might still be saved.

Brigadier General Lon Non stood alone in the operations room, maps still marking the aborted offensive down Route 6. He felt each casualty report over the last weeks like a physical blow. Thousands of soldiers lost, and nothing to show for the blood spilled.

The door opened and an American advisor entered, his expression grim. "General, the last FANK battalions have withdrawn up the highway. The Khmer Rouge hold the southern half."

Lon Non merely nodded, unsurprised. Once the offensive stalled outside Kampot, he knew it was only a matter of time.

"We came so close," Lon Non said quietly. "Even with your country's training and airpower, it wasn't enough to dislodge them."

The advisor shook his head. "Your men fought bravely. But once the communists reinforced, the jungle terrain favored them heavily."

Bitterness rose in Lon Non's chest. "So much sacrifice, now the Route 6 lifeline remains cut. Half our country is lost..."

A long silence followed. Both men understood the implications. With Sihanoukville Port isolated, FANK would struggle to resupply, while Khmer Rouge arms flowed unimpeded from North Vietnam.

Lon Non rolled up the offensive maps. "Tell your superiors in Saigon we are grateful for your support. But Cambodia's survival now hangs by a thread. We must forge our own path from here."

Departing alone, Lon Non felt the weight of failure pressing down. But in his heart, the spark of defiance still burned. The war was not yet over.

In the end, Operation Chenla II resulted in over 10,000 FANK troops killed and thousands more wounded or captured. Khmer Rouge losses were estimated to be comparable.

The military defeat was compounded by severe psychological damage. The failed offensive left FANK's remaining units demoralized and fragile, while energizing and emboldening the communist insurgency.

Militarily and psychologically, the damage suffered during Chenla II was catastrophic. The Cambodian army would never fully recover from the blow of abandoning the campaign to reopen Route 6.

In the aftermath, the government shifted to a defensive posture, focused on retaining control of the capital, key garrisons and Mekong river supply lines. This consolidation ceded much of the countryside to the Khmer Rouge, enabling their recruitment and expansion.

Though fought valiantly with American aid, Operation Chenla II proved a pivotal turning point in Cambodia's civil war. The failed campaign dashed hopes of driving back the communists and set the stage for greater FANK losses in coming years. Its legacy was a weakened army unable to prevent being gradually surrounded by Khmer Rouge forces, leading to final defeat in 1975.

Saigon, South Vietnam

General Abrams entered the ops center, scanning the situation maps. His mood had soured dramatically. Cambodia's defeat along Route 6 was a severe blow to containment efforts on the border.

"General Minh, what's your assessment of the border situation?" Abrams asked the South Vietnamese commander. "How does Cambodia's loss affect your forces?"

Minh's jaw tightened. "The situation is dire. The communists now have unchecked sanctuaries to mass forces and store supplies for assaults down the entire frontier."

He jabbed a finger at the maps. "We are facing multi-division attacks along Highways 1, 22 and 13. My battalions are outnumbered defending this vast border."

Abrams nodded, mouth set in a grim line as he traced the red expanding blob. "Every inch they gain in Cambodia brings enemy forces closer to Saigon. Your men will bear the brunt holding the line."

"My concern is being outflanked from Cambodia," Minh replied. "Their sanctuaries are untouched; they can amass forces at will for assaults into the Delta and threaten the capital."

Abrams nodded gravely. "I understand your situation. You have my full authorization to use air and artillery power across the border. Disrupt their supply lines and staging areas."

Minh's eyes flashed. "While your air support is welcome, your defensive strategy is failing. We don't need half measures. We must destroy the communist's Cambodian sanctuaries completely. The only true solution is sending American troops to clear those sanctuaries once and for all."

Abrams held up a hand placatingly. "You know ground intervention is not possible. My hands are tied in Washington."

"Yet you seem comfortable tying ours," Minh retorted, "Forcing my army to shoulder the burden alone while you evacuate your forces."

Abrams bristled at the accusation. "I've committed everything I can to bolstering the ARVN. But we're withdrawing down to 50,000 troops as it is. My options are limited."

Minh shook his head bitterly. "Limited options, while the enemy enjoys unlimited sanctuary? This war will not be won by bombing trails and roads. We must seize their staging areas and destroy the NVA units and supplies clusters inside Cambodia."

"I gave my best advice in Washington," Abrams

insisted. "But the decisions are made. We must make do with available resources."

"And what resources will be left when America abandons us?" Minh pressed angrily. "How do you suggest we stem the communist tide then?"

Abrams held up a conciliatory hand. "Our commitment is not open-ended, I acknowledge that. But for now, maxims utilization of air and artillery is essential to disrupt their operations."

Minh uncrossed his arms, marginally appeased. "I will employ those assets to maximum effect. But it will be near ruin given the scale of enemy attacks."

"When you require more support, don't hesitate to request it," Abrams affirmed. "Defending Cambodia's border means protecting Saigon too."

Both men felt the weight of the deepening crisis. The scales were tipping as communist forces expanded unchecked from Cambodian sanctuaries.

Finally Abrams met Minh's eyes. "I cannot promise how this ends. But I swear I will back you with what influence I still possess. We will get through this."

Minh nodded slowly. Despite their differences, defeating the communist onslaught united them. That shared cause had to sustain them through the dark days ahead.

As the Nixon administration pursued Vietnamization, handing the war effort over to South Vietnam, General Abrams grappled with his waning influence. After building up American forces to over half a million troops, now he was charged with withdrawing them rapidly.

Abrams had faith in the ARVN's courage, but harbored doubts about their logistical capabilities and air power needed to confront vast communist forces. He worried the accelerated pullout timeline was driven by politics rather than military reality.

Abrams was a seasoned soldier who followed orders. As US troops departed and bases closed, he worked dutifully to bolster South Vietnamese capacities despite constraints.

In private moments though, Abrams chafed at hollow assurances from Washington. He knew hasty withdrawal could jeopardize hard-fought gains. The communists were unlikely to quit while military victory loomed as US involvement decreased.

Abrams's role was to implement strategic decisions, not challenge them. He focused on maintaining US air support critical to the ARVN's survival. Though no longer directing ground operations, Abrams hoped America's lingering firepower commitment might offer South Vietnam a fighting chance.

As American forces rapidly departed Vietnam, the burden of continuing the war fell squarely on General Minh and the South Vietnamese army. Given charge of ground operations just as US troops were evacuating, Minh felt profound pressure.

He maintained a stoic face around American commanders, but privately Minh harbored deep concerns. The ARVN had grown dependent on US fire support, logistics, and mobility. Now they were forced to confront the formidable communist forces increasingly alone.

Like many South Vietnamese officers, Minh was skeptical of Vietnamization. He doubted both the timetable for withdrawal and assurances that America would provide ongoing air power. Promises from

Washington rang hollow as B-52s and fighter jets disappeared from Vietnamese skies daily.

Minh focused on rapidly building ARVN capacities, but felt South Vietnam was being abandoned prematurely for political expedience. He hid his bitterness at being reduced to merely a recipient of diminishing American aid.

Whatever the frictions, Minh channeled his energies into preparing the army to fight self-sufficiently. South Vietnam's survival now depended on the ARVN's tenacity and skill. Minh was determined not to fail, even against long odds and absent the allies who had started this war.

A Master's Stroke

White House, Washington DC, USA

The chanting from the National Mall drifted through the thick White House windows. "Hell no, we won't go!" The anti-war protesters had been gathering for days, streaming into Washington D.C. like tributaries feeding a raging river. Their signs and slogans all blended together into one indignant roar.

President Nixon pressed his forehead against the windowpane, his jaw clenched tight. No matter what he did to deescalate the war in Vietnam, the protests only seemed to grow larger and louder.

"I don't get it, Henry," Nixon said as Kissinger entered the Oval Office. "I've brought home more boys in the last year than that peacenik Johnson did in four. And yet they scream as if I've done nothing."

Kissinger came to stand beside the president at the window. "It's not enough for them," he said. "They want the whole thing ended now."

Nixon pounded his fist on the window sill. "I'm doing everything I can to untangle the mess Johnson left me. Don't they see that?"

"It's not about logic, Mr. President. It's emotion. They're running on pure anti-war fervor."

"And the press fuels their fire," Nixon said bitterly. "If the media would give us some credit for Vietnamization, maybe public sentiment would start to turn. But instead they focus on the mistakes and the body count."

Nixon turned away from the window in frustration. He couldn't stand to look at the teeming crowds another moment. "This damned war is going to taint my presidency forever if we don't change the narrative," Nixon said, pouring himself a scotch as he and Kissinger sat by the Oval Office fireplace.

Kissinger nodded. "It's overshadowing everything else you've accomplished. Détente, ending the draft..."

"Exactly," Nixon said, pointing at him. "I refuse to go down in history as the Vietnam War president. There has to be more to my legacy than that."

He took a sip of his drink, his eyes distant and contemplative. "When people think of Richard Nixon, I want them to think of bold foreign policy. Historic diplomacy. A president who wasn't afraid to reimagine America's role in the world. I want my legacy to be one of peacemaking, not war-waging."

Kissinger realized it was the moment he had been waiting for...

"It's time for bold action," said Kissinger. "We need to remind the American people that their president is a man of vision. A man seeking peace."

Nixon raised an eyebrow. "What did you have in mind?"

"China," Kissinger said simply. "If we can open relations with Beijing, the whole political landscape could shift in our favor."

Nixon froze, looking incredulous. "China? You can't be serious."

Kissinger held up a hand. "Hear me out, Mr. President. I know they're Communists, but—"

"Not just Communists," Nixon interjected, "they're the enemy, Henry! Red China wants to destroy us and everything we stand for. What would our allies think if we embraced Mao?"

"Precisely why it's such a bold gambit," Kissinger said. "No one would expect it. But we could use détente with China as leverage against the Soviets and North Vietnam."

Nixon shook his head, frowning. "I don't know...this could backfire terribly. The American people still despise Red China for good reason."

Kissinger stepped closer, speaking earnestly. "Sometimes peace requires befriending old enemies. China's influence on North Vietnam could end this war sooner. Doesn't pragmatism demand we at least consider it?"

Nixon remained silent, staring out the window and rubbing his chin. Kissinger could see the wheels turning, the president's instincts for power politics at war with his anti-communist ideology. "Détente with China could very well drive a wedge between the communist world. The Soviets would be beside themselves."

"That's true. They might even ask to come to the bargaining table themselves."

"Exactly, Mr. President. I see great potential upside in a move like this."

"Opening up to China would be a huge political risk," Nixon said as he paced slowly behind his desk. "Can you imagine how the American people would react to their anti-communist president strolling through Beijing?"

"It would certainly take some explaining," Kissinger agreed. "But think of how it would confound our enemies. The Soviets would be rocked to the core. And North Vietnam would feel pressured with China at the peace table."

Nixon nodded. "You're right about the strategic advantages. The prospect of a China-US alliance could force North Vietnam's hand in the peace talks."

"Exactly," said Kissinger. "It would suggest we have options beyond the quagmire of Vietnam."

"You know what, Henry? Maybe it's just crazy enough to work. Mao Zedong is a ruthless dictator. But I promised the American people peace with honor. If this could achieve that..." Nixon trailed off, then met Kissinger's gaze. "Set up a backchannel. Discreetly. Let's see if the old bastards in Beijing will even talk."

Kissinger suppressed a smile. "Yes sir, Mr. President."

Kissinger strode from the Oval Office feeling a growing sense of uncertainty. The president's faith in him was flattering, yes, but also daunting. Opening relations with China would be no simple diplomatic matter.

As he walked the carpeted hall, Kissinger muttered under his breath. "How in the world am I going to make this happen?"

He envisioned the endless obstacles - securing covert communications with Beijing, arranging the summit without causing a domestic uproar, and somehow persuading two bitter ideological rivals to find common ground. The hurdles seemed staggering.

Kissinger entered his office, closing the door tightly behind him. He sat down heavily at his desk, the wood creaking beneath him. Resting his forehead in his hands, he let out a weary sigh. Maybe the idea of befriending Red China had been rash, more hypothetical than realistic. Could he really pull this off?

Of course, Kissinger couldn't voice these doubts to Nixon. The president was counting on his renowned strategic abilities to open this bold new channel. But the truth was, Kissinger had no clue where to start with China. No contacts, no backchannels, no leverage to get them to the negotiating table.

As the afternoon sun shifted across his office, Kissinger racked his brain for a plan. Finally, he unfolded a world map, tracing his finger along potential routes into Beijing.

"There has to be a way," he muttered. Failure was not an option - not when Nixon was determined to "make history." For better or worse, Kissinger had set this unpredictable gambit in motion. Now he had to see it through.

Willard Hotel – Washington DC, USA

Kissinger sat alone at a secluded corner table in the Willard Hotel's lounge, contemplating how to initiate covert contact with China. The darkened wood and leather furnishings provided privacy for Washington's powerful to discreetly discuss affairs of state.

He sipped bourbon, considering his limited options. Direct communication was out of the question. The State Department had no formal ties with the People's Republic, and the CIA presence in China was woefully inadequate. A friendly ambassador could be an asset, but State was filled with holdovers from the anti-Red China Kennedy and Johnson administrations.

Kissinger watched as a senator and lobbyist huddled nearby, speaking in hushed tones. Everyone in this town had a backchannel, he mused. Now he needed to find one to Beijing. "There must be a side-door, an unorthodox channel we can utilize," Kissinger muttered to himself. Getting a message directly to Zhou Enlai would be ideal.

Just then, an idea struck - the Pakistani foreign minister was scheduled to visit Beijing next month. If he could convince the minister to secretly relay an invitation, it might reach Zhou Enlai's ears.

Kissinger quickly drafted a carefully worded message on the Willard's crested stationery. "The President would like to normalize relations with the People's Republic," it began.

Folding the note into his jacket, Kissinger finished his drink and exited the lounge. If this gambit worked, Nixon would have his historic diplomatic opening, and Kissinger the chance to reshape the Cold War landscape. The wheels were in motion.

Pakistan Embassy – Washington DC, USA

The next day, Kissinger arrived at the Pakistani Embassy for a clandestine meeting with Ambassador Sultan Khan. After being ushered into a plush sitting room, Kissinger got straight to business.

"Thank you for agreeing to this discreet discussion," he said in a low voice. "As you know, Pakistan's relationship with China could be useful in a delicate matter."

Khan raised an eyebrow but remained silent, waiting for Kissinger to continue.

"Simply put, President Nixon wishes to explore normalizing relations with the People's Republic," Kissinger said. "Any direct request would be...complicated at this stage. But we believe a trusted partner like yourself could act as an intermediary."

Pulling out the folded note, Kissinger handed it to Khan. The ambassador scanned it quickly, his expression giving away little.

"You're asking me to secretively pass along this message in Beijing," Khan said slowly.

"I realize it puts you in a difficult position," Kissinger acknowledged. "But leaders in both Islamabad and Washington would be grateful."

Khan leaned back, stroking his beard as he contemplated the ramifications. Passing a secret message from Washington to Beijing would jeopardize Pakistan's delicate balancing act between the U.S. and China. If exposed, Pakistan could lose trust and support from either side.

Professionally, Khan would be going well beyond his role as ambassador, dabbling in high-stakes foreign policy better left to presidents and premiers. And on a personal level, Zhou Enlai was a long-time friend - would relaying America's covert overture endanger that relationship?

Khan realized Nixon's request could threaten Pakistan's strategic interests in Asia. And yet, facilitating communication between the two adversarial powers could also strengthen Pakistan's position as an intermediary. The risks were profound, but so too were the potential rewards.

After several tense moments weighing the gamble before him, Khan met Kissinger's expectant gaze. Perhaps Pakistan could discreetly nudge two giants closer together, serving its own interests while aiding Washington and Beijing. The chance to reshape history was worth the hazard.

"Very well," Khan finally said. "I will relay your message during my visit. Zhou Enlai is an old friend, after all. Just don't be surprised if his response is less than warm. China's distrust of America runs deep."

White House – Washington DC, USA

Over the next few weeks, Kissinger waited anxiously for word from Ambassador Khan. Had his message been delivered to Zhou Enlai? Or had Khan thought better of the risky proposition and kept quiet in Beijing?

The wait was agonizing. Kissinger threw himself into work - policy meetings, drafting memos, diplomatic receptions - all the while wondering if his bold gambit had been received. Or dismissed. Or worse, openly rebuked, jeopardizing any future overtures.

"Any word yet?" Nixon asked, intercepting Kissinger in the West Wing hallway.

Kissinger paused, swallowing his frustration. "Not yet, Mr. President. It's only been two weeks since I met with Ambassador Khan."

"Well, what's taking so long?" Nixon pressed. "Did Khan even deliver the message to Zhou?"

"I believe he did, but we can't rush this process. Reaching out to China will take finesse and patience."

Nixon frowned. "My patience is wearing thin. I need action, progress. Something to show the American people."

Kissinger chose his words carefully. "Establishing

this connection is delicate. If we come on too strong at first, the door may slam shut permanently."

"So you're saying I should just sit and wait while the clock ticks?" Nixon scoffed.

"Yes sir, unfortunately that's the best approach for now," Kissinger said calmly. "I know it's frustrating, but a diplomatic opening with China can't be forced. Persistence and discretion are key."

Nixon's expression remained stern, but he gave a curt nod. "Alright Henry, we'll do it your way. But I expect substantive progress soon. Our legacy is on the line."

"I understand Mr. President. You have my word that I'm working every angle," Kissinger assured. Satisfied for the moment, Nixon continued down the hall.

Five weeks after Kissinger's clandestine meeting at the Pakistani Embassy, he received intriguing news. Khan wanted an urgent meeting.

Pakistani Embassy, Washington DC, USA

Rushing to the Embassy, Kissinger was led once again to the quiet sitting room. Khan's expression was unreadable.

"Well? Did you pass along the message?" Kissinger asked anxiously.

Khan nodded. "I gave Zhou Enlai your letter. He read it carefully, then set it aside without a word."

Kissinger felt his heart sink. "So, he rejected the overture. I suppose that's that."

"Not quite." Khan leaned forward. "Two days later, Zhou gifted me a private letter to bring back to you. I think you will find its contents are... intriguing."

"You read it?" said Kissinger.

"Of course not. But Zhou did inform me of the general sustenance of the letter."

Eagerly taking the letter, Kissinger saw the swift brushstrokes and red seal - a communication directly from the top levels of Beijing. The door had cracked open to China.

Sliding the letter into his suit coat pocket, Kissinger thanked Khan profusely for taking the risk of delivery. Then he rushed directly from the Embassy to his office in the White House.

White House – Washington DC, USA

Sitting at his desk, Kissinger's hands trembled as he opened the letter, the flowing Mandarin characters leaving him frustrated. His grasp of written Chinese was still elementary. He could only pick out a few key phrases: "American communication," "study closely," and "reply shortly."

Desperate for translation help, Kissinger hurried to the State Department's Office of Language Services. There he found an expert linguist to interpret the full message from Zhou Enlai.

The translator read slowly, allowing Kissinger to jot down notes: "Acknowledges receipt of message via Pakistani channel...will consider seriously...potential for further discussion."

It was guarded, but not a firm rejection. Kissinger leaned back, relief washing over him. Zhou had left the door slightly ajar.

Without fluency in Mandarin, Kissinger knew he was at a strategic disadvantage in forging this connection. He resolved to ramp up his language lessons, needing to understand China's coded diplomatic language to navigate this delicate opening.

For now, though, Kissinger had enough to inform Nixon. Mandarin fluency could come later; today, their foot was in China's door.

Kissinger hurried to the Oval Office, still digesting the translated letter from Beijing. He found Nixon at his desk, looking up expectantly.

"What's the word from China?" Nixon asked.

Kissinger took a breath. "The message is guarded, but overall positive. Zhou Enlai acknowledged receiving our communication via the Pakistani channel."

"That's good, right?" Nixon said, though his tone was uncertain.

"Yes, Mr. President, it confirms our backchannel approach succeeded. Zhou wrote they will seriously study the matter and may reply again shortly."

Nixon considered this news. "So, no concrete promises yet?"

"No sir, it's still early. But the fact that they are studying the idea of rapprochement is encouraging," Kissinger said.

Nixon stood and began pacing slowly. "I don't like vague assurances. Did Zhou give any indication they're willing to meet?"

Kissinger chose his words carefully. "Not explicitly. But we've caught their interest. Further reciprocal messages may warm relations enough for a summit."

"Maybe so, but they're still Red China, don't forget," Nixon said, pointing his pipe sternly. "If Zhou just keeps things ambiguous, trying to string us along, I'll need more than words on paper eventually."

Kissinger nodded. "I understand, Mr. President. But patience and persistence are key now. The door has opened a sliver - I believe we can push it wider."

Nixon paused his pacing, considering Kissinger's counsel. "Alright. We'll play it your way, for now. But don't let them think I'll wait around forever. I expect real progress."

"You have my word. Our next messages will nudge them closer." Kissinger knew the path ahead remained precarious, but they had taken the first pivotal step.

Over the next few months, Kissinger and Zhou Enlai exchanged a series of carefully worded letters through their Pakistani backchannel. Each message was intended to incrementally build trust and thaw relations.

Kissinger took pains to strike the right tone - acknowledging past tensions but suggesting shared interests could form the basis of a renewed relationship.

Zhou's replies were always formal, even terse, though no longer wholly rejecting reconciliation. But Kissinger noticed Zhou never went beyond vague generalities or direct commitments.

By early 1971, Nixon was growing impatient. "These exchanges aren't getting us anywhere," he fumed, reading Zhou's latest noncommittal letter.

Kissinger counseled continued engagement. "We're inching the door open slowly but surely. We just need the right opportunity now, something to spur momentum."

The letter exchanges were stalling. "We need a bold public gesture to break the impasse," Kissinger told

Nixon.

Sitting in his office late one night, Kissinger had an idea - what if he could arrange for China's ping pong team to be invited to the U.S.? The goodwill symbolism would be immense.

Kissinger discreetly spoke with the US ping pong association and asked that they extend an invite to China's Ping Pong team for a series of exhibition games. They agreed to try but were weary of China's reaction to such an invitation. Kissinger assured them China would seriously consider the invitation.

When China accepted several weeks later, Kissinger informed Nixon as if unaware of the upcoming exhibition matches.

Nixon took the bait perfectly. "This is an incredible opportunity! We should welcome them at the White House."

"Great idea, Mr. President. A White House visit will show America's good faith," he told the president. "A symbolic gesture before the people."

The Chinese ping pong team arrived in the U.S. to great fanfare all arranged discreetly by Kissinger. He left nothing to chance.

Nixon welcomed the Chinese athletes on the South Lawn, shaking hands awkwardly as cameras flashed.

Later, Nixon posed with the team in the Oval Office. "Let's get that gift I prepared," he told Kissinger through gritted teeth.

Returning, Kissinger handed Nixon a wrapped American ping pong paddle signed by the president himself. Nixon presented it to the Chinese team captain as cameras clicked away.

After the successful PR visit, Kissinger exclaimed to Nixon, "You've made history, Mr. President! That handshake will be front page news across China."

Within days of the team returning to China, Zhou Enlai extended an invitation for Nixon's envoy to Beijing.

Rushing to tell Nixon, Kissinger could hardly contain his excitement. "This is it, Mr. President! China is ready for direct contact."

Nixon laughed heartily. "Great news, Henry. My ping pong maneuver is paying off handsomely."

Allowing Nixon to take the credit, Kissinger swelled with satisfaction. He had masterfully orchestrated a "ping heard round the world" to catalyze the diplomatic opening. Sometimes diplomacy just needed the right photo op.

Now that China had invited an American envoy, Kissinger focused on making the trip a success. He worked closely with Winston Lord, a diplomat well-versed in Chinese language and culture, to prepare for their clandestine mission.

"We'll be the first U.S. officials in Red China's capital since 1949," Kissinger told him. "Everything must go perfectly."

He outlined the visit's delicate goals - build rapport with Zhou Enlai, explore common interests, assess obstacles still remaining. Lord soaked up every detail. He knew well that he was about to become part of history.

July 9, 1971 – Beijing, China

Kissinger and Winston Lord secretly flew from Pakistan to Beijing aboard a Pakistani jet. As the plane descended through thick cloud cover, Kissinger gazed out the window, eager for his first glimpse of the Chinese capital. Suddenly, the grey veil parted, revealing the sprawling cityscape of Beijing stretching to the horizon.

Squat Soviet-style buildings dominated the view, along with a few striking temples and palaces from imperial days. Broad boulevards cut through a sea of cinderblock apartments and warehouses. Plumes of smoke rose from coils of factory pipes.

It was a drab yet mesmerizing vista - the nerve center of the world's most populous Communist regime. Kissinger spotted Tiananmen Square and the Forbidden City, iconic landmarks he had only seen in intelligence photos.

Now he was circling above them, about to make history on the ground below. As the tarmac neared, Kissinger felt China's mysterious expanse opening up, heavy with opportunity and uncertainty. Their aircraft wheels kissed the runway - the point of no return. Beijing awaited.

As Kissinger descended the plane's steps, a Chinese delegation stood waiting on the tarmac. At the head was a distinguished man in a grey Mao suit - Vice Foreign Minister Chiao Kuan-hua.

"Welcome to China," Chiao said in crisp English. He nodded briefly to Kissinger and Lord but did not extend his hand.

Kissinger nodded back respectfully. He had expected the lack of direct physical contact - it would take time before such casual intimacy could occur between high-level diplomats of their two systems.

For now, a simple dignified greeting without handshake was all the protocol that could be managed. But Kissinger knew well the significance of their presence here today - two worlds converging after decades of hostility and separation.

He joined Chiao heading toward the idling fleet of black sedans, ready for the short silent drive into history. The moment felt solemn and profound, handshake or not.

The short car ride to their government guest house took place in tense silence. Beijing's wide boulevards and drab Soviet-style buildings made clear they were deep in communist territory.

"Remember, speak only when spoken to at first," said Kissinger knowing that Lord probably knew the protocol, but not wanting to leave anything to chance.

Arriving at the walled compound, Kissinger and Lord were shown to their separate quarters in one of the traditional pavilion-style buildings. The rooms were spacious, with lacquered furnishings and calligraphy scrolls decorating the walls.

After freshening up, they were served tea and traditional delicacies - dumplings, smoked duck, and noodles - by white-jacketed attendants in a dining room overlooking a manicured garden courtyard.

Kissinger knew each dish was carefully selected to impress the American guests. "Remain politely neutral in your reactions," he whispered to Lord. "Don't appear too enamored or resistant."

In between meetings, they were encouraged to stroll the guest house grounds and view artwork displays. Security agents followed at a distance as they walked among rock sculptures and bonsai trees, both eager for glimpses of everyday life beyond the compound walls.

At night, Kissinger struggled to sleep, knowing the course of history could hinge on their discussions over the coming days. He knew much persistent work remained to push open China's doors.

The imposing edifice of the Great Hall of the People loomed large as Kissinger and Lord's car approached. Completed in 1959, the monumental granite structure dominates the western edge of Tiananmen Square.

Passing through cavernous entry arches, they walked beneath towering red columns topping 100 feet in height. Hammered gold lanterns cast dim light on the polished marble floors. The vast space was dim and hushed, befitting the seat of the highest levels of Chinese power.

Guards then escorted them to Zhou Enlai's personal office on the third floor. Despite its sparse furnishings, the large office projected grandeur with a panoramic view of the Square.

An expansive mural stretched across the entire back wall of Zhou's office. It depicted a classic Chinese landscape scene - jagged mist-shrouded mountains rising above a flowing river and meadows dotted with blossoming trees.

In the foreground, small figures in traditional clothing appeared to be peasants farming, hauling bundles of rice, and carrying baskets of tea leaves up winding paths. Some fished along the riverbanks as cranes soared overhead.

The pastoral imagery evoked traditional Confucian ideals of harmony between man and nature. Yet the figures also seemed to embody communist virtues of rural workers united in building a prosperous society.

Kissinger studied the rich hues of the hand-painted

mural, struck by the juxtaposition of ancient aesthetic beauty with the office's austere communist environs. The contrast captured something profound about China's identity under Mao's rule.

Kissinger sized up the slender, distinguished man rising to greet them from behind an immense wooden desk - Zhou Enlai, Premier of the State Council. Zhou's refined manners and accented but fluid English spoke to his education in elite missionary schools and abroad.

His expression was sober, even inscrutable, yet his eyes remained alert and piercing. Kissinger knew Zhou's skills as a diplomat and negotiator were renowned. He would measure his words carefully, revealing little too soon.

When they shook hands, Zhou's grip was neither firm nor limp, as if calibrated to exactly the strength required by protocol and no more. Kissinger was determined to emulate such discipline in these high stakes talks.

Though Zhou's receding hairline and lines around his eyes betrayed his seventy years, he exuded an energetic intellect. This consummate statesman would be a formidable counterpart across the negotiating table in the days ahead.

Zhou greeted them solemnly across his expansive desk. "I hope your journey was acceptable. Shall we begin discussions?"

Speaking slowly, Kissinger conveyed America's interest in renewed relations, while Lord interpreted into Chinese. Zhou listened impassively, occasionally nodding, but gave little away behind opaque smiles and pleasantries.

"Premier Zhou, thank you for welcoming us,"

Kissinger began. "Our nations have been isolated from each other for too long. We hope this will mark a change."

Zhou nodded politely. "I am pleased you made the journey. We have much to discuss."

Kissinger continued speaking, taking Zhou's brevity as a cue. "President Nixon deeply regrets the hostility that has divided us. He believes it is time for a new chapter - one of open dialogue and mutual understanding. We recognize the deep differences in our philosophies of government," Kissinger went on. "But peace between us is paramount. Neither benefits from perpetual conflict."

Zhou stroked his thin beard, listening intently without comment.

Kissinger pressed forward in Zhou's meditative silence. "The United States is committed to normalizing our relations. We are prepared to take tangible steps to build trust. But we will need creativity and courage on both sides."

At last Zhou spoke. "Minister Kissinger, your sincerity is evident. China also seeks peaceful ties, on principled terms. But past tensions cannot disappear instantly. Let this be the first of many earnest discussions."

Kissinger felt relieved. Zhou was receptive despite his guarded tone. This would be an ongoing courtship demanding vision and patience. But a foundation had been laid.

Kissinger and Zhou spoke for another hour, cautiously feeling each other out on a range of issues. Kissinger emphasized America's desire for open communication and military de-escalation. Zhou reiterated China's stance on Taiwan, Vietnam, and nuclear arms.

Their exchanges remained diplomatic yet noncommittal, each careful not to concede too much ground too quickly. But Kissinger was heartened by Zhou's engagement on even difficult topics.

Back at the guest house, Kissinger anxiously debriefed Lord. "What's your read?"

Lord chose his words carefully. "Zhou's controlled, but not rejecting reconciliation. We have more work to build true trust."

Kissinger knew Lord was right - this would be a gradual courtship requiring discretion. But as he stared out at the strange skyline of Beijing, success felt tantalizingly close.

Toward the end of the second day of meeting with Zhou, Kissinger decided to suggest something bold - the possibility of a state visit by President Nixon.

"If Premier Zhou would entertain it, President Nixon would be honored to visit China in an official capacity," he proposed. "It would signal a new era in our relations."

Zhou's expression remained unreadable. "An intriguing notion," he replied neutrally. "One requiring much careful preparation."

Kissinger nodded, not wanting to press the point too firmly too soon. But the idea was on the table.

As the meeting concluded, Zhou clasped Kissinger's hand firmly. "I appreciate your sincerity, Minister Kissinger. I look forward to our next discussion."

In those two days in Beijing, only preliminary steps had been taken. But riding back to the airport,

Kissinger allowed himself a smile. Seeds had been planted.

White House – Washington DC, USA

Returning to Washington, Kissinger wasted no time in briefing Nixon on every detail of his visit. He described Zhou's mannerisms, the negotiating climate, and the possibility left open for an eventual presidential summit.

"So, they're clearly interested but playing hard to get," Nixon observed. "We'll have to keep wooing them if we want this historic trip to happen."

Kissinger nodded. "Our next messages must strike the perfect balance - expressing clear interest while allowing Zhou to set the pace."

In the months that followed, Kissinger focused single-mindedly on continuing to court China through backchannel communications. He made plans for another pre-summit visit to finalize arrangements.

October 1971 – Beijing, China

Kissinger made a second secret journey to Beijing to meet Zhou Enlai, finalize arrangements for Nixon's trip, and continue thawing US-China relations.

"Welcome back, Minister Kissinger. Please sit," Zhou greeted formally in his office. "I trust your flight went smoothly."

"Thank you, it did," Kissinger replied as he settled into his chair. "I'm grateful for your hospitality again. My president is eager for this opportunity."

Zhou nodded. "Likewise. This will be an historic moment for our nations after long hostility."

The two statesmen discussed protocol and logistics for the presidential visit. Kissinger then steered the talk toward possible joint communiqués outlining shared principles and a common desire for peace.

Zhou remained noncommittal on specifics but open in principle. Kissinger strived to balance charm and tenacity, sensing progress without pushing too fast too soon.

By meeting's end, the last hurdles were cleared for Nixon's momentous trip the following February. Kissinger felt elated as he left Zhou - his patient, persistent diplomacy had positioned change between two giants. The world would soon bear witness.

February 17, 1972 - Beijing, China

The world watched in awe as Air Force One descended through the clouds over Beijing, wings tipping to greet crowds gathered below. President Nixon had arrived in China.

As the jet taxied to a stop, Kissinger straightened his tie, swelling with accomplishment. His bold vision years ago had led to this improbable moment.

Nixon and Kissinger stepped onto crimson-carpeted tarmac flanked by soldiers standing at crisp attention. A military band played both countries' national anthems as Chinese dignitaries approached in formation, their faces betraying restrained smiles.

As Nixon shook Zhou's hand, he said earnestly "The people of America have waited a long time for this moment."

Zhou nodded solemnly. "As have the people of China. Let us make the most of this opportunity."

Stepping into the gleaming terminal, Nixon and

Zhou passed under a fifty-foot portrait of Mao gazing benevolently upon the arrival of his American guests. Cavernous halls echoed with applause from assembled crowds, many waving bouquets of flowers.

Outside, along Beijing's broad boulevards, crowds lined the motorcade route - ordinary Chinese hoping to glimpse the first US president to visit their capital since its 1949 revolution. Nixon stood and waved through the smoked-glass windows.

At the Great Hall banquet, Nixon toasted Zhou before a feast of Peking duck, fish Maw soup and other exotic delicacies. In a banquet toast, Nixon raised his glass to "new understanding between old adversaries."

Zhou followed, lauding "peaceful exchange after years of hostility."

Chinese cultural troupes entertained under suspended lanterns as the leaders dined at an expansive mahogany table surrounded by sixty feasting diplomats.

The incongruous sight of America's staunch anti-Communist president banqueting in the belly of Mao's regime left Kissinger reflecting on how far persistence and imagination had brought them here against all odds.

Every detail - from waving schoolchildren to the painting of a dove Nixon gifted to Zhou - reinforced the sensation of etching themselves into the annals of history.

Over the next six days Nixon met extensively with Zhou, forging diplomatic inroads. Kissinger sat in on each critical session as they outlined principles for normalizing relations and easing decades of suspicion. Conferring in Zhou's office, Nixon said "We must build trust, step-by-step."

"Agreed," replied Zhou. "Candid diplomacy will allow us to resolve our differences."

Every night back at the state guest house, Nixon congratulated Kissinger. "This trip is making history, Henry! Well done." Kissinger had helped guide his president here through sheer audacity and persistence.

Nixon knew a highlight of the visit would be meeting Mao Zedong, despite reports the aging chairman had been sick and out of public view for weeks. Even in frail health, Mao insisted on receiving Nixon for a short symbolic meeting.

Nixon entered Mao's residence unsure what to expect from the infirm leader. "Chairman Mao is most pleased you have come," Zhou assured Nixon. "He wants the people to see our friendship taking root."

Despite his illness keeping him mostly sidelined, Mao made sure to engineer that critical handshake for the cameras, underscoring his personal stamp on this rapprochement he knew carried deep significance for China's future.

Nixon was ushered into a large room where Mao waited in a wheelchair. As Nixon approached, Mao rose slowly but deliberately from his wheelchair, clasping Nixon's outstretched hand as cameras flashed around them.

Mao's frailty was evident, but his grip was firm and his gaze steady as he locked eyes symbolically with America's president. This simple act of physically standing to greet his guest conveyed the enormity of the occasion.

While reviewing summit photos, the shot of Mao rising from his wheelchair captivated Nixon more than any other. It encapsulated the determination of two formidable leaders to propel their nations forward together.

"Chairman Mao wanted you to know how profoundly he values this partnership," Zhou told Nixon after. "That symbolic moment was deeply important to him."

Nixon knew the images of him standing hand-in-hand with Mao would resound powerfully worldwide - visible evidence of China reconciling with its fiercest Cold War nemesis.

Though only a brief encounter, that moment accomplished a key summit aim - showing the American president in fellowship with the face of China's communist revolution. A bold signal of changed attitudes resonating symbolically with both nations' citizenry.

Near the end of the visit, Nixon and Zhou appeared together on national TV. "The people of our two countries should be friends," Nixon declared. Eight hundred million Chinese heard him speak.

Boarding Air Force One to depart Beijing, Kissinger took one last look at the city that had once seemed unreachable. Now they were leaving as partners on the path to peace.

In just six remarkable days, Richard Nixon and Henry Kissinger utterly transformed global relations, capping years of painstaking diplomacy to thaw tensions with formerly isolated China. Nixon's public handshake with Mao sealed a seismic rapprochement once unthinkable between the two powers. Both gained strategically, with China splitting the communist bloc and America gaining leverage over rivals. Hostilities rapidly melted as the two moved toward partnership. Despite differences, Nixon and Kissinger had achieved a masterstroke by opening China after decades of estrangement, reshaping Cold War paradigms with immense ongoing reverberations.

Red Fiery Summer

Hanoi, North Vietnam

A chill wind gusted through the streets of Hanoi, rattling the shuttered windows of the nondescript government building. Inside, General Vo Nguyen Giap strode down the darkened hallway, his footsteps echoing solemnly. Reaching the door at the end, he paused to collect himself before entering the sparsely furnished meeting room.

Seated at the lone table beneath the glare of a single light was Le Duan, General Secretary of the Vietnamese Communist Party. His face was cast in shadows that did nothing to conceal the hardness in his eyes. Giap had expected to be summoned, but this late at night could only mean one thing—the Politburo was preparing to launch a major new offensive against the South and they wanted their famous general's stamp of approval.

Even though the Tet Offensive was Le Duan's idea, General Giap was blamed for its failure. He had lost much of his influence. Only when South Vietnam's invasion of Laos had failed miserably did Giap's stock go up. Once again, Le Duan planned on shielding himself from any military failure by using Giap. He knew Giap was too patriotic to refuse to help in any way he could. He would become Le Duan's scapegoat if necessary. It had become his lot in life.

Without preamble, Le Duan pushed a map across the table toward the general.

"The ARVN has suffered grievous defeats at our hands in Laos and Cambodia," he said. "Now is the time to deliver the coup de grace before they can recover from those losses. One giant push is all that is needed to topple the South Vietnamese government. With the government in shambles, the Americans will have no choice but to pack their bags and leave Vietnam for good."

Giap studied the map, immediately noting the mass of markers and unit designations along the Demilitarized Zone separating North and South Vietnam. At least twelve NVA infantry divisions and hundreds of tanks and artillery pieces were poised to strike. It was a massive, planned invasion force.

Le Duan jabbed a finger at the map. "We will strike here, all along the frontier. Our forces will overwhelm the meager ARVN defenders and open the path south."

His mind still sharp, the aging Giap considered the battlefield. The North Vietnamese troops would be operating close to their supply sources near the border. That was good. And American forces had been steadily withdrawing, leaving the ARVN depleted and demoralized after years of grueling combat. That was good too.

But doubts gnawed at Giap. "The Americans will likely still respond with their bombers, as they did during Tet and other offensives," he said carefully. "Our supply lines will be vulnerable."

Le Duan's eyes narrowed, his voice rising. "You speak as if the Americans still have the will for war. Nixon's policy of so-called 'Vietnamization' has utterly failed despite his propaganda. The U.S. withdrawal continues irrespective of ARVN's defeats in Laos and elsewhere. The Americans want out. This invasion will show them the door."

Le Duan stood and paced animatedly as he spoke. "One crushing offensive blow now will collapse the Thieu puppet regime before Vietnamization can take effect. Then we will be negotiating with the Americans from a position of strength and can dictate the terms of their surrender!"

Giap held his tongue. He vividly remembered the devastation B-52 Arc Light raids had wrought on their armies during previous failed offensives. And there were still American advisors on the ground supporting ARVN units.

But directly challenging Le Duan was unwise. The general secretary's volatile temper was infamous, and his influence within the Politburo was unmatched. Better for Giap to voice caution through more subtle means.

"You are most wise, Secretary," Giap said evenly. "But have we fully considered all that such an offensive would mean if it does not achieve complete victory quickly? The ARVN troops may surprise us and put up stiffer resistance than anticipated, especially with U.S.

air support. And a massive attack now could disrupt the ongoing Paris Peace Talks just as they are gaining momentum—"

Le Duan waved a hand dismissively. "The negotiations in Paris are a mere sideshow, General! The Americans pretend at peace while secretly funneling aid and weapons to our enemies in Saigon. We will show them and the world our true strength and total commitment to achieving victory no matter the cost!"

The general secretary sat again, pouring over the maps and charts before him, almost in a frenzy as he strategized aloud.

"While our main force drives south down the coast from the DMZ, we will launch additional diversionary attacks from Laos and Cambodia to stretch the ARVN to the breaking point."

He traced proposed axis of advance from Laos toward Hue and from Cambodia east toward Saigon. "Secondary drives through the Central Highlands will sever South Vietnam in two and prevent Saigon from reinforcing the crumbling northern front."

Giap studied the broad front being proposed. It was an extremely ambitious and complex plan, but not militarily unrealistic given ARVN's weakened state and low morale after recent defeats. Capturing and holding provincial capitals could allow declarations of liberated zones under the Provisionary Revolutionary Government, demonstrating the South's instability for all to see.

But seizing all of South Vietnam in one massive campaign still struck Giap as optimistic at best. A colossal gamble staking everything on total victory or ruinous defeat.

"The Politburo has devised a truly bold and daring

strategy," Giap finally pronounced. "If perfectly executed, the decadent puppet regime will certainly be fragmented and overwhelmed. Our socialist revolution will carry the day and reunify our nation after so many years of struggle."

Le Duan grinned wolfishly at Giap's assessment and poured celebratory glasses of Hanoi rice wine. They toasted the coming offensive and the imminent defeat of the loathed American imperialists.

In Le Duan's fervent mind, the very hour of destiny for their long-promised victory was now fast approaching. The Americans would surely abandon South Vietnam once and for all when faced with ignoble defeat.

After further congratulatory drinks, Giap prepared to take his leave. As he reached the door, Le Duan's parting words gave him chills. "Ready the plans and prepare all forces without delay, General. We attack as soon as weather permits, likely in the new year. Let this be the beginning of the end for our enemies! Then we shall see who dictates terms to whom..."

Despite his misgivings about the operation, Giap knew he had no choice but to follow orders. "It shall be done, Secretary. We will strike mightily as you direct, for the good of revolution and our people."

Giap stepped out into the blustery night, the door closing firmly behind him. As he hurried toward his waiting car, Le Duan's dramatic words echoed hauntingly in his mind. The coming months would severely test the combat readiness and morale of the People's Army. Giap only prayed that victory would indeed swiftly follow, rather than the disastrous quagmire he secretly feared.

March 30, 1972 – Quang Tri Province, South Vietnam

The Demilitarized Zone (DMZ) stretched jaggedly along the 17th parallel, a no man's land separating North and South Vietnam. Barren and scarred by past conflict, its fortified fences and watchtowers stood ominously between two nations still technically at war. As dawn's light filtered through distant mountains, an eerie calm hung over the frontier. But beneath the surface, tensions were about to boil over.

Having moved up quietly over the last couple of weeks, North Vietnamese troops and tanks lay hidden beyond the tree line, awaiting the signal to attack.

Inside their cramped bunkers, ARVN defenders kept uneasy watch, unaware the hammer was about to fall.

After months of secret preparations, the North's military machine now stood poised to unleash its Easter Offensive. A monumental campaign to smash through the DMZ, blitzkrieg south, and crush the Saigon government once and for all.

Nguyen Le Toan crouched low behind the mound of earth, peering through the early morning darkness at the enemy defenses across the field. The young North Vietnamese soldier gripped his AK-47 tightly, his heart pounding. This was it, the long-awaited invasion of South Vietnam. He had been too young to fight during the Tet Offensive, but now he was trained and ready to kill the ARVN he faced. Toan glanced left and right at the hundreds of his comrades taking up positions for the assault, their faces locked with determination.

Somewhere out there in the gloom, American

advisors and ARVN troops were waiting, dug into bunkers and trenches, M-16s and machine guns ready to cut them down. But Toan's superiors had assured them victory was certain. The puppet ARVN army was weakened from years of demoralizing war and the Americans were going home. This time, the revolution would succeed in reuniting Vietnam under the communist party.

Toan wondered if his brother, who had joined the the South Vietnamese years before, was out there among the bunkers. Would he recognize him before putting a bullet between his eyes? A flare shot up from the enemy lines, casting harsh white light over the open field. Toan tensed, expecting enemy fire, but only silence followed.

To his right, an T-54 tank rumbled into position, the ground vibrating under Toan's hands and knees. More tanks and heavy artillery lined up for the barrage. The flak guns mounted on some of the tanks swiveled back and forth, searching for aerial threats. Jet fighters and bombers had devastated their forces many times before. But their spies reported the South Vietnamese Air Force was grounded by monsoon storms today.

The minutes crawled by, sweat dripping down Toan's forehead. His hands trembled slightly on his weapon. Was the assault going to be called off? A bird called out just as the horizon glowed red with dawn's first light. Toan peered through his gun sight at the enemy bunkers, his finger tightening on the trigger.

With a deafening roar, the North Vietnamese artillery opened fire, shells screaming overhead toward the enemy positions. The ground heaved and enormous geysers of dirt fountained up from the ARVN bunkers. Toan watched wide-eyed as smoke billowed and debris rained down. He had never seen anything like it – the true monster of war. The T-54 tanks lumbered forward, firing as they went, their treads churning the muddy earth.

Over the radio, the code for the assault came through. With his heart in his throat, Toan leapt up and ran headlong toward the enemy lines, firing on full auto. All around him, thousands of North Vietnamese soldiers charged across the shell-pocked field, yelling at the tops of their lungs.

Enemy tracer rounds zipped past as Toan ran hunched over, bullets snapping the air around him. He slid into the nearest crater and took cover behind the torn edge, gasping for breath. The earth rumbled as more T-54s rolled forward, firing relentlessly into the enemy lines.

Toan peered over the rim of the crater at the rows of ARVN bunkers, now wreathed in smoke and dust. The shelling had been devastatingly accurate.

"Forward, keep moving!" his sergeant barked, waving men on as he fired his AK from the hip. More North Vietnamese troops ran past Toan's crater, some falling in sprays of blood from ARVN fire. Toan swallowed hard, then scrambled out, joining the assault again.

Just ahead, an ARVN bunker was still active, the machine gun chattering as it swung toward the oncoming NVA. Toan dove for cover as the bullets chewed up the earth around him. Two soldiers carrying RPGs sprinted past him. With a hollow thump, one of the grenades shot into the bunker slit, silencing the machine gun.

Toan was up again, charging with the others toward the perimeter trench lines. He hurdled down into the narrow earthworks, nearly stumbling over the body of a dead ARVN soldier. The man's hands were still clenched around his M-16 rifle. Toan grimaced and moved deeper into the trench, eyes darting warily.

Ahead, muffled shouts in Vietnamese drew his attention. Toan raised his AK and crept toward the sounds. Turning a corner, he saw three ARVN soldiers standing over the body of one of his comrades. One of the soldiers, a young man with a wispy mustache, was going through the dead man's pockets.

Toan felt rage boil up inside him. "Don't move!" he barked, leveling his rifle on the group. The ARVN soldiers froze, eyes wide. The mustached one started to bring his rifle around, but Toan fired a burst into his chest. The other two dropped their weapons and raised trembling hands.

Toan approached slowly, not lowering his AK. "Why are you fighting your own people?" he demanded harshly. "Can't you see this war is unjust?"

One soldier, who looked barely eighteen, spoke hesitantly. "I'm just trying to stay alive, comrade. My family needs me."

Toan considered him a moment. "Run. Get away from this madness if you want to live."

The young soldier nodded thanks and took off down the trench line. Toan turned to the remaining ARVN, who stared back defiantly. "I'll never turn traitor! Death to the Communists!" the man spat.

Toan's face hardened. He squeezed the trigger, cutting the man down in a hail of bullets. As the soldier's body crumpled, Toan felt only resolve. The revolution marched on.

Toan stepped over the bodies and continued down the trench, AK ready. The sounds of fierce fighting echoed all around him now. His comrades were overwhelming the perimeter defenses, but pockets of ARVN resistance still remained.

Coming around a bend, Toan spotted two NVA soldiers pinned down by an ARVN machine gun nest across the trench. One of the men was wounded, a dark stain spreading across his thigh as he tried to return fire.

Toan rushed over, shouting over the din. "Stay down! I'll flank their position."

The uninjured soldier nodded, still squeezing off shots from his SKS rifle. Toan climbed out of the trench and circled around, using craters and debris for cover. He could see the machine gun bunker ahead, sandbags stacked around its slit.

Getting as close as he dared behind a shell-blasted tree, Toan primed a grenade and hurled it. The explosion tore through the sandbags and viscous machine gun fire rattled out as the wounded ARVN tried to drive him back. Toan gritted his teeth and rushed forward, firing on full auto. Bullets ripped into the bunker opening and the machine gun went silent.

Toan slung his smoking AK and waved the all-clear to the trapped NVA soldiers. As they regrouped, a thunderous artillery barrage began falling dangerously close, blasts shaking the ground.

"We have to keep moving! The enemy is targeting these coordinates!" Toan yelled over the eruptions. They climbed from the trenches and sprinted for the tree line ahead. Dirt fountained around them as they ran. A shell exploded directly in front of Toan, the concussion slamming him down.

Ears ringing, he struggled up and saw the two NVA soldiers sprawled lifeless, torn apart by shrapnel. Jaw clenched with anger, Toan turned and continued toward the trees. He dove into the underbrush just as a shell obliterated the spot he'd just occupied.

Toan lay prone, breaths coming in ragged gasps as the artillery subsided. All around the tree line, NVA infantry were rallying and tending wounded. Stretcher teams carried the most critical back toward the rear. Toan checked his ammo and reloaded.

The radio on his belt crackled to life. "All call signs, this is Le Duan. The first phase is complete. Regroup and prepare to continue the advance."

Toan allowed himself a tight smile. The general secretary's voice on the radio meant the Politburo was directly commanding this offensive. He felt proud to be a part of the revolution, a part of history. His sacrifice would help drive the imperialists out and unite Vietnam. Toan rose with reinvigorated spirit. The revolution ground on.

Lieutenant Tran Ngoc crouched in the rubble of the ARVN command bunker, straining to hear over the ringing in his ears. The North Vietnamese artillery barrage had been devastating, but he was still alive. For now.

He crawled from the debris and blinked smoke from his eyes. All around, the base was in ruins, craters still smoldering from the bombardment. Bodies of ARVN soldiers and NVA alike littered the ground.

But the attack wasn't over. Tran could hear the chatter of rifles and thump of grenades as enemy infantry advanced through the ruins. His men were still fighting, hopelessly outnumbered.

Tran checked his rifle and limped toward the sound of fighting. He had to rally the survivors before it was too late.

Coming around a ruined building, he spotted a squad of ARVN infantry pinned down behind a rubble pile by NVA troops in the treeline. Two of his men lay motionless, another screamed as his comrade tried to stem the bleeding from his shredded leg.

Tran raised his M16 and fired controlled bursts into the trees, driving the NVA back into cover. The ARVN squad glanced around in surprise as he slid in beside them.

"Sir! We thought you were dead!" the sergeant said.

"Not yet, but we will be if we don't fall back," Tran responded. "Get your wounded ready to move. I'll cover you."

The young ARVN soldiers scrambled to improvise stretchers under Tran's covering fire. When ready, they retreated as Tran laid down suppressive bursts at the tree line.

Reaching a crater, Tran and the men took cover. The sergeant looked at him with despair. "It's over, we can't stop them."

Tran gripped his shoulder firmly. "We're still in this fight. Help is coming - B52s are being diverted. Their bombs will squash our enemy like bugs. We just need to hold on."

The young man seemed to take heart. Tran peered cautiously over the crater rim. A hundred meters away, NVA infantry were advancing through the smoke behind two T-54 tanks.

Tran's mind raced as the enemy approached. They had to make a stand here or be overrun. "Sergeant, take your men south down that trench. I'll go north and catch them in crossfire."

"But they have tanks. We only have our rifles and a

few grenades," said the sergeant.

"We fight with what we have," said Tran. "If we kill their supporting troops, the tanks will have no choice but to stop their advance until more troops move up."

The sergeant nodded and moved out. Tran sighted down his rifle at the NVA around the lead tank. He may die today, but he'd take some enemies with him.

The T-54's turret rotated toward Tran's crater just as a whistling sound built in the distance. Tran glanced up to see flights of American B-52s overhead, dropping strings of bombs.

The earth erupted around the tanks as 500-pound bombs walked their explosive lines of devastation toward the NVA. Tran shielded his face from the blasts, feeling the shockwaves in his chest.

When he looked again, the two tanks were smoldering wrecks, enemy bodies littered around them. More bombs crashed down, destroying vehicles and artillery.

Tran allowed himself a fist pump. The American bombers had arrived - dealing a crippling blow to the North's invasion force. He and his men would live to fight another day.

From the turret of his T-54 tank, Sergeant Nguyen Tan watched in dismay as the American B-52s pummeled the battlefield. Their momentum had been so strong pushing through the ARVN defenses. But now, devastating bombs were transforming the advance into a hellish rout.

All around Tan, T-54s and PT-76 tanks burned, charred bodies strewn around them. Troops ran for cover only to disappear in eruptions of dirt and fire. The air filled with oily smoke, metallic scent of blood, and screams of the wounded.

Tan ducked down into the turret hatch as more bombs whistled down dangerously close. Shrapnel pinged off the tank armor. His driver, Private Tran, glanced back wild-eyed.

"We have to retreat, Comrade Sergeant! We're being slaughtered!"

Tan weighed their options quickly. The infantry assault had disintegrated into chaos. Most communication lines were down. They had no air support to combat the bombers.

He gave the order to withdraw. The tank roared in reverse before swinging south away from the aerial onslaught. Tan peered out at the devastation, Le Duan's words echoing in his mind.

"Our people in the South are ready to rise up. One decisive victory will tip the balance against the imperialists once and for all."

The Politburo had believed the South was ripe for revolution. Instead, their assault had been blunted by the puppet ARVN army and American firepower.

But the battle was not over. Tan resolved that his tank would find a way to stay in the fight. As they retreated, he used the radio to hail other intact units, directing them to rally at Phase Line Delta.

Soon, they arrived at the rendezvous - a ragtag group of T-54s, armored cars, and infantry that had escaped the bombing. Tan gave instructions, organizing a defense.

They would hold this position to cover the withdrawal of remaining forces. When the order came to retreat into North Vietnam, they would do so in an orderly fashion.

Tan rotated the turret, scanning for enemy

movement. In the distance, plumes of smoke rose from the devastated battlefield. Closer, wrecked vehicles and dead livestock marked the path of their advance.

A young private approached Tan's tank, face begrimed with dirt and smoke. "Why have we stopped, Comrade Sergeant? Shouldn't we continue north?"

Tan fixed him with a hard look. "We hold here. Our army does not run in disarray like cowards."

The private ducked his head, chastised, and hurried off.

Tan had pledged his life to Ho Chi Minh's revolution. He would rather die with honor than abandon their objective so easily. If another opportunity arose to strike against the puppet regime, his men would be ready.

When the reinforcements and resupply they had been promised finally arrived, the NVA regrouped. With their artillery batteries paving the way, the tanks and infantry attacked once again. The offensive was far from over.

Presidential Palace - Saigon, South Vietnam

General Abrams strode into the ornate conference room, still dressed in stained fatigues after flying in from the embattled northern front. President Thieu rose from his chair to meet him, the faces of his advisors and generals sullen beneath the crystal chandelier.

"What is the situation, General?" Thieu asked without preamble. "Our forces are falling back across the entire front."

Abrams wasted no time on pleasantries. "It's a

damned dire situation, Mr. President. Intelligence failed us completely. The North has committed their entire army to this offensive - at least fourteen infantry divisions and several hundred tanks."

He jabbed a finger at the large map on the wall showing the North's unrelenting advance. "They pummeled our border outposts with artillery before sending in armor and infantry. We're looking at a least 70,000 NVA troops across the DMZ so far."

The South Vietnamese officers muttered anxiously. Thieu's face remained impassive, but Abrams saw the strain in his eyes. This could be a death blow if they didn't act swiftly.

"My commanders are consolidating units to make a stand along the My Chanh River," Thieu said. "But we desperately need your bombers to blunt their momentum."

Abrams nodded. "I've already set our air power into motion. B-52 strikes are being flown continuously up and down the front. Phantoms and Skyhawks are hitting their supply lines."

He moved to the map, pointing out areas. "If we can isolate and destroy their armored spearheads here and here, the infantry will be exposed in the open."

Thieu considered the map a moment before turning back to Abrams. "You and I have had our differences, General. But will America stand with us now in this crisis? Or will you abandon us when victory is within the enemy's grasp?"

Abrams met the president's gaze firmly. "I've made my views clear to Washington. We leave now, and South Vietnam will fall. I'll resign my command before I let that happen."

He put a hand on Thieu's shoulder. "We're shoulder

to shoulder in this fight. I've already requested diversion of bombers from SAC bases around the Pacific. Arc Light is just the beginning."

Thieu managed a small smile. "I am heartened to hear it, my friend." He turned to his staff. "Notify all division commanders. We will halt the enemy advance and drive them back across the DMZ."

As the men dispersed to their tasks, Abrams studied the map. The coming weeks would test ARVN's courage and training to the limit. But he would be damned if he let commies flying VC flags take Saigon on his watch.

No force on Earth could overcome the commitment and firepower America would bring to this fight. He pitied the NVA should they keep coming south.

Near the DMZ, South Vietnam

Major Henderson ducked as another shell impacted close by, showering dirt over the sandbagged bunker. The North Vietnamese bombardment had been going on for hours, and showed no signs of letting up.

Henderson checked his watch again. Where the hell was that air support? He poked his head above the bunker rim, peering through swirling smoke at the tree line. Enemy infantry were massing for assault, AK47s and RPGs glinting in the dawn light.

"Get ready, boys, here they come!" Henderson yelled to the South Vietnamese troops crammed into foxholes nearby. He chambered a round in his CAR-15 rifle. No air power meant they would have to blunt this attack themselves.

The NVA infantry surged from the trees, sprinting

through the churned up field toward the ARVN lines. Henderson drew a bead and dropped one, then another. The ARVN troops opened up, filling the air with lead.

Still the enemy kept coming, screaming defiance through the firestorm. They needed those jets here now before it was too late.

"Concentrate fire left flank!" Henderson ordered as the charge threatened to overwhelm a section of ARVN defenses. Tracers converged, cutting down the attackers. But more emerged from the tree line, charging through their own dead.

An RPG round impacted the bunker above Henderson, collapsing part of the roof. He narrowly rolled away as sandbags and debris rained down. The radio crackled to life on his belt.

"Advisor station, this is Eagle Lead. Standby for gun run, inbound hot!"

Henderson broke into a grin. "About goddamned time!" he yelled into the handset. "Give them hell, Eagle!"

Seconds later the first F-4 Phantom screamed low over the treetops, cannons blazing. Thunderous explosions ripped through the enemy ranks as napalm and cluster bombs detonated. More jets joined the fray, unloading their deadly payloads.

Henderson cheered along with the ARVN as corpses and shredded earth rained down. The NVA assault wavered then collapsed into panicked retreat, men throwing down weapons in their haste.

When the Phantoms finally circled back around, nothing lived or moved between the tree line and ARVN trenches. Henderson sagged back against the bunker in relief. That had been close. Too close.

But they had held. Henderson gazed with pride at the cheering ARVN troops. Despite overwhelming odds, they had stood their ground. With American training and air power, the South Vietnamese could defeat the communists. Henderson was more convinced of that than ever. It would be hard bloody work, but freedom would prevail in the end.

Thua Thien Province, South Vietnam

General Vo Nguyen Giap stood stoically atop the forested hill, peering through binoculars at the devastation unfolding below. What had promised to be a decisive victory was turning rapidly into an unmitigated disaster.

All morning he had been receiving fragmented reports from the front. The initial artillery strikes had obliterated the South's border defenses. But then the American B-52s arrived, halting his armored columns in their tracks and inflicting horrendous casualties.

Fighter bombers were now savaging what remained of his invading force. The once pristine valley below was obscured under a pall of smoke and fire. Even from this distance, Giap could see smoldering vehicles and bodies littering the churned up battlefield.

His staff stood nearby, awaiting orders. Giap remained silent, grappling with the grave implications of this defeat. The Politburo had staked so much on this offensive - believing the South ripe for revolution and the Americans weary of war.

Instead, their actions had crippled the People's Army for a generation and weakened Hanoi's position irrevocably. Giap felt the sting of failure personally. His strategies had won them victory over the French. Why not now against the imperialist successors?

A young officer approached hesitantly from the command radio. "General Giap, units are requesting permission to withdraw across the DMZ before they are annihilated."

Giap kept his gaze fixed on the unfolding tragedy below. After a long moment, he gave the order. "Full retreat. All forces are to disengage and cross back into the safety of the North."

He turned to his staff officers with fire in his eyes. "We will rebuild and strengthen the People's Army. Train new divisions and modernize our weaponry. When the time is right, we will strike again until final victory."

The men nodded somberly before dispersing to coordinate the retreat. They left unspoken the reality - it would take years to recover from this defeat. And the Politburo's patience was not unlimited.

Giap stayed atop the hill until dusk fell, overseeing the remnants of his invading force as they fled back across the DMZ from the advancing ARVN. Even in the depths of failure, he felt admiration for the South's soldiers. They had fought valiantly for their cause, despite being outnumbered.

As night enveloped the battlefield, Giap descended to his waiting jeep. South and North alike had paid a terrible price this day. Such was the great tragedy of war - no matter which side claimed victory.

The revolution's time would come. But for now, difficult days awaited in Hanoi.

Operation Pocket Money

May 5, 1972 – South China Sea

The decision to mine Haiphong Harbor had been years in the making. As early as 1969, President Nixon and his advisors had discussed closing the port to cut off North Vietnam's main supply line. But they held back, wary of provoking China and the Soviet Union. By 1972, however, Nixon felt he had no choice.

Frustrated with years of inconclusive negotiations, Nixon opted for dramatic military escalation in 1972 to pressure North Vietnam into making concessions at the peace table. He hoped renewed bombing and mining campaigns would punish Hanoi for negotiating in bad faith, isolate them from their communist allies, and demonstrate American strength to voters back home. Nixon gambled that his hardline approach would finally compel the compromise needed to end the war on favorable terms for the U.S.

North Vietnam's Easter Offensive earlier that year had made major gains in South Vietnam. ARVN forces were battered and reeling. If the North wasn't stopped, the South could collapse. Drastic action was needed.

In late March, Nixon ordered renewed bombing of the North under Operation Linebacker. He also gave the go-ahead to mine Haiphong, although the planning was kept secret. Only a handful of officers knew the true purpose behind the Navy's intensified activity off the North Vietnamese coast.

Among them was Lt. Commander Pete Marzano, operations officer aboard the USS Worden. For weeks, he'd noticed subtle changes in their patrols. More time spent lingering off Haiphong. Closer surveillance of the harbor entrance and channel depths. Orders from the brass to collate data on shipping traffic and anchorages. Something big was in the works, and Marzano had a good idea what.

Still, when the coded flash traffic arrived in early May, it came as a shock. Marzano read the message with widening eyes: COMMENCE MINING HAIPHONG HARBOR EFFECTIVE 120200Z MAY. This was it. The point of no return.

Marzano burst into the wardroom, where Commander Lewis grated over the ops schedule. "Sorry to interrupt, sir. Just got an eyes-only for you."

Lewis scanned the message, face neutral. "Very well," Lewis said. "Alert the department heads and prepare the ship for special operations. I'll brief them myself at 1300."

Marzano left to carry out the orders, mind racing. Dropping mines across Haiphong's harbor mouth would choke off over seventy percent of North Vietnam's imports. Food, weapons, fuel. If it worked, it could turn the tide of the war. But that was a big if.

At the wardroom briefing, Lewis outlined the

mission. Twelve Navy ships would spend four nights sowing over 11,000 mines across Haiphong's channels. It was risky. Minesweeping trawlers, patrol boats, and MiGs would oppose them. But Lewis radiated stoic confidence. "We've drilled for this, gentlemen. It's our time to act."

Marzano spent the next forty-eight hours in a whirlwind of planning. Triple-checking locations and water depths with the charts and pilots. Coordinating with the aviation and boat crews seeding the mines. Liaising with the destroyers guarding the seaward flank. By May 8th, everything was ready. The fleet anchored off Haiphong, awaiting the final order.

May 7, 1972 - Haiphong Harbor

Sweat pooled under Marzano's uniform as he stared out from the darkened bridge. The night air was muggy, electric with tension. He glanced at the bridge clock: 0115. Just forty-five minutes to go time. Out there, in the darkness, lay their objective: the drab contours of anchored freighters, the loom of Haiphong's docks and warehouses, the unseen mouths of channels key to stopping the North's war machine.

Marzano unconsciously flexed his grip on the bridge rail. Decades later, historians would debate the mining's legality and morality. But legality meant little tonight. Sometimes in war, fate called men to make history. Their time had come.

Marzano checked his watch again. Thirty minutes to go. Around him, the bridge crew worked in hushed efficiency, faces taut with anticipation. Marzano's palms were slick with sweat. He wiped them discreetly on his trousers and glanced at Lewis.

The commander stood rigid; hands clasped behind his back as he stared into the darkness. A model of composure, but Marzano sensed the coiled intensity beneath. These next hours would test them all.

At ten minutes prior, Lewis broke the silence. "Operation Pocket Money is a go. Launch helicopters."

Marzano relayed the order. Moments later, the throbbing rotors of Sea Stallion helicopters filled the night. One by one, they lifted off, laden with parachute-equipped Mk52 mines. The aerial minelaying had begun.

Five minutes to go. Marzano issued the second order: "Deploy motor whaleboats." With muted rumblings, the ship's cranes lowered two boats over the side. Each boat's crew started their outboard motors and sped away, towing long cables with twenty Mk36 mines apiece.

One minute prior. Marzano tensed. Any moment now, North Vietnamese radar would detect the helicopters and boats. Defensive fire could erupt at any second. He saw Lewis straighten almost imperceptibly as they watched the sweep second hand close the final gap.

"Execute," Lewis said.

Marzano gave the flash order by signal lamp. Far off the port beam, a Destroyer winked an acknowledgement and released its whaleboats. All across the task force, minesweepers turned and accelerated towards their seeding zones in the channels.

Marzano kept his eyes glued to the lights of the receding whaleboats. Plumes of phosphorescence marked their wake as they sped inward. Two miles to go. He tracked their progress by stopwatch, imagining the minemen aft preparing to deploy the first Mk36.

One mile. Thirty seconds to release point. Sweat trickled down Marzano's cheek. His throat was dry as chalk.

Now. The first Mk36 entered the water with a muffled splash, then another...another, rapidly unspooling from the boats in straight lines across the channel mouth. The aerial minelaying helicopters were doing the same farther inland. The die was irrevocably cast. Haiphong Harbor was now a death trap for any ship that entered.

Marzano let out the breath he'd been holding. No explosions yet, no enemy response. The first phase was complete. Around him, the bridge crew exchanged relieved looks and quiet murmurs.

It was hardly over. Three more nights remained before the operation was complete. Each night would mean threading the needle between radar installations, dodging patrol boats, and escaping unscathed. But as the whaleboats returned safely to the ship, Marzano allowed himself a slight smile.

To maximize speed, payload size, and access to the farthest reaches of Haiphong's channels, Navy planners deployed squadrons of A-6 Intruders and A-7 Corsair IIs to conduct aerial mining in coordination with the seaborne effort. The jets could quickly penetrate defended airspace and sow parachute-equipped mines in areas too shallow or obstructed for mining boats to reach. Their inclusion provided redundancy if the boat operations were disrupted, flexibility to adjust to changing conditions, and drew fire away from the more vulnerable boats. Using both jets and boats capitalized on the strengths of each platform to ensure comprehensive, swift seeding of the harbor.

They'd caught Hanoi off-guard and drawn first blood. Maybe now, with its vital supply lines severed, North Vietnam would finally feel the pain needed to bring peace. That was the hope, at least. The reality, only time would tell.

The next two nights followed in nerve-racking repetition. Marzano coordinated the aerial and seaborne mining while North Vietnamese trawlers and patrol boats attempted to intercept.

Close calls were frequent. On the second night, two of their whaleboats escaped a pursuing trawler by mere yards, escaping into a smokescreen laid down by a destroyer.

The third night, a patrolling Mig nearly caught a returning A-6 outside its attack profile, only to be driven off by a Combat Air Patrol F-4 Phantom from the Coral Sea.

By the early hours of May 9th, the minefields were complete. Over 11,000 mines now carpeted Haiphong's harbors and channels. Any vessel attempting to pass would do so at near-certain peril.

Marzano stood again on the bridge as the first pale light filtered over the horizon. Off the port lay the hulking shapes of darkened freighters anchored offshore, unaware of the lethal trap now lying beneath their keels.

"Your strategy appears successful, Commander," Marzano said. "They've had three nights to stop us, yet the mines are laid. Their supply lines are cut."

Lewis nodded. "We've done our task well. But now the true test begins."

He was right, Marzano knew. They may have sealed off Haiphong, but the North Vietnamese were a relentless foe. They would search relentlessly for gaps in the minefields, sacrificing ships and men if needed. Constant vigilance would be required to maintain the blockade.

The coming days confirmed Lewis's prediction. Each morning, Marzano watched the surveillance reports with apprehension. Small enemy minesweepers would carefully test the edges of the minefields, trying to chart safe channels for the freighters.

Time and again, North Vietnamese trawlers struck mines attempting to clear a path. Muffled detonations flashed across the waters, followed by plumes of smoke as the broken ships quickly sank. The losses were heavy, but still they kept coming.

When several sweeps failed, the North Vietnamese began sending large cargo ships to deliberately trigger the mines. Each massive explosion made Marzano flinch. But the tactic revealed the mine locations, allowing sweeps to gradually clear narrow passages.

As North Vietnamese minesweepers and civilian freighters began slowly breaching passages through the aerial and seaborne minefields, U.S. commanders ordered new waves of air strikes to reseed critical areas. Squadrons redeployed to the USS Coral Sea and USS Kitty Hawk unleashed strikes around the clock, braving intense anti-aircraft fire to parachute fresh mines into the harbor's main channels. For ten days, A-6 Intruders and A-7 Corsair IIs flew dangerous sorties, dropping hundreds of mines to keep Haiphong closed, buying precious time until new naval mining operations could begin. The deadly net was kept tight.

After two tense weeks, the Worden was ordered

away from Haiphong to refit. Marzano left with a profound respect for the North Vietnamese sailors ready to sail into the minefields again and again. Such relentless sacrifice in pursuit of victory, he thought, was something only equally hard choices could break.

As the Worden departed into the South China Sea, Marzano glimpsed the smoke still rising from Haiphong's harbor. The loss of those ships meant food and weapons that would never reach the battlefields. Just a small measure of North Vietnam's pain, he knew, in this grinding war of wills and sacrifice. The mines were only the opening gambit. How much more pain would both sides endure before the end?

The aerial reseeding bought time, but closed channels inevitably reopened. After two weeks, the Navy returned to finish the job.

Marzano was back off Haiphong as part of the rotating fleet maintaining the blockade. The North Vietnamese had redoubled their efforts to sweep paths through the minefields, progressing foot by bloody foot.

Now the Navy would bury them again.

As night fell, Marzano watched the first wave of A-6s thunder off the carrier deck northwards, bomb bays packed with freshly activated mines. Their target: the narrow channel just breached by minesweepers that morning.

Moments later, a radio crackled to life on the bridge. "Vampire, Vampire, Vampire! MiGs inbound, twenty miles out!"

Marzano rushed to the radar screen. Sure enough, two fast moving blips had appeared, vectoring to intercept the Intruders.

The radios erupted in terse shouts as F-4s from the Combat Air Patrol raced to meet the threat. Marzano listened helplessly to the aerial battle raging in the darkness.

Tracers arced through the night sky as the MiGs swept in. On the radar screen, Marzano saw one F-4 break left to engage. The other held course, trying to cover the A-6s as they jettisoned their mines. Mines that would not make it to Haiphong if the F-4s failed.

The aerial dogfight whirled closer. Marzano pictured the F-4 pilot straining against tight G-forces, trying to get his guns on target for a split-second kill. Closer...closer...

Abruptly, one MiG veered away, dropping from radar. "Scratch one bandit!" came the exultant cry over the radio.

The second MiG broke off too, outmatched. In a few fiery minutes, the danger had passed.

Marzano let out a long breath as the A-6s radioed mission complete. The reseeding was a success, the channel blocked again. Around him, the bridge crew exchanged relieved smiles.

Over the coming week, the cycle continued. Minesweepers advanced, only to be thrown back by renewed strikes. Each small breach came with staggering loss of life.

Late one night, Marzano stood alone on the empty bridge, staring at Haiphong's fires. How much longer could this go on? What would it take for sanity to prevail? He thought of the Vietnamese fishermen unable to go to sea, the rice spoiling in freight holds, the hungry families waiting in vain for word from sailors who would never come home.

This was the brink they were driving towards, where more death and deprivation would birth only bitterness. Some pain must be endured to find peace. But too much pain only spawned new hate. What was the line where justified cause became pointless cruelty?

Marzano didn't know. He only prayed leaders on both sides had the wisdom to turn from this abyss before the chance was lost forever. The lives of too many innocent souls depended on it.

By late May, the mining campaign had settled into an exhausting war of attrition. Both sides were bloodied but resilient.

Haiphong's channels remained largely blocked, choking North Vietnam's seaborne supply lines. Yet the human toll mounted each day as minesweepers worked relentlessly to breach the blockade.

Marzano and the Worden had returned to port for repairs, granting a short reprieve from the tensions offshore. But as Marzano walked to the commissary, Haiphong was never far from his thoughts.

How much longer could this stalemate drag on? Would Nixon stay the course despite diplomatic pressure and domestic unrest? Or would the North Vietnamese finally be compelled to negotiate a peace? There were no easy answers.

Marzano's reverie was broken by shouting nearby. A group of sailors jostled around a radio, faces alight. "What's happened?" Marzano asked.

"Peace terms!" came the reply. "Hanoi's agreed to negotiate if we stop the bombing and mining. It could finally be over!"

Marzano hurried closer, hardly daring to hope. Details were still coming in, but it seemed a breakthrough had finally been reached. After all these years of war, peace talks looked set to begin in earnest.

As word spread, cheers and applause broke out across the base. Officers arrived to officially confirm the news. Plans were already being made to scale down operations off North Vietnam's coast.

That night, Marzano celebrated with his crewmates long into the early hours. But amidst the revelry, he couldn't shake a sober thought. Their jubilation was justified, but he knew the North Vietnamese people were celebrating too tonight – fishermen, mothers, children, wives waiting at quays that would never again see their sailors return.

Marzano realized then that he felt no anger towards those he'd fought these long months. Only sadness for the lives sacrificed on both sides. And hope that the spirit of reconciliation might overcome bitterness and vengeance. Leaders must summon the greatness to look beyond past wrongs and forge a just and lasting peace. Too much blood had been spilled already.

The next weeks passed swiftly as the Navy prepared to stand down from combat operations. With the peace accords signed, the monumental task of clearing Haiphong Harbor began. An Armada of minesweepers, mine hunters, patrol boats, and helicopters converged to tackle the sprawling minefields seeded over the last two months. Systematically, they began detonating and deactivating the thousands of remaining mines using a combination of timed self-destructs, acoustic triggers, magnetic sweeps, and explosive charges.

The work was painstakingly slow and methodical to avoid accidental explosions. Navy EOD divers accompanied the sweeps, risking their lives to attach small demolition charges to individual mines before moving to the next. Meanwhile, MH-53 helicopters towed giant electromagnetic coils overhead to deactivate magnetic fuses. Gradually, the mines were neutralized, and mile by mile, Haiphong Harbor was restored to peacetime status. After sixty days of round-the-clock clearance efforts, the channels were finally declared mine-free once more.

At last, the Worden departed the Gulf of Tonkin bound for home. Standing on the forecastle, Marzano watched the jungle coast recede into haze astern. He thought of the courage displayed by all who had fought and died here – American and Vietnamese alike. Now perhaps their sacrifices would know some redemption.

Peace would not come easily or quickly in these scarred lands. But as the Vietnamese coast faded from view, Marzano dared to hope that humanity's better angels might yet prevail. That wisdom could still chart a course away from devastation towards healing.

Linebacker

April, 1972 - White House, Washington DC, USA

By 1972, peace negotiations had failed to end the Vietnam War. North Vietnam invaded the South in an offensive codenamed Nguyen Hue, flouting the Paris Peace Accords.

President Nixon was visibly upset. "Three divisions across the DMZ and halfway to Hue before we could even react. How did our intelligence fail so completely?"

General Wheeler straightened his glasses. "We're still piecing together the details, but it appears the North has been massing forces for months under strict radio silence. They achieved complete surprise with this offensive."

Henry Kissinger steepled his fingers gravely. "And now over a third of South Vietnam has been overrun within the first weeks. At this rate, Saigon may fall by summer."

Nixon rose and paced. Once again, the North was flouting agreements and threatening to undo years of bloody progress. "What are our options here, gentlemen?"

Admiral Moorer gestured to a map of North Vietnam marked with targets. "We hit them where it hurts most - their supply lines. Columns of Soviet tanks and trucks are pouring down the Ho Chi Minh trail as we speak. Our B-52s can turn that trail into a junkyard within days."

General Abrams nodded. "A new bombing campaign could cripple North Vietnam's ability to reinforce their offensive. It might just buy the ARVN time to regroup and hold."

Nixon weighed the proposal. He had ended Lyndon Johnson's bombing campaigns in order to start negotiations four years ago. Going back on that vow would cost him politically. But he saw no other choice if South Vietnam were to survive the onslaught. "If we do this, it needs to be absolute devastation," Nixon said firmly. "Power plants, rail yards, warehouses - everything sustaining their army in the South. Make them pay an unprecedented price, more than they ever dreamed we'd inflict again."

Wheeler leaned forward eagerly. "With your approval, we'll bring our full air power to bear. Rolling Thunder will look restrained compared to the campaign we envision. Codename Operation Linebacker."

Nixon stopped pacing, resolved. "Get Linebacker

planned and executed. Throw everything we've got at them until they withdraw every last soldier back across the DMZ."

The men filed out with new urgency, cognizant that millions of fates now rested on the bombers they would unleash.

Nixon retreated to his office and sank into his chair, alone with the weight of his decision. The cost of renewed war would be bitter, but the alternative was unthinkable.

In response to the North Vietnamese offensive, Operation Linebacker was the largest aerial bombardment campaign against the North since Rolling Thunder ended in 1968.

Linebacker's goal was to halt the flow of North Vietnamese supplies and weapons fueling the Nguyen Hue Offensive. Cutting the North's ability to sustain its armies in the South was key to driving the North Vietnamese leaders back to negotiations.

Pentagon, Arlington, Virginia, USA

The mood was grim in the windowless operations center deep beneath the Pentagon. For months, Secretary of Defense Melvin Laird had been seeking a diplomatic solution to end the Vietnam War. But the North's massive Nguyen Hue Offensive had erased all hopes of peace.

Now, Laird monitored reports of entire South Vietnamese divisions being mauled and driven back under the onslaught. His military advisors were unanimous - only immediate and overwhelming air power could stabilize the situation.

Laird weighed the decision for hours, knowing it could extinguish his last hopes of a negotiated settlement. But there was no denying the desperation of the field dispatches. A refusal to unleash America's bombers could mean defeat and collapse within weeks.

With a heavy heart, Laird authorized plans for Operation Linebacker - an air campaign more intense than any yet seen in the war. He ordered bombers into action within ninety-six hours, hoping speed and shock could turn the tide on the ground. There would be a terrible cost, but the alternative – the fall of South Vietnam - was unthinkable.

In the days that followed, Laird worked closely with the Joint Chiefs, pouring over target lists and strike packages. They mobilized every bomber wing in PACOM for round-the-clock missions that would decimate North Vietnam's infrastructure.

When the first B-52s left Andersen Air Force Base, Laird knew there could be no turning back. The war's final bloody act was underway. Now he could only steel himself for the mounting casualties soon to fill endless rows of telegram sheets on his desk.

May 9, 1972 - Andersen Air Force Base, Guam

The rumble of eight Pratt & Whitney jet engines shook the runway as Colonel Risner watched the first B-52 lift off for the start of Operation Linebacker.

"Skyswept One airborne," came the report from the control tower. The bomber's outline shrank to a pinpoint on the horizon and vanished into the night sky.

Eleven more B-52s from the 92nd Bombardment Wing followed, each carrying over 100 bombs weighing up to 750 pounds each. Risner tracked them climbing to 35,000 feet on his radar scope, cruising in cells of three aircraft that filled a five-mile-wide block of airspace. Their target was the Lang Chi hydroelectric plant north of Hanoi, a key source of power for North Vietnam's war machine.

Risner turned to his operations officer, Major Vic. "What's our current force composition looking like?"

Vic scanned the flight status board. "We've got F-4s from the 58th and 469th Squadrons launching now for MiG sweeps ahead of the bombers. Wild Weasels are tasked for SAM suppression once the strike is underway."

"And we're sure those power plants are still operating? I don't want the bombers making milk runs."

"Recon photos are less than twelve hours old," Vic confirmed. "All targets remain active."

Risner nodded, hoping more Wild Weasel fighters could be diverted to escort the lumbering bombers. SAM batteries dotted the North Vietnamese landscape. Each bomber would need to traverse multiple missile engagement zones to strike their objectives and make it home.

"The Wild Weasels are making their run," said Vic.

Risner nodded, hoping they were enough...

Sky Over North Vietnam

Captain West wiped the sweat from his eyes as he banked the F-105F Thunderchief into a forty-five-degree dive, aligning on the SAM site guarding the approach to Hanoi. In the backseat, his electronic warfare officer Lieutenant Mahoney called out that their AGM-45 Shrike missile had locked onto the radar emissions.

"Magnum away!" West called out as he squeezed the trigger, feeling the aircraft lurch upwards as the anti-radiation missile left the rail. Five tense seconds passed, then a bright flash erupted from the site below, secondary explosions ripping through the missile battery.

West yanked the stick back, pulling up just above the trees at over 600 knots. The force pinned him to his seat for a moment before the Thunderchief leveled out. There was no time to admire their work - Mahoney already had three more Fan Song radar emitters displayed on his scope. More SAM sites were lighting up like a deadly constellation ahead as dozens of B-52 Stratofortresses rumbled toward Hanoi.

"Rhino Lead, this is Wild Weasel One-One," West radioed. "Path is cleared to first set of BUFFS. We'll take out the next sites along the bomber route."

"Copy One-One," came the strike leader's reply.

West steeled himself as he turned to the northeast, the Thunderchief seeming to snarl with determination as they raced back into the lethal zone. The Wild Weasels had cleared a path for now, but it was up to the bomber crews to survive the flak and fighters and deliver their payloads. And they would be back again tomorrow, and the next day, until Hanoi was theirs or the Weasels were all dead.

Andersen Air Force Base, Guam

"Skyswept flight entering enemy airspace," the radio crackled. Risner leaned forward, picturing the bombers' methodical advance toward the target. The first SAM warnings came quickly as the surviving radars locked onto the intruders. Minutes later, the radar scope blossomed with missiles rising to intercept.

"Here we go," Risner muttered, gut tightening. The bombers were still fifteen minutes from their target and already swimming through a swarm of SAMs. He watched helplessly as angry red tracks converged on the blue blips of the B-52s.

Then the red tracks slowed, wobbled, and began disappearing one by one as the B-52s metallic chaff bundles sowed confusion among the radar-guided missiles. Only a few SAMs continued undeterred, their supersonic speeds closing rapidly with the subsonic bombers. Pilots' tense warnings and missile proximity alerts filled the radio channel.

Risner visualized SAMs detonating just below and aside the bombers, their frag warheads spraying deadly shrapnel upward. Many of his men would die. The B-52s rocked violently amid the concussive blasts but stayed in formation, still tracking toward the target.

One bomber at the rear drifted out of its cell, damaged but maintaining course. "Skyswept Seven took a hit, but we're still in the game," its pilot reported.

Risner mopped the sweat from his forehead, willing the bombers through the lethal zones ahead to deliver their payload. The B-52s pressed onward, their alien shapes gliding high above the darkness blanketing North Vietnam's hills and valleys. Spotlights probed upward from anti-aircraft guns, trying in vain to spear the aircraft soaring four miles above.

The SAM attacks had thinned out, but Risner knew the most dangerous leg was still ahead - the bomb run itself. The bombers would have to descend to 12,000 feet, well within range of anti-aircraft fire, to accurately deliver their payload on the power plant.

Risner envisioned the aircraft banks shifting, bright flares dropping to illuminate the target, bomb bay doors cranking open. The planes would be most vulnerable now, committed to their attack profile as hundreds of enemy artillery gunners took aim.

Twelve long minutes passed as Risner waited on edge, unable to aid the crews from half a world away. Finally, the strike leader called "Bombs away!" Risner pictured the 750-pound warheads plunging from the bomb bays, whistling down through the night air. Then blooming eruptions flashed across the target area as 500,000 pounds of ordnance impacted in seconds.

The B-52s banked hard, clawing for altitude and speed as artillery shells burst around them. Once clear, the strike leader reported "Bombs on target. All aircraft exiting." On his map, Risner drew an "X" through the power plant. Its output had just been reduced to zero.

Around him, the operations room burst into muted celebration. The crews had it made it through the gauntlet once more. Risner knew such success would become rarer as North Vietnam's defenses intensified. The worst was still ahead.

One strike down, but Linebacker had just begun. Andersen would execute hundreds more sorties in the coming weeks to systematically paralyze North Vietnam's ability to wage war. The cost would be high, but there was no going back now.

Risner monitored a trio of B-52s as they exited the target area, cruising low over mountain ridges back toward Guam. Trailing smoke, a damaged bomber lagged further behind its formation with each mile, slowly losing altitude.

"Skyswept Six, what's your status?" Risner called.

The pilot responded through bursts of static. "Took...SAM strike to our rear stabilizer. Aircraft control deteriorating...unable to maintain speed or heading."

Risner froze as he imagined the crippled bomber barely above the mountain peaks, limping for home. A controlled crash landing in the ocean was now the crew's only hope.

The radar blip for Skyswept Six slowed further and descended toward the green topographic overlay. "Bailing out," the pilot said finally. "Aircraft lost." Then only silence.

Risner lowered his head. Ten men gone, the first of many if Linebacker was to succeed. The price was already proving greater than he'd dared imagine.

Pentagon - Arlington, Virginia, USA

General Wheeler pushed the reconnaissance photos across the table to Secretary Laird. "These are the first damage assessments from last night's strikes around Hanoi and Haiphong."

Laird examined the photos showing smashed rail lines, collapsed bridges, and buildings reduced to rubble. "And the loss estimates?"

Wheeler removed his glasses. "Seven B-52s shot down, at least a hundred air crew killed or missing. Heavy casualties, but within projected limits for penetrating that deeply."

Laird nodded solemnly. Each lost bomber had a ten man crew. Over 100 gone in the first day's operations. And yet he knew it was a minor toll compared to what was coming.

"Initial analysis is the strikes degraded

transportation networks and supply flow by twenty percent," an intelligence officer reported. "But North Vietnamese defenses remain largely intact."

Wheeler outlined the plan for the next wave. "We'll concentrate follow-on strikes around Hanoi and key transportation nodes. Our goal is to completely paralyze war materiel shipments down to the battlefields in the South by the end of the month."

Laird absorbed the briefing, feeling events sliding toward an irreversible climax. "Issue the strike orders," he said finally. "We have to stay the course now, whatever the costs here on the homefront. I'll personally answer for the losses to the president."

As the officers departed to initiate the next night's raids, Laird sat alone with the recon photos showing the first wounds scored against the enemy. He reminded himself that behind each ruined target were North Vietnamese troops who would now never reach the South. It was the only ledger that mattered.

Staring at the photos, Laird hardened his resolve. There could be no mercy for the aggressor, not while their tanks still rolled, and bombs still fell on allied soil. The bombers must get through until that machinery of invasion ground to a halt, no matter how many men it took.

Near Hanoi, North Vietnam

First Lieutenant Davies gripped his control wheel tight as the B-52 descended into the jaws of North Vietnam's air defenses. Outside his window he could see the entire strike force of over thirty bombers arrayed in their cells around him, silver giants that turned the night sky into day with their engine blasts.

His eyes flicked between the radar scope and the dark void ahead, watching threat symbols blossom as SAM radars locked on. "Hang tight boys, here they come!"

The B-52 bucked as missiles detonated nearby, peppering the wings and tail with shrapnel. Alarm lights flashed angry red across Davies's console. He could already feel the aircraft growing sluggish, bleeding speed and altitude from the damage.

"Number four engine out, number two on fire!" his co-pilot called. Davies craned his neck to look back, seeing the right wing sheathed in angry flame. It was out of his hands now - they would have to gut this one out and hope the bomber held together long enough to strike the target and limp back to the Gulf for a crash landing.

The bone-jarring impacts came closer together as they approached the target airfield. Davies ignored the instruments warning of catastrophic structural failure and kept his shaking hands on the controls. Just two more minutes to release their payload and get clear.

"Steady boys, bombs away on my mark!" Davies called. The crippled bomber seemed to rally for one final effort as he lined up the runway. "Mark!" He felt the aircraft lurch upward as thirty-six 750-pound bombs dropped into the darkness. A silent prayer went with them that their sacrifice here would shorten the war.

A hundred miles back, Captain Austin added throttle as he saw contrails of SAMs rising ahead of the bomber formation. The flight of F-105 Thunderchiefs he led were the bombers' only escort, tasked with suppressing enough missile sites to get the strike force to their targets in one piece.

"Target radar at eleven o'clock, batteries visible below," Austin's wingman reported. The Thunderchiefs screamed down, pumping missiles into the SAM launchers before pulling up just above the jungle canopy. Blossoms of secondary explosions told Austin they had hit their mark.

For three tense hours, the Thunderchiefs raced ahead of the bomber track, firing on missile sites the moment they activated. But Austin knew they were only knocking down a fraction of the SAMs as dozens of red tracks continued unabated toward the bombers. Their fuel tanks were running dry now - time to turn for home and hope other fighter waves could protect the bombers still deeper in North Vietnam.

The tales Austin heard back at Da Nang base that night told of bombers limping back with shrapnel scars, gaping holes torn in wings and fuselages. Five bombers had been lost that day, dozens more made it to deliver their payload. Austin bowed his head for the crews that had not returned. Their losses only deepened his resolve to defend the bombers on their next flight into the maelstrom.

August 1972 - Hanoi, North Vietnam

In an underground bunker beneath the rubble of Hanoi, the North Vietnamese Politburo met to assess the devastating American bombing campaign. Operation Linebacker had been raging for over three months, bringing death and destruction on a scale not seen since WWII.

Prime Minister Pham Van Dong pounded a fist on the conference table in a rare show of anger. "Half our oil reserves are ashes! Three major power plants demolished in a week! How can we sustain the offensive like this?"

General Vo Nguyen Giap removed his cap and wiped his brow. "Our divisions at the front are now critically low on supplies. We've had to halt attacks across three provinces."

Foreign Minister Xuan Thuy threw up his hands. "Yet still the Americans want more concessions at the peace table before halting their bombs! Their terms grow harsher as our position worsens."

A young officer rushed into the bunker and snapped a sharp salute. "Comrades! Radio intercept shows 100 more bombers crossing our coastlines from the east."

The leaders sat in silence as the bunker tremored from distant detonations. The Americans were increasing the pressure, sensing victory close at hand.

Giap spoke first. "The Politburo must consider... limiting objectives for this offensive. We cannot defeat the puppet regime in the South this year." The words tasted bitter, but their military situation was dire.

Dong weighed the unthinkable prospect of de-escalating the attack that had carried such high hopes. Perhaps it was time to preserve their gains rather than pursuing a now-impossible total victory.

"If we must, we can resume offensive operations once we rebuild our strength," Dong said. "But not with a thousand American bombers overhead. We must get Linebacker halted before it destroys us completely."

The leaders nodded solemnly. It was a grave decision, but negotiating now from weakness was preferable to total collapse.

Pentagon – Arlington, Virginia, USA

By October 1972, Operation Linebacker had pounded North Vietnam without respite for over five months. Every major target on the Pentagon's lists had been destroyed - power plants, bridges, petroleum depots, rail yards, and airfields. Entire regions lay in ruins, their power and transportation grids shattered.

But the bombing had failed to force the North Vietnamese to retreat. Their troops continued advancing in the South, absorbing horrific casualties to gain ground week by week. The Linebacker strikes had stalled the offensive but had not turned the tide outright.

In Washington, Secretary Laird read the daily casualty lists with a heavy heart. Over 1,000 US aircraft had been lost, and crew casualties had far exceeded initial estimates. With the presidential election just weeks away, there was growing pressure to end the ultimately futile bombing.

White House – Washington DC, USA

On October 22nd, President Nixon ordered a halt to Linebacker. The campaign had delivered more destruction than any since World War II but had not achieved its strategic aim. Laird privately assessed that only invasion and occupation of the North could now force unconditional surrender.

As B-52s returned to base with bomb bays empty, US commanders knew that Linebacker had inflicted a heavy toll. But it had failed to break the enemy's will to continue the invasion. They steeled themselves for the difficult fight still to come on the ground in the South.

The war's end was still almost three agonizing years away. But the sacrifices of Linebacker had bought critical time, preventing total collapse and setting the stage for eventual peace talks.

By December 1972, peace talks had stalled again despite months of negotiations. North Vietnam was refusing to compromise or offer concessions that would ensure the South's sovereignty. Their army continued to occupy portions of the South.

With the anti-war movement growing stronger at home, Nixon felt he was out of options. He authorized a massive bombing campaign against the North codenamed Linebacker II. It became known as the Christmas bombings.

For eleven days, B-52s dropped over 15,000 tons of bombs, targeting infrastructure around Hanoi and Haiphong. The White House strategy was to inflict devastating blows that would force North Vietnam back to earnest negotiations.

The Linebacker II bombings caused widespread damage across the North and some of the highest US losses of the war - 15 B-52s shot down, ninety-three airmen killed. But the North remained defiant despite this onslaught.

By December 29th, with no sign of capitulation from the North, Nixon halted Linebacker II. It had failed to achieve its purpose, instead galvanizing international opposition for its severity.

The mounting political pressure convinced Nixon to accept the North's terms and sign the Paris Peace Accords in January 1973, finally bringing US direct involvement in the war to an end.

Though Linebacker II failed to force North Vietnam's hand, it was one of the final blows that made clear the war could not be won militarily. The accords allowed the US to withdraw with "peace with honor" - the most dignified outcome possible after years of grinding conflict.

Operation Gemstone

White House – Washington DC. USA

The Oval Office was quiet except for the ticking of a clock on the wall. President Nixon sat at his desk, reviewing notes for an upcoming speech. A knock at the door disturbed his concentration. "Come in," Nixon said, slightly irritated at the interruption.

H.R. Haldeman entered, holding a thick folder. "Sorry to bother you, Mr. President. But there are some plans here I think you should approve - Operation Gemstone."

He started to hand the folder to Nixon, who waved it away.

"I don't need to see the details, Bob. You know what needs to be done."

Haldeman hesitated. "If something goes wrong, it could be damaging, sir."

Nixon fixed him with a stern gaze. "Then don't let anything go wrong. You have your orders. Take care of it, and leave me out of the specifics."

"Of course, Mr. President." Haldeman tucked the folder under his arm.

"Just tell me you have it under control, Bob."

Haldeman nodded. "Of course, sir. My team knows what to do."

"Good," Nixon said, returning to the papers on his desk. "I'll leave you to handle it then."

Satisfied, Nixon waved him away. After Haldeman departed, Nixon sat back reflectively. A successful operation could give his campaign the edge it needed. Nixon pushed away any nagging thoughts of what could go wrong. There was an election to win.

May 28, 1972 - The Old Ebbitt Grill – Washington DC, USA

H.R. Haldeman sat across from James McCord in a booth at The Old Ebbitt Grill. In hushed tones, he gave final instructions for the Watergate break-in operation.

"You're clear on what we need?" Haldeman asked.

McCord nodded. "Any intel that gives us an edge over the Democrats - campaign strategy, donor lists, dirt on their candidates."

"Good," Haldeman said. "And remember - "

"Discretion assured," McCord interjected. "No trail back to you or the president. We're ghosts. My guys know how the game is played, Bob. They're professionals."

Haldeman studied him closely. "See that it stays that way. Pull this off cleanly and there will be a bonus."

"My men work for more than just money," McCord replied evenly. "They know what's at stake here."

Haldeman slid the floorplans over and stood. "Do it right and Nixon wins. Good luck tonight."

He watched McCord disappear into the night. The

operation was in motion with no turning back now. Haldeman could only hope their risky gamble would pay off. All he could do was sit back and hope the break in was a success.

Howard Johnson's Motel – Washington DC, USA

The night was thick with humid air as the team gathered at the Howard Johnson motel across from the Watergate complex. Jim McCord, Virgilio Gonzalez, Frank Sturgis, Eugenio Martinez, and Bernard Barker - the crew hand-picked for the secret operation they were about to undertake.

Jim McCord laid out the plans in a hushed tone. "OK, gentlemen, you all know why we're here. The target is the DNC headquarters on the 6th floor. Our objective is to bug their offices and photograph campaign documents that can give Nixon an advantage."

The team reviewed the floorplans and security details one more time. Frank Sturgis cleaned his glasses nervously. Eugenio Martinez flicked his lighter absently. McCord could sense the anxiety in the room.

"I know the stakes are high, but you were chosen because you are the best. In and out, quick and clean. If we get caught, we don't know each other. No ties back to the White House."

The team all nodded solemnly. They understood the implicit order - successful deniability was more important than loyalty if captured.

McCord shook each man's hand. "For the president," he said quietly. One by one the men stood and exited silently into the night, ready to carry out their mission. Dressed in suits and carrying briefcases to appear as normal businessmen, they crossed the street discreetly toward the Watergate complex, swallowed by the darkness.

McCord pulled a brimmed hat low as he entered the parking garage. McCord led the team to a predetermined stairwell, avoiding the lobby and elevators. At the basement-level stairwell door, McCord taped the latch and hinges with surgical tape to allow easy re-entry later.

Ascending six flights, they arrived outside the DNC office door and got to work. McCord manually picked the office door lock while Sturgis and Barker kept watch.

Safely inside the DNC headquarters, the burglars got to work quickly and quietly. McCord set up a monitoring device to listen for any approaching footsteps in the hallway outside. Meanwhile, Barker was busy photographing documents using a palm-sized camera, snapping photos of pages containing lists of financial donors and campaign strategy notes.

Martinez took inventory of the office supplies, placing small pieces of tape inconspicuously on desks and file cabinets to determine if anyone entered before they returned to check on the function of their devices. In another room, Sturgis dusted for fingerprints, looking for signs of who had been in the office recently and where they sat.

Gonzalez focused on the phones, carefully unscrewing mouthpieces to implant tiny voice-activated radio transmitters. He tuned them to an obscure frequency so they could listen in remotely later.

Every few minutes, McCord double-checked the

hallway monitor. So far, their illegal entry seemed undetected. But tension was high and time was limited. They couldn't risk being caught in the act.

After nearly two hours gathering intelligence, photographing documents, and rigging surveillance devices, the team packed up and slipped away into the night unseen. Despite the nerves, Operation Gemstone's first phase was a success.

The next day, a nondescript van was parked near the Watergate complex, looking utterly ordinary to passersby. But inside, the burglary team sat hunched over radio receivers, magnetic tape reels spinning as they listened intently through headphones.

The tiny transmitters Gonzalez had planted throughout the DNC offices filtered in a stream of ambient noise - the ringing of telephones, muffled voices from down the hall, the click of heels on hardwood floors.

McCord made notes, identifying the locations of each invisible bug based on the background sounds. Occasionally they picked up snippets of actual conversations, and Sturgis highlighted transcripts of discussions related to campaigns or fundraising.

By the end of the day, they had filled numerous tapes. Satisfied with the surveillance setup, McCord ordered the team to get some rest. It had been over twenty-four hours since any of them slept. McCord needed his team sharp as the mission continued. Gonzalez carefully packed up the equipment in the van.

Operation Gemstone's infiltration was succeeding so far, unbeknownst to the Watergate inhabitants being monitored day and night.

Joining them was Alfred Baldwin, a former FBI agent hired by McCord for the monitoring operation. For weeks, Baldwin listened intently through headphones, making notes on conversations picked up from the DNC offices.

By mid-June, Baldwin had filled numerous tapes. But he noticed the audio quality deteriorating, with long gaps of static and garbled voices. He reported the issue to McCord - they were missing too much.

McCord realized some of the bugs must be defective. An urgent inspection was needed. Over two weeks had passed since the initial break-in. McCord ordered his team to discreetly return to the DNC offices on the night of June 17th to check and replace the faulty listening devices.

Just after midnight on June 17th, Frank Willis a Watergate security guard, was making his rounds in the garage when he discovered a strip of tape on the basement stairwell door's latch. Finding this odd, he removed the tape. He assumed a worker had mistakenly taped it and thought nothing more of it.

An hour later, McCord and his team entered the garage and approached the stairwell. When he went to open the stairwell door, he noticed that the tape was missing. He picked the lock to open the door, then re-taped the latch to ensure they could escape quickly.

The team ascended to the DNC offices. As before, McCord picked the door's lock and they entered. The team split up to inspect their surveillance equipment.

In the phone room, Gonzalez discovered two of his wiretaps had ceased transmitting, possibly discovered and removed. He swiftly replaced the devices with new ones.

Barker found his hidden microphones in the office ceilings were still operational but had poor sound quality. He adjusted their frequency for better clarity.

A janitor's cart stood unattended in the hallway. In it, Martinez planted a fresh walkie-talkie bug they could use to monitor conversations remotely. When finished, Martinez went back inside the DNC offices.

In the garage below, security guard Willis was again doing his rounds when he found the stairwell door had be re-taped. He called the police and reported an illegal entry.

Across the street at the Howard Johnson's Motel, Baldwin had been assigned to be the outside spotter. He was distracted while watching a film on television – Attack of the Puppet People and did not notice the police cars pulling up in front of the Watergate complex.

After connecting with Willis, the police ascended to the sixth floor and began searching the offices turning on the lights in each office.

When Baldwin finally glanced out the motel window and noticed the sixth floor lit up like a pinball machine, he immediately called McCord on his radio. It was too late.

Moments later the police entered the DNC offices with their weapons drawn and arrested Virgilio Gonzalez, Bernard Barker, James McCord, Eugenio Martínez, and Frank Sturgis. The five burglars were handcuffed and taken into custody.

It was past midnight when the phone rang in Haldeman's home. Groggily picking up, he heard an aide on the other end, "Sorry to wake you, sir, but there's been an incident at the Watergate complex tonight."

Haldeman felt his pulse quicken. "What happened?"

"Five men caught breaking into the DNC offices, arrested on site," the aide explained. "Turns out they were McCord's team."

Haldeman swore under his breath. "Are you sure it was them?"

"Yes, sir. No doubt."

Haldeman's mind raced. "Get down to the courthouse and find out what's going on."

"Yes, sir. Are you going to inform the president?"

"Don't be an idiot. Of course, I'm going to inform him. In the morning. No need to wake him until we have more information. Get your ass moving."

Hanging up, Haldeman stared into the darkness, knowing everything hung in the balance now. This was a nightmare scenario that could unravel everything they had worked for.

Haldeman spent the remaining night hours anxious and sleepless, running through every possible outcome in his mind. At first light, he headed straight for the White House, bracing to break the catastrophic news to Nixon.

At the police station, the five men were separated for questioning. Detectives grilled Gonzalez first. "Start talking. What were you doing breaking into the Watergate?" the detective demanded.

Gonzalez shrugged nonchalantly. "We just wanted to ruffle some feathers. Give the Nixon guys a hard time."

"Cut the act. You're trained operatives, not pranksters."

"Think what you want," Gonzalez replied casually. "We're just citizens expressing our displeasure with the current administration."

The detective slammed his fist on the table. "You're going to need a better story than that. Who hired you?"

Gonzalez leaned back, unfazed. "Like I said, we needed no one's help to orchestrate this little act of protest."

One by one, the rest stuck to the same script, denying any political ties and claiming theirs was an independent act of vandalism against Nixon. But the detectives sensed they were seasoned professionals working for someone higher up the chain. Cracking them would be difficult.

The arrests sparked immediate curiosity from the press. Reporters swarmed the courthouse, pressing the accused men with questions. McCord hid his face from cameras while Martinez chain-smoked anxiously, and Barker stared straight ahead in silence. Nobody was talking, but it was early in the investigation.

At the White House, Haldeman hesitated outside the Oval Office door, his heart pounding. He knocked lightly and entered the oval office. Nixon was sipping his morning coffee, reading the newspaper. Nothing about the break in or arrests on the front page. Haldeman was relieved. He cleared his throat. "Mr.

President, there's been a development requiring your attention."

Nixon peered at him over his reading glasses. "This early, Bob? It better be important."

"It's regarding Gemstone," Haldeman said grimly. "There were complications."

Nixon lowered his newspaper, his expression darkening and said, "Complications?"

Haldeman hesitated briefly then continued, "There was an incident at the Watergate last night. A team of five men were caught breaking into and burglarizing the DNC headquarters."

Nixon straightened abruptly. "Our team?"

"Yes, sir. They were arrested at the scene, currently in custody."

Nixon muttered a curse under his breath. Haldeman added, "The men identified themselves as anti-Nixon activists upon arrest. Their arraignment is in a few hours."

"You said you had this under control, Bob."

"Yes, Mr. President. I did. I am not completely sure what happened."

"Then maybe you'd better find out."

"Of course, Mr. President."

The gears in Nixon's mind were turning. "Tell Mitchell and Hoover. They'll know how to cut this thing off at the knees."

"Absolutely sir," Haldeman affirmed. "I'll coordinate with Mitchell and Hoover to kill wider speculation."

"Keep me updated discreetly."

"Of course, Mr. President. I'm on top of it."

"That used to be so reassuring, Bob. Now... not so much."

Haldeman had no reply. He had set disaster in motion. Dismissed, he began the desperate work of limiting the damage.

At the arraignment of McCord's team, Bob Woodward of the Washington Post studied the five burglars intently as they were brought into court. He noted their ages, facial features, demeanors, and attire in his notepad.

When James McCord was called, Woodward observed his military-style cropped hair and disciplined posture. While the others avoided eye contact, McCord scanned the room like a tactician, his expression humorless.

Woodward wrote: "McCord - military background? Get full bio."

After the hearing, Woodward got to work learning all he could about McCord. He uncovered past connections to the CIA, Army Counterintelligence, and a private security company McCord had left abruptly before the break-in.

Woodward pressed sources at the federal courthouse until they finally admitted McCord was also employed by the Committee to Re-elect President Nixon. For Woodward, this was the first major break in deciphering what happened at Watergate. Through meticulous notes and tenacious follow-up, Woodward transformed a mundane hearing into front page news that launched his legendary career.

As the arraignment concluded, Haldeman received an urgent call from his trusted aide Lawrence Higby. "We have another situation, sir. That rookie reporter Woodward from *The Post* dug up a connection between

McCord and the Committee to Re-elect Nixon. They're going to run the story tomorrow."

Haldeman felt nauseous. This was their worst fear coming true. "How the hell did he uncover that link so quickly? Have our people been talking?"

"I'm not sure yet, but Woodward found a solid source he's relying on," Higby replied uneasily.

Pacing his office, Haldeman's mind raced through options. "Go directly to Bradlee at *The Post*. Insinuate publishing this could compromise national security interests. We need forty-eight hours minimum to get ahead of this."

"Yes, sir, I'll apply maximum pressure to delay their printing."

"Also contact Pat Gray at the FBI," Haldeman continued. "Have warrants drawn up to raid *The Post's* offices and investigate their sources. Fabricate pretenses if needed - we can claim stolen documents, anything plausible."

"Consider it done, sir," Higby affirmed.

Haldeman hung up, sweat beading on his forehead. He instantly dialed the White House operator. "Get me Hoover at the FBI right away."

As Hoover came on the line, Haldeman spoke urgently, "Edgar, we have a situation requiring your immediate assistance..."

Deploying every resource at his disposal, Haldeman desperately maneuvered to *undermine The Post's* investigation. But the toothpaste was already squeezing out of the tube - Woodward had cracked Watergate open. Controlling the damage would only get harder as the administration's web of deceit began to unravel in the coming weeks.

Over the next few days, Haldeman worked

feverishly behind the scenes trying to stall *The Post's* reporting by Woodward and his partner Carl Bernstein. The young Woodward had been paired with veteran reporter Bernstein to follow the Watergate leads.

Haldeman called in favors with executives at the paper's parent company to have them muzzle Woodward and Bernstein's story.

At the same time, he nudged the CIA to have the FBI narrow the scope of their Watergate investigation by classifying it a simple burglary. "A localized event, nothing more," Haldeman urged Hoover.

The Post's duo's trail was hot. They uncovered that the Watergate burglars had received substantial payments from a slush fund connected to CREP. Haldeman recommended returning the money, making it seem like an independent operation.

As new revelations trickled out daily, the White House spun and deflected. "This is nothing more than political mischief," press secretary Ron Ziegler told reporters. "We have no further comment."

But privately, Haldeman warned Nixon they were sitting atop a volcano. Hush money was arranged for the burglars to buy their silence. CREP officials connected to the plot were told to take vacations to avoid questioning.

Haldeman was a man on fire sealing any leaks, urging the FBI to suppress evidence, and keeping Nixon isolated. But the more he tried to conceal Watergate, the more it spiraled. Haldeman could sense the coming eruption, powerless to stop the pressure building below the surface.

As Woodward and Bernstein's exposés gained traction, the Senate soon caught wind, establishing a committee to investigate Watergate. Haldeman recommended staffers erase any Nixon connections from their files. Meanwhile, he had the CIA tell the FBI to back off its probe of the money trail.

When Woodward tracked down Nixon's personal lawyer linked to the burglary team's payoffs, Haldeman knew the jig was up. He pushed for the lawyer to flee the country to avoid questioning.

Nixon maintained distance, acting unaware of White House ties to the scandal. Behind closed doors, he urged Haldeman to do whatever it took to shield him from blowback. "Plug every damned leak!" Nixon fumed.

By summer's end, the web of lies was collapsing. Key CREP officials resigned. Money swapping hands was exposed. The burglar's Nixon ties emerged.

Haldeman was exhausted from working overtime trying to bury Watergate. The cover-up was blown wide open. As more officials lawyered up, Haldeman realized he himself could become a liability. The scandal's impact was now unavoidable.

By September, the avalanche was unstoppable. The Senate called Nixon's closest aides to testify, where they stonewalled and feigned ignorance. Woodward revealed Nixon's team had a secret slush fund tied to the break-in.

Haldeman urged the president to make sacrifices to contain the damage. Overwhelmed by paranoia, Nixon agreed. Campaign manager John Mitchell resigned. Top advisor John Dean was fired. Haldeman cleaned house, ousting all linked to the scandal.

But the firings only fueled speculation of a cover-up. Haldeman recommended Nixon take decisive action to regain credibility with the public.

In a dramatic move, Nixon instructed his new

attorney general to appoint an independent special prosecutor with unchecked power to investigate Watergate. It was a Hail Mary to restore faith in the White House.

The ploy backfired. Archibald Cox, the chosen prosecutor, immediately subpoenaed Nixon's tapes from the hidden recorders in the oval office. Haldeman pushed for refusing to comply.

"We cannot hand over evidence against ourselves," he urged Nixon. The president was losing control of the spectacular mess Haldeman had tried frantically to conceal. The Watergate monster was now loose, with Haldeman helpless to tame it.

Special Prosecutor Cox's subpoena for Nixon's tapes put the president in checkmate. Haldeman advised refusing to turn them over, knowing the recordings likely implicated them in the cover-up.

Nixon agreed to stonewall, claiming executive privilege. But the ploy failed - Cox took them to court and won.

When Nixon still refused to release the tapes, Cox issued new subpoenas and indicated he would take drastic action. Haldeman urged Nixon to fire him.

On October 20th, 1973, in the infamous "Saturday Night Massacre" Nixon ordered his attorney general to axe Cox. The AG and Deputy AG both resigned in protest, but Cox was dismissed.

The discharge ignited a firestorm. Calls for Nixon's impeachment flooded Congress. The president was losing his grip as the Watergate inferno raged.

In a desperate gamble, Nixon appointed a new

special prosecutor and turned over doctored transcripts of select tapes. But the actual recordings contained clear proof of his obstruction of justice.

Now cornered, Nixon made a fatal mistake - he ordered the FBI to stop investigating the scandal. This final abuse of power triggered introductions of impeachment resolutions.

By summer 1974, the Supreme Court ordered Nixon to surrender the actual tapes. Upon their release, bipartisan impeachment and conviction became certain. The scandal that started with a bungled burglary would end a presidency. With no moves left, Nixon resigned in disgrace on August 8th, 1974.

Unconventional Warfare

August 6, 1972 – Plain of Jars, Laos

For over a decade, Laos had been embroiled in civil war. The communist Pathet Lao, backed by North Vietnam, were battling royalist forces for control of the small Southeast Asian country. By 1972, the communists had gained significant ground, now controlling large swaths of territory in northern Laos.

The United States had been covertly supporting the royalists, led by General Vang Pao and his Hmong army. Vang Pao's guerrilla fighters, trained and supplied by the CIA, were essentially all that stood in the way of a complete communist takeover. After years of exhausting combat, his forces were faltering.

Dale Freeland watched these developments with growing unease from his post as CIA station chief. Despite America's secret bombing campaign, the communists were advancing. And now they were poised to seize control of the strategic Long Tieng airfield deep in Hmong territory.

Long Tieng was the lifeline for Vang Pao's resistance. All CIA weapons and supplies flowed through this remote jungle airstrip carved into the mountains. If Long Tieng fell, it could spell the end for Vang Pao's fighters.

In early 1972, the North Vietnamese army launched a massive offensive toward Long Tieng. Vang Pao's men valiantly held off the initial attacks. They took heavy losses and were running dangerously low on ammunition and medical supplies.

Freeland knew he had to act fast to resupply Vang Pao before his defenses collapsed. The monsoon rains had turned Long Tieng's dirt runway into a muddy mess, grounding the cargo planes loaded with guns and ammo in South Vietnam and Thailand airfields.

With the airlift stalled, Freeland conceived a daring mission. He would send a single C-130 transport plane packed with supplies on a dangerous night flight through heavy weather and enemy fire to keep Vang Pao's forces in the fight.

As the most experienced fixed-wing pilot in Southeast Asia, Coyle was asked to fly the perilous airlift. He decided to fly with the smallest crew possible so as not to risk additional lives. His co-pilot Walker doubled as navigator and his flight engineer Wilson doubled as loadmaster. The three airmen would put all on the line to reach Vang Pao's forces.

It was an enormous risk. The lumbering C-130 would be easy prey for communist anti-aircraft batteries guarding Long Tieng. Freeland knew the secret war in Laos hinged on sustaining Vang Pao's defenses. The mission had to succeed.

As Coyle's C-130 took off into the stormy night sky,

Freeland could only hope his gamble would pay off. The fate of Laos hung in the balance. Operation Phou Phiang II would either keep Vang Pao's resistance alive or doom them to defeat if the plane went down. The coming hours would decide.

The C-130 plunged into the monsoon storm, massive black thunderheads looming all around. Rain lashed the windshield as Coyle switched on the plane's weather radar to navigate through the tempest.

A brilliant flash lit up the cockpit, followed instantly by a deafening boom. The plane bucked violently. "Lightning strike!" yelled Walker. "We just lost the radar."

Coyle gripped the yoke, getting the plane back under control. "Alright, we'll have to fly by sight alone from here. Keep your eyes peeled for any breaks in this soup!"

They flew on through the dark clouds. With each flash of lightning, the ominous silhouettes of mountains appeared and vanished like ghosts around them.

Coyle strained his eyes for any sign of the ground. But the rain was too thick, the clouds impenetrable. They were flying blind through steadily rising terrain.

"See anything, Walker?" Coyle asked. His co-pilot shook his head grimly. Wilson called out from the back that radar was still down.

Suddenly, lightning illuminated a massive peak dead ahead. Coyle pulled back on the yoke with all his strength, forcing the C-130 into a steep climb. The plane's fuselage skimmed a rocky outcropping at the top of the mountain with an awful screeching sound.

"Jesus! That was too close!" yelled Walker as they cleared the ridgeline. Coyle leveled off, his heart pounding. "We can't take another hit like that, not in these mountains!"

For what felt like hours they flew on, surrounded by dark crags jutting from the shadows. Blind except for split seconds of lightning flashes revealing the deadly terrain.

Fatigue set in as Coyle and Walker strained at the controls, desperately trying to anticipate each new peak and turn in time. One wrong move would send them crashing into the rocks.

As the heavy clouds finally began to break, Coyle glimpsed the valley opening up before them. He let out a deep breath and wiped the sweat from his brow. "We made it through the worst of it," he told Walker. "Let's get our bearings and find Vang Pao's runway."

As the storm faded behind them, a new danger presented itself. Tracer fire suddenly zipped past the cabin and explosions burst all around - enemy flak batteries spotting them!

Coyle banked the C-130, jinking left and right to escape the barrage. More guns opened up, filling the air with bursts of shrapnel.

"So much for the easy part!" Coyle grunted through clenched teeth. One piece of flak ripped through the tail with a fiery explosion. Alarms blared a warning in the cockpit.

Walker assessed the damage. "Controls are still responding, but we better find that runway quick. We're losing hydraulic pressure."

Coyle radioed Long Tieng for an update. Through bursts of static came the response: "Continue heading 2-7-0. We will lay down suppressing fire."

Artillery explosions lit up the valley as Hmong guerillas below provided cover hammering the enemy anti-aircraft positions. Coyle pushed the damaged C-130 on through the bombardment, trusting his heading. Tracer fire still ripped through the night sky as Coyle scanned desperately for the runway.

Small orange light began blinking on one at a time, illuminating the airfield between the hills.

The Hmong guerrillas were lighting oil-soaked piles of wood, providing a visual for the plane landing in the darkness and rain.

Through the windshield, Coyle glimpsed the landing strip outlined by the flickering flames. "Those fires ain't gonna last long in this downpour," said Walker.

"It's now or never," said Coyle.

With Walker's help, Coyle lined up the approach, squinting through the fires' dim, smoky light. The wounded C-130 descended rapidly toward the short runway. The fires were already sputtering out as the plane neared the ground. "I'm putting her down!" Coyle yelled.

The C-130 hit the muddy runway hard, skidding through puddles and nearly fishtailing. Coyle slammed the brakes, bringing the plane to a precarious stop just yards from the end of the strip, flames dying all around them.

Walker let out a huge breath. "Couldn't have cut that much closer. Nice landing, Skipper."

Coyle nodded, his heart pounding. "Let's unload this cargo quick."

"It would be a crying shame to come all this way only to have the aircraft and its cargo destroyed on the runway," said Walker.

"You really need to work on your attitude, Walker. More positive vibes."

"Will do, Skipper. But attitude don't stop mortars."

Coyle shrugged in surrender.

As the aircrew exited the plane, Hmong fighters rushed to the runway smothering the flickering runway fires with dirt and wet burlap sacks. Coyle watched them quickly extinguish each small blaze, plunging the airfield back into darkness concealing the plane before enemy spotters pinpointed their position.

Walker gave a thumbs up to the muddy silhouettes hurrying around the aircraft. "Nice thinking. They just bought us some time."

Coyle nodded, impressed by the Hmong's tactical adaptability. "Let's not waste it. Get that cargo ramp lowered so we can unload these supplies."

Working swiftly in the rain, the aircrew and Hmong began offloading the vital cargo destined for Vang Pao's forces. Their lives depended on getting it done before the enemy's mortars zeroed in on the aircraft through the black night.

As more cargo was unloaded, a huge lightning strike illuminated the aircraft at the end of the runway. "That can't be good," said Walker.

"There you go again. Positive thoughts dammit!" said Coyle.

Moments later, enemy mortar rounds shrieked in and exploded around the airfield. "See?" said Coyle.

"Are you saying I'm responsible for the lightning now?" said Walker as he continued to unload.

"I'm saying your negative attitude ain't helping," said Coyle.

As Coyle pushed a large crate toward the ramp, he thought of his lost friend McGoon always harping on him not to be so negative. He smiled to himself as another mortar exploded near the ramp wounding two

Hmong fighters. With dozens of crates still in the back of the aircraft they had run out of time. "Everybody out!" shouted Coyle.

But the Hmong wouldn't give up, grabbing more cargo and carrying it out of the aircraft. Coyle realized they were willing to die to save the ammunition and weapons they so desperately needed to fight off the Pathet Lao. Coyle grabbed another crate to help them as more mortars exploded in front of the cockpit, shattering the windshield and shredding the instruments with shrapnel.

Coyle and the Hmong picked up the pace, working as fast as possible. A deafening blast rocked the plane from the right side. A mortar had exploded next to the landing gear, collapsing it. The aircraft violently shifted as crates tumbled and spilled their contents – live ammunition skittered across the deck. "She's going up. Everyone out now!" Coyle bellowed. The remaining Hmong scrambled from the burning aircraft.

A remaining Hmong fighter was pinned by a heavy crate, crying out in pain. Coyle rushed over and with enormous effort lifted the container enough for the man to pull free. Coyle helped the fighter hobble toward the rear exit.

Another mortar detonated against the cockpit, blowing a large hole in the fuselage. Flames erupted inside as aviation fuel ignited. Ammunition cooked off, sending machine gun shells spinning through the air. Two Hmong grabbed their comrade from Coyle and carried him out of the burning aircraft. Coyle did a quick sweep of the hold. Seeing no one left aboard, he turned and sprinted for the ramp.

Just as he jumped down to the runway, a direct mortar hit turned the center of the aircraft into a massive fireball. The force of the blast flung Coyle to the ground as flames consumed the C-130.

His ears ringing, Coyle staggered away from the inferno that seconds earlier had been a functioning plane.

Reaching the safety of the edge of the runway where Walker and Wilson were waiting, he turned back to see a huge secondary explosion rip the aircraft apart. Twisted debris littered the runway. "Well, I guess we are walking home," said Walker.

"At least we got most of the cargo out," said Wilson. "Hopefully it'll be enough for a few more days of fighting."

"Yeah, but then what?" said Walker.

Forward Operating Base, Laos

Freeland unfurled a large map on the table, the assembled field commanders crowding around. It depicted Long Tieng surrounded by communist forces - four full NVA regiments. "Vang Pao's 2,500 Hmong fighters have been holding out for weeks, but they're cut off and supplies are dwindling," Freeland briefed. "Ammunition, medical provisions, food - it's all running dangerously low."

Murmurs swept the room as the dire situation sank in. "What's the enemy's troop strength around the city?" a Royal Lao commander asked.

Freeland pointed to the map. "We estimate 20,000 NVA and Pathet Lao troops including the 174th, 866th, 148th and 335th regiments. Plus T-34, T-59, and PT-76 tanks, K-63 armored personnel carriers, 85mm and 122mm field guns, not to mention hundreds of mortars and recoilless rifles. They also have substantial anti-aircraft guns and artillery protecting their troops and surrounding Long Tieng."

"What do we have on our side?" said a commander.

"Not enough. A hodgepodge of Hmong guerillas and Thai mercenaries. Six battalions in all. The one thing we do have in our favor is air power. We have eighty T-28 Trojans in the Royal Lao Air Force, plus twenty F-4 Phantom IIs and six A-1 Skyraiders from the Americans. We will also have one B-52 Arc Light strike daily and five fixed-wing gunships on call."

Another commander gave a low whistle. "Even with the aircraft, those are long odds. We'd be marching into a meat grinder."

Freeland nodded gravely. "You're not wrong. But Vang Pao's force is the last allied holdout left in Laos. If Long Tieng falls, Laos will follow."

The weight of his words fell heavy on the men. The stakes were immense. One commander still looked concerned. "Even with those resources, 20,000 battle-hardened NVA and Pathet Lao...it's a tall order."

Freeland's face was grim but resolute. "This will be bloody. But it's our only viable chance to save Vang Pao and keep Laos in the fight. The freedom of the nation hangs in the balance."

The men nodded solemnly, understanding the desperate stakes. "Return to your units and prepare to move out in forty-eight hours," Freeland ordered. "Dismissed."

As the commanders left to ready their battalions, Freeland hoped the resolve he saw in their eyes would sustain them against the formidable odds ahead. Victory over the communists during this operation could save Laos. But defeat would surely be the end.

Long Tieng, Laos

The morning sun cast its pale light over Long Tieng, glinting off the dew dripping from the thick jungle foliage surrounding the remote airfield. A low mist hung over the primitive runway, lending an eerie tranquility totally at odds with the violence soon to erupt here.

Inside the perimeter, Hmong fighters made final checks of their weapons and crafted meager meals from their dwindling rations. Some penned last letters home, while others prayed or smoked in silence, mentally steeling themselves for the battle ahead. A mood of grim determination permeated the ragged defenses.

Along the tree line, North Vietnamese and Pathet Lao troops camouflaged their positions and set sight lines for mortars and machine guns that would soon spew fire upon their enemy. Artillery pieces were calibrated to rain shells upon the airstrip and primitive fortifications. Fresh ammunition was brought up from rear areas to supply the onslaught.

High above, spotter planes circled, waiting to call in airstrikes to support the garrison and hammer communist rear areas. At airfields just over the border in Thailand, fighter-bombers sat fueled and armed, pilots ready to scream into the skies the moment the call came in.

For now, an eerie quiet surrounded Long Tieng as both sides prepared for the pivotal battle about to commence. The very fate of Laos hung in the balance.

In a matter of hours, the tranquil jungle would erupt into an inferno, and heroes would be made.

Bounpheng crouched in the trench, wiping the sweat from his eyes. The eighteen-year-old gripped his AK-47 tightly to stop his hands from shaking. "Steady now, little brother," said his platoon sergeant Toulay, placing a hand on his shoulder. "We'll make it through this day."

All around him in the camp, Hmong fighters made final preparations, their faces taut with apprehension. For weeks they had been hemmed in at Long Tieng, resources dwindling, death raining down. Today they would try to break out or die trying.

Several kilometers away, Viet trudged through the misty jungle under the weight of his rucksack and RPG launcher. "How much further till we can rest?" he complained aloud.

No response from his exhausted comrades. The young North Vietnamese soldier was bone-tired from the long siege. But today his unit would surge forward to deliver the final blow against the enemy base. Victory - and rest - were close at hand.

In a foxhole near the airstrip, Royal Lao Army Captain Sensoa checked his watch nervously. The preparatory bombardment should be starting any minute. He peered through his binoculars where the tree line concealed massed communist forces. This push had to succeed, or the fate of Laos would be sealed. Every soldier felt the weight of this final battle on their shoulders. Sensoa shouted into the radio, "What's the delay on that artillery barrage? We're sitting ducks out here!"

On a ridge overlooking Long Tieng, Pathet Lao platoon leader Khamphong scanned the besieged base through his captured American binoculars. After so many hard months, the enemy was nearly at the breaking point. One last assault would extinguish them. Khamphong felt only grim determination - today there would be no mercy. "Wait for my order to attack," he told his men. "We must be patient and—"

He was cut off as a deafening explosion erupted thirty meters away. Khamphong dove for cover, ears ringing. His radio squawked, "Incoming rounds! Take shelter!"

Inside Long Tieng, Bounpheng flinched as the first artillery shells whistled overhead toward communist positions. The pounding sound of the preparatory barrage erupted, the ground shaking. Across the camp, final prayers were offered. Then the order came - fix bayonets. Bounpheng steadied himself. May God grant him courage this day. Toulay shouted to Bounpheng and his other troops over the din, "Lock and load! For Laos!"

Nearby, Viet was startled as the artillery began crashing down without warning. Airburst shells shredded the canopy, pelting him with smoldering shrapnel. The morning stillness erupted into cacophony, the world aflame. Viet cowered in his hole frantically - what fresh hell was this? Viet cried out "We need to retreat!" But his words were lost in the chaos.

Captain Sensoa watched as B-52s hammered the tree line with explosive payloads. Napalm saturated the jungle in liquid fire. He silently thanked their American allies for this vengeance. Over the intercom, the signal came from headquarters. Sensoa steadied himself and gave the order into the radio, "Advance now! Push forward!"

Platoon leader Khamphong was thrown to the ground as a string of bombs erupted thirty meters down the ridge line. His eardrums rang from the concussions. Troops ran in all directions through the smoke and falling debris. Before Khamphong could regain his feet, the Royalists' ground assault emerged from Long Tieng, headed right toward his position. Scrambling up, Khamphong screamed "Return fire!" But his decimated platoon could only take cover as the enemy surged forth.

Bounpheng charged forward with his comrades, adrenaline surging through his veins. Tracers zipped overhead as machine guns tried to stem the human tide. An explosion flicked Bounpheng to the ground like a stunned flea. For an instant he lay shocked, then got up and kept moving through the gunfire. Adrenaline surging, Bounpheng charged forward with his comrades. Tracer rounds zipped past, but he felt no fear, only determination. "Onward!" he yelled. They would not stop until freedom was won.

Bounpheng plunged into the smoke-filled jungle, bayonet fixed on his AK-47. All around him came the crackle of rifle fire and cries of the wounded as his platoon advanced into withering enemy fire.

Charging forward, they collided with an enemy platoon in close quarters. Bayonets and rifle butts swung wildly in vicious hand-to-hand combat.

Bounpheng parried a rifle strike from a young North Vietnamese soldier, then drove his blade into the man's chest. Wrenching it free, he checked behind to make sure his brothers were still with him. They were.

The allied platoons gained ground in the confused melee before the tree line suddenly erupted with enemy machine guns and recoilless rifles, scything through their ranks. Men fell on all sides, the jungle floor turning slick with blood.

"Get down!" Sergeant Toulay bellowed, pulling Bounpheng behind a thick tree trunk as bullets ricocheted around them. With grim determination, Bounpheng reloaded his rifle and returned fire at the muzzle flashes blinking in the foliage.

All along the line, the attack stalled in the withering fire. A Lao platoon to their right tried to advance but was mowed down before they could rise from the underbrush. Screams of the wounded carried over the din.

Toulay exchanged despairing looks with Bounpheng. It was a slaughterhouse, and ammo was running low. Word came by runner that supporting armor had been ambushed and decimated behind them. No reinforcements would be coming. Grabbing Bounpheng's shoulder, Toulay shouted over the gunfire: "Fall back, we have to retreat!"

Reluctantly Bounpheng withdrew with the remnants of his platoon. All around, scores of his brothers-in-arms lay unmoving on the red jungle floor. This day was supposed to break the siege, but it had turned into a gruesome defeat.

Reaching their forward trench line, the bloodied men grimly reloaded their dwindling ammunition. The enemy had halted their advance for now, but their superior numbers and guns still surrounded Long Tieng on all sides.

As distant airstrikes pounded the jungle, Bounpheng thought of home. Would he ever again see his family and village? But he shook off those thoughts. The battle was far from over. Gripping his bloodstained rifle, he steeled himself for the fight ahead. Laos's future remained in the balance.

Suddenly, figures charged from the jungle. "Here they come!" Bounpheng yelled, opening fire with his platoon. The enemy fell in droves but more emerged, fanatically surging toward Bounpheng's trench.

Reaching the barbed wire, the attackers threw themselves upon it like a human wave, trying to force a breach for their comrades behind. They were mowed down by blistering fire from the trench. But a few managed to cut through and stumbled toward Bounpheng, riddled with bullets yet still coming.

Leaping up, Bounpheng bayoneted one and shot another point blank before a burst of fire from Sergeant Toulay's submachine gun cut down the last of them. The trench line held.

"Pour it on, don't let up!" Toulay shouted to his men. The air sang with returned rifle fire.

Behind the dead and dying before their wire, the second enemy wave massed. Then with a cry, they charged forth, throwing grenades and firing obsolete bolt-action rifles. One grenade dropped into the trench, blowing a Hmong fighter apart before he could grab and hurl it back out.

"Grenades, return fire!" Toulay ordered. A barrage of grenades sailed out of the trenches, breaking the enemy's momentum. Under deadly fire, the advance disintegrated into confusion with the wounded and dying crying out pitifully on the battlefield.

Bounpheng fired methodically at enemy soldiers trying to crawl back to the jungle. The trench line had held again, but they couldn't take much more.

Toulay slapped Bounpheng's back, yelling over the din. "We bloodied their nose today, but they'll be back again soon. Dig in and stay sharp!"

Bounpheng nodded, blinking sweat from his eyes. Around him men dragged the dead from the trench and frantically deepened fortifications. This war seemed without end. But if called again to fight, he knew he must be ready. Freedom demanded it.

As darkness fell, Bounpheng peered into the gloom searching for any sign of enemy movement. But all was silent except for distant artillery and airstrikes. This day the defense of Long Tieng had held. Bounpheng offered a prayer of thanks, but knew tomorrow could be far bloodier. Grimly he reloaded his rifle and kept watch, as the war ground on.

The night had passed without attack, both sides licking their wounds. But with daylight, the battle would renew. The tree line was shrouded in morning mist. Everything seemed still.

Bounpheng sat in silence, absently running his thumb over the worn wooden stock of his AK-47. The sounds of preparations echoed around the bunker - the scraping of blades as knives were sharpened, the clink of ammo clips being loaded. Outside, muffled thuds signaled the American bombers softening up enemy positions.

After a while, Platoon Sergeant Toulay approached and put a weathered hand on Bounpheng's shoulder. "How're you holding up, little brother?"

Bounpheng nodded, not taking his eyes off his rifle. "I'm ready, Sergeant. Just want it to start."

Toulay gave a solemn smile. "I know the waiting is the hardest part. But take heart - we'll break their siege today and send these communists running!"

His voiced boomed with confidence, lifting the spirits of the nearby men. But his eyes betrayed worry that their predicament may be hopeless. Still, Toulay knew his role was to kindle the courage of these youths who had never known peace.

The staccato report of artillery suddenly cracked outside, followed by the drone of approaching aircraft. Toulay straightened. "Lock and load boys! This is it!"

The men scrambled to readiness. Bounpheng took a deep breath and thought of his mother and father far away. He believed he would see them again someday. But now was the time to fight.

As the roar of battle erupted, Bounpheng surged up the trench ladder, Toulay's words ringing in his head - "For Laos!" Adrenaline flooded his veins as he charged into the smoke, AK-47 blazing.

Viet peered through the dense foliage as the first artillery shells rained down ahead of the enemy advance. Trees erupted in flames, shrapnel slicing through the ranks. The assault was underway.

Scrambling from his foxhole, he assembled with his platoon along the front trench. Their machine guns and mortars stared down the slope at the approaching columns of Royalist troops.

"Steady boys," Sergeant Thuong said, hand raised for them to hold fire. "Let them come into our kill zone."

Viet chambered a round in his AK-47, fingers slick

with sweat. As the enemy drew nearer, their bayonets glinting through the trees, his mouth went dry with fear. This was his first major battle.

At last, Thuong's hand dropped. "Open fire!" The jungle erupted with flame and Viet convulsively fired on full automatic along with his comrades.

Mowed down in droves, the attackers wavered. But Viet was stunned to see a surge of enemy fighters emerge from the smoke, charging straight at their position. Wild yelling and gunshots split the air as the two forces collided.

Viet fired from the hip, spraying rounds desperately as a Hmong fighter barreled toward him, face contorted in fury. At the last second, Viet seized his entrenching tool and swung with all his might. The shovel caught the man across the temple, dropping him instantly.

All around raged hand-to-hand combat. Viet heard Thuong cry out as he was run through with a bayonet. Suddenly a Lao soldier tackled Viet, choking him against the trench floor. Viet gasped for breath, reaching for his pistol. He fired point blank into the man's chest, the weight lifting as the body went limp.

Stumbling up, Viet looked around wildly. Most of his comrades were dead. The enemy had breached their line. He turned and ran back into the jungle, heart hammering.

Reaching the next defensive trench, he and other survivors dug in, awaiting the pursuing Royalists. But strangely the attack never came - the enemy must have suffered heavy losses too. The machine guns and mortars had done their grim work.

As night fell, Viet slumped in the trench, numb with

shock. He had survived, but scores of his brothers had not. The enemy was still out there, but their assault had been halted for now. This battle was far from over. He had fought this day - now he must fight again tomorrow, until Long Tieng was won or he was dead.

Bounpheng crouched in the trench, rifle smoking. His last clips of ammunition were spent. All around the perimeter, his comrades were down to scarce handfuls of rounds. Without resupply, Long Tieng would soon be overrun.

Nearby, Coyle exchanged desperate looks with his aircrew. When the ammunition vanished, there would be nothing left to hold back the human waves of enemy troops surging at the perimeter. Their situation seemed hopeless.

Suddenly, a small plane crested the ridgeline, barreling right for the battered airstrip. Tracer fire erupted from the jungle. The pilot jinked wildly but kept on course as mortar blasts erupted around him.

"Is that one of ours?" said Wilson.

"Crazy bastard's never gonna make it," said Walker.

Coyle and his crew watched in disbelief as the plane continued toward the airstrip, weaving wildly to avoid thick curtains of tracer fire erupting from the jungle. Anti-aircraft artillery explosions bracketed the aircraft, black puffs of smoke sending shrapnel into the plane's wings and fuselage. Undaunted the fearless pilot held his course and leveled out as he reached the valley floor.

Touching down on the ruined runway, the plane jolted and skidded over shell craters before finally sliding to a stop. Even before it halted, the cargo door dropped open and Hmong fighters poured out of the trenches, sprinting for the aircraft under heavy fire, frantically unloading crates of ammunition as more mortar fire rained down exploding around them. Several fell from shrapnel and were carried off by their comrades.

Coyle ran to the plane and clapped the pilot on the shoulder - it was his old associate Willis from Air America.

"Freeland sent me to get you out," Willis shouted over the gunfire. "Said he couldn't lose the only pilot and crew stupid enough to fly a C-130 through the mountains of Laos during the middle of a monsoon." Coyle waved his crew aboard with several wounded Hmong soldiers. Closing the cargo door, the plane accelerated down the chewed-up airstrip, shells exploding just yards behind the tail. It lifted off while taking heavy fire, then ducked back over the ridgeline.

As they gained altitude, Coyle peered out at smoke rising from Long Tieng. Against all odds, the garrison still held and he and his crew had survived.

Gripping his comrade's shoulder, Coyle gave a nod of deep gratitude. The battle might go on, but hope remained.

The earth shook as enemy armor rumbled from the jungle – NVA Russian-made tanks and personnel carriers streaming toward Bounpheng's trench. He and his comrades fired desperately with rifles and machine guns, but the cacophony of enemy machine guns drove them to cover.

Bounpheng watched as his platoon's recoilless rifle team loosed a shell against the lead tank, but it deflected off the angled armor. The tanks crashed through the barbed wire, their treads churning men into the mud.

"Fall back!" Toulay yelled as the position was overrun. They retreated through the camp, rallying the last of the defenders. The end seemed imminent as more enemy armor breached the lines.

Then, a roar echoed down the valley. American F-111 Aardvark fighter-bombers hugged the valley floor, aligning on the enemy tanks. Bounpheng watched in awe as they released anti-tank clusters of bomblets.

Fiery eruptions engulfed the armor, steel hulks burning and some flipping over from the concussive force of multiple explosions. The Aardvarks made another pass, strafing the enemy tanks and APCs with the anti-armor shells from the aircrafts' 6-barrelled 20mm Vulcan cannons piercing their armor. Surviving crews abandoned their crippled vehicles and fled under the aerial onslaught.

The garrison cheered, galvanized by this miracle. Reinforcements rushed forward to plug the breaches and hold the line.

Bounpheng gazed up as the gleaming aircraft banked away, contrails streaking the sky. Gripping his rifle, he turned to face the enemy once more. The battle still raged, but Long Tieng would not fall that day.

Smoke billowed from the smoldering ruins of an enemy radar station as the allied column emerged from the mountains. Colonel Phan scanned the hilly terrain ahead through binoculars. The ridge lines were wooded, but the valley between was open farmland - tough going for armor.

"Fan out those platoons," he ordered his company commanders. "We'll advance along that central ridge to their main line."

Phan watched as the lead elements fanned out. His tanks churned up muddy water as they crossed flooded rice paddies, moving to support the infantry platoons advancing along an elevated berm between fields.

From the turret below, his gunner reported enemy movement ahead. Phan focused his optics, spotting North Vietnamese troops dug in at the tree line edge of a potato field 500 meters ahead.

"Enemy platoon ahead, end of that potato field," Phan radioed. "Have mortars lay smoke."

Seconds later, white phosphorus rained across the treeline, billowing thick smoke as the return fire intensified. "All units...fire!" Phan ordered.

The ridge erupted with flame as allied tanks and APCs unleashed .50 cal and 40mm cannon fire into the smoke cloud. Mortars and recoilless rifles added their salvos. Inside the churning haze, secondary explosions signaled ammo caches igniting.

"Cease fire!" Phan called. As the smoke cleared, he saw dozens of enemy dead and wrecked log bunkers. "Forward, keep the momentum!"

His column pressed on up the ridgeline, strafing more bunkers. An enemy AAA gun opened fire from higher ground, forcing the lead tanks to withdraw.

Phan grabbed the radio. "Cobra 11, we've got AAA on hill marker Juliet-5, can you assist?"

"Roger that," came the helicopter pilot's response. "Rolling in hot."

Phan watched as the Cobra gunship crested the ridgeline, unleashing a salvo of rockets and 20mm cannon fire. The enemy gun blew apart in a satisfying explosion.

"Nice shooting, Cobra. Drinks are on me when we take Long Tieng."

"I'll hold you to that, ground pounder. Good hunting."

With the high ground neutralized, Phan's forces pressed forward, edging closer to the main communist trench lines. Dug in infantry slowed their advance with heavy small arms fire.

Phan directed tank and mortar support to clear strongpoints. But the enemy seemed to have endless reserves, replacing each unit knocked out. If they didn't break through soon, his column could be surrounded and destroyed.

As they entered the tree line, withered fire suddenly erupted from camouflaged spider holes and trenches. An RPG team knocked out the lead tank, blocking the advance.

"Ambush, infantry in the trees!" Phan yelled. The column ground to a halt, unable to spot the concealed enemy shooting from all sides. Control was rapidly lost as men retreated back down the muddy berm.

Phan urgently radioed for smokescreens and gunship support. But his lead elements were surrounded, taking heavy casualties. By the time gunships pushed the communists back, it was too late - the ambush had devastated the head of the column.

Surveying the burning tanks and wrecked APCs mired in the field, Phan knew the breakthrough attempt had failed disastrously. He had underestimated the enemy's reserves and defenses. It would take a rethink and much more firepower next time.

Just then, artillery fire began raining down from behind their advance. "They've got our rear, pull back!" Phan yelled over the radio.

Under heavy fire, his battered units withdrew down ridge. He had failed to crack the siege this time. Phan knew he would keep trying, throwing everything into the attack until they broke through or died trying. The fate of Long Tieng and Laos depended on it.

Phan observed grimly as the remaining armored vehicles retreated back down the muddy berm, leaving several immobilized tanks smoldering behind. Medics worked to evacuate the wounded as sporadic artillery fire targeted their withdrawal.

Regrouping in the foothills, Phan urgently radioed command about the failed breakthrough attempt. "The ambush decimated our vanguard," he reported. "We'll need heavy air assets to soften their defenses for the next push."

"Roger that," came the reply. "B-52 strikes are being coordinated. Pull your units back and standby."

Over the coming days, waves of B-52 Arc Light strikes pummeled the enemy trench networks and supply lines. Phan watched from the mountains as massive detonations blanketed the valley day and night.

When word came of the next assault, his forces would be ready. Stronger infantry contingents would protect the vulnerable armored advance, while gunships provided close air support. Sappers would check for spider holes and traps.

Studying maps, Phan saw a ridge that could provide flanking fire on the enemy's northern trenches. Taking that high ground would enable them to split the communist lines.

For the moment, he kept spirits high and prepared for the next major push. Though progress was slow with heavy losses, Phan knew persistence would win out. The siege had to be lifted, no matter the cost. There was no choice but to keep grinding the enemy down.

As the last B-52 contrails faded, the low rumble of new aircraft echoed over the mountains. Phan glanced up to see flights of American F-4 Phantoms and A-1 Skyraiders streaking overhead.

The valley erupted in smoke and fire as they swooped in low, pummeling the enemy's trench networks with bombs, rockets and cannon fire. Napalm saturated the jungle, engulfing swaths of vegetation in raging flames.

When the fighters finally banked away, the landscape was cratered with still-smoldering ruins. supply depots and ammunition caches burned uncontrollably. The air assault had obliterated miles of communist fortifications.

Gazing at the devastation, Phan knew the window of opportunity was open. The enemy was reeling, defenses fractured, and supplies destroyed. The time to strike was now.

He radioed command, ready to unleash their assembled forces before the enemy could recover. Victory remained distant, but with allied airpower laying waste to the valley, the odds now favored an aggressive blow.

The ground assault would be bloody, but supported from above, Phan knew his reinforced battalions stood a chance of cracking the siege wide open. The goal was finally within reach - they had to seize it decisively.

As jets streaked back to base, Phan prepared to lead the charge himself when the order came down. The men's morale was high, spirits lifted by the aerial display of might. He would channel that energy into a knockout punch that could finally turn the tide.

Phan surveyed the valley stretching before him

from the mountain overlook. The previous assaults had failed with heavy losses, but intelligence reported a potential weak point in the enemy's southern flank.

One last daring night attack through there, and they might finally break the siege of Long Tieng. Studying the map, Phan outlined his plan to his battalion commanders.

"We'll advance down this ravine under cover of darkness and infiltrate here, behind their trench network," he indicated. "With the element of surprise, we can cause chaos and open a corridor into the city."

"This plan is terribly risky, sir," said Colonel Ratanak. "That ravine will be a death trap."

"The enemy will see us coming and cut us to shreds," another officer added.

Phan raised a hand to silence the objections. "I understand your concerns. But we're out of options and out of time. Vang Pao's forces can't hold much longer."

He made eye contact with each man, voice hardening with resolve. "Yes, this is a long shot. But it's the last card we have left to play. I would never ask this of you if there was any other way."

Ratanak still looked uncertain. "Sir, if we fail here, it could mean the end."

Phan put a hand firmly on his shoulder. "I know, old friend. But we can't dwell on fear of failure. We must dare greatly for any hope of victory."

Seeing Ratanak's hesitant nod, Phan addressed them all. "I won't lie, gentlemen. The odds are long and lives will be lost. But we fight on because we must."

His gaze burned with conviction. "If this war has taught us one lesson, it's that we can endure and achieve far more than we ever believed possible.

Remember that today."

The men straightened with grim determination. Phan gave a final rallying order: "For our homeland and for freedom - whatever the cost!"

The commanding general had granted them this one last roll of the dice before accepting ceasefire negotiations. Failure now would doom the Hmong and Laos itself.

As the light faded, and the assault force prepared to descend into the ravine, Phan gave a final order: "Armor units stay in position here with engines off. You'll advance only on my signal at the start of the attack."

It was a risky move, assaulting entrenched enemies without armor support. But the element of surprise was paramount. Phan knew the spearhead had to be a stealthy infantry infiltration.

Leaving the idle armor concealed under jungle cover, Phan led his softly-treading battalions down into the ravine... His men were swallowed up by the dense, oppressive jungle. Vines as thick as pythons draped from gnarled tree limbs, brushing against the uneasy soldiers. The moist air was choked with swirling mist and the stench of decaying vegetation.

Every shadow seemed to harbor hidden threats. Strange animal cries pierced the dusk, along with the drone of insects swarming in the half-light. Loose rocks and thick mud made the descent treacherous, as if the jungle itself were trying to deter their advance.

Phan tried to silence the nagging doubts in his mind. Had he just led these men into a tomb from which they'd never emerge? No, he couldn't afford such thoughts. This hellish place had to be their path to victory.

Phan led his battalions silently through the jungle ravine as it began to level out, senses alert for any sign of the enemy. The only sounds were the soft footfalls on damp soil, creaking of leather harness, and occasional clipped bird call signals between squad leaders.

Reaching a winding section, the point man suddenly halted and raised a clenched fist. Phan froze, his pistol raised. The metallic click of a safety lever echoed somewhere ahead, then silence again.

Phan glanced back and whispered "Enemy patrol. Ready weapons." His men tightened grips on rifles and unsheathed machetes in anticipation.

Creeping forward, Phan peered through the vegetation. In a clearing ahead, two enemy soldiers stood smoking, oblivious to the threat just meters away.

Phan flashed a hand signal and two skirmishers slipped like ghosts through the brush. Muffled cries rang out, then nothing. The skirmishers reappeared and gave a thumbs up.

Phan led the column past the enemy bodies, now silent in a spreading pool of blood. A few hundred more yards and they would be behind enemy lines.

Everyone was tense. Adrenaline kicking in. Last second check of their weapons. Ready to fire.

Flitting through the shadows like ghosts, they reached the rear of the enemy lines undetected. The dense foliage opened up ahead into the enemy's rear staging area. Phan steeled himself - the chance they'd been waiting for was upon them. He whispered a prayer that the wilderness they'd just traversed would not become their graveyard.

Phan gave the signal to attack with a hand signal. Every foot they could advance without the enemy discovering their presence was a gift from God. The battalions poured from the underbrush, crashing into the unsuspecting communist positions.

The element of surprise allowed the allies to overrun the first line of trenches in savage close combat. Phan fired his pistol at fleeing silhouettes, rallying the men forward.

"Press the attack! We've got them reeling!" he yelled. This was their moment to achieve a breakthrough. He radioed his armor commander. He heard the engines starting in the distance. They would be there soon. Heart pounding, he charged ahead.

As they advanced further, sudden blistering fire erupted from concealed bunkers and foxholes that had seemed abandoned. Phan watched in dismay as his lead platoons were ripped apart.

It was an ambush. The communists had feigned retreat, drawing them deeper into a trap. His men were quickly pinned down as they dove for cover. Phan radioed his armor commander, "We're under heavy fire. We need armor now."

He heard the armor engines rev higher as they gained speed. Every second would count. Phan watched as the first, then the second tank emerged from the forest. He smiled. His men were saved.

Then, disaster. Hidden enemy RPG teams emerged from cover and flanked both sides of the armored column. The RPGs blew the first two allied tanks sky high. The enemy teams maneuvered for better firing positions as more tanks emerged from the jungle. Without ground troops to support the armor, more enemy RPGs fired and more tanks exploded.

Realizing his entire task force was in deep trouble, Phan desperately radioed for emergency air support as RPGs and heavy machine gun fire pinned his units down. "Broken Arrow, Broken Arrow!"

Soon the roar of jet engines echoed across the hills. F-4 Phantoms screamed over the tree line, dropping payload after payload on the enemy positions.

Explosions rocked the enemy trenches and defensive positions as 500- and 1000-pound bombs unleashed avalanches of fire and shrapnel. The aircraft made repeated runs, engulfing the enemy trenches in eruptions of smoke and soil.

The enemy bunkers and foxholes were too well-fortified, while the ravine provided too much cover. And with allied forces trapped in the impact zones, the bombs only added to the chaos.

Men who had survived the ambush were now cut down by friendly fire, their screams silenced by the unrelenting aerial barrage. All cohesion vanished as units dissolved into desperate retreat under the aerial onslaught.

Finally, Phan screamed into the radio, "Abort strike! Abort strike! You're hitting friendlies!" The fighters peeled away, afterburners searing the night sky.

In the smoldering aftermath, all that remained of Phan's task force was a scattered mass of dazed and wounded men. The air support had arrived too late and delivered only death. Around Phan, the jungle still bristled with enemy forces, determined to finish them off. By the time Phan ordered retreat, it was a disorganized rout.

Bringing up the rear, he provided covering fire as his decimated battalions fled back up the ravine. Enemy gunners cut down scores of men in the open.

As he turned to follow his men, a burst of machine gun fire tore into Phan's legs and back. He collapsed to the muddy ground, vision darkening. The frantic footsteps retreated into the distance as his lifeblood seeped into the earth.

His final thoughts were of Long Tieng still surrounded, the siege unbroken, Laos was lost. As the blackness consumed him, Phan knew his gamble had failed. There would be no victory. He had led these men here to die in vain.

As the distant sounds of gunfire, RPGs, and mortars destroying the allied task force finally faded, Bounpheng leaned against the trench wall, bandages covering his shrapnel wounds. All around him, the remaining defenders slumped in exhaustion.

For months they had endured relentless attacks and deprivation, clinging to survival while the world seemed against them. Many times it appeared their defeat was imminent.

Yet somehow, against all odds, they had endured. Long Tieng still stood, defended by these battered but unbroken men. Though just a fraction of those who had stood here months ago, these warriors had achieved the near-impossible.

When all seemed lost, they had found strength to withstand the onslaught until allied reinforcements had arrived. Though darkness and danger still lay ahead, for now they had won. Bounpheng offered a quiet prayer of thanks before closing his eyes to rest, finally at peace.

In the aftermath, with the relief force destroyed, the Laotian government agreed to peace talks that ultimately saved Vang Pao's Hmong forces from being overrun.

Four Thai battalions were flown in to reinforce Long Tieng for the time being. But Phan would never know of this - his body lay abandoned and forgotten in that ravine, another casualty of a senseless war.

A Long Conversation

1966 – Warsaw, Poland

As the veteran diplomat's plane descended into Warsaw, Averell Harriman gazed out the window in melancholy reflection. The city still wore the scars of war - buildings pockmarked by bullets, rubble strewn lots yawning amidst the reconstruction. Twenty years earlier, he had watched Warsaw burn from afar as Nazi bombs pounded its proud defiance into submission.

Now the poles were allies, drawn together with America against the creeping menace of communism. But to Harriman, Warsaw embodied the deeper failures of diplomacy that led to such wars.

As he rode through the bleak streets to the secluded safehouse, he vowed to avoid such catastrophic breakdowns in the conflict brewing in Vietnam. If talks could keep the bombs from falling on Hanoi as they had Warsaw, then he would seize that chance, no matter how slim.

Stepping into the discreet living room where

veteran diplomat Janusz Lewandowski waited, Harriman felt the weight of history's judgment upon him. The safehouse was sparsely furnished, with drawn curtains that blocked out the sounds of Warsaw and a haze of cigarette smoke blending together in the gloom. Lewandowski rose silently to greet his guest. "Thank you for making the long trip, Mr. Harriman," he said in accented English. "I realize the risk you are taking in meeting this way."

Harriman waved off the pleasantries, "If there's any hope of progress, some risks are worth taking."

Lewandowski poured two glasses of vodka as Harriman settled into the worn leather chair across from him.

As an Eastern Bloc representative, Lewandowski had rare access and communication channels with North Vietnamese officials that Western diplomats lacked. This allowed him to act as a go-between to begin exploring potential negotiating positions between Washington and Hanoi.

While Poland was allied with the U.S. at that time against the Soviets, Lewandowski was still valued as a neutral third party who could shuttle messages and test waters on both sides of the conflict in Vietnam. His Eastern Bloc role gave him credibility with the North Vietnamese that opened doors.

For Harriman, this was an opportunity to find a different path. He would listen closely to this patient Pole across the table. Failures of diplomacy had scarred too many cities already.

The two men sat back, observing each other closely as the pause lingered. Harriman saw a patient wisdom behind Lewandowski's tired eyes. This was a man who understood compromise and conviction in equal measure.

Finally, Lewandowski broke the silence. "While not officially conveying Hanoi's views, I can share my...impressions of possible flexibility, if the conditions warrant it."

Harriman raised an eyebrow. "Flexibility does interest us. I too can offer observations, not formal positions, that may reveal mutually acceptable paths."

The veteran diplomats shared a look that only their rare breed understood. Today they would deal in nuance and whispers. But their quiet words might someday cool the fire of war. The dance had begun.

The path to peace remained daunting, but Harriman and Lewandowski's tireless diplomacy had cracked open the door to negotiations.

1967 – Paris, France

The specter of peace in Vietnam hovered over the Parisian skyline like a distant mirage. Years of bloody conflict had worn down all sides, yet the fighting dragged on. Both Hanoi and Washington desired a way out, if only the other would bend first.

The City of Light glittered outside the window of the nondescript apartment building, but inside Averell Harriman sat in tense silence. Across from him, a North Vietnamese diplomat he knew only as Mr. Mai smoked cigarettes one after another, his face an inscrutable mask.

Their meeting followed months of carefully orchestrated messages through Lewandowski and other intermediaries. Hanoi had finally agreed to direct backchannel talks, secretly authorized by President Johnson and Secretary of State Rusk. But years of war and mistrust sat between the two diplomats like a phantom.

Harriman decided to break the ice with sincerity. "Neither of us are here officially, but I believe we both want this war to end. Can we not have an honest discussion, as men if not diplomats?"

Mai tapped his ashes deliberately before responding. "There is too much history between us for honesty alone. But I am authorized to explore your intentions."

"Then let us explore," Harriman said, leaning forward. "Tell me which of your priorities are inflexible, and I will do the same. Perhaps then we can find common ground."

Mai paused to consider his response carefully. "Complete cessation of bombing of the North is non-negotiable for any substantive talks. And we will never abandon our compatriots in the South."

Harriman nodded, unsurprised but disappointed. "Those are not easy concessions for us either. But understand this - we cannot agree to any deal that allows the North to overrun the South. Their right to self-determination must be respected."

"Self-determination imposed by American guns is hardly fair," Mai countered.

"And reunification by Northern tanks is better?" Harriman replied pointedly.

Mai bristled at this but held his tongue. After a moment, he continued. "On matters of the South, we may have...flexibility. If other conditions are met."

Harriman's pulse quickened, though his face remained neutral. "Other conditions? Such as?"

"As I said, bombing must cease entirely and permanently," Mai insisted. "And the DMZ must be respected, on both sides."

Harriman weighed his next words carefully. "If verifiable assurances on the DMZ and Southern self-determination were guaranteed, my government could be persuaded to consider a conditional bombing pause. I cannot promise more at this time."

Mai took a long drag on his cigarette as he absorbed Harriman's words. "Let us then explore the specifics of these conditionalities further."

The two men leaned forward, voices lowered but urgent. The delicate stroll towards compromise had begun. They talked late into the night, gingerly circling core issues without commitment. Harriman searched for any clue to shift Hanoi's stance, while Mai subtly signaled which concessions his superiors might consider. No agreements emerged, but they parted with a nod of understanding.

As dawn broke over Paris, Harriman felt a spark of hope. Numerous obstacles remained, but finally the once-impossible idea of negotiations seemed conceivable.

As the backchannel talks continued into the summer of 1967, Harriman and Mai found themselves bogged down on the issue of bombing pauses. Hanoi demanded unilateral halt with no conditions, while Washington insisted on strict reciprocity.

"Your bombers must stop their terror against us with no restraints," Mai pressed at one tense session. "Only then can we show good faith."

Harriman shook his head firmly. "A complete pause is impossible. But a mutually agreed restricted bombing zone could be viable."

Mai slammed his hand on the table in a rare show

of frustration. "Limited bombing is still bombing! Would you accept foreign bombs falling on your homes?"

"And would you accept foreign troops invading your homeland?" Harriman shot back pointedly.

The two envoys sat in angry silence as the stalemate deepened. Finally, Harriman softened his tone. "This war wounds both our nations. Can we not take even small steps to stop the bloodshed?"

Mai's expression shifted from anger to resignation. "You know our pain well, Mr. Harriman. I will convey your proposal to consider a restricted zone. But the bombing must truly stop for talks to progress."

Harriman sighed, the glimmer of compromise receding once more. Yet he forced himself to remain hopeful. "We will await Hanoi's response," he said simply.

Through the summer they struggled to find common ground on bombing and other issues. But Harriman reminded himself that the path to peace was long, and never smooth. Their work in Paris remained the best chance to inch the mirage of peace closer to reality.

As 1967 drew to a close, the Paris backchannel talks were at risk of collapsing. Despite months of secret meetings, neither side could agree on the conditional terms for halting the bombing. Domestic political pressures were rising in both Washington and Hanoi, making flexibility harder.

"I fear we are at an impasse," Harriman confessed solemnly during one late night session. "The bombing remains the barrier neither of us can overcome."

Mai nodded grimly, the ever-present cigarette

burning low between his fingers. "Our superiors grow impatient. Yet I agree, no real progress can occur while your planes menace us."

Harriman ran a hand over his weary face, mind racing. Was this how diplomacy failed, not with a bang but a whimper? Then an idea struck him.

"Perhaps a temporary pause, say, just for the holidays to build trust?" he proposed. "No conditions, but a good faith gesture on our part. To restart talks in the new year."

Mai considered this silently. "A pause...not unconditional cessation?"

"A limited gesture, for now," Harriman affirmed. "We must walk before we run."

Mai crushed out his cigarette, contemplating the offer. "I will communicate this to Hanoi. But they will expect more concessions down the road."

"One step at a time," Harriman pressed. "Will you carry this idea to your leaders?"

Mai nodded slowly. "I will do so. For the sake of the progress made here already."

As they parted, Harriman felt the first real glimmer of hope in months. The marathon towards peace often came down to a single step. Now, at last, they just might take one together.

Harriman paced the faded carpet of the apartment, glancing impatiently at his watch. Mai was late, very unusual for the normally punctual diplomat. Could Hanoi have rejected the proposed Christmas bombing pause? Harriman feared the fragile progress made might unravel if the North rebuffed even this limited gesture.

Finally, footsteps sounded on the stairs. Mai

entered, face unreadable as always. But he carried a bottle of rice wine. "My superiors agree to a bombing pause over the holidays, as you proposed," he said without preamble. "They wish to build trust."

Relief broke across Harriman's face. "This is most welcome news. I will inform Washington immediately."

Mai set two glasses on the table and began opening the wine. "This pause must lead to full cessation," he cautioned. "But your proposal allows talks to resume."

"One step at a time," Harriman said, raising his glass. "This is progress."

They drank the tart wine in rare celebratory spirits. Both knew much work remained, but for this moment, the endless complexities of diplomacy faded into the background.

Across the world, as 1967 gave way to 1968, bombs would briefly stop falling from the skies. And two patient diplomats allowed themselves a glimmer of hope that peace just might be possible after all. The New Year had dawned with a chance.

February 1968 – Warsaw, Poland

The biting cold of the Warsaw winter could not diminish Harriman's buoyant mood as he strode into the familiar safehouse. Lewandowski awaited him beside a crackling fire, both men grinning. "So, the holiday pause came through?" Lewandowski asked rhetorically.

"It did indeed!" Harriman confirmed. "Twelve days without our bombers over the North. A small but vital step."

Lewandowski poured cognac in celebration. "My contacts report it was well received in Hanoi. But they wonder - will the bombing truly end?"

Harriman sipped his drink pensively. "I cannot promise that yet. But momentum is building in Washington for continued pauses. Johnson faces pressure to reach a settlement."

"Hanoi feels that pressure too," Lewandowski noted. "Your pause put hardliners there on the defensive."

Hopeful silence settled between the two elder statesmen. Then Lewandowski raised his glass. "To perseverance and peace."

"I'll drink to that," Harriman said. "The longest journeys start with a single step."

Their eyes met with shared understanding. The road ahead remained long, but walking it together, they just might reach the destination - a negotiated end to the bloodshed.

March 1968 – Paris, France

The sound of shouts and breaking glass echoed from the streets below as Harriman and Mai met again in Paris. Student protests and labor unrest had exploded across France, putting both men on edge.

"Your people seem as weary of war as mine," Mai commented as a chorus of chants rose up.

"Governments may prop up wars, but the people suffer its costs," Harriman mused.

They turned their focus to the business at hand. The holiday pause had led Johnson to approve further temporary bombing restrictions. But a gulf still separated the two sides.

"Hanoi insists all bombing must cease if talks are to move forward," Mai reiterated firmly.

Harriman pushed back just as hard. "Scaling back the bombing shows our sincerity. Your side must reciprocate on political terms in the South."

Fatigue and frustration permeated the room as they rehashed the same arguments that had blocked progress for months. Another barrage of shouts interrupted from below.

Mai shook his head as the noise faded. "While nations posture, people yearn for peace. The tide is turning against this war everywhere."

"You're right," Harriman acknowledged. "But governments move slowly, even as their citizens rush ahead."

"Then we must keep pace with the people's hopes, not the inertia of bureaucracy," Mai pressed.

Harriman nodded thoughtfully as outside the clamor resumed. "Perhaps you have a point..."

The shouts below mirrored the world's desire for an end to war. Harriman sensed a sea of change coming. The channels of power might yet follow the will of the people demanding peace.

April 1968 – Paris, France

The April skies in Paris were overcast, matching the gloomy mood as Harriman and Mai met again. Days earlier, Martin Luther King Jr. had been assassinated in Memphis, unleashing turmoil and riots across America.

"Your country weeps over the loss of a great man," Mai offered solemnly.

"And yet the war drags on," Harriman lamented. "My government remains torn."

Their talks reflected the internal divisions warring within Johnson's administration. Progress had slowed again as U.S. policy seemed in flux.

"Hanoi cannot wait indefinitely while Washington debates itself," Mai warned. "The bombing must end now, or else..."

His voice trailed off, but the implication was clear. North Vietnam's patience was wearing thin.

Harriman tried to sound a hopeful note. "President Johnson agrees with your goals of de-escalation and negotiated peace. But the political complexities are immense."

Mai gave him a hard look. "Complexities do not concern the peasants hiding from your bombers, or the fathers burying their sons."

Chastened, Harriman fell silent. Both countries had lost far too much already. How much more before peace prevailed?

"I will communicate Hanoi's urgency regarding the bombing," Harriman finally assured Mai. "But they must understand our good faith efforts."

Mai simply nodded as he stood to leave. As long as the bombs fell, words meant little. Action was needed now on both sides, or the chance for peace might spiral away for good.

May 1968 – Paris, France

As blossoms bloomed along the Seine, the atmosphere turned urgent at the Paris talks. After launching the Tet Offensive at the beginning of the year, Hanoi had launched Mini-Tet – a second massive offensive in South Vietnam, overrunning cities and bases. American casualties mounted sharply.

"This second offensive proves we will not yield," Mai declared. "Now will you cease the bombing without condition?"

Harriman slammed his fist on the table in anger. "Attacking while negotiating is outrageous! How can we trust Hanoi's intentions?"

"And we should trust American bombs?" Mai shot back.

The veteran diplomats nearly came to blows before Harriman restrained himself. "Enough endless circles. I am returning to Washington to speak directly to the president. The time has come for decisive action, one way or another."

Mai nodded solemnly. "I will do the same in Hanoi. The days of talking in circles are past."

Both men understood the urgency of this pivotal moment. All their tireless work toward peace could unravel if leaders on both sides failed to take bold steps now. Diplomatic patience was spent.

As Harriman flew back across the Atlantic, he gazed down at the sea below. Were the months of secret talks a fool's errand? Or the groundwork for a diplomatic breakthrough to silence the guns? He prayed Johnson would seize this crisis to push through to peace before more lives were lost. The time for half-measures had passed.

June 1968 – White House, Washington D.C.

Harriman's footsteps echoed urgently along the White House halls. After weeks of grinding diplomatic wrangling, he had returned to deliver his blunt assessment directly to the president.

As Harriman was ushered into the oval office, Johnson sat hunched, the weight of the worsening war clearly bearing down. Harriman dispensed with niceties, "We cannot keep stalling, Mr. President. Hanoi will only bend so far without reciprocation."

"Damned Reds will give nothing!" Johnson fumed. "Just keep attacking while we show good faith."

Harriman pressed on. "Their offensive is desperate brinksmanship. But we must call it. Our hand now, or more lives wasted."

Johnson stood abruptly, pacing as he weighed his options. Harriman held his breath.

Finally, Johnson turned to him. "Help draft my speech. I will announce a full bombing halt. But by God, those North bastards better come to the table for real."

Relief broke across Harriman's face. "This is the bold step needed, Mr. President. It will bring Hanoi along."

Johnson waved his hand dismissively, suddenly looking very tired. "I hope you're right, Averell. Or else we stayed in that damned war for nothing."

Harriman chose his next words carefully. "If we want peace, we must risk it. This opens the door, but both sides must step through."

Johnson simply nodded before turning away, signaling the meeting was over. After years of struggle, they had reached the turning point. What came next Harriman prayed would be peace, not ruin.

July 1968 – Paris, France

Amid fireworks bursting over Paris for Bastille Day, Harriman awaited Mai's arrival with nervous anticipation. After Johnson's dramatic bombing halt, Harriman had sent word for urgent renewed talks.

Footsteps finally sounded outside the apartment door. Mai entered, his expression unreadable as always.

Harriman stood to meet him. "Thank you for coming promptly. President Johnson has taken a bold step. Will your leaders be ready to talk seriously now?"

Mai carefully lit a cigarette before responding. "Hanoi welcomes the bombing halt after so many years. They are prepared to engage in substantive discussions."

Relief broke across Harriman's face. "At last! With both sides willing, we have a real chance for peace."

"There are still difficult matters to resolve," Mai cautioned.

Harriman waved his hand dismissively. "Of course, of course! But thanks to your reasonableness and our president's courage, we have turned the corner."

Mai allowed a trace of a smile. "Your upbeat American spirit will be needed in the challenging days ahead. But for now, let us celebrate this important step forward."

As the Bastille Day fireworks continued outside, both men raised a toast with American bourbon. Years of painstaking work had led to this pivotal breakthrough. Harriman could already glimpse the light of peace on the horizon.

August 1968 – Paris, France

A somber mood filled the negotiating room as Harriman and Mai resumed formal talks. Despite the bombing halt, immense obstacles remained. Disagreements over political solutions in South

Vietnam constantly threatened to derail the delicate process.

"Our allies in the South cannot accept a forced coalition with the NLF (Viet Cong)," Harriman insisted. "Free elections must be guaranteed."

Mai refused to yield. "The NLF cannot be barred from governing. Our compatriots have fought too long for their rights."

Back and forth they went, with distrust running high on both sides. Meanwhile, clashes continued in the countryside, raising tensions.

As talks dragged late one weary night, Harriman decided on candor. "If we cannot build trust, I fear no progress will be made. What can be done to move us forward?"

Mai considered this, taking a long drag on his cigarette. "I acknowledge the complexity for your policymakers. Perhaps smaller agreements first could improve the climate."

Harriman nodded, sensing an opening. "Solidifying details like troop withdrawals from the DMZ? Concrete steps to demonstrate good faith?"

"Just so," Mai agreed. "To cultivate further trust between our governments at the highest level."

Harriman smiled cautiously. "I believe that would be most welcome after the stalemate we've endured."

They shook hands firmly. Much hard bargaining lay ahead. But both men felt heartened that the path of negotiation, however difficult, was the one they continued to walk together.

January 1969 – Paris, France

Harriman gazed pensively at the Paris skyline, pipe

smoke wreathing his head. Below, protest chants echoed his own uncertain thoughts. A knock, and Mai entered. "Not an easy goodbye after our long road together."

"No, though we reached our destination in the end." Harriman searched for more words, but none sufficed.

Mai lit a cigarette, his sharp eyes studying Harriman's tired face. "You have doubts about handing over the torch?"

Harriman huffed wryly. "My trust in Lodge is limited at best. He can be tough that's for sure. And I suspect you have similar feelings about his counterpart."

"Xuan Thuy is...rigid in his convictions," Mai conceded diplomatically. "But the people want peace. The tide is flowing, regardless of who holds the helm."

Harriman nodded, unconvinced. "I pray you're right, my friend. That others may finish what we started."

Mai clasped his shoulder firmly. "What we started will not be easily undone. Take heart in that."

Outside, the protestors' chants swelled, underscoring the uncertainty ahead. But Harriman took comfort in Mai's stoic faith. Their work was done; the future would unfold as it may.

January 1969 – Paris, France

A new era dawned as formal peace negotiations began in Paris. With Nixon now President, Harriman was dismissed from diplomacy. In his place came Henry Cabot Lodge, a stern Yankee aristocratic.

The grand Hôtel Majestic's conference room had

been converted for the newly launched peace talks. Ornate murals and gilded trim belied the somber mood within. Grizzled diplomats in rumpled suits chain-smoked under glittering chandeliers that caught the winter sunlight streaming through tall windows.

Outside, protestors' distant chants echoed up the tree-lined Avenue Kléber. But inside, all was muted decorum as the adversaries prepared to parlay.

At the head of the long wooden table, Harriman shook hands with his successor, Lodge. The patrician New Englander towered stiffly in contrast to Harriman's rumpled weariness. "I inherit the considerable foundation you laid," Lodge acknowledged to Harriman. "But much work remains to secure a just and honorable peace."

"I agree. The path you follow remains challenging," Harriman said. "Commitment and patience above all. And never forget we negotiate to save lives, not score points."

Lodge smirked at the lecture from a man he considered his lesser, then nodded solemnly. "I appreciate your counsel. This is far too important for ego or politics."

Harriman wished his successors Godspeed and left, fading into retirement from diplomacy and a long deserved rest.

Across the table, Xuan Thuy led the North Vietnamese team, his tone militant. Still, he extended diplomatic courtesy to Lodge. "The beginning of wisdom is to call things by their true names. Let us speak frankly in our search for resolutions."

As the first formal sessions began, demonstrators chanted outside demanding immediate withdrawal. Inside, the veteran negotiators settled in for deliberate, arduous talks. The longest journeys unfolded step by step.

February 1969 - Paris

The mood was tense as formal peace talks resumed. Lodge slammed down a fist in frustration as Xuan Thuy refused to budge on political issues.

"Your stubbornness risks destroying all progress made!" Lodge fumed.

"And your arrogance may scuttle good faith bargaining," Xuan Thuy shot back.

Across the city...

As the acrimonious stalemate dragged on, Mai discreetly visited Harriman at his hotel. Over tea, they lamented the deteriorating climate.

"Lodge lacks your patience and persuasion," Mai remarked. "He attacks where you sought common ground."

Harriman sighed. "I fear both sides are digging in. Ego and mistrust poisoning the well."

"What wisdom can you impart to bring things back from the brink?" Mai asked.

Harriman considered this, then replied. "Remind Lodge and Xuan Thuy that ending senseless death must transcend politics."

Mai nodded thoughtfully. "I will reflect deeply on what you have said. Men of peace must unite against men of war."

They parted with a hearty handshake, renewed purpose kindling in their eyes. Harriman's work here was done, but his hard-won wisdom would continue guiding others down the challenging road ahead. The fate of peace lay in determined hands.

February 1969 – Paris, France

Gilt-edged shadows crept across the negotiating room in the Hôtel Majestic as tempers flared. "Our concessions are met only with greater demands!" Lodge's fist slammed the lacquered table, startling the aides lining the walls. "Where is the reciprocity?"

American delegates shifted uncomfortably, exchanging worried glances.

Across the table, Xuan Thuy's eyes narrowed as his Vietnamese team sat motionless behind him. "Reciprocity? While your military continues aggression across our homeland?"

Lodge sprang from his chair, pacing as a flush rose on his neck. "How can we build trust when your puppet NLF breaches every agreement?"

"Do not speak to me of trust and breaches." Xuan Thuy's voice was ice. His deputies silently nodded their approval. "Over 200,000 of our people slaughtered by your bombs, and yet we come to this table."

The room rang with indignant silence. American and Vietnamese aides alike sat frozen, pens suspended over notebooks. All eyes followed Xuan Thuy as he leaned forward, his gaze unblinking. "Your new president claims honor. But hollow public words will not write peace. Only actions."

Lodge slowly retook his seat, jaw clenched, his team exchanging uneasy looks behind him. Outside, protest chants swelled, then faded like the tide. Neither lead negotiator spoke. The ruined landscape of war lay between them. How could they hope to bridge it with just words?

The negotiating gulf had never seemed wider. Surrounded by their uneasy delegations, Lodge and Xuan Thuy sat frozen at the crossroads, uncertain of the next step.

March 1969 - Paris

As spring bloomed outside the Majestic, a chill remained inside the negotiating room. Lodge and Xuan Thuy continued to trade barbs and accusations rather than concrete proposals.

Lodge sat gripping his pen, knuckles white as he glared across the table. "Your forces continue offensive operations! Our offers of de-escalation are met with more bloodshed."

His team shifted in agitation behind him. Xuan Thuy met Lodge's fiery gaze, unmoved. "These so-called offers seem empty when your puppet regime enlarges by force."

Murmurs of dissent rustled through the North Vietnamese delegation. Xuan Thuy raised a hand for silence before continuing. "Meaningless rhetoric while people suffer and die. These are not the words of peace."

Lodge's face reddened as he started to retort, but an aide whispered urgently in his ear. After a tense beat, Lodge leaned back, tone icier than before. "I see no purpose continuing today if your side remains deaf to reason."

"Nor I, given your detachment from reality." Xuan Thuy signaled his team to gather papers and depart. As they filed out, Xuan Thuy turned for a parting shot. "When words align with deeds, then we will have reason to meet again."

The Americans sat in angry silence as the door closed behind the North Vietnamese and Viet Cong diplomats. Bright spring light mocked the darkening mood within. How could both sides keep talking past each other, as if no lives hung in the balance?

April 1969 – Paris, France

Gloomy skies mirrored the downcast atmosphere as talks resumed at the Majestic. Lodge came prepared with a new proposal - US withdrawal from isolated rural outposts in exchange for North Vietnamese pulling back from urban areas.

Xuan Thuy studied the map delineating zones silently. His deputies conversed in hushed tones behind him. Finally, he spoke, "Your offer has some merit." Murmurs rippled through both delegations at this concession. "But adequate verification methods must be established."

Lodge maintained a poker face, but a glimmer of optimism showed in his eyes. "Naturally. Neutral observers could be approved."

"Observers alone are inadequate." Xuan Thuy tapped the map. "Joint military commissions with free access are required."

Lodge hesitated, considering. His staff radiated anxiety. Then he nodded. "If combined with partial ceasefire commitments in those zones, joint commissions could be arranged."

Xuan Thuy leaned back, lighting a cigarette as he weighed Lodge's words. "This requires further analysis. But it represents the beginning of substantive dialogue."

Relief settled around the room like an easing of pressure before a storm. Lodge slid a fresh document across the table. "My team has drafted preliminary terms for discussion."

Xuan Thuy glanced over them, face still impassive. But the ice had cracked, letting in slivers of light. "We will study your proposal thoroughly."

He rose to leave, his deputies donning coats to follow. The first concrete steps had been taken, fragile yet full of possibility. The long road ahead appeared less shrouded for now.

May 1969 – Pari, France

Honeysuckle scented the air as Lodge once again arrived at the Majestic, pausing to take a deep breath before entering the fray. How he wished these days of contending with Xuan Thuy could conclude with a simple walk in the park, away from the clamor of war. But duty kept their paths confined to this gilded chamber.

Xuan Thuy's mask of stern resolve could not conceal the fatigue haunting his eyes. The burden of carrying his people's defiant hope through endless, uncertain talks weighed on his aging shoulders. But he would not be bowed by the imperialist puppet masters. Justice must prevail.

As expected, tensions rapidly resurfaced. "Your so-called 'neutral' observers have clearly sided with the puppet regime!" Xuan Thuy pointed a bony finger, mustering a show of strident fervor.

Lodge bit back his instinctive acid rebuke. A loving letter from his wife back home in his suit jacket rested over his heart, reminding him of his better angels.

"False accusations only undermine trust..." he began steadily.

Even in locked horns, glimpse of the human behind the hostile facade could be found. Stubborn conviction from one side calling forth patience from the other; a weary statesman raging against a diplomat clinging to hope - their fates were bound, even at impasse.

June 1969 – Paris, France

Humidity hung heavy as thunder rumbled outside the Majestic. Inside, Lodge loosened his tie, sweat beading as tensions escalated.

"Your so-called 'relocations' are merely euphemisms for continued aggression!" Xuan Thuy's fist hammered the table, rattling forgotten teacups.

Lodge sprang up, the old oak chair screeching against marble floors. "How dare you! We are extracting troops from conflict areas in good faith!"

"Good faith?" Xuan Thuy barked a caustic laugh. "When your CIA lackeys continue black operations against civilian targets?"

Aides muttered darkly as the two statesmen faced off. Lodge trembled with restraint, the streets of his beloved Boston seeming a universe away.

Lightning flashed outside stately windows, casting the ornate room into sudden relief - oil paintings of regal French statesmen looking on in stern reproach from their gilt frames. *How foolish men's endless wars must seem to those lofty ghosts*, Lodge mused.

The storm's ferocity seemed to shake loose their own rage. As rain lashed the pavement below, their tone turned less heated, more weary resignation.

"This achieves nothing." Lodge extended an olive

branch. "Shall we adjourn for today and return when skies and tempers clear?"

Xuan Thuy paused, then gave a single nod. "That may be best."

They parted solemnly, the storm receding to a gentle patter. There was time yet to find common ground before hatred and fear consumed them entirely.

July 1969 – Paris, France

Soft dusk light filtered into the Majestic's negotiating room as Xuan Thuy chain-smoked in brooding silence. He barely glanced up as Lodge entered and said, "I understand your frustration, but surely some small steps can be taken? Confidence-building measures, even minor ones, could restart momentum."

Lodge's appeals to reason dropped into the yawning gulf between them. Xuan Thuy simply shook his head.

Shadows deepened in the room's corners, the two statesmen avoiding each other's gaze. Then Xuan Thuy gestured to the window. "Men walked the moon this week, and we cannot walk ten feet to agreement. What madness is this?"

Lodge followed his gaze up to the emerging stars, so remote and unaware of humanity's struggles below. He let out a weary chuckle. "You're right, of course. We quarrel over inches of soil while reaching for the heavens."

Xuan Thuy's perpetual frown relaxed briefly. "Our leaders forget the vast universe we inhabit together."

Twilight deepened into velvety night. Somewhere out there, courageous men charted undiscovered realms. Perhaps the negotiators could yet follow their audacious lead - take one giant leap away from the past toward a future beyond war.

This stormy planet was but a pale blue dot in the cosmic dark. Even bitter enemies could walk in peace if they realized how small their differences were.

August 1969 – Paris, France

Rain pattered softly against the Majestic's windows as Xuan Thuy entered. But no prickly retorts awaited him today. Instead, a beaming Henry Cabot Lodge extended his hand in greeting.

"What's this?" Xuan Thuy said, hesitating. "You look as pleased as the cat who caught the canary."

"Can't two negotiators simply shake hands?" Lodge replied. When Xuan Thuy tentatively shook, Lodge grinned wider. "Excellent! For today marks a promising development."

He slid a document across the table. As Xuan Thuy scanned it, his perpetual scowl relaxed into surprise. "A proposed timetable for phased troop withdrawal? This is unexpected."

"But hopefully welcome," Lodge said. "A chance to turn our gaze from the past toward the future. Both our nations want this war to end. Too many of our young men have died."

Xuan Thuy considered carefully, as if glimpsing a door long sealed now cracked open. "This merits close analysis, but your government's change in tone is...not unwelcome."

Lodge pressed the opening. "Who knows what may flow from the right gesture at the right time?"

Outside, the rain had stopped, leaving behind glistening boulevards full of possibility. The mood in the negotiating room turned lighter as well. Perhaps their moment had come.

Crimson leaves swirled outside the Majestic as the negotiators resumed sessions. Cautious optimism tinged the atmosphere for once rather than acrimony.

Lodge extended an offering of French pastries, a genteel gesture suggesting new rapport. Xuan Thuy scrutinized him shrewdly, then selected a croissant.

"Your withdrawal timetable requires adjustment, but not rejection." Concessions flowed easier with sweets on the table.

"Adjustment is reasonable. What terms could make it more equitable?" The give and take of diplomacy filled Lodge with energy.

As they hashed through details, even thorny issues seemed surmountable. Until Xuan Thuy paused, brow darkened once more. "But meaningful peace requires addressing your regime's political oppression."

Lodge's cheerful mood wavered. "You know my government cannot dictate internal affairs..."

Xuan Thuy rose abruptly to leave. "Then these talks are mere theater." He turned at the door with a piercing look. "Courage to change course is required from you as well."

Lodge sat in sober silence as the door closed. Xuan Thuy was right - peace demanded they untangle the full web of complicity, not just military matters. Could Lodge persuade Washington to loosen its grip on South Vietnam? The answer might determine success or failure.

Across Paris

Rain pattered on the tin roof of a nondescript house in

the Paris suburb of Choisy-le-Roi. Inside, a new channel opened between implacable foes.

Henry Kissinger waited anxiously in the bare living room, surprised when a short, slender man in a drab suit entered. Le Duc Tho shook Kissinger's hand firmly, neither betraying emotion.

"Paris is lovely this time of year, though I wish the skies were clearer," Kissinger ventured. Le Duc Tho nodded politely if vacantly.

Kissinger had convinced Nixon the public stalemate in Paris required covert diplomacy. But gauging this inscrutable veteran communist would be challenging.

"Shall we begin substantively?" Kissinger probed. "Your Mr. Mai and I have already established some background."

"Background is air without foundation. Let us discuss concrete matters." Le Duc Tho's voice was smooth but unyielding as granite.

Kissinger sweated under his diplomatic facade. "Naturally. We have proposals for mutual troop reductions we can review as a starting point."

Le Duc Tho waved his hand dismissively. "First we must address core political questions. The character of the Saigon regime. A coalition government. Free elections."

Kissinger shifted in his seat. "Those remain sensitive areas. But de-escalation creates conditions for broader solutions."

"Our peoples need political resolution, not lingering conflict." Le Duc Tho's eyes bored into him.

As talks stretched fruitlessly, Kissinger cursed himself. How could he sway this uncompromising ideologue? The rain strengthened, underscoring his

313

frustration.

Finally, Le Duc Tho stood, polite yet unyielding. "When you are ready for serious discussion, not hollow maneuvering, we will meet again."

He departed, leaving Kissinger alone with the drumming rain. The chance for progress had slipped from his grasp this time. But he vowed to bring more substance next time. There must be a way to inch Hanoi toward peace.

September 1969 – Paris, France

Kissinger waited anxiously in the safehouse, rehearsing his arguments. This channel must not fail like Lodge's public deadlock.

Le Duc Tho entered briskly. "You requested urgency. What substantial offer brings me here?"

Kissinger spoke carefully. "We propose mutual withdrawal from the DMZ by year's end. This localized de-escalation could lead to..."

Le Duc Tho cut him off. "Partial steps skirt core issues. Our peoples need total ceasefire, yet you fear upsetting your puppets with real peace."

Kissinger blinked, keeping his tone measured as doubts crept in. "Realities in the South are complex. We cannot dictate their political future, but seek to end the conflict between North and South."

Le Duc Tho leaned forward. "Peace depends on South Vietnam's people determining their own destiny, free of outside control."

Kissinger hesitated. Had he misjudged how far he could sway Nixon's policy?

Hotel Majestic

Lodge smiled blandly across the negotiating table, hiding his unease. Xuan Thuy was suspiciously quiet lately. What new ploy was he planning?

"We hoped for counterproposals to our DMZ withdrawal concept," Lodge probed gently. Silence followed.

Xuan Thuy finally spoke. "Mr. Kissinger suggested your plan. But we only engage in serious negotiation. When you have real authority, we will respond."

Lodge paled internally. Kissinger's backchannel was undermining his credibility. How could he regain momentum?

Xuan Thuy rose to leave abruptly. "When your left hand knows what your right is doing, we can talk again."

Lodge pushed down his anger. Kissinger's meddling had only made peace more remote by exposing their internal divisions. He cursed the arrogance that gripped Washington, trampling real diplomacy.

Across Paris

Kissinger rubbed his temples wearily after another barren meeting with Le Duc Tho. He had failed to sway Nixon toward the flexibility Hanoi demanded. Nor could he reveal the limits of his power, or all leverage would be lost. He was tied on both ends, pulling vainly to inch the knot of war loose. But each side kept yanking back.

November 1969 – Paris, France

Kissinger waited, glaring at his watch as he paced. Le

315

Duc Tho was now fifteen minutes late, a grave insult.

When he finally entered, Kissinger erupted. "Your disrespect for my time is unacceptable! I am making every effort here in good faith while you obstruct progress."

Le Duc Tho did not react to the outburst. "And was it respectful to escalate bombings as we tried negotiating? Your 'good faith' is saturated in blood."

"How dare you!" Kissinger fumed. "I will not be lectured when your troops continue attacking as we offer ceasefires!"

"Enough." Le Duc Tho headed for the exit. "Contact me again when you are ready for serious talks, not narcissistic theatrics."

"Please, we were making real headway earlier." Kissinger scrambled to contain the damage. "Surely we can find some common ground?"

Le Duc Tho paused, then spoke coldly. "My side is done with 'common ground' that is always on your terms. Offer real concessions or we shall cease these futile talks."

He left without another word. Kissinger collapsed into his chair, cursing himself. Months of delicate backchannel work teetered toward collapse thanks to his temper and pride. He had to regain Hanoi's faith quickly or Nixon would shut this fragile door for good. Time was bleeding away.

Hotel Majestic

At the Majestic, Xuan Thuy was fuming as Lodge urged calm. "Dr. Kissinger is not authorized to negotiate on my government's behalf. Please let us continue our substantive work here."

Xuan Thuy was unmoved. "Your side plays games while bodies pile up. When you have one voice and one will for peace, we will talk again."

He stormed out as Lodge protested in vain. Watching the door slam shut, Lodge felt only contempt for Kissinger. His arrogance had poisoned Hanoi against any talks. Now Lodge's efforts lay in ruin, and Kissinger lacked the dignity to even inform him. Peace had never seemed more distant.

December 1969 – Paris, France

Kissinger waited anxiously in the safehouse, his relationship with Le Duc Tho teetering after last month's blowup. His pacing stopped when Le Duc Tho entered silently.

Kissinger spoke solemnly. "Thank you for coming. I know trust has been damaged, but we cannot afford to lose what we've built so far. Please, let us move forward in good faith."

Le Duc Tho considered him coolly. "Moving forward requires demonstrating respect, not platitudes. Your actions must reflect your words."

Kissinger swallowed his pride. "You're absolutely right. I let frustration undermine my diplomatic restraint. It will not happen again. I still believe we can make real progress if both sides stay committed to ending this conflict."

Le Duc Tho finally sat. "More belief than progress so far. But the goal remains worth pursuing, through proper channels."

Heartened, Kissinger slid over a document. "Then let's start rebuilding. I have new proposals on political representation in the South..."

They spoke urgently but respectfully late into the night. Common ground remained elusive, but the tone had been reset. As they parted, Kissinger felt hopeful once more. With patience against impossible odds, diplomacy could still weave peace.

Hotel Majestic

At the Majestic, Xuan Thuy remained withdrawn, responding to Lodge's ideas tepidly.

Sensing Xuan Thuy's lingering distrust, Lodge spoke earnestly. "I know backchannels created tensions. But I believe in the progress we can still make here and now, without preconditions. Please reconsider."

Xuan Thuy took a long sip of tea before responding. "Your side remains too tangled for real negotiation. But I will relay your sentiment to those who can affect policy."

Lodge nodded gratefully. "That's all I ask. Keep faith in our process moving forward."

After Xuan Thuy left, Lodge felt hopeful for the first time in months. Whatever Kissinger was maneuvering separately, Lodge could still steer their ship steadily toward peace. He would cling to that purpose against storms ahead. The chance still remained if they kept their compass true.

February 1970 – Paris, France

Kissinger waited anxiously in the safehouse, their last meeting ending bitterly without even a date set for this one. Le Duc Tho finally entered, wordlessly.

Kissinger spoke solemnly. "We cannot continue

missing opportunities for progress. I ask you plainly - do you believe our talks still have value?"

Le Duc Tho considered him gravely before responding. "These conversations once held promise. But no longer. Your side seems unable to offer real change, only repetition."

Kissinger's heart sank, but he nodded in acceptance. "I'm disappointed, but I understand your position. And I appreciate your candor."

Le Duc Tho extended his hand politely. "I wish you luck with your formal delegation. We prefer to deal directly with their authority for any future talks."

Shaking his hand somberly, Kissinger knew this risky backchannel had collapsed for good. Hanoi had lost faith in his ability to sway Nixon. Now the chance for a negotiated peace would live or die at the main table alone.

"Farewell then. I hope our larger discussions can still bear fruit." Kissinger saw Le Duc Tho out with a heart weighed by failure. This path to peace was closed. But pray God another one remained open.

Hotel Majestic

At the Majestic, Xuan Thuy arrived unexpectedly, catching Lodge off guard. "My superiors feel the moment is right for more substantive negotiation. Shall we begin?"

Lodge could hardly contain his surprise. "That's...welcome news! I have several new proposals we could discuss."

Xuan Thuy raised a hand. "First, a point of clarification - we will engage only through your formal delegation directly, not through other channels.

Agreed?"

Relief swept over Lodge. "Completely agreed. Our sole focus will be the progress we can make in this room."

Xuan Thuy gave a rare hint of a smile. "Good. Then I believe we are ready for serious dialogue."

As they dove into brisk talks, Lodge felt immensely gratified. At last, this could be the long-awaited turning point. Kissinger's hubris had met its reckoning. Now real diplomats could steer a true course to peace.

May 1971 – Paris, France

A torrential downpour drowned out the usual city bustle as Lodge and Xuan Thuy sat negotiating. The past year of intense discussions had inched them closer, but mistrust lingered.

"Our concessions cannot be one-sided," Lodge argued firmly. "Reciprocal restraint by your forces is essential."

Xuan Thuy bristled, the familiar impasse looming again until thunder cracked loudly outside.

In the ringing silence, Xuan Thuy seemed to reconsider. "Perhaps...some simultaneous steps could be taken. Confidence must start small to grow."

Lodge sensed the ice cracking and went all in. "What if both sides pulled back from the DMZ as a start?"

"And ceased activities in Laos?" Xuan Thuy added. "To alleviate tensions?"

Lodge could scarcely believe they were finding common ground after so long. "That would be more than agreeable. We could formalize terms."

Xuan Thuy allowed himself a rare smile. "It seems

we have a foundation to build trust upon."

They shook hands firmly as thunder rumbled again. Finally, after years of deadlock, both sides were ready for reciprocity. Inch by painful inch, they had crept toward understanding. Much disputed territory lay ahead. But today, a real milestone. The skies were still dour, but Lodge felt a ray of hope peeking through the clouds. If they kept moving together, step-by-step, they just might outlast this storm.

October 1972 – Paris, France

A crisp autumn breeze swirled leaves around the Majestic as Lodge and Xuan Thuy prepared to meet. An air of optimism had grown since their breakthrough last year. But final obstacles remained.

When they sat, Xuan Thuy spoke first. "Your gestures to remove troops are promising. Let us consolidate with a definitive timeline for complete withdrawal."

Lodge nodded. "We are prepared to finalize withdrawal details. But political power-sharing remains complex."

"Our allies must have an equal voice in any unity government." Xuan Thuy's tone allowed no give.

As debate resumed, an aide suddenly rushed in and handed Lodge an urgent cable. His eyes went wide as he read it. "I have unexpected news. President Nixon has authorized full concession on a coalition government."

Xuan Thuy looked stunned. "He agrees to power-sharing with the FLN?"

"Yes, with implementation details to be negotiated." Lodge extended his hand. "Can we finally bridge this last gap?"

Slowly, Xuan Thuy shook his hand. "I believe so. Our most difficult obstacle is cleared."

They embraced firmly, feeling history's tide turn. After seemingly endless dark days, the first ray of peace emerged. Together, they had persevered.

Much work remained to cement the ideals into reality. But this was the moment that made it feel achievable. The storm had broken. Light could shine through at last.

January 27, 1973 – Hotel Majestic - Paris, France

A new year's optimism warmed the negotiating room as Xuan Thuy and Lodge prepared to finalize the accords. But the road here had been long and arduous.

Years of agonizing efforts had slowly softened their hardened stances. Troop withdrawals, ceasefires, and power-sharing had all been painstakingly negotiated.

Now, as aides distributed documents, Xuan Thuy halted them. "One matter remains unaddressed - support for reconstructing our devastated nation."

Lodge's shoulders slumped as this final roadblock emerged. "Reparations will face immense opposition in the U.S. What terms does Hanoi seek?"

"Not reparations." Xuan Thuy held up a hand. "Worldwide appeals show solidarity. We ask only endorsement of reconstruction aid, not direct payment."

Considering this, Lodge felt the knot in his chest release. "Endorsing international assistance efforts is far more viable. I believe we can accommodate that request."

Xuan Thuy smiled and extended his hand. "Then

we have an agreement."

At noon, with winter sun streaming through tall windows, the diplomats solemnly signed the accords with a heady mix of accomplishment and relief. Photos captured the historic handshake - once implacable foes now joined in promise of peace. Applause erupted in the room and cheers echoed from crowds below.

"We have moved mountains together to arrive at this moment," Xuan Thuy remarked poignantly.

Lodge nodded. "For all the hard roads ahead, may we continue walking the path of healing."

The Vietnam War for America was finally ending after so many bitter years of loss. The future waited to unfold in peace.

The Corsicans

Conein tossed back another glass of scotch, barely feeling the burn as the amber liquid slid down his throat. The smoky haze and clatter of the underground casino swirled around him, blurred at the edges by alcohol. He glanced at his dwindling pile of plaques and dragged a hand down his face.

The casino was tucked away in the basement of a nondescript building in Cholon, run by Franchini and the Corsican mob. But once inside, it opened into a surprisingly posh space with chandeliers, red velvet upholstery, and marble floors. The low-ceilinged room filled with cigarette smoke despite efforts to whisk it away through vents. Raucous shouts came from gamblers crowded around baccarat tables and roulette wheels. Servers in crisp vests wove through the tables refreshing drinks and flirting with patrons to keep them betting.

Mattheu Franchini, the owner of the casino and head of the Corsican mob in Southeast Asia slid into the seat next to him, his usual charming grin replaced by a look of concern. "You're bleeding chips tonight, mon ami. Maybe it's time to call it."

Conein waved a hand dismissively, eyes still on the

spinning roulette wheel. "I'm good for it. Just need a change of luck."

"At this rate, your luck will change for the worse." Franchini gestured to the croupier for a refill on Conein's drink. "You've had a rough month. Let me cover your losses tonight."

Conein bristled at the offer of charity but bit back a retort. Franchini was only trying to help. And he wasn't wrong - between the lost revenue from the Laos opium operation and the constant hemorrhage at the tables, Conein was drowning in debt.

He took a brooding sip of the refreshed scotch. "What's your angle, Mattheu? You don't make offers like this out of the goodness of your heart."

Franchini spread his hands. "An investment. I hate to see a friend struggle." He lowered his voice. "And it just so happens I have a business proposition - one I think you'll find very interesting."

Conein turned to face him fully, "Go on."

"The customs tax on liquor importation is bleeding me dry. But with properly counterfeited tax stamps, I could import freely and sell at triple times the profit."

Franchini watched him closely. "You have connections at the Bureau of Taxation, yes?"

"Yes."

"Then you could purchase a sheet of uncut stamps that we could copy. I would supply the materials and split the profits with you thirty-seventy."

"I assume you would get the seventy."

"I am open to negotiation. But we both know where we will end up. Shall we say forty-sixty?"

"We shall say fifty-fifty, and I have not agreed yet."

"It is a good opportunity, Luc."

"I didn't say it wasn't. But as the printer I'd be

taking most of the risk."

"Yes, but we are talking about a lot of money."

Conein swirled the ice in his glass, temptation and doubt warring within him. Getting mixed up in one of Franchini's schemes was playing with fire. But the promise of easy money and wiping his debts clean was too attractive to ignore outright.

"Fifty-fifty, and I do all the work?"

"We have to put the stamps on the bottles."

Conein chuckled, "Well, then that seems fair. How do I know you won't bleed me dry like the taxman?"

Franchini clapped a hand on his shoulder. "Because we are friends, Luc. I would never cheat you." His eyes hardened slightly. "Or break your thumbs when you can't pay your gambling debts."

The implied threat hung in the air between them. Conein grimaced into his drink. Backed into a corner by his own reckless mistakes, he didn't have much choice.

He met Franchini's expectant gaze. "Alright, I'm in. But this stays between us, understand? No loose lips."

Franchini grinned broadly, "Of course, of course! Your name will never pass my lips." He stood, straightening his impeccable suit. "I'll have my people deliver the materials to your office by the end of the week. A pleasure doing business with you, mon ami."

With a wink, he disappeared into the crowd of gamblers. Conein stared after him, tension coiling in his gut.

A few moments later, a waiter brought over a large stack of plaques, set them in front of Conein, then said, "On the house from Mr. Franchini."

He had just shaken hands with the devil, but at least he was a generous devil.

Conein's Warehouse

A few days later, Conein was back in his office, bleary-eyed from another long night of gambling and drinking. On his desk were the counterfeit printing blocks he had carved by hand using a sheet of government stamps he had purchased from the tax bureau as the model. A sharp rap at the door made him flinch. "It's open," he called.

Two of Franchini's men entered carrying a large crate between them. They deposited it on his desk with a heavy thud. "Compliments of Mr. Franchini," one said in a gravelly voice.

Conein waved them away and cracked open the crate. Inside was a printing press, typesetting blocks, sheets of stamp paper, and inks. Nestled in packing straw were two bottles of fine French cognac.

He let out a low whistle. Franchini wasn't messing around - this was serious equipment. For a moment, doubt crept in again. He was in dangerous territory that would be hard to explain if discovered.

Then he remembered his debts, both financial and moral. He owed Franchini for getting him out of trouble before. And he needed to regain his financial footing after the Laos losses. The government of South Vietnam took taxation serious and punished offenders with hard labor. This venture was high risk, high reward.

Mind made up, he lifted out the printing supplies and got to work experimenting with the right formula of inks and paper. After a long day tinkering with ratios, he held up a sheet of finished stamps and compared it to the sheet of stamps he had purchased.

The counterfeit stamps were flawless, indistinguishable from government-issue.

Over the next few days, Conein worked diligently preparing the counterfeit tax stamps. After printing the sheets, he used a large blade on a paper cutting board to slice them into individual stamps. It was tedious work, but necessary to mimic the real thing.

It wasn't his first time producing forged documents - during WWII he had partnered with Franchini and the Corsicans printing fake German Reichsmarks to fund Allied intelligence operations. Danger was familiar territory for him.

Finally, rows of stamped sheets were stacked and ready for use. Conein leaned back, stretching his cramped muscles. He had just committed a major crime that would land him in prison for a long time if discovered. But the promised profits made the risk worthwhile.

Now he just had to deliver the stamped sheets to Franchini without being caught. Conein glanced at his watch - just past midnight. The quiet streets would provide cover for the late-night transfer.

He bundled up the sheets and loaded them into a briefcase. After one last visual inspection to ensure quality, he snapped the case shut. Time to meet his partner in crime and see this deal through.

Conein stepped out into the humid night, briefcase in hand. He had decided to go on foot to avoid police roadblocks that were frequent in the capital at night. The air was heavy and still, signaling an incoming storm. He hoped to make the delivery before the skies opened up. Gripping the briefcase tighter, he set off through the dark alleys towards Franchini's warehouse on the docks.

He stuck to the shadows, ducking into doorways whenever headlights approached. The contents of the case were damning evidence if discovered by the wrong person. After fifteen tense minutes, he arrived at the meeting point.

Franchini emerged from the warehouse flanked by two armed guards. He greeted Conein with a broad grin. "Luc, mon ami! Do you have the merchandise?"

Conein held up the briefcase. "Right here. Your 5,000 stamps, perfectly printed."

"Magnifique!" said Franchini. "Come inside where we will have more privacy."

Inside the warehouse, Franchini took the case, popping it open to inspect the contents. He nodded in satisfaction. "Impeccable work. We will begin distribution immediately."

"I want my profits applied to my debt until it is paid off, but I could use a small advance to tide me over," said Conein.

"Of course," said Franchini holding up his hand and using his fingers to suggest the thickness of bills Conein requested.

Conein raised his chin suggest more. Franchini doubled the size of the bills. Conein nodded acceptance. Franchini moved to the safe behind his desk. Spinning the dial, he opened the safe and removed two thick stacks of money. Closing the safe and spinning the dial, he handed the money to Conein.

"Thanks, Mattheu. I appreciate it," said Conein.

"Do not mention it, Luc. This is just the beginning," Franchini said, clapping him on the back. "With your skills and my distribution network, we will make a fortune!"

Conein pocketed the cash with a tight smile. Easy money, just as promised. But an uneasy feeling still lingered in his gut.

Over the next few weeks, business boomed. Conein's warehouse produced stamp after stamp, siphoning hundreds of thousands in tax revenue from the government's coffers. Franchini's liquor flowed freely through Saigon's bars and nightclubs, generating huge profits and capturing more of the market.

Across Saigon...

At the Tax Bureau headquarters, Director Trang sat across from Head Inspector Phuc. "This counterfeit stamp operation has cost us nearly one million in lost liquor tax revenue so far," Trang said. "We need to put a stop to it immediately."

Phuc nodded. "My revenue enforcement team suspects organized crime. Perhaps the Corsicans or Triad."

Trang stroked his chin thoughtfully. "A possibility, but we have no solid evidence. And both the Corsicans and the Triad have friends in high places that will protect them."

"Then we get the evidence we need," Phuc said. "Audit known smuggling fronts, monitor warehouse cargo transfers—"

Trang held up a hand. "Carefully, Inspector. Heavy-handed tactics could tip them off."

He sat back, pondering their options. "Let us deploy undercover agents to infiltrate the supply chain. They can trace the contraband back to its source without raising suspicion."

Phuc considered this, then nodded slowly. "Yes, subtlety is key here. I will have my best agents embed themselves discreetly."

"Good. It is a finesse job, not a brute force one," Trang said. "Whoever is responsible has grown arrogant. Time we remind them no one is above the law."

Both men rose, newly energized by having a plan in place. The counterfeiting ring's days were numbered.

Associate Press Bureau

Karen sat across from Quigley, the AP's bureau chief, as he skimmed her story proposal, face impossible to read.

After an agonizing silence, he set down the page and took off his glasses. "Karen, going after Franchini and the Corsicans is playing with fire."

Karen leaned forward. "I know it's risky, but the Corsican mob lost one of its biggest revenue streams when the Montagnard were overrun by the Pathet Laos. They lost all their poppy fields in Laos. It ground their drug smuggling business to a halt. Now they're scrambling for new revenue... illegal revenue. They're exposed. Their guard is down. If there was ever a time to publish a story on the Corsican mob in Southeast Asia, this is it."

"I don't think the mob's guard is ever down, Karen. But I get your point. They are scrambling."

"We have an opportunity, Quigley. We need to strike now."

"Strike now? You've been spending to much time with the Marines. If you do this, you're going to be on your own. I'm not going to assign a journalist to this story until we have enough evidence."

"I agree. I work better alone anyway. I'll bring the evidence."

"One misstep, you pull out," he said firmly. "Corsicans play rough."

"You have my word on it. I don't have a death wish, but this is a story that needs to be told."

"I agree. Go get 'em, Karen."

She left the office, adrenaline and unease mixing within her. But she had her chance, and she wasn't about to waste it.

Across Saigon…

Karen sat at an outdoor coffee shop down the block from Franchini's warehouse, camera ready, covered with a newspaper. Her motorbike was parked on the street in front of her. After two hours of monotonous stake-outing, two sleek black cars pulled up in front of the warehouse.

She grabbed her camera and racked focus as Enzo, one of Franchini's enforcers, emerged from one car and from the other car none other than Lucien Conein. Karen snapped photos, mind racing as they entered the warehouse. What was Conein, a former CIA operative, doing with the mob?

An hour later, the men emerged from the warehouse. Karen turned away in her seat as the cars pulled away in opposite directions. This was her chance to get answers. She decided to follow Conein.

Keeping a safe distance, she tailed Conein's car through the busy streets of Saigon. He pulled into a warehouse district and parked at a building with no markings. Karen stopped her motorbike a block away and watched as Conein unlocked the building, two men in suits stepped out from their concealed positions. Conein was surprised to see them.

"Mr. Conein? Revenue Department," the agent flashed a badge. "We need to perform an inspection on these premises."

Conein paled slightly but kept his tone even. "Of course, gentlemen. I have nothing to hide."

He unlocked the warehouse and led them inside. Karen crept in behind them, staying hidden and snapping photos as the agents searched. They quickly discovered the printing press and stacks of counterfeit tax stamps. One of the agents held up a sheet of the counterfeit stamps. "I don't suppose you have a permit for printing these?"

Conein shifted nervously. "Of course, it's just, ah, filed away somewhere. Let me take a look. I'm sure I can find it."

He pretended to rummage through his office. The agents shared an impatient glance. Conein opened his safe and withdrew several stacks of money. He walked out of the office and approached the agents

"Perhaps we can forget about the permit for now," Conein said, returning with cash in hand. "As a donation to the Revenue Department's charity fund."

The agents exchanged a look, then shook their heads in unison. Conein added more bundle to the stack. Again, the agents refused. Conein placed the remaining money on his desk. It was more than they made in a month. Finally, with a subtle nod from his partner, the senior agent pocketed the money. "Your permit must have been misfiled. We'll confirm your paperwork is in order from the office." He shot Conein a hard look. "This establishment better be fully compliant on our next visit next week. Do you understand?"

"Of course. It's business."

"Exactly. And we would hate to shut yours down if you accidently came up short each and every week."

With that thinly veiled threat, the agents departed. Conein cursed them once they were out of earshot. He walked into his office and called the Corsican warehouse, "It's Conein. I need to talk to Mattheu. What do you mean not there? I just left him. Okay, fine. When he comes back tell him we have a problem and I need to talk with him right away."

Conein hung up and went back out into his warehouse. Karen peered out from her hiding place and saw Conein operating a printing press, pausing to inspect a sheet against something in his hand. She couldn't quite make out what he was printing.

When Conein stepped away to his office to answer a ringing phone, Karen seized the opportunity to move in closer. On the press she found a sheet of real liquor tax stamps that Conein was using as a guide. Then she spotted a stack of printed sheets - they were perfect counterfeit stamps.

Karen grabbed one sheet and folded it into her bag just as Conein's footsteps approached. She dove behind pallets, barely hidden from view as he returned.

Karen watched as Conein used a blade to cut the stacked sheets into individual stamps. He placed the stamps into a briefcase and left the warehouse.

As soon as he was gone, Karen slipped out. She tailed Conein's car from a distance. The damning counterfeit sheet felt like it was burning a hole in her bag. She needed to catch him delivering the stamps to Franchini.

Conein drove recklessly through Cholon's crowded streets until screeching to a stop outside Franchini's warehouse. Two guards blocked the entrance, arms crossed.

"I need to see Franchini. Now." Conein's tone left no room for argument.

One guard disappeared inside. A minute later he returned and beckoned Conein in.

Franchini was in his office, laughing over drinks with a businessman. His smile faded when he saw Conein's expression.

"What is wrong, my friend?"

"We need to talk. Privately." Conein's eyes flicked to the businessman.

Franchini grasped the situation immediately. He ushered his guest out while Conein closed the office door.

"Okay, Luc. You have my attention. What is the problem?" said Franchini.

"Two revenue agents showed up at my warehouse."

"I see. You paid them the appropriate bribe?"

"Of course."

"Then what is the problem?"

"They know about the counterfeiting. We need to shutdown. At least until things cool down. I don't want to spend the rest of my life behind bars."

"You know I wouldn't let that happen."

"Yes, but you don't control everything, Mattheu."

"Well, that's debatable, but I get your point."

"We've made good money, but we have to quit while we are ahead."

Franchini swirled his cognac. "This is a

complication, but not the end. We have come too far to quit now."

"If we keep going, it's only a matter of time before we're caught."

"Then we adapt," Franchini said. "Shift the operation, bribe any official who gets curious. There are always possibilities."

He could see Conein was still hesitant.

"This is unlike you, my friend. You never have shown fear."

"I know, I know. It's stupid. I'm getting older and I have a family I need to look after."

"Admirable. But fear is not for people like us."

"You're right. It's not. I just need to get my head screwed on straight."

Franchini refilled their glasses and leaned back conspiratorially.

"You've seen the profits, Luc. Why walk away now? We are so close to breaking into the American PX store system. Think of the fortunes from selling tax-free to US soldiers!"

The promise of even greater rewards softened Conein's stance. The PX stores represented an untapped goldmine. Still, the risks were climbing.

Franchini seemed to read his thoughts. "I understand your caution, mon ami. We will improve security - rotate warehouses, use new courier routes. And if anything goes wrong, my people will provide us a warning."

Conein swirled his cognac thoughtfully. The profits had been excellent so far. And with Franchini's connections, they could probably evade the authorities for a while longer. Why give up when the real payday was within reach?

He met Franchini's expectant gaze and raised his glass. "Alright. We change up locations and personnel. Nobody new. Only those we trust."

Franchini grinned and clinked their glasses together. "Now you are thinking like a true businessman! We will be more prudent. The PX stores will make today's profits look like peanuts."

Conein couldn't suppress a twinge of excitement at the prospect. He had come this far - why stop before a big score? They just needed to be cautious.

"You have more stamps for me?" said Franchini.

"It's not the full order, but your men can get started while I finished the rest of the printing," said Conein pulling the stamps from his briefcase.

Outside the office, Karen listened intently while snapping photos through a gap in the blinds. This was the proof she needed - Conein giving the forged stamps to Franchini.

Suddenly a strong hand clamped down on her shoulder. Karen spun around with a gasp to see one of Franchini's henchmen looming over her.

"Boss! We got a little rat out here," he shouted. Karen struggled uselessly as he dragged her into the office and threw her to the floor.

Conein was surprised to see her, "What are doing here, Karen?"

"My job. You weasel," said Karen.

"You know her, Luc?" said Franchini.

"She's Tom Coyle's daughter and a photojournalist for the Associated Press."

"Coyle, he flew for us, yes?"

"My father flew for you?" said Karen. "Doing what exactly?"

"None of your damned business," said Conein.

"And if you're smart, you'll keep your mouth shut."

"You have quite the death wish, no?" said Franchini to Karen.

"My editor knows that I am here. If I don't show up at the office, he'll send the police to look for me."

"The police do not worry me, little one," said Franchini. "Most are in my pocket. And those that aren't can easily be bought or disposed of."

Franchini turned to Conein, "I'm sorry, but we cannot let her live, Luc."

"I know, I know. But we need to think this through. Coyle is CIA. He can cause trouble, especially if we want to do business with the PXs."

"He's never going to find her. My men will see to that."

"We've got her. There's no rush, is there?"

"The police may come looking for her."

"Then we'll deal with them as you said. I just don't want to do anything stupid when we're this close to a pile of gold."

"You are wise, Luc. I suppose we have a few hours. That should be enough to consider all the possibilities," said Franchini before turning to his henchman. "Put her some place safe where she cannot cause any more trouble. And keep an eye on her."

Karen struggled as she was carried away. Conein's mind was racing. "You agree with me, yes?" said Franchini.

"Yes, of course. I just want to be cautious."

"Be cautious then. But be quick. The longer we wait, the more danger we both are in."

Karen was tied up and tossed in a storage room by the henchman. "Be a good girl and I'll make it quick when the time comes."

"Up yours, you overgrown slug," said Karen.

The henchman smiled, then gave her a fast punch in the face knocking her unconscious. "I warned you," he said as he left locking the door behind him. Outside the storage room, he grabbed a chair and sat across from the door, keeping guard.

Conein could hardly catch his breath. He knew what he had to do, but it was the last thing he wanted. Still, there were no good options. Franchini had Karen and he wasn't going to let her go. Any disobedience in the matter would be seen as betrayal and it was not realistic for anyone to betray the Corsicans and expect to live. There was no real choice... just death. "Are you alright, Luc?" said Franchini. "You look as white as a ghost."

"I'm fine. I just really need to pee."

"Then I suggest you do that."

"Right. I'll be back in a moment. By the way, just in case the cops show up with those revenue agents, how many men do you have here today?"

"I don't know twenty, maybe twenty-five."

"Twenty-five... that should be enough to hold off a small army."

"Probably, yes. Are you expecting an army?"

"No. I'm just overthinking things."

"You're starting to worry me, Luc. You really need to calm down or you'll have a heart attack."

Conein laughed, "I should be so lucky. Where's the toilet?"

Franchini pointed. Conein left.

Conein stood in the front of a mirror, staring, his face covered with water. "Are you really going to do this?"

he asked himself.

After a long moment, he answered the question, "Yeah, I guess you are."

He used the rotating drying towel in a metal box on the wall to dry his hands and face, then pulled out his pocketknife and cut the drying towel from its box. He wrapped the towel loosely several times around his left hand keeping his fingers spread wide. With his right hand, he pulled out the small caliber automatic pistol he kept in his ankle holster and chambered a round. He felt nauseous . It was like being caught in a nightmare and no matter what he did or said, he couldn't wake up. He tucked the pistol in his front pant pocket and left the toilet.

Instead of turning back to Franchini's office, Conein moved deeper into the warehouse. He stepped quietly glancing around corners, pushing himself to go further. Finally, he saw the henchman guarding the door to the storage room. He took a deep breath and approached. "Times up for the reporter," he said to the guard.

The guard nodded, not unhappy. He opened the door and started to enter. Conein held up his hand stopping him, "Nope, my friend. Franchini wants me to do it. Some kind of loyalty test."

"What happened to your hand?" said the henchman noticing the towel wrapped around his hand.

"Broke a glass. I really got cut back on my drinking."

The henchman grunted. Conein stepped in front of him and entered the storage room. "Where the hell is she?" said Conein.

The henchman panicked and rushed into the room to see Karen still unconscious on the floor. Conein stepped up beside him, placed his hand with the drying towel on the side of the henchman's face, then place the end of his pistol's barrel between his left thumb and index finder and pulled the trigger twice with his right hand. There two dull thumps as the pistol fired through the towel muffling the sound from the muzzle blast. Two .22 caliber bullets entered the henchman's temple. He went down like a sack of coal. He twitched several times on the ground, then finally stopped moving as blood pooled up around him. The towel around Conein's hand was on fire. He dropped the towel on the floor and stomped on it until the flames were extinguished. Conein moved the dead henchman's feet and shut the door. He moved to Karen and gently smacked her face until she came around.

"What are you doing here?" said Karen.

"Saving you, kiddo," said Conein.

Karen saw the henchman on the ground, motionless with a pool of blood. "Jesus," said Karen shocked.

"Don't mind him. He's harmless," said Conein as he moved to untie her.

"Why are you doing this?"

"Does it really matter?"

"Yeah, it matters."

"I suppose it's out of some weird kind of loyalty to your father. We're not friends. But we're not enemies either."

"You're his boss."

"Not anymore. When the Montagnard fell, his job was over."

"Smuggling opium?"

"You know, I could just leave you tied up here."

"No. I appreciate your help. I'll shut up."

"Good. And don't be so judgmental about your father. He's one of the good guys."

"And you?"

"Not so much… but I'm trying."

The last knot was loose. Karen was free. "Now what?"

"Now, you haul ass back to your little news office."

"What about my camera and film?"

"They are the price you pay for sticking your nose in other people's business."

"I'm not leaving without that film."

"Yeah, you are. If Franchini catches you, he gonna kill you."

"What about you?"

"Me? Don't worry about me. I always take care of myself."

Conein moved to the door and opened it slightly to peer out into the hall. Nobody had come to investigate the muffled shots. "Let's go."

Conein and Karen made their way out of the warehouse through a back door. They moved around the side of warehouse to the front where Conein's car was parked. Conein opened the trunk. Inside was a small arsenal. He pulled out a bandoleer of 40mm grenades and slipped it over his head and shoulder wearing it Poncho Villa style. He did the same for a bandoleer of 9mm magazines. He slipped on a web belt with extra pistol magazines and a holster holding a M1911 semi-automatic pistol. The pistol's magazines only held seven bullets, but whatever those seven bullets hit… stopped. Finally, he pulled out a Heckler & Koch MP5 sub machinegun and a Hawk MM1 multi-grenade launcher with twelve-round rotating drum. It was loaded. "You can't be serious?" said Karen watching him. "They'll kill you."

"They'll try."

"I didn't ask you to do this."

"It ain't about you, princess. When Franchini finds out I let you go, he's gonna put out a contract to have me killed. I'm gonna beat him to the punch."

"You're insane."

"Yeah… a little. I think it's time you left."

After a long moment, Karen started to walk away, then stopped and turned, "Thank you."

"You're welcome," said Conein as he raised the MM1. "Fire in the hole," said Conein with a grin.

Realizing what was about to happen, Karen took off running down the street toward her motorbike. Conein took aim with the MM1 and shot two grenades into the front doors of the warehouse offices. The wooden doors splintered in hundreds of wood shards from the explosions. The wood remaining on the hinges burned. "I bet that got their attention," said Conein.

Next, Conein shot the MMI like a pistol from the hip. He didn't need to aim. One entire side of the warehouse was covered with glass windows. Three grenades sailed across the parking lot and crashed through several windows. Two seconds later, the explosions shattered most of the windows sending a ball of flame and shards of glass toward Conein. He ducked down beside his car for cover. As the fire inside the warehouse quickly spread as bottles of liquor exploded adding to the fuel. He could hear men inside the warehouse, some screaming in pain, others barking out orders to put out the flames. He wasn't sure how many men were inside the warehouse trying to save the liquor and other contraband.

Two Corsican henchmen ran out of the office section through the shattered wooden doorway and opened fire at Conein with sub machineguns.

Conein set the MM1 on the hood of his car and fired three rounds without revealing himself. Conein's accuracy was impressive for firing blind. The explosions from the grenades showered the two Corsicans with shrapnel cutting them down.

As he rose to look for targets, a sniper on the warehouse rooftop took aim and fired. Conein was hit in the side. It spun him around and he fell. It took him a moment to regain his focus. He picked up the MM1 and launched two grenades toward the sniper in a poorly aimed barrage. Both grenades sailed over the sniper and landed on the opposite side of the warehouse with two loud explosions. The sniper took another shot as Conein hid behind his car. The bullet landed in the front fender just inches from his left ear. As the sniper chambered the next round Conein rose with the MM1 and took careful aim. The sniper also took aim. Conein rolled to one side as the sniper fired and missed. Conein took aim again and fired. The single grenade landed in front of the sniper. The explosion took his head off. His rifle slid down the roof and land with a clatter in the parking lot.

Conein checked the wound in his side. It wasn't good. Blood oozed out. At least it wasn't an artery or his liver. He ripped off one of the sleeves of his shirt and stuffed the cloth in the wound to slow the bleeding. It hurt like hell. Another ripped strip of clothes tied it in place. He had only killed three Corsicans and he was already badly wounded. Hardly a result worthy of his legendary reputation. Pitiful. He steeled himself for the next round as he reloaded the

MM1 with more grenades. The men he was about to kill were his friends. He had worked with many of them over the years. He blocked the thought from his mind. They would kill him if they got the chance, friendship or not. Loyalty to Franchini was rock solid within the brotherhood.

He rose from behind the cover of his car and moved toward the broken doorway. Nobody was in sight and that worried him. Maybe Matthau had been lying and there were only a few Corsicans working today. One could always hope.

He entered the office section of the warehouse and stared down the smoke-filled hallway. At the end of the hall was a barricade of turned over desks. They had built a fortress. Four Corsicans rose and fired their weapons down the hallway at Conein. He pivoted around the corner using the wall for cover. He placed the barrel of the MM1 on the edge of the corner wall and fired three more grenades. The fireball from the explosions reached all the way to Conein's position licking the walls with flame. The Corsican's guns fell silent.

Conein knew he had to reach Franchini if he was to have any hope of stopping his henchmen. He also knew that Franchini knew this and would be waiting. He swung around the corner ready to fire, but nobody was alive, and the fortress of desks was burning. Bodies lay on the floor. Conein supposed that the additional smoke was a good thing and kept him hidden as he moved through the building. He heard explosions in other parts of the buildings. He didn't know what they were about but was willing to accept whatever help he could get taking down the Corsicans. Deciding grenades in close quarters was not the best idea, he switched from the MM1 grenade launcher for the MP5 sub machinegun letting the MM1 hang by its strap on his shoulder. The heavy weapon hit him in the side where his wound was located. He winced in pain, then switched the launcher to the opposite shoulder as he moved cautiously down the hallway constantly checking his six.

Finally, he reached Franchini's office. He prepared himself for a gunfight and reached for the handle… then stopped. He considered what he would do in such a situation and reconsidered opening the door. He moved to a nearby janitor's closet and retrieved a mop. He again readied himself standing to one side of the doorway instead of directly in front of it. He used the mop to turn the door handle. The lock clicked open and nothing happened. He gave the door a shove with the mop. The door disappeared in a massive explosion of wood shards. Multiple Claymore mines had sent thousands of ball bearings through the doorway along with a ball of flame. Everything burned. He knew Franchini was not inside, but he checked the office anyway. Nothing.

He checked his wound again. He was leaking, but not badly. He moved back out into the hallway and moved toward the warehouse. If Franchini was still in the buildings there was little doubt that he had heard the explosions from his Claymore boobytrap. There was a good chance Franchini thought he was dead. That was to his advantage. The Corsicans would need all hands to put out the fire in the warehouse. He knew where they were, but they didn't know he was still alive. Conein figured there were probably thirteen to eighteen Corsicans left in the buildings if Franchini hadn't lied. That was a big if, but there was little he could do about it. Bad odds no matter how he looked at it.

He came to a stairwell leading to the mezzanine offices overlooking the warehouse. He started up the stairs. If the Corsicans attacked him while he was climbing the stairs there was little hope he would survive. There was no cover. He pulled out his M1911 pistol and chambered a round against his leg. Pointing the pistol downstairs and the MP5 upstairs he continued upward with his head swinging back and forth like a boy watching a pendulum.

When he finally reached the door, it was locked. He doubted that it was boobytrapped. He was about to fire a short burst from the MP5 into the door handle, then stopped. He didn't want to alert Franchini and the Corsicans that he was still alive. He pulled the Kbar from his web belt and pried the lock. The door swung open. He moved inside the first office. He saw the janitor and two female office workers hiding behind a desk. Their eyes were wide with fear. Conein put his finger to his lips motioning for them to be quiet, then waved toward the door. They nodded and left quickly.

Conein moved on to the check the remaining offices. They were empty. Through the windows overlooking the warehouse, Conein could see the Corsicans fighting the multiple fires. There was no sign of Franchini. At the end of the offices, he saw a metal catwalk leading to another set of stairs on the opposite side of the warehouse. He considered for a moment, then moved to a hinged window. He opened the window. He stuck the barrel of the MM1 grenade launcher out the window and fired the remaining nine grenades in rapid succession. Some of the grenades ricocheted off the ceiling beams landing randomly throughout the warehouse, while others bounced off the stacks of liquor boxes, then tumbled to the floor. The explosions followed one after another.

Conein was unsure if he actually hit any of the Corsicans, but he was sure he had created more mayhem in the burning warehouse. He dropped the MM1 and ran for the door to the catwalk.

He made his way across the catwalk passing each stack of liquor boxes with their accompanying alleyways for access. As he passed the alleyways, he fired the MP5 down at the Corsicans battling the fire. In less than a minute, he had killed or badly wounded eleven of the henchmen. The odds of his survival were still long, but getting better as each Corsican dropped. Still, no Franchini.

The fire in the warehouse was out of control. Smoke filled the ceiling and moved down to the catwalk. Hacking and coughing, Conein could barely breathe. He reached the metal stairs at the end of the catwalk and then heard... "Have you gone mad? Why are you doing this, Luc?" said Franchini behind him on the catwalk. Conein turned to face him. Neither raised their weapons toward the other.

"You were going to kill her. I couldn't let that happen," said Conein

"She's a goddamned journalist and she's gonna get you and I thrown in jail."

"Probably. I'm not saying it's the smartest move."

"You would choose her over me? I thought we were friends."

"We are friends, but we're also the bad guys. And I'm tired of being a bad guy."

"Bad guy. That's a myth. There is no good or bad. Life is not that simple."

"Yeah. I kinda wish it was."

"Each situation we face dictates our behavior, not morality."

"I flunked psychology in college."

"You should read more."

"I wish we didn't have to finish this."

"Walk away, Luc. I can forgive everything if you just walk away."

"We both know that's not gonna work."

"No matter what happens here, you know Corsicans never forget. You will never be able to rest no matter where you go. They will hunt you down."

"Yeah. I know the rules. What's done is done. Our conversation is over."

"As is our friendship. Goodbye, Luc."

"Goodbye, Mattheu."

They both raised their weapons at the same time and fired. Mattheu was stitched with bullets from the MP5 and fell dead on the catwalk. Conein was hit in the thigh from Mattheu's .38 pistol and fell backward down the metal stairs. Conein landed in a heap at the bottom of the stairs. His sub machinegun was halfway up the stairway and out of his reach. Both his legs were broken, a shattered femur stuck out of the side of his trousers. More blood.

Three Corsicans ran toward him, their pistols raised. They had watched Franchini die. Now it was his killer's turn. Conein pulled his .45 from its holster and fired. The Corsicans dove for cover. Two of the Corsicans returned fire at Conein, while the third moved down an aisle to circle around and flank him.

Conein pulled out a full magazine, then emptied the current magazine before reloading. He thought for a moment, then came up with an idea. Instead of firing at the two Corsicans, he fired at the stack of liquor boxes behind them. Bottles broke. Whiskey gushed out of the bottom of the boxes, pooling on the floor and surrounding the Corsicans. They realized what Conein had done, but it was too late. Conein fired two shots on the concrete next to them and the whiskey ignited from the sparks. Blue flames enveloped the two Corsicans setting their clothes on fire. They fell to the floor and rolled trying to put the flames out, but the floor was covered with burning whiskey and was soaked up by their clothes making things worse. They screamed as they burned.

The third Corsican ran down the aisle next to Conein firing his pistol. A bullet hit Conein in the neck barely missing an artery. More blood and pain. Conein took aim as best he could and fired until his pistol locked back empty. The Corsican was only hit once from the barrage of bullets, but the shot was true and hit him in the heart. He fell dead.

Conein pulled himself up against a stairway column and reloaded his M1911 with his last clip. He was operating on instinct, not thinking. As he waited, he thought about his family and wished he had saved more money rather than gambling and drinking away his profits. He thought about Franchini and the Corsicans, his friends and now his enemies. He thought about Granier and wished he had one last chance to put a bullet in him. He felt his head swirling. His eyes blurred. He fell on his side. He was dying from blood loss. No Corsicans came. He didn't know why. He doubted that he had killed them all, but maybe the fire had taken some. And maybe others had run off after Franchini died because there was nobody left to pay them. It didn't matter. He had killed enough and was resigned to his fate. He closed his eyes and hoped he died before the fire got him. He hated the idea of burning alive. Death was washing over him. He could feel it. He was grateful. In a moment, no more pain.

Then someone grabbed him by one of the bandoliers and pulled him across the floor backward. He grew angry. He assumed it was the Corsicans trying to keep him alive so they could torture him. Idiots. He'd be dead before they had their fun. "Get up, dammit!" said a woman.

A woman? Why the hell was woman dragging him? Then he stopped and he heard a thump. The woman had fallen next to him and said, "Conein, you've got to get up."

Conein looked over at the woman. It was Karen. "I can't. My legs are broken. Leave me. I'm dead anyway."

"Don't be a pussy."

Karen climbed to her feet and ran off. Conein was happy. Peace, finally. Then Karen returned with a unfolded box and laid the cardboard sheet next to Conein. "Roll you, bastard."

Conein obeyed and rolled onto the sheet of cardboard. Karen grabbed the front of the sheet and pulled. Conein slid much faster on the cardboard. "Where are your keys?" said Karen as they left the warehouse and entered the office area also burning fiercely. Something exploded, knocking Karen over. Flames increased. Conein reached in his pants pocket and handed her his keys. She struggled back to her feet and pulled Conein out the shattered front doors. Conein realized what was coming next – the stairs. "No. Wait…" Too late.

Karen didn't stop. She dragged Conein down three steps. Conein screamed in pain each time he landed on the next stair. More blood. She left him at the bottom of the steps and ran to his car. She started the engine and backed up almost running him over. Conein knew she wasn't going to stop until he was in the car. The thought made him cringe. He did what he could to pull himself into the backseat while she pushed and shoved his broken legs. Once inside, she slammed the door shut and jumped back in the driver's seat. She raced out of the parking lot and onto the street just as firetrucks were arriving. She drove like a maniac. "Stay awake," said Karen.

"Are you shitting me? I'm in so much pain sleeping is the last thing on my mind."

"Good. When and where were you born?"

"I'm not playing your fucking game."

"Do you want to live?"

Conein thought for a minute, then… "November 29, 1919. Paris, France."

"What were the names of your parents?"

"Lucien Xavier Conein and Estelle Elin."

"Where did you go to high school?"

Six minutes later, she skidded to a halt in front of a hospital. Nurses ran out to the car and placed Conein on to a gurney. More pain. More blood. "Morphine," he mumbled.

Karen watched as Conein disappeared inside the hospital. She had done what she could. Now, it was up to Conein and the doctors. She wondered if it all really mattered. The surviving Corsicans would surely hunt him down. That was a problem for another day. Right now, she wanted a hot shower and a stiff drink. Later, she'd go camera shopping.

Epilogue

In 1972, President Nixon declared his War on Drugs. After three very painful months in an American hospital, Conein was finally released. He knew the Corsicans would be waiting, but fortunately so was Nixon. He made Conein the head of covert operations in the newly formed Drug Enforcement Agency (DEA). Conein became one of the most protected and powerful men in the world. He made his first task to take down the Corsican mob in a little project called, "The French Connection."

Truth is often stranger than fiction... especially when dealing with Lucien Conein.

Letter to Reader

Dear Reader:

I hope you enjoyed *Spectre of War*. While there were many chapters that I was proud of writing, it was a book that left me a bit sad when I was finished. But then again, it's war, right? It should be sad. Anyway, I hope you liked it. The next novel in the Airmen Series is ***Twilight of War*** – Book 20. Here's a quick snapshot: As the last American ground troops leave Vietnam, the war continues to rage as if the peace accords meant nothing. Now, the CIA and offshore American airpower were South Vietnam's only allies between North Vietnam and annihilation. Granier, Coyle, Karen, and Scott remain along with thousands of American civilians. I can't tell you anything more or I will spoil it.

Oh, and there're lots of historical battles and suspense. I hope you like it.

Sharing my work with your friends and reviews are always welcome. Thank you for supporting The Airmen Series.

Regards,

David Lee Corley, Author

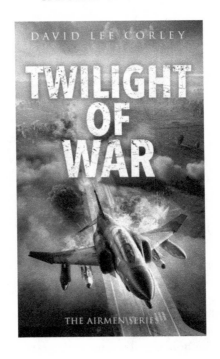

Author's Biography

Born in 1958, David grew up on a horse ranch in Northern California, breeding and training appaloosas. He has had all his toes broken at least once and survived numerous falls and kicks from ornery colts and fillies. David started writing professionally as a copywriter in his early 20's. At thirty-two, he packed up his family and moved to Malibu, California, to live his dream of writing and directing motion pictures. He has four motion picture screenwriting credits and two directing credits. His movies have been viewed by over fifty million movie-goers worldwide and won a multitude of awards, including the Malibu, Palm Springs, and San Jose Film Festivals. In addition to his twenty-four screenplays, he has written fourteen novels. He developed his simplistic writing style after rereading his two favorite books, Ernest Hemingway's *The Old Man and the Sea* and Cormac McCarthy's *No Country For Old Men* An avid student of world culture, David lived as an expat in both Thailand and Mexico. At fifty-six, he sold all his possessions and became a nomad for four years. He circumnavigated the globe three times and visited fifty-six countries. Known for his detailed descriptions, his stories often include actual experiences and characters from his journeys.

Printed in the USA
CPSIA information can be obtained
at www.ICGtesting.com
CBHW011004020124
3105CB00005BA/454